AF618157

By Samantha Sotto Yambao

Before Ever After

Love and Gravity

A Dream of Trees

The Beginning of Always

Water Moon

The Elsewhere Express

LOVE
AND
GRAVITY

LOVE AND GRAVITY

A NOVEL

SAMANTHA SOTTO YAMBAO

Dell
New York

Dell
An imprint of Random House
A division of Penguin Random House LLC
1745 Broadway, New York, NY 10019
randomhousebooks.com
penguinrandomhouse.com

2026 Dell Trade Paperback Edition

Originally published as an ebook in the United States by Ballantine Books, an imprint of Random House, a division of Penguin Random House LLC, in 2017.

ISBN 979-8-217-30255-0
Ebook ISBN 978-0-399-59324-6

Printed in the United States of America

1st Printing

Book Team: Production editor: Cara DuBois • Managing editor: Saige Francis • Production manager: Richard Elman • Proofreader: Cyrus Chin

The authorized representative in the EU for product safety and compliance is Penguin Random House Ireland, Morrison Chambers, 32 Nassau Street, Dublin D02 YH68, Ireland. https://eu-contact.penguin.ie

For Oma and Opa

In the eighteenth century and since, Newton came to be thought of as the first and greatest of the modern age of scientists, a rationalist, one who taught us to think on the lines of cold and untinctured reason. I do not see him in this light. I do not think that any one who has pored over the contents of that box which he packed up when he finally left Cambridge in 1696 . . . can see him like that. Newton was not the first of the age of reason. He was the last of the magicians, the last of the Babylonians and Sumerians.

—An excerpt from "Newton, the Man," an address to the Royal Society Club in 1942, written by John Maynard Keynes

The Truth

When Sir Isaac Newton died in 1727, he left an intellectual legacy that changed the world but neglected to leave a will to settle the rest of his estate. While most of his fortune was expediently distributed among his heirs, the contents of a large metal chest proved harder to divide.

The chest contained a trove of Newton's handwritten personal journals, notebooks, and manuscripts. Dr. Thomas Pellet, a member of the Royal Society, was appointed to determine which among the scientist's writings could be published. Of the collection's eighty-one items, he deemed only five acceptable for the public's eyes. The rest were labeled NOT FIT TO BE PRINTED, packed up in boxes, and promptly forgotten.

Until July 13, 1936.

An auction for Isaac Newton's private writings opened at one in the afternoon at Sotheby's New Bond Street premises, and at its close, British economist John Maynard Keynes went home with a significant portion of the collection and the two-hundred-year-old secrets the Royal Society had chosen to hide.

LOVE
AND
GRAVITY

1

ISAAC

Nitimur in vetitum semper, cupimusque negata.
—OVID

Woolsthorpe Manor
1666
Isaac is twenty-four.

HISTORY IS WHAT MEN CHOOSE to remember. Truth is what a man cannot forget. Isaac recalled everything about the night he wrote his last letter to her. It was Tuesday, he was young, oak gall ink stained his cuticles, and he was more in love with Andrea Louviere than he had been the day before, and the day before that. He inhaled through his teeth and sealed his letter with molten wax.

Red, the shade of good claret, seeped from under his copper seal and cooled in the shape of a rose. Isaac lingered over the wax petals, debating whether they were blooming or withering away. Beginnings and endings were oftentimes difficult to tell apart. He nudged his letter deeper into the halo of the tallow candlestick on his desk, undecided.

Sheep lard sputtered around the candle's wick, scenting Isaac's small bedroom on Woolsthorpe Manor's second level with wisps of burning fat. A dim orange flame flickered over the grooves of his wax initials. The tip of the *I* bled into the seal's border and the grooves of the *N* were thinner than he would have liked, but he did not doubt that Andrea would know whom the letter was from. He pressed the seal to the bow of his mouth and dented it with a whisper and a kiss.

"Andrea."

The syllables melted, honeyed and soft, over his tongue. They were a pale imitation of Andrea's lips, but he made do. Since she'd left, her name was all he had of her. He spoke it into his pillow each night before he slept. Hope did not require a reply. It grew with every letter he wrote. He added his most recent one to the lopsided stack on his desk and wrapped a black ribbon around the bundle. "Always," he said, tugging the ribbon tight.

A breeze, perfumed with evening dew, ripe apples, and a flock of longwool sheep, swept through the gap in the mullioned window above his desk and whipped the ribbon into a frenzy. Isaac caught the flailing strips between his long, tapered fingers. The velvet felt frailer than when he had taken it from his half sister's sewing basket, but there was no point in hunting for an alternative. The heaviest chain in Woolsthorpe was not going to keep his mind still. Destiny was a hefty thing, and tonight he was binding two.

Isaac knotted the ribbon a second time. He reached across his desk and grabbed the window latch. A handsome young man with wavy dark hair, a chiseled jaw, and a hint of a cleft peeking from beneath a day's worth of scruff on his chin brooded from a glazed pane. Isaac rubbed the wrinkle between his brows, smoothing the crease on his reflection's forehead. He left the window ajar and let the breeze have its way. Andrea's letters were going to have to fend for themselves before the night was over, and the wind was the least of his worries.

He slid his hand along the edge of his desk, finding the notches that marked the days Andrea had been away. When he ran out of desk, he had stopped keeping count. He didn't need nicks to remember how long it had been since she had slept by his side. The cold spot on his bed stepped up to the task, sparing his fingernails from further abuse.

Isaac had never fought sleep as much as when Andrea was molded into his chest, warm, soft, and smelling of sweet cream. Her hair, red golden like the barley fields at sunset, was his favorite place to stand his ground. He nuzzled it until his dreams forced him to surrender.

His fingers reached the end of the etched trail. He heaved a sigh and looked up. Fog crept over the apple orchard and coiled against his window. His shoulders loosened. Delivering Andrea's letters was going to be easier in the dark. He gathered them along with his sealing wax and candle, rose from his chair, and, with one brisk stride, transformed.

Though they never admitted it, Isaac's schoolmates in Cambridge shared the same opinion of him: Isaac was two men. The first blended into his books, with only the air rising and falling in his chest to distinguish him from their pages. But when he surfaced from his thoughts and drew himself to his full height, the second Isaac owned the room. The lines of his lean, muscular frame sliced the air when he took the slightest of steps, and the wildfire in his hazel irises made it impossible to look at anything or anyone else.

Isaac did not have an audience this evening, but his bedroom's heavy oak furniture paid him the same hushed respect. He walked past a bookshelf he'd built and knelt by his bed. He lifted its custard quilt and pushed aside the traveling trunk stowed beneath it. The trunk scraped the room's lime-ash floor, heavy from the textbooks he had brought home with him from Cambridge. It had been a year since his alma mater, Trinity College, had shut its doors for fear of the plague raging through London, and Isaac had not relished the idea of biding his time at Woolsthorpe. Andrea had since changed his mind. She might not have found him otherwise.

Isaac hauled a small wooden box from behind the trunk. A

pair of butterflies, drawn in a corner of the writing box's slanted lid, watched him with their wings half-open, forever waiting to take flight. Isaac caressed them with his thumb, hoping that some of their patience would rub off on him. He sat on his haunches, admiring the flowers carved along the sides of the box, the trademark of the joiner he had commissioned to craft it. His eyes stopped at the two small intertwined circles scratched into the center of its front panel. His handiwork was crude compared to the joiner's, but he didn't mind. It was not meant as décor. He had copied the symbol from John Wallis's book *Arithmetica Infinitorum.* Wallis had invented it to represent infinity; Isaac employed it to carry a promise and a prayer.

Isaac lifted the box's sloping lid. A small pile of packages wrapped in parchment sat inside it. He plucked the largest of the parcels from the box as quietly as he'd done when he had stolen it from Trinity's library. Not once, in the five years that had passed since his crime, did he regret committing it. None of his schoolmates would ever appreciate the fifteenth-century edition of the Roman poet Ovid's tales as much as Andrea would. He stroked the book's spine through its wrappings. The ridges of the winged nymph embossed on its leather binding rubbed against his fingertips. Isaac wished her a safe journey. She was going somewhere he could not. He returned the book to the box, laid his letters on top of it, and sealed the box's entire lid with red wax.

Isaac squeezed his hand between his feather mattress and bed frame. There was one last thing he needed to do before he sent Andrea's letters on their way. He drew out a small knife from beneath the mattress and tested its blade on his thumb. A red bead glistened in the candlelight, dribbled down his hand, and slipped under the black leather strap around his wrist. The 1952 Omega Seamaster fastened to the strap told him to hurry. He pressed the tip of the knife into the box's lid and etched two words onto it with short, hasty strokes.

COME HOME.

THE TOOLSHED SEEMED twice as far without his lantern, but Isaac did not wish to wake the farmhands or his family. His half brother, Benjamin, could snore through a thunderstorm, but his mother and two young half sisters were light sleepers. His late-night experiments had woken them on more than one occasion. Explaining the nature of gravity, white light, and fluxions was infinitely easier than having to confess his correspondence with Andrea. In their eyes, she would be the devil's work. In his, she was the sin that he would commit over and over again.

Mud squished under his boots' leather and wood soles. He paused at a fence post, adjusted his grip on the writing box, and summoned a lantern of memory to light his way. Except for the years he was away at school in Grantham and Cambridge, he had spent his life at Woolsthorpe and knew its grounds almost as well as he did every inch of Andrea's body. But there was no contest which of them was more pleasant to explore in the dark. From the moment he had entwined his fingers through hers, he knew that no other place would ever feel like home.

Isaac tripped over a plow and fell to the ground, staining his breeches with mud. The writing box tumbled next to him. He scrambled to collect the box and limped down the length of the barn.

The tip of his boot found the toolshed first. He groped inside the small outbuilding, passing over the sheep shears, hay rake, and wooden beadle. A ditching spade brushed against his knuckles. Isaac pulled it out and held it under a sliver of moonlight. It was smaller and weighed less than he remembered, having been a boy when he had last handled any of his late father's tools. He clutched it at his side and followed the fragrant trail of apples in the air.

Isaac set the wooden box by the foot of one of the taller apple trees in the orchard. He took a measured pace and shoved the spade into the ground. Its blade slammed against a rock. White heat shot up Isaac's wrist. Isaac staggered into the apple tree's curved trunk, knocking a verse from *Amores,* Ovid's first book of poetry, from a dusty shelf of Latin lessons in the back of his mind.

Nitimur in vetitum semper, cupimusque negata. We are ever striving after what is forbidden, and coveting what is denied us.

Isaac slumped against the apple tree's trunk. The centuries had not blunted the truth of the Roman poet's verse. A laugh cut Isaac's teeth. It was the cruelest of jokes that of all the obstacles that lay in his box's path, the one thing that he had power over was a rock. He drove the spade's blade under the stone, pried it loose, and flung it over his shoulder.

A mound of soil grew next to the apple tree. Isaac wiped the sweat from his brow and leaned over the hole. It was blacker than the night and almost as deep as the secrets he was going to bury in it. He nestled the box between two thick roots and covered it with soil, smoothing the ground with the back of his spade. He stepped away from his night's work and held out his arms in front of him. His palms were red and blistered, but they did not burn as much as they felt empty. He found a sharp rock and scraped two tiny intertwined loops into a whorl in the tree's trunk. The infinity symbol was far smaller than the one he had carved into the writing box. It was intended only for Andrea's eyes.

Moonlight spilled over his watch's glass face. Time's two tiny silver hands sparkled. Isaac begged them to be as kind to his letters as they had been to Ovid's ancient tales. The sealed pages bearing his words were on their way to Andrea, and all that was left for him to do was wait. He tugged the ruffle of his sleeve over the Omega and turned in the direction of the manor. The wind chilled the streaks of sweat on his back, urging him to sprint to the nearest fireplace. He reminded himself that there was no need to hurry. The three centuries before Andrea would be born was a lot of time to kill.

2

ANDREA

Every particle in the universe attracts every other particle with a force that is directly proportional to the product of their masses, and inversely proportional to the square of the distance between them.

—ISAAC NEWTON'S UNIVERSAL LAW OF GRAVITATION

San Francisco

Present Day

Andrea is seven.

APPLE PIE À LA MODE. Four ice cubes. The "Butterfly Lovers" Concerto. And a crack. These were the details of the afternoon Andrea met the boy who lived behind her wall. She turned seven that day and was good at remembering things that made her smile.

The red velvet birthday cake her father, Andrew Louviere, burned black was less memorable. He warmed a slice of leftover apple pie in the microwave, topped it with Häagen-Dazs vanilla bean ice cream, and stuck pink-and-white-striped candles on it instead. Only three fit on the melting scoop, but Andrea didn't complain. Apple pie à la mode for breakfast was a pretty good deal. She had another serving with a double scoop of ice cream for her afternoon snack. Cello practice always made her hungry.

Andrea scraped up the last crumbs of the buttery crust from her plate and washed them down with chocolate milk. Ice cubes tinkled against the tall glass. There were four of them. She knew because she listened closely. Three sounded thin. Five was too noisy. Four was just right. Her dad indulged her little requests, believing that such quirks came with the territory of raising a musical prodigy. Andrea wasn't sure what the word *prodigy* meant at that time, but she knew that her dad smiled whenever he said it. She sipped her chocolate milk and called on her four ice cubes to do an encore.

Every *clink, clank,* and *clunk* against the glass was pitch-perfect. The music room of the cornflower-blue Victorian home in San Francisco made everything sound good. If the room had had a fridge and an air mattress, Andrea would have lived in it. Its acoustic foam–paneled walls didn't laugh the way the kids at school did when she told them how Gabriel Fauré's Elegy made the air smell like rain or how Saint-Saëns's Allegro Appassionato painted rainbows on the ceiling. Juilliard had offered her the same shelter when she was six, but Andrea had begged her dad to turn the music scholarship down. The conservatory's teachers didn't read stories from pop-up books, and its classrooms didn't have any crayons, or goldfish named Steve. Her dad dried her eyes with a white handkerchief, smiled, and told her that Juilliard could wait.

Andrea drained her chocolate milk. Her father set his bone china teacup down next to her glass and straightened the pages of his cello duet arrangement of Chen Gang and He Zhanhao's "Butterfly Lovers" Concerto on the stainless-steel music stand. "Knock, knock," he said, tapping Andrea's knee with his bow.

"Who's there?"

"Little old lady."

"Little old lady who?"

"Hey, I didn't know you could yodel."

Andrea giggled. The joke was as corny as the first time he'd told it, but her father's warm baritone made her want to do nothing else but curl up inside his voice. "My turn. Knock, knock."

"Who's there?"

"Spell."

"Spell who?"

"W-H-O."

"Good one, kiddo." Andrew chuckled and handed his daughter her cello. The instrument was scaled for her size and looked like a doll's toy in his hands. "Let's start from the top, shall we?"

She rested the hand-carved maple cello on her chest. "Ready."

Andrew pushed up the sleeve of his plaid sweater and checked the time on his 1960s Patek Philippe Calatrava, the latest addition to his collection of vintage timepieces. He explained to Andrea, almost as often as he told her knock-knock jokes, that watches and cellos were kindred spirits. Both measured time's pulse. The former expressed it with gears and springs, the latter with strings and notes.

"What time is it?" Andrea asked.

"Three-thirty. Are you tired? We can call it a day if you want."

She swung her legs from the stool and considered her options. She had finished her warm-up of scales, arpeggios, and long tones, practiced her Popper études, and gone over her repertoire twice. SpongeBob, however, wasn't on until four.

"Nah. I'm good, Andrew. Let's start." Andrea's *s*'s whistled out of the gap where her two front teeth had fallen out.

"You're the boss, birthday girl. But please, I've told you a million times. Don't call me Andrew."

"Okay, Andrew." She grinned and curved her fingers around her pernambuco bow.

Andrew rolled his eyes and positioned his 1914 Neuner and Hornsteiner cello between his legs. He tapped his daughter's shoulder with his bow and pointed to the full-length mirror leaning against the wall. "And watch your posture this time, missy."

Andrea nodded as though she meant it. No matter how many times her father explained the importance of being aware of her posture, arm motion, bow position, and finger height when she played, she loathed checking her reflection. Music was so much easier to see when her eyes were closed. The mirror's only practical use, as far as she was concerned, was to make sure that she didn't play Tchaikovsky or Bach while wearing a chocolate milk moustache.

Andrew pressed the red button on his mini audio recorder and gave Andrea her cue with a wink. She winked back. She arranged her fingertips over the fingerboard and drew the bow across the cello's strings.

The silky strains of "The Butterfly Lovers," a song inspired by an ancient legend thought to be the Chinese equivalent of *Romeo and Juliet,* flowed out of the two cellos. Notes, sweet and floral like perfectly steeped green tea, swirled around the music room. They twirled in the spot where the grand piano that belonged to Andrea's mother used to be and drifted past the framed concert posters her dad had accumulated before his early retirement.

AN EVENING WITH ANDREW LOUVIERE

CHRISTMAS WITH THE NEW YORK PHILHARMONIC
AND ANDREW LOUVIERE

ANDREW LOUVIERE GIVES BACH

The last poster was from his farewell performance, a benefit concert for the National Nerve Cancer Foundation before his hair fell out. His auburn curls, as thick and unruly as Andrea's, had since grown back. *Remission* had sounded like a scary word when he first told her about it, but it became her favorite when she learned what it meant.

The Butterfly Lovers' tale swelled around them, finding and

filling every corner of the music room. Listening to Andrew Louviere play, no one would have guessed that his limb-sparing surgery had left him with a metal rod in his bow arm. But he heard his flaws more sharply than anyone else did. After his surgery, he played only for an audience of one. He told Andrea to listen closely and learn from his mistakes, but all she ever heard was the joy in his strings. It echoed the happiness coursing through hers.

The telephone ripped the Butterfly Lovers apart. Andrew pressed pause on the recorder and answered it. When his irises brightened from slate to sea blue, Andrea knew that it wasn't her mother on the other end of the line.

Andrew clasped his hand over the receiver. "Sorry, kiddo. Do you mind if we take a break? I need to take this call."

Andrea fixed her eyes on her glittery purple sneakers and shrugged. "Sure."

He ruffled her hair and walked out of the room. "Hi, babe," he whispered. "I've missed you, too. How was the seminar?"

Andrea ran her forefinger over the cello's purfling, the inlaid border that prevented cracks from spreading through the instrument's wood. She dug a chewed fingernail into it. If someone had invented something similar for families, she was convinced that hers would not have cracked. She dipped her bow onto the cello's strings and lifted it in a brisk spiccato style, hurling the opening strains of Metallica's "Enter Sandman" out the door. Her dad hated heavy metal as much as she enjoyed giving it a classical twist. Today, the song wrestled with her fingers. It had been ten months since her parents' divorce, but it still rang in her ears and made everything sound a little off-key.

New notes nudged her fingertips and tempted her to stray from the percussive strains she knew by heart. She chased them over the fingerboard. She could never resist the promise of a shiny new song for long. Her father urged her to write her compositions down, but Andrea wasn't convinced it was necessary. The music came and went as it pleased and by the time he got her to sit still at her desk, it was gone. She flipped through her dad's music sheets and filled their staff lines with fluffy striped cats instead.

Andrea glided her bow over the cello and made the new tune speak. Finding its notes was like popping a Jelly Belly into her mouth and guessing its flavor. The last three tasted like a mix of green apple, cinnamon, and French vanilla. The song twisted and turned, and just when she thought that it was trying to be happy, it squeezed a fat, hot tear through her lashes. She looked up at the mirror and followed the tear's path down her reflection's cheek. A bright white light streaked over the wall behind her. Andrea jumped up and knocked her cello to the floor.

The wall grew dark. Andrea crept to it and gave it a poke. Acoustic foam pushed against her fingers. She exhaled. Her dad was right. She was tired.

His laugh frothed through the doorway. The sound was still new to Andrea. It was half an octave higher than the chuckle he reserved for her knock-knock jokes. He had found it three months earlier in the cereal aisle when a five-foot-four Pilates instructor's slender hand collided into his as they both reached for the last box of gluten-free organic muesli. He let Sylvia Miller Takashi have the cereal and went home with Froot Loops, her phone number, and a giggle that made him sound a lot younger than forty-two. Andrea hated it instantly.

She clamped her hands over her ears and ran up to her room.

Four leather-clad cellists flicked their long blond hair from their usual spot on her bedroom's purple wall. On any other day, she would have smiled back at the poster of the Finnish heavy metal cello quartet. She stomped past Apocalyptica to her desk and yanked its drawer open. *Johann Sebastian Bach* greeted her from inside it. She pulled out the small red Moleskine journal with less care than it deserved. The boyish laughter burrowing into her middle ear didn't give her time to feel guilty.

The notebook had come in a FedEx packet a week ago, along with a pop-up card that sang a tinny version of "Happy

Birthday." Julia, Andrea's mother, let Hallmark do the talking for her but scribbled the last two words at the bottom of the card herself.

Love, Mom

Andrea imagined her mother saying them out loud. Her voice was naturally clipped, and Andrea always had to search her eyes to tell if she was happy, angry, or sad. Andrea fidgeted by the phone every Saturday, waiting to hear it. Their weekly talks were brief, just as they'd been when Julia lived at home.

"You're lucky, Andrea," Julia had said one damp afternoon when Andrea was five and still played the piano. Of the few words she spoke to Andrea in a day, these were the three that she said most often. Julia never said them with a smile. "This is all so easy for you, isn't it?"

"Is it supposed to be hard?" Andrea asked, her fingers dancing over the grand piano's keyboard.

"Yes."

Andrea did not know much about envy then. She just knew that being "lucky" made Julia carve a stiff smile whenever she played a piano piece better than Julia did. Andrea switched to the cello as soon as she was big enough to hold one.

Her dad did not try to stop Julia when she left them to live in New York. Andrea did. She couldn't get her mother to like her more if she wasn't around.

Andrea cracked open the journal Julia had sent. She did not know whether her mother had selected it because it was an easy gift to mail or because the wind had magically carried the words she sobbed into her pillow each evening to Julia's Upper East Side apartment. She didn't bother to find out. She was just happy to find a friend she could talk to. She named him after her favorite composer. *Johann Sebastian Bach* was hard to spell, but she had stuck with it. "Diary" was boring.

Her strawberry-scented pen trembled over one of *Bach*'s crisp, white pages. An army of words trampled over one another on their way to the pen's tip. She gripped her pen, forming bold block letters the way Mrs. Leary had taught her in penmanship class. Andrea stopped writing and flung the pen across the room. She was going to burst before she wrote down everything boiling inside her. There was a quicker way.

Andrea pulled her second cello out of her closet. She spread rosin over its bow's hairs, letting the dark amber cake coat each strand to help them grip the cello's strings. She rested the cello against her chest. Its shape and weight were identical to her practice instrument, but she could tell that it was not her old friend. Its polished maple felt colder. She drew her bow over the steel strings her dad had meticulously selected to produce the best sound in a large and highly reverberant room—the exact sort of place she did her best to avoid. Every string was out of tune.

The last time she had used the instrument was when she performed at the San Francisco Symphony's "Sounds of Music" Youth Concert at the Davies Symphony Hall earlier that month. Her dad had bribed her to accept the orchestra's invitation with an autographed copy of Apocalyptica's latest album. Nothing less would have swayed her. She loved the band almost as much as she hated performing in front of an audience, especially one made up of fidgeting fourth graders.

Andrea switched on her pocket-size chromatic tuner and made her bow speak over the A string. *A-sharp* flashed on the tuner's digital screen. She twisted the peg at the top of the cello's neck while plucking the string and turned the knobs of the fine adjusters on the instrument's ebony tailpiece to get the proper tension. She played the string and checked the tuner. A digital *A* appeared on its screen. She tuned the other three strings by ear and dove into the prelude from Bach's Cello Suite No. 1 in G Major. She stopped after three notes. They were too happy. She shook the stiffness from her wrist and let her bow take the lead.

Green apples, cinnamon, and warm vanilla drifted out of the cello's steel strings. She held her chin up and squared her jaw. She refused to let the song make her cry again. White light flashed over the wall on the opposite end of her bedroom. Her bow screeched over the D string. The light retreated into the purple wallpaper. If Andrea was older, she might have been relieved to watch it disappear. But she was seven and the Tooth Fairy had just left a dollar under her pillow. She believed in magic, and this time she wanted to see more.

Andrea coaxed the song back with steady bow strokes. White light glowed over the wall and expanded to the size of one of her mom's Christian Louboutin shoe boxes. She inhaled sharply and caught a whiff of a cool evening, ripe apples, and damp grass seeping through her wall. A faint greasy smell that reminded her of burning bacon wafted after it. She leaned closer. A jagged glowing crack broke through the wall. Shadows turned into shapes behind it.

A candle.

A window.

A bed.

A desk.

A boy.

Andrea clung to her cello to keep from jumping out of her skin. The boy, who appeared to be around her age, was hunched over his desk as Andrea played. His wavy dark hair curled at the collar of his loose linen shirt. A fire, brighter than the flame of his half-melted candle, flickered in his hazel eyes as he assembled a miniature wooden cart. Andrea recognized the look. She saw it whenever she chanced upon her reflection while she played the cello.

The boy hammered a wooden wheel into place. Andrea strained to hear the slightest thud, thump, or scrape. Only silence escaped through the crack. The boy pounded away, equally deaf to Andrea's music. The candle in the corner of his desk flickered. The boy sheltered its flame with one hand and reached for the window's turnbuckle with the other. His fingers froze over the wrought-iron handle. His eyes shifted in their sockets and met Andrea's. He choked on a silent gasp.

Andrea raised her bow and gave him a small wave. It seemed like the polite thing to do. The boy tumbled off his chair. He scrambled to his feet, his lips quivering. He wrangled his mouth into a lopsided grin and waved back. He took a step forward.

Andrea leapt out of her chair and staggered back from him. He raised his hand, gesturing her to come closer. Her legs refused to do anything except tremble. The boy grabbed three small brown objects from his desk. From where Andrea stood, they looked like pieces of bread. The boy grinned and tossed them over his head. His bright hazel eyes twinkled as he juggled. One by one, the pieces vanished as they fell into his hand. Andrea gasped. The boy held his empty palms out to her, beaming proudly. A chunk of bread slipped out of his sleeve and fell to the floor. The boy's cheeks burned bright red. He scratched the back of his head and chewed the corner of his lower lip. He lowered his eyes and peeked at Andrea through his thick lashes.

Andrea stared at him. The boy's sleight of hand trick had failed, but not before his magic had sailed through her wall. It found her chest and melted the lump of fear inside it. She exhaled. A chuckle hitched a ride with her breath, tickled the back of her throat, and bubbled out of her. She clapped for her new friend. She wasn't sure if the boy could hear her applause, but she hoped that he could tell that he had made her happy.

A smile spread across the boy's handsome face. The golden embers in his eyes burned brighter. He plucked the chunk of bread from the floor. He held it to the crack and swept his other hand over it. Two more pieces of bread appeared on his palm. He stuffed them into his mouth and grinned.

Andrea burst into laughter.

The boy inched forward, his ruddy cheeks stuffed with bread, as though he was approaching a tiny animal that he did not want to scare away.

Andrea did the same. The glowing borders of the crack dimmed. Wallpaper crept over the hole between her and the boy, shrinking it to the size of a deck of cards. The boy ran to the wall, questions swirling in his irises. A purple bunny print sealed the crack before any of them made it to his lips.

"Wait!" Andrea sprinted to the wall and banged her fists on it. "Come back. Who are you?"

Knuckles rapped on her door. "Andrea?" her dad said. "Are you okay in there?"

Andrea did not have enough breath to answer.

The doorknob rattled. "Andrea? Let me in."

She walked to the door. That is, she thought she did. There was an equal chance that she crawled. She couldn't bring herself to remember or care. She unlocked the door, her head clouded with apple-scented fog.

Her dad crouched and cupped her shoulders. "What was all that shouting about? Are you all right?"

"There's someone in my room."

"What?" He jumped to his feet. "Where?"

Andrea threw her arms around his waist and pointed to the wall. "There."

Her father frowned. "In the wall?"

She nodded. "There was a crack and there was a boy inside it."

Andrew knelt beside her. "Listen, kiddo. I know you don't like that I'm dating Sylvia. I understand. Really, I do. But you don't have to make up stories just to—"

"I'm not lying. He was real. I saw him. He juggled bread and made it vanish. He knew magic. You have to believe me, Daddy." Andrea choked on tears. "Please."

"Okay, okay. Don't cry." Her dad dried her eyes with his handkerchief. "Why don't we go for a walk?"

Walks were Andrew Louviere's universal solution. Before his retirement, along with handfuls of orange M&M's, it shook off his nerves before his concerts and his excess of adrenaline after them. After his wife left, he liked to take Andrea on long ones around their neighborhood. San Francisco's steep and sloping streets bought him time to answer Andrea's questions about when her mother was coming home.

"Why don't you believe me?" Andrea asked.

Her father wrapped his arms around her and sighed into her hair. "I do believe you, kiddo."

"Really?"

"Yes."

"Pinky swear?"

Andrew hooked his little finger around Andrea's pinky. "Pinky swear."

Andrea laid her cheek against his sweater and breathed in the scent of Ivory soap and citrusy cologne. "Knock, knock."

"Who's there?"

"Olive."

"Olive who?"

"Olive you, Daddy." She hugged her father tight and thought about the story she would tell *Johann Sebastian Bach* that evening about the boy who lived behind her bedroom wall.

THERE WAS A new book on Andrew Louviere's nightstand the next day: *Imaginary Friends: Should Parents Worry?* At dinner, Andrew asked Andrea about her friend's name. Andrea stabbed the vegetarian meatloaf Sylvia had sent over and told him it was George. A pea rolled across her plate. Andrew smiled and said that it was okay to invite George to come with them when they went on a picnic with Sylvia at Crissy Field that Sunday. He told her to tell George to bring a sweater in case it got cold. Andrea drank her chocolate milk and drowned out his voice with the tinkling of four ice cubes.

3

CONFESSIONS

Be patient and tough;
one day this pain will be useful to you.
—OVID

San Francisco
Present Day
Andrea is nine.

ANDREA HAD FORGOTTEN HIS FACE. Two years had passed since she'd seen the boy in her wall. She played his song the best she could remember it, but he would not come. One morning, she woke up and realized that she no longer remembered the color of his eyes. On some days, she was convinced that they were blue. On others, she swore that they were leaf green like hers. Most days she didn't care. She had more urgent concerns. A date was circled on their kitchen calendar with a red Sharpie and it was getting close. She had to get away before her father's wedding day.

"But why can't I live with you?" Andrea pressed the phone to her cheek, wishing she could squeeze through it and pop out on the other end.

"You know what my touring schedule's like," Julia said, repeating the answer she'd given Andrea for the past two weeks. "I'm leaving for London next week."

"I'll go with you."

"But you have school, your cello lessons . . ."

"I don't care about school. Or music."

"You don't mean that."

Andrea blew her nose into her sleeve. "I do."

"You came with me on tour last summer and you hated it, remember? You called your father every night complaining about how bored and miserable you were."

"It will be different this time, Mom. I promise."

"And what do you think will make it different?"

"Pink." Andrea had never eaten a week-old dead fish, but she guessed that the taste the color left in her mouth came close to it. "Sylvia wants me to wear pink. I hate pink and I hate her. I don't want to be a flower girl at her stupid wedding. I don't want to be here when she moves in."

"I'm sorry, Andrea. I have to go. I'll call you from London, okay?" her mother said. "By the way, did you get the birthday gift I sent you?"

Julia had sent her another journal just like the ones she had given her on her last two birthdays. Andrea wanted to tell her that she didn't need a new one. She'd had less to say to *Johann Sebastian Bach* ever since she stopped writing about the boy in her wall.

"I did. Thanks."

"Do you like the color?"

"Yes." Julia never bothered to ask what color she wanted, but this year, she chose well. Chocolate, even if you couldn't eat it, was comforting. "Mom . . ."

"Yes?"

"Take me with you."

"Andrea . . ." Julia said. "Everything will be fine."

Andrea might have believed her mother had she not paused

after saying her name. Silence made the truth easier to hear. The date her father had circled on their kitchen calendar was not going to go away.

CLANK. CLINK. CLUNK. Andrea pulled her blanket over her head. Glass clattered through the purple duvet. Andrea groaned and rubbed away the tears crusted on her lashes. She rolled over and searched her bedroom for the sound. Golf ball–size hail pelted her bay window. Andrea sank into her pillows and sighed. It figured. It was the perfect day for the sky to fall. The little red ink circle on their kitchen calendar had found her. It crept into her bedroom, wrapped itself around her neck, and squeezed. Andrea wheezed, struggling to breathe. The day of her father's wedding had arrived.

DIANE LEE, THE wedding planner, handed Andrea a small basket wrapped in pink lace that matched the taffeta tiers she was drowning in. Diane fiddled with Andrea's curls, her forehead scrunched as though the fate of the world depended on her successfully taming Andrea's hair under a wreath of pink silk flowers. Andrea had not made her job any easier. She had not bothered to comb her hair or brush her teeth when she got dressed that morning. She didn't think anyone would notice her anyway. She was short for a nine-year-old and blended in with the rest of the wedding décor.

Diane tucked a curl behind Andrea's ear. It sprung free for a third time. Diane gave up with a muffled groan and turned her attention to the flower basket. She held her arm in front of Andrea. "Watch," she said, flicking her wrist to scatter imaginary petals over the aisle. "Slowly and gracefully, okay, dear?"

Andrea nodded without looking at her.

"Good." Diane smiled. "Come. Follow me, dear."

Andrea shuffled behind her, doing her best not to trip on her floor-length skirt. She took her place behind the ring bearer, Sylvia's six-year-old nephew, Zach.

"Hi," Andrea said softly.

Zach didn't hear her. His tongue was curled upward out of his mouth as he tugged at the white gold rings fastened on the ring cushion. Andrea had never seen anyone look more determined. She wondered if the wedding would have to be called off if the rings came loose, rolled onto the floor, and got utterly lost beneath the endless layers of her dress. A string trio's version of the Beatles' "All You Need Is Love" kept her from finding out. Zach marched down the short aisle in time with the song. Andrea's feet refused to join him. She could not see beneath her skirt, but she was certain that her pink shoes had grown roots.

Diane tapped her shoulder. "Go on, dear."

Andrea wrung the handle of her flower basket. Her eyes darted around the church, searching for help. Her father waved at her from the other end of the aisle.

"You can do it, kiddo," he mouthed slowly.

Andrea read his lips. She drew a breath and pried one foot off the floor. She took another step and tripped on taffeta. Petals exploded over the aisle, neither gracefully nor slowly. Andrea considered remaining sprawled on the floor next to them. That way, she could hide her tears.

Warm arms helped her to her feet. "You're okay, kiddo. You're okay." Her father dried her eyes with a pale pink satin handkerchief and straightened the wreath in her hair. "I'm here."

Andrea buried her face in the crisp collar of his black tuxedo and sobbed. "I hate pink. I hate this dress. I hate this stupid awful thing in my hair."

"Oh, good. I was worried."

Andrea scrunched her forehead. "Worried?"

"I wanted the wreath for myself, but I thought you liked it." Andrew took the wreath from her head, planted it on his, and grinned. "It looks better on me, don't you think? It brings out my eyes."

Andrea pressed her lips to keep a giggle in. It burst free.

Andrew smiled and took her hand. "What do you say, kiddo? Shall we try this again? Together?"

Andrea nodded and let Andrew lead her down the aisle, a flower wreath half-slipping off his head. She took small steps. It was the last walk she would have him to herself and she wanted to make it last as long as she possibly could.

ANDREA ANGLED HER chair at the wedding reception to keep as much of the two-tier gluten-free vanilla coconut wedding cake as possible between herself and the sixty-five guests. She adjusted the cello in front of her, relieved that she did not play the flute. The latter would not have made much of a shield. Behind the cake's pink sugar flowers and her cello's broad maple back, she stopped trembling enough to play her father's request. The first movement of Schubert's Arpeggione Sonata streamed out of her cello's strings.

Applause roared over her last note. Andrea managed a small smile, but she felt too nauseous to take a bow. She knew what was coming next. She watched her father stand up and button his tux. He tapped his champagne flute with a spoon and cleared his throat. He glanced at Sylvia, his eyes sparkling more than the facets of his glass.

"I have an announcement to make." He dangled a pair of pale pink organic cotton baby booties in front of his guests.

Clinking of glasses and cheers erupted, nearly drowning out the name of the baby girl Andrew and Sylvia were expecting in the fall. Andrea didn't have to strain her ears to catch it. It had been ripping the walls of her stomach ever since her father had told her what it was. *Wendy* was made up of only five letters, but each was as sharp as broken glass.

WENDY MARIE TAKASHI LOUVIERE couldn't wait for autumn. She was born in the summer just before dawn and weighed four pounds and two ounces.

"Andrea, your sister is . . ." Tears watered her dad's voice as they walked down the long white corridor to the neonatal intensive care unit. "She's going to be inside a glass box and there will be a lot of tubes sticking out of her body. Don't be afraid."

Andrea wasn't sure if he was talking to himself or to her, but she nodded just the same. She clung to him, inhaling the scent of air-conditioned air, antiseptic, and freshly mopped floors. Her dad tightened his grip on her hand. Her knuckles hurt and her fingertips turned white. She didn't mind. Her dad didn't say when they were bringing Wendy home, but as soon as they did, he was going to have someone else to take on long walks.

Wendy's incubator was tucked into a corner of the room, surrounded by machines with blinking lights. The clear tape over her eyes and the tangle of multicolored tubes attached to her body matched the picture Andrea's dad had painted in her head. But there were two things he didn't tell her. Wendy was a lot smaller than Andrea had expected, and so much easier to love. She looked up at her father. "Can she hear us?"

Andrew rested his hand on her shoulder. "I'm sure she knows we're here."

"Hello." Andrea pressed her fingertips against the incubator's glass. Wendy's small pink hands looked like a doll's next to hers. They were curled into fists but Andrea could tell that Wendy was going to play the piano well. Johannes Brahms's Cello Sonata No. 2 in F Major was going to be their song. That is, it would be when their dad was within earshot. When he wasn't, she was going to teach Wendy Apocalyptica's version of Metallica's classic "Nothing Else Matters."

"She looks like you," her father said.

Andrea smiled. "Of course she does. I'm her big sister."

THE SKY WAS the wrong shade of blue. It was too bright. Neither had the sun nor grass dressed appropriately for the occasion. Only the small group of people that gathered around a small white casket wore black. Tears streamed down all of their faces, but Andrea couldn't hear anyone sob. The metal pulleys were also quiet. They didn't creak as they lowered Wendy's coffin into the ground. "Nothing Else Matters" ran in a loop in her head and blocked out every sound.

The silent song was the only music at the funeral. The funeral parlor's director had offered Sylvia and her father a selection for the service: Schubert's "Ave Maria," Pachelbel's Canon in D Major, Elgar's "Nimrod" from Enigma Variations, Williams's *The Lark Ascending,* and Barber's Adagio for Strings, op. 11. Andrew rejected all of them. Nothing was sad enough to mourn the daughter he had not been able to hold.

Andrea agreed. Wendy's coffin was tiny, but it somehow managed to hold all of their hearts. Andrea tossed a rose over it. A thorn pricked her thumb. She sucked a bead of blood from her finger. The thorn, her sister, and the boy in her wall had one thing in common. They required only the briefest of moments to slip under her skin.

Sylvia put her arm around her. Andrea hugged her back. She didn't know whether Sylvia or her dad would hold her again if they knew what she had done to their daughter.

ANDREA THREW HER legs over her bed and planted her cello between them. One of the first lessons her father had taught her shoved its way to the front of her mind. A cello's tone production and volume depended on a combination of factors, the most important of which were the bow's speed, the weight applied to the string, and the point of contact of the bow hair with the string. Andrea drew her bow and realized her father was wrong. What mattered most was what you wanted to say and how badly you wanted to say it. She begged Wendy to listen to her apology.

The cello wept a flutelike sound. The sul tasto effect was used when cellos needed a soft tone that blended in with the rest of the orchestra. Andrea chose it because she wasn't sure if she was prepared to hear what she needed to say. Her sister was gone because, for the past seven and a half months, she had knelt by her bed and prayed to God to take her back.

Andrea's small fingers floundered over the strings. She took her dad's old advice to conserve her movements and hold her bow higher. She raised her arm a quarter of an inch, relaxed her wrist, and leaned in the direction of the upcoming note.

An old melody weaved its way back into her hand. It was not the confession she had intended, but she let it have its way. Green apple, cinnamon, and French vanilla sprang from her cello, stringing along the memory of a boy's bright hazel eyes. White light flashed on her purple wallpaper.

A pulsing glow outlined the crack widening between a lavender rabbit's printed ears. The hole grew to half of the size of Wendy's casket, opening a window into the boy's world. His candlelit bedroom was smaller and had a lower ceiling than the one Andrea had seen two years before. The boy inside it had also changed. He was older and filled more of his wool tunic and breeches. He sat with his legs crossed beneath him on the floor, grinning at a miniature windmill.

A brown mouse ran inside a steel wheel at the bottom of the mill, spinning its white cloth sails. Bits of ground corn flew out of the mill and scattered around it. The mouse raised its head and sniffed the air. It jumped off the wheel and chased after the corn. The boy caught it by its hind legs. The mouse wriggled free and scurried into the shadows. The boy's eyes darted after it. They found Andrea instead. His jaw raced hers to the floor. Andrea's won.

Andrea lost her grip on the bow. It bounced off the carpet,

leaving notes to fade in the air. The crack dimmed. The boy steadied his cleft chin and ran toward the wall, his smile growing wider with every stride. He wasn't juggling bread chunks or making them disappear, but the spring in his step tickled the corners of Andrea's mouth. Wendy's death stained every inch of her, but in the boy's bright, happy eyes, she was still the same girl who lived behind his wall and made him smile.

The boy cupped his hands and blew into the hollow of his palms. A mouse's head popped up from between his fingers, wiggling its whiskers. The boy beamed and set the animal on the floor.

Andrea clapped. The boy's greatest magic trick was not pulling things out from thin air. It was finding her when she needed a friend the most.

The boy took a bow. His mouth molded silent words. *What is your name?*

Andrea read his lips. The crack shut as she replied. She grabbed her bow and pummeled her wall with notes, each one louder than the one that came before.

Her bedroom door flung open. Her father marched through it, tears glistening in the hollows of his cheeks. He had aged ten years since he'd buried his younger daughter. "Andrea, it's late." His voice croaked out of him and made Andrea's name sound like it was covered in rust. "You'll wake the neighbors."

"The boy's back!" Andrea yelled over the music. "He has a windmill. And a mouse. A brown one. It ate his corn and ran away."

"Please, Andrea." A vein throbbed in his left temple. "Stop."

Andrea made up more notes. She didn't care if they were sharp or screeched. One of them had to be right. The boy was real and she could prove it. His song was somewhere in her strings. If she placed her fingers over the right ones, she would find it.

"I said *stop.*" Her father snatched her bow and broke it over his knee.

4

DOUBT

Once doubt begins, it spreads rapidly.

—JOHN MAYNARD KEYNES

San Francisco
Present Day
Andrea is ten.

DOUBT IS A SMALL AND weightless thing. But it is patient. For months, Dr. Matthew Colin watered Andrea's on his brown leather couch for one hour every Wednesday after school without so much as a sprig to show for his trouble or Andrew Louviere's money. The boy in her wall, his mouse, and his mill were real, and there was nothing Dr. Colin could say to convince Andrea otherwise. Her detailed journal entries of the boy's two visits were all she needed to relive the moments she'd had with him. *Johann Sebastian Bach* believed in magic and was on her side.

Nathaniel William Davis was another matter.

His ash blond hair flopped over his pale blue eyes as he walked into Andrea's fourth-grade math class in a vintage Metallica T-shirt that was two sizes too big for him. He clutched two drumsticks in one hand. The way his knuckles hardened around his drumsticks belied his breezy stride. Andrea clung to her bow the same way when she felt afraid and alone. He took the seat in front of Andrea and planted his black backpack on the floor. He stuffed the drumsticks into it. Andrea stared at the drumsticks sticking out of his bag and sucked in a breath and half a lungful of hope. She was not disappointed. Nate turned out to be the only other person in her class who played a musical instrument, even if, by her father's definition, electronic drums didn't count. Though Nate never spoke to her, she was content to imagine that one day, when he passed her a worksheet over his shoulder, he was going to glance her way. Every morning, she practiced how she would smile back at him in her bathroom mirror.

Nate never turned around to see her grin. He was more interested in performing drum solos that left a trail of dents on desks, lockers, and cafeteria tables. A fifth grader's sandwich got in the way of a downstroke one afternoon. It took its accidental beating with a quiet squish. Its owner was more vocal. He growled and grabbed Nate by the collar. Andrea jumped in and offered her lunch bag to keep the peace. Luckily, Nate had ruined the lunch of the only student in school who happened to like vegetarian meatloaf more than grilled ham and cheese. Nate threw in his chocolate milkshake and tater tots to seal the deal. The next morning, he passed a worksheet to the seat behind him, glanced over his shoulder, and smiled at the girl who had saved him with baked tofu.

NATE ROLLED HIS eyes at Andrea. "Seriously, Dre? Santa?"

Andrea sank into her seat in the cafeteria. In all the time that they had spent every lunch period together, this was the first time she could not think of something to say back to him.

Nate smirked. "Don't tell me you believe in Rudolph, too?"

Andrea gulped down her milk.

"Oh God." He chuckled. "You do."

"Shut up. I don't." Andrea avoided his eyes. Nate had just murdered Santa and summarily executed Rudolph with a snicker. She was never going to jump out of bed on Christmas mornings ever again. She hid her grief behind her lunch bag.

"Then why do you look like someone just died?" Nate laughed.

"I hate you." Andrea stomped away.

"No, you don't," Nate called after her.

Andrea outran his voice, swearing never to speak to him again. Years later, she would forgive his skepticism. She would have scoffed at anything remotely odd or magical, too, if her mother was being treated for schizophrenia. Nate had believed his mom when she had told him about the voices in her head and the fairies flying around their living room until his grandparents explained that they were why her doctors had to take her away.

But Andrea didn't know any of this that afternoon. She marched down the hall, swallowing a mixture of hot tears and every intention she had of telling Nate about the boy who lived in her wall.

"Dre, wait up." Nate caught up with her. "I'm sorry."

Andrea folded her arms and glared at him.

"Forgive me?"

"No."

"See you on the bus?"

She walked away without answering. She didn't need to. Whether they argued or not, they always saved a seat for each other on the bus. They spent the ride debating about the colors and shapes of songs. Even though their conversations usually ended with Andrea punching his arm and turning her back to him, they both knew that they were going to sit together again the next day. Nate made being strange a less lonely place, even if she had to keep her stranger secrets to herself.

ANDREA COULDN'T SAVE the boy in her wall for long. Santa and his reindeer were dead and she was ten years old. Doubt had taken root and she had gotten too old for imaginary friends. Dr. Colin gave her a vanilla cupcake with purple sprinkles and asked her how she felt about her tenth birthday. Andrea told him that it didn't feel very different from being nine—except that she knew that music couldn't open holes in walls and that the boy who lived in her wall wasn't real. Dr. Colin smiled, told her that it was their last session together, and gave her a red velvet cupcake to take home.

Andrea ate her cream cheese–frosted reward on her early evening walk with her dad. When she licked off the last of it from her fingers, they stopped for ice cream. Unlike a boy who lived in a wall, a chocolate-sundae detour was a secret her father was happy to keep between them.

ANDREA RESTED HER chin on her hands and stared at the computer screen. She rubbed her eyes and yawned. Her science report made her wish for the nights she still believed in magic. Scouring her wall for glowing cracks was more fun than researching Isaac Newton. She pushed her chair away from her desk. "Tuna? Come here, girl."

Sylvia and her dad had given her the Persian kitten for her birthday. Tuna crept out from under her bed and curled into a small orange ball at her feet. Andrea tickled her new kitten's tummy with her toes. Tuna purred. Next to the tinkling of four ice cubes, it was Andrea's favorite sound.

Sylvia's round stomach poked through Andrea's half-open bedroom door. Andrea's brother was due in a month and the family had taken a vote and had decided to name him Sebastian, after Andrea's favorite composer. Sylvia peeked inside the room, her pin-straight blue-black hair skimming her waist. "How's the science project coming along? Need any help?"

"Can you make Isaac Newton less boring?"

She smiled. "I'm afraid not. But it's taco night if that makes you feel any better."

"It does." Her mouth watered. Like her tofu tacos, Sylvia had grown on Andrea. Her stepmother's cooking had stopped tasting like liver right about the same time hugging her before she left for school had stopped giving Andrea hives. In the time that Sylvia had been married to her dad, Andrea had learned two things: Tofu was not the work of the devil and people weren't like bags of salted caramel popcorn. She didn't have less of her dad even if she had to share.

"I made whole-grain walnut brownies for dessert," Sylvia said.

"It's official. You are my favoritest person in the world. And I don't care that it's not a real word."

Sylvia laughed. "I think we have just enough votes to put it in the dictionary." She winced and grasped her stomach.

"You okay?" Andrea sprinted to her.

Sylvia exhaled through her mouth. "I think that was just your brother agreeing with me. The little guy can kick. And punch."

"Wendy had such small hands." Andrea regretted the words as soon as they slipped from her lips. She could not think of the brother she was going to have without remembering the sister she had sent away. She looked at her feet. "I'm sorry."

Sylvia hugged Andrea as close as her belly would allow. "There's nothing wrong with remembering her. I think it would make her very happy. Wendy wasn't with us long, but she'll always be a part of this family. Love isn't measured by time."

"Do you miss her?" Andrea asked.

Sylvia's face crumpled. She clutched her tummy and groaned. "Get your dad. Hurry."

JENNY DE LOS SANTOS had been Andrea's babysitter since she was six and that evening, while her dad and Sylvia were at the hospital, Jenny and Andrea had their quietest dinner together. Andrea could not fret, talk, and pretend to eat cold vegetarian tacos at the same time.

"Don't worry." Jenny reached across the table and patted her hand. "Everything will be okay. You'll see."

Andrea fixed her eyes on the crystal hearts glued to Jenny's neon-pink nails, trying to forget the one other night that she had said those same words. It was Wendy in Sylvia's tummy that evening and Jenny's nails were painted lime green. Andrea nodded, emptied her untouched plate into the sink, and went up to her room.

She settled in front of her laptop and clicked on a post about Isaac Newton's personal collection of books. Tuna staked her claim on her lap. She stroked Tuna's back and read the article. Of the 1,752 books the scientist kept in his private library, only one was related to music, a treatise on the vibration of strings. Tuna couldn't care less, and purred.

Andrea clicked on a link that directed her to a site devoted to Newton's childhood inventions. She skimmed over his sundials and water clocks and stopped at an illustration of the floating paper lantern he had made to light his way to school on gray winter mornings. She imagined how it must have scared his neighbors. He wasn't as dull as she had thought. She scrolled down the page to see his next creation.

A miniature wooden windmill with cloth sails appeared on the screen. Andrea's hand froze over the keyboard. She tore through the text beneath the photo that explained how a twelve-year-old Newton had made a replica of a mill being constructed on a hill near his grammar school in Grantham. To keep his model from being dependent on the wind, he designed it to be powered by a "mouse miller" that ran inside its steel wheel.

Andrea's mouth fell open. The dark-haired boy buried under a year's worth of $150-an-hour therapy sessions climbed back to the top of her mind, his hazel eyes as bright and clear as the night she had watched him chase after his runaway mouse. This picture proved he was real. And a thief. He had stolen Sir Isaac Newton's windmill. A "Butterfly Lovers" Concerto ringtone sliced through her accusations. Andrea grabbed her phone. "Hello?"

"Hey, kiddo." Her father's voice scraped the sides of his throat.

She pressed the phone to her ear. "Dad?"

He caught his breath. "Sebastian can't wait to meet his big sister."

She squealed. Her father's words edged out every thought, including those about the young thief in her wall. "When can I see him?"

"You can visit him tomorrow. I love you, kiddo."

"I love you, too, Dad. Oh . . . and . . . um . . . tell Sylvia that I . . . uh . . ."

"She knows you do."

ANDREA DRAGGED NATE into the music room after school the next day. "Come on. Hurry up."

"What are we doing in here? Is your dad home?"

"Nope. He went back to the hospital to bring Sylvia a few things." Andrea took a seat and arranged her cello between her legs. "Sit down. I want you to listen to something."

"I thought you didn't like having anyone around when you played."

Andrea rubbed her hands on her jeans. Playing in front of other people turned her palms to ice, but her new baby brother was someone that she needed to celebrate with someone else. She had missed first period to visit him and had seen his tiny hands and tufts of brown hair, but he still didn't feel real. If God saw how thankful she was for him, she figured that he wasn't going to change his mind and take him back. "Just be quiet and listen, okay?"

Nate shrugged and settled onto her dad's stool. He pulled a

drumstick out of his backpack and twirled it. "What song are you going to play?"

"Sebastian's."

"Really? When did you write it?"

She drew her bow. "I'm about to."

Every happy thought Andrea had ever had flowed into her cello. Warm apple pie and vanilla bean ice cream. Four ice cubes and Tuna's purr. Wendy and her small pink hands. Andrea squeezed her lids shut to block the darker memories she had of her sister, but she was too late. They tumbled out of her in a rusty chain, dragging along a melody she had spent a year trying to forget. The boy's song spilled out of her cello and pushed against the music room's foam walls.

Nate gasped.

Andrea's eyes flew open. A bright white crack glowed between her dad's Vienna and New York concert posters. She stopped playing. "Nate, do you see—"

The crack vanished.

Nate blinked at the wall.

Andrea grabbed his arm. "I knew it. I knew it was real."

"I have to go." Nate jumped off the stool.

"What? Why?"

He scampered to the door.

"Wait. Don't go." Andrea chased after him. "You have to tell my dad. You have to tell everyone. Dr. Colin was wrong. I'm not crazy. I didn't imagine it. You saw the crack, too."

"I didn't see anything." He kept his head down and scurried down the hall.

"Of course you did."

"I told you," he hissed. "I didn't see anything." He rushed out the front door and slammed it behind him.

Andrea grasped the doorknob. And let it go. Nate could wait. The boy in the wall could not. This time, she was going to be ready for him. She ran back to the music room.

Andrea pressed a black marker onto a blank music sheet. A

million words raced to the paper and slammed into the pen's felt point. An inkblot spread over the page. Not a single word in her ten-year-old vocabulary seemed like the right thing to say to the boy in her wall. She settled on five letters. She angled the music stand toward the wall and planted her message on it.

The boy's song surged down her arm and steered her bow, urging it to leap from string to string. White light ripped through an acoustic panel in the middle of a vibrato. She peered through the crack. Moonlight washed over a dark shape curled on a bed. The figure turned to its side. Light pooled over the boy's face and glistened on the wet streaks on his cheek. Heat rose up Andrea's nape. This was not the right time to intrude. Her hasty note seemed silly in the midst of the boy's tears. She lifted her bow from the cello's strings. The crack dimmed. She begged it to close faster. The boy's eyes fluttered open. He wiped his face on his pillow and read the message on the music stand. A smile lit his hazel eyes as the crack closed.

Andrea's heart dropped to her stomach. She gripped her cello, wishing that she had kept the wall open. She readied her bow. *Four Seasons* chimed from the doorbell. Andrea ignored it. She glanced at the music stand and reread her hasty note.

Hello!

She grimaced at the smiley face she had drawn on the *o*.

Vivaldi summoned her to the door again. She set her bow down. She and the boy would have to continue their talk when she came up with something better to say.

5

EYES

The cause is hidden; the effect is visible to all.

—OVID

San Francisco
Present Day
Andrea is fourteen.

REGRETS, LIKE L-SHAPED COUCHES, TAKE up a lot of space. For four years, they pushed against Andrea's ribs. The crack refused to open after that afternoon in the music room with Nate, and there wasn't a day that she didn't wonder what would have happened if she had chosen the boy over answering the front door. Instead of signing for a delivery of Sylvia's organic lemongrass tea, she might have gotten proof that she wasn't crazy.

Some days were better than others, but all her nights were the same. They were always too short. Her failed attempts to find the boy made the sun rise sooner. She erased half of the measures she composed before collapsing into bed at dawn. She didn't need to play them to know that they weren't going to crack her wall open. She carved her frustration into her desk and ruined enough ballpoint pens to make her dad start buying them in bulk. On the odd night that she felt hopeful, she ventured to play her compositions. Her wall didn't think much of her work, but *Johann Sebastian Bach* didn't rub it in. He never complained when she filled his pages with updates on her progress or lack of it. He never said much, really, even when she added something entirely new to her daily report.

Dear Mister Johann Sebastian Bach,
The concert is next week. I don't know why I ever agreed to do it. Kill me now.
Andrea

The Mariinsky Youth Philharmonic Orchestra had invited her to be their guest soloist on their U.S. tour. The chance to be led by their world-renowned conductor, Anatoli Dotsenko, outweighed any aversions she had to performing in public. As the concert grew close, the scales tipped the other way. Sweater sleeves hid her hives, but Nate saw her heart in her throat through her braces as he walked her home from the bus stop.

"So are you going to tell me what's bothering you or what?" he said.

"Do I have a choice?"

"No." He pushed his hair out of eyes that mimicked the color of the sky right after it rained.

"Fine. It's the concert. Happy?"

"What about it?"

"I'm going to suck."

He grinned. "What's new?"

Andrea punched his arm.

"Ow. I'm kidding. I'm kidding. You'll do great."

Andrea rolled her eyes. "You've never even heard me play."

He dropped his gaze to the pavement. "I have, remember? I didn't get the chance to hear a lot, but I heard enough."

Andrea stopped walking. Since the crack had appeared in the music room, this was the closest Nate had come to talking about what had happened. She searched his face for a sign that he recalled more about that afternoon than just her little performance.

"You're good, Dre," he said. "Really good."

Andrea shoved her hands into her pockets. "It's easier to be good without an audience waiting for you to make a mistake."

"They're not there to catch your mistakes. More than two thousand people bought tickets to enjoy your music. Don't you think that's cool? Even just a little?"

"Gee." Ice filled her stomach. "Thanks for reminding me. I owe you one."

"Not yet."

"Yet?"

"You'll see." He grabbed her hand and tugged her along the sidewalk toward her house. "Hurry."

NATE'S EYES ROAMED around the music room, his fingers absently twirling the chain of a round, coin-sized, plain metal pendant he had worn for as long as Andrea could remember. He had told her the pendant was a gift and joked that if she looked into it, she could see the future. Today, she wanted to believe him. Knowing how the concert was going to turn out could help her decide whether or not to run away.

"You're lucky." He tucked his pendant under his shirt.

Andrea flinched. *Lucky* still wasn't her favorite word.

He patted a foam panel. "You get to play in a place like this and I have to practice in a spot next to a moth-eaten couch and the spare freezer in my grandparents' garage."

"If you showed up for more of your cello lessons with my dad, you'd get to practice in here, too. He doesn't offer free lessons to just anyone, you know. Except for the two of us, he doesn't give lessons to anyone. Period."

He shrugged. "Cello really isn't my thing."

"But you're good at it."

He planted himself on her dad's stool. "We're not here to talk about how good I am. We're here to prove how good *you* are."

Andrea's eyes hardened. "What are you talking about?"

"Play for me."

"Are you serious? No way."

"Sorry, but I've got a front-row seat. You're not canceling this show."

Andrea scratched the hives spreading over her arms. "Let's just stick with a pep talk, okay? Besides, I have a ton of homework and I still haven't studied for our math test tomorrow."

"Quadratic equations? The quiz will be a breeze."

"For you. I barely passed the last one."

Nate grasped numbers the way Andrea understood notes. He had tried to convince her that music and math were just different ways of expressing the same rhythm. He quickly learned that they got their math homework done faster if he kept his mouth shut and did it for her. In exchange, Andrea didn't complain about their spy movie marathons. She even made popcorn.

"I'll help you study." He handed Andrea her cello. "*After* you play. I'm not leaving until you do."

"And you'll tell me if I suck?"

"I was the guy who killed Santa, remember? I'll always tell you the truth."

NATE'S STAMP OF approval dissolved in the pit of her stomach on the night of the concert, along with the Shake Shack french fries she'd had for lunch. The only thing that kept her from bolting out of Carnegie Hall's emergency exit and catching the first flight back to San Francisco was the three-digit number jostling around her fourteen-year-old head: *One hundred and thirty-seven.*

Counting steps was her preshow routine. Compared to her dad's ritual of walking around the block while picking out orange M&M's, Andrea didn't think hers was that strange. She looked up from the last carpeted step of the Isaac Stern Auditorium's balcony, inhaled the restrained elegance of the white and gold interior of Carnegie Hall's largest performance space, and choked on it.

Two thousand eight hundred and four red-cushioned seats were arranged around the curvilinear hall with one end in mind: to direct their occupants' full attention to every mistake she was going to make. Vomit lapped at the back of her tongue. She grabbed Nate's pendant from her neck. She peered into the small disc's smooth surface. The only future she saw in it was smudged with cold sweat. She tucked it away and stuck her hand in the back pocket of her jeans. She pulled out the yellow Post-it Nate had stuck on the pendant when he lent it to her. He had also given her a kiss on the cheek. Both, he said, were for luck. She wasn't sure if she was supposed to kiss him back so she didn't. She unfolded his note.

Breathe.

She took Nate's advice. Inhaling was easy. Exhaling was not. She wheezed.

Sebastian waved at her from the balcony's steps.

"See, buddy?" Her dad turned to her four-year-old brother. "I told you we'd find her here."

Andrea shoved Nate's note into her pocket.

"One hundred thirty-six?" her dad asked, his wavy auburn hair falling over his brows.

"Thirty-seven."

Sebastian tugged the frayed edge of Andrea's Metallica T-shirt. "Why are you up here?"

Andrea swallowed bile and tried to smile. "Just checking out the view. It's cool, right?"

Sebastian nodded. "Dad got tired going up the steps. He's old."

Andrew smirked. "He insisted on looking for you. He's been wanting to tell you a joke he came up with."

Andrea ruffled Sebastian's curls. His wild hair wasn't the only thing he had gotten from their father. "Let's hear it."

"Knock, knock."

"Who's there?"

"Carnegie."

"Carnegie who?"

Sebastian giggled. "Carnegie Hall."

"Good one, Bas." Freckled four-year-olds were funny whatever they said.

Her dad looked out at the stage. His slate eyes shifted to blue. "This is it, kiddo. We're finally here. Excited?"

Acid rose up Andrea's esophagus. She sank into a chair. "*Excited* is not the word that comes to mind."

"Hey, buddy," he said to Sebastian. "Why don't you see if you can count the seats in this row?"

"But I'm hungry."

Andrew fished a packet of M&M's from his pocket. "Here. Don't tell Mom."

Sebastian grinned and ran to the far end of the row.

"Don't eat the orange ones," Andrew called after him.

"Do they really help?" Andrea asked.

"Better than the red ones." He sat down. "You should give them a try."

"I'll pass. I don't think Dotsenko would like it if I threw up orange M&M's all over his stage. I don't suppose you'd like to come out of retirement and take my place?"

Her father patted her hand. "It's your time to shine. That scholarship at Juilliard's still on the table, you know. We can drop by tomorrow to visit the campus if you'd like. I have a feeling you'll find that their seats have shrunk quite a bit since the last time you were there."

"I don't think they'll want me after tonight."

"Of course they will. A few of my friends on the faculty will be at the concert. We'll have to beat them off with a stick after the show."

"You mean after Dotsenko gives me a whack over the head with his baton? I don't think he likes me very much. He hasn't smiled once during rehearsals."

"He never smiles. That's just how he is. Look, don't worry about him. Just focus on your playing and enjoy yourself."

Andrea wrung her fingers. "I can't."

"You were just as nervous before you promoted the concert on the *Today* show and that turned out great."

"I played for three minutes. This is a full-length concert. It doesn't even have intermission." Andrea buried her face in her hands.

"Kiddo, trust me. You'll be fine."

"I'm not ready."

"Listen to me, Andrea. You're ready for this. You've always been ready," he said, speaking as though he were declaring something as indisputable as gravity. "No one deserves to be on that stage more than you. You were born to do this. Tonight is when everything really begins. Do you want to take a quick walk around the block to shake off your nerves?"

"I'll pass. If I set one foot out the door of this place, I won't be coming back. I think I'll stick with counting steps."

Her dad smiled. "Whatever works for you, kiddo."

Andrea leaned on his shoulder. "Will you hate me if I mess up?"

He put his arm around her and gave her shoulder a squeeze. "You won't mess up."

ANDREA'S GREEN SILK empire-waist gown matched her eyes and shimmered in the spotlight. She was certain that the audience could see her legs shaking beneath it. Her neck felt worse. The auditorium's air-conditioning made every hair on it stand on end. She gripped her bow, wishing that it was her dad's hand.

She scanned the front row. Sylvia's turquoise dress stood out in the sea of black. She smiled when Andrea caught her eye. Andrea tried to smile back but her lips had iced over. Sebastian's dimpled grin thawed them. He threw his arms in the air and waved, his legs dangling from his chair. As far as buffers went, Andrea's parents could not have asked for a more freckled or cuter one between their seats. Her mother's latest boyfriend, Matt Willoughby, provided extra distance.

A burst of applause swept Andrea back to the stage. Frost snaked up her spine. Anatoli Dotsenko shuffled to the podium. The wiry silver-gray nest on his head bobbed as he walked, the only part of him that acknowledged the audience's cheers. He bowed at the podium and raised his baton, his mouth set in stone. The brass section responded with the opening fanfare of Shostakovich's Festive Overture. Winds followed, filling the melody's sails. The song soared. Andrea positioned her fingertips over the fingerboard and waited for her section's cue. Her knees knocked against the back of her instrument. Dotsenko flicked his baton her way. She drew a breath and set the music trembling in her fingers free.

Andrea was still flushed from Shostakovich's crescendo when the orchestra began Tchaikovsky's Variations on a Rococo Theme. She flipped the page of her music sheet. Her ribs squeezed her lungs. Her solo was coming up. She sat on the edge of her seat as the French horn finished a strain. She clasped Nate's pendant. Dotsenko directed his baton at her. She glanced at the front row and caught her dad's wink—and lived in it.

The audience vanished. The auditorium disappeared. The stage faded away. Andrea was back in her music room, cradling her quarter-size cello. She was seven again, playing for no one but herself and following no other conductor than joy. She improvised with vibratos and double stops, letting the melody have its way. White light flashed in her eyes. She blinked, telling herself that it was the spotlight bouncing off the music sheet stand. Bright hazel eyes blinked back from the crack ripping through the middle of her musical score, hidden from the audience and the rest of the orchestra. Andrea reeled, her bow moving mechanically over the strings.

The boy in the music sheet took a step back from the crack. He was much taller than the last time Andrea saw him and teetered on the cusp of becoming a man. Time had taken great care in shaping his face, chiseling it into elegant angles. The dark, warm pools in his eyes invited her to take a swim. Only the cello between them kept her from falling in. He sprinted to his desk and scribbled on a notebook. He tore the page and held a question up to the crack.

Name?

"Andrea!" Her voice reverberated through the auditorium.

Silence dripped from her cello. Each drop echoed and filled Andrea's ears. A sharp whistling sound pierced the hush. Andrea looked up. Dotsenko's steel glare sliced the air and cut cleanly through her rib cage. Andrea stood up and broke apart. Pieces of her soul spilled out and landed with a wet thud by her feet. She dragged one foot in front of the other, counting each endless step away from her cello and the 2,804 pairs of eyes boring a hole in the base of her skull. The future that hung on a silver chain around her neck grew heavier. Its metal clasp bit into her nape. Andrea stopped and turned to the audience. She had overcounted the eyes on her by one pair. Two slate eyes, partially hidden by a curtain of wavy auburn hair, were firmly fixed on the floor.

6

PUZZLES

His peculiar gift was the power of holding continuously in his mind a purely mental problem until he had seen straight through it.

—JOHN MAYNARD KEYNES ON ISAAC NEWTON

San Francisco
Present Day
Andrea is seventeen.

THE METAL DISC DANGLED FROM Nate's neck and grazed Andrea's collarbone. Nate pressed closer and kissed her. He had gotten much better at it over the past year, she thought. She couldn't quite recall the exact day they started kissing, but she did remember how Nate had once tried to hold her hand during a Bourne movie and how she had spilled their bucket of popcorn avoiding his grasp. Kissing required only curiosity. Holding hands meant a willingness to be held captive by someone's fingers. Her hands' last and only long-term relationship had been with her cello, and since she walked off Carnegie Hall's stage, she hadn't dared to hold on to much. Tonight, in the shadows of Nate's bedroom, she was feeling extra curious.

Nate's fingers found the buttons of her blouse. They trembled as he undid the first one. "Are you sure you want to do this, Dre?"

"Yes," she said, her voice quivering as much as Nate's hands. "Do you?"

Nate's mouth closed over hers. He unbuttoned her blouse and pulled it off her.

Andrea kissed him back deeper and longer than she had ever dared. When they kissed, she heard the music they both used to love. When they didn't, she remembered why only one of them continued to play their songs. Nate both soothed and ripped open old wounds. On this night, three years ago, the only passion she had ever known had been extinguished in an icy auditorium. Pressed against the warmth of Nate's bare skin, Andrea did not care that the heat radiating through her came from a different kind of fire. All that mattered was that here, in this moment, wrapped in Nate's arms, she felt something other than the cold emptiness inside her. Music had no mass or volume, but the hole it had carved out from Andrea made her feel that she was made up of little more than spiderwebs and air. She clung to Nate to give herself weight. They fell into his bed, a tangle of limbs and need. Andrea fumbled with the zipper of his jeans. Nate tensed, let her go, and retreated to the edge of the bed.

"What's wrong?" Andrea pulled his blanket over her bra.

"Maybe we should wait."

"For what?"

"Your first time should be special."

"It will be. It's going to be with you. I . . . I thought you wanted me, too."

"More than you can imagine. But are you sure you're ready for this? If we do this, everything will change."

"I want things to change. *I* want to change." She buried her face in her hands. "I'm sick of being me."

Nate held her hand. "Please don't say things like that."

"Say things like what? The truth? Everything I was and could have been ended in front of two thousand people three years ago. I'm a fucking walking joke, Nate."

"You're not a joke, Dre."

"Yeah. I suppose not. A joke's funny. I'm just pathetic."

"Come on, Dre, you're seventeen."

"So?"

"You haven't even begun to live."

"Then let me start. Now. Tonight." She cupped his cheeks. "Make me feel alive."

Nate inhaled deeply and cradled her against his chest. "Can you hear it?"

"Hear what?" Andrea frowned.

"Close your eyes."

"Why?"

"Just do it, okay?"

"Fine." Andrea shut her eyes. "They're closed."

"Good. Now listen."

"I can't hear any—" A rhythm drummed in her ear. Nate's heart was beating faster than his voice let on.

"Can you hear it now?"

"Yes," she whispered against his skin.

"My heart's pounded two beats faster since I walked into that classroom in fourth grade and pretended not to notice you trying to smile at me from your seat. It's been racing for almost half of my life, running toward you. I go to bed every night with a silly smile on my face because I know I'll be seeing you in the morning. And on the days that I don't get to see you, every inch of me misses you. If that's not how I make you feel now, Dre, sleeping with me isn't going to make you feel any different. I can't make you feel alive." He handed her blouse to her. "I . . . don't think we should do it. Not like this. Not tonight."

Andrea did not move or make a sound. Tears burned behind her eyelids and if she breathed, they were going to fall and never stop. She had grown up knowing that two things came to her very easily: music and Nate. She didn't have to try to be good at either of them. They were her life's givens, the legs on which everything else stood. She was born with the music inside her and all she had to do was let it out. Nate was just as simple. All she had to do was let him in. But now he pushed her away. Nothing was ever going to be easy again.

She stood up and pulled on her clothes. "You're right." She wiped her eyes with the back of her sleeve. "You can't help me. How can you? I've lost everything. I've lost my scholarship, my music, and my future. My dad can't even look at me the same way. Music was all that I was good at. It's who I was. Do you have any idea how it feels knowing that for the rest of my life, I'm going to have to pay my rent, put food on my plate, and pay my bills by pretending to be someone else? Look at me, Nate. What the hell do I have left?"

Nate gathered her in his arms. Tears rimmed his eyes. "Me."

ANDREA HOBBLED TO her front door shortly before noon on Sylvia's birthday with a second coat of bright yellow nail polish drying on her left foot. Her toes were the easiest part of her to paint a semblance of cheer on. Smiling was harder since she had left Nate's bedroom the night before.

She opened the door and smudged the polish on her big toe. An elderly, angular man in a gray forties-style fedora, matching suit, and cinnamon wing tip shoes smiled at her from the rubber welcome mat. He stood with his shoulders pulled back, his spine stretched, and his chin up, as though the top of his head was pulled taut by an invisible string.

"Yes?" She balanced on her bare heels. "Can I help you?"

He pulled off his hat and revealed a full head of wavy white hair. "I have a package for a Ms. Andrea Louviere." An English accent chiseled his words.

"I'm Andrea."

He narrowed his deep-set brown-green eyes, crinkling the

fine lines around them. The wrinkles might have made a weaker face look tired, but on his, it had the effect of making him appear statelier. Like the notches on a handsome antique, each line promised a story. "The cellist?"

Bile churned in her stomach. "No."

"Ah. I must have the wrong address then. I apologize." He placed his hat on his head.

Andrea gripped the doorframe. "Wait."

He stopped and turned. "Yes?"

"You have the right place. I am . . . was . . . a cellist."

"Was?"

"I don't play anymore."

"Why not?"

"I don't see how that is any of your business, Mister—"

"Westin. Oscar Ian Westin. And you're quite right. It isn't any of my business. I was just curious. It's an old habit of an old man, I'm afraid. I am sorry if I offended you." He reached into his suit jacket and pulled out what appeared to be a yellowed letter sealed with red wax. "This is for you."

Andrea took the letter from him. Must and age filled her nostrils. She tried not to gag. She turned the letter over. It didn't have a return address.

Mr. Westin adjusted the rim of his fedora. "Thank you for your time, Ms. Louviere. Good day." He strode down the walkway.

"Hang on," she called after him. "Who sent this?"

"Andrea?" Her dad's baritone drifted from behind her. "Is there someone at the door?"

She tucked the yellowed letter beneath her mint sweater and shut the front door.

Her dad poked his head out of the music room. "Who was that?"

"Just some delivery guy," she said, trying to keep Mr. Westin's letter out of sight. "He had the wrong address."

"Oh. Okay."

Her music career had ended on Carnegie Hall's stage, but Andrea knew that every time the postman stopped by or her father's email inbox pinged, he still hoped to find an invitation for her to perform. She had never seen spam and the Sears catalog crush anyone more. Until she found out what Mr. Westin's delivery was, keeping it from her dad was the kindest thing to do.

"Sylvia wants sushi for her birthday so I made dinner reservations at Zushi Puzzle," he said. "You can bring Nate, if you'd like."

"I'll give him a call."

Andrea could have told her father that she had been the one who was craving sushi and that Sylvia was being kind, but she made it a point to keep their conversations short. It was difficult to look directly into his eyes for long. Most people would not have noticed the slight quiver behind his lash line, but she did. She wasn't sure what it was the first time she saw it. Now she was certain.

Over the years that she had played her cello, she had received a variety of looks ranging from jealousy to awe. The look in her father's eyes was brand-new. As more people, including Nate, cast it her way in the months that followed the concert, she grasped what it was. Pity, like dust, made eyes twitch. The only difference was that no matter how much water you splashed over it, you could never flush it out.

HER CELLPHONE RANG. She laid Mr. Westin's delivery on her bed and pressed the phone's speaker button. She had not spoken to Nate since she had slipped out of his bedroom. "Hey, you."

"See you on the bus?"

She gripped the phone. It was the weekend and there was no school bus to catch, but the question was still their code for checking if things were okay between them. She wasn't sure if what had happened the previous evening counted as a fight. Lately, a lot of things they did had grown more difficult to define. She didn't have a name for what they had become to each other. If they had slept together, they would have woken up with a label for their relationship, and all labels, whether they were pasted on cat food, peanut butter, or people, came with expiration dates. She may not have understood her feelings for Nate, but she knew that she could not imagine riding the bus without him at her side. She nodded, forgetting that Nate could not see her.

"Dre?" Nate asked. "See you on the bus?"

"Yes. We're good. You were right. About everything. I . . . I wasn't thinking straight. It was just that last night was—"

"I know. Carnegie Hall. I realized it after you left."

"I'm sorry."

"It's okay, Dre," he said, his tone lighter. "So do you . . . um . . . want to talk about it some more? I can come over and . . ."

She glanced at the musty letter on the bed. "No. That's okay. But Dad made reservations for Sylvia's birthday dinner later. How do you feel about sushi?"

"Sounds good."

"Great. See you at Zushi Puzzle at eight."

Andrea set the phone down and reached for Mr. Westin's delivery. Tuna jumped onto the bed and planted all her eleven and a half pounds over the wax-sealed note. Andrea tugged the letter from beneath Tuna's hind leg. Red wax scattered over her lilac duvet. Andrea cracked the brittle seal and unfolded the letter. The edge of its first page was torn, as though it had been ripped from a notebook. It contained a single word written in brown-black ink.

Name?

The night Andrea had screamed her answer to the very same question in the middle of Carnegie Hall's main stage bled out of an old wound, hot, sticky, and bright red. She crumpled the page and hurled it across her bedroom. Tuna jumped on the paper ball and tossed it between her paws. Reason pounced on it the same way. In both matches, the rumpled sheet lost. The letter had to be a prank. Even after three years, Google made the details of her humiliation easy to find. All you needed to type was "Prodigy chokes at Carnegie Hall."

Andrea crushed the rest of the letter in her fist to make Tuna another toy. A line scribbled across the top of its second page screamed a plea.

Andrea, stop. Pray, take a breath. I swear to you, this is real. I am the boy behind your wall and you are the girl behind mine. Do not cast my words away.

Her heart lurched. If this was a trick, it was a cruel one. Tears burned behind her eyelids.

You are seventeen and the time has come at last to tell you how everything began, how I have come to love you above all else, and how you will come to love me.

Andrea sucked in the deepest breath she would ever take in her life and dove into the sea of elegant, minuscule handwriting. A story of a young boy, a wall, and a crack rippled in every direction.

Woolsthorpe Manor
1650
Isaac is seven.

A drop of melted mutton fat teetered by the wick of one of the two tall tallow candles on the oak dining table. A thin dark-haired boy peered into the shiny bead, watching the orange light swirling inside the liquid wax.

"Don't let your stew grow cold, Isaac," his grandmother

scolded. The candlelight softened the lines of her square face, bringing out her resemblance to her daughter Hannah.

Isaac swiveled his spoon around a thick pottage of bacon and sorrel. "Does light have color, Gran?"

"Color? I . . . um . . . well . . ." A V-shaped crease crinkled between her eyes. "Would you care for more bread?"

Isaac shook his head. "No, thank you."

His grandmother pushed another slice of buttered rye onto his plate. "You really should eat more."

Isaac washed back a sigh with watered-down orrisroot ale.

His grandmother tilted his chin toward the candlelight. "You are much too thin. What will your mother say when she sees you?"

Isaac tore a piece of bread and shoved it into his mouth. He hoped that if he chewed long enough, he would not have to give his grandmother an answer. He wasn't entirely sure that she required one. She knew as well as he did that her daughter's visits were few and far between.

Since his mother had moved to North Witham to raise a family with her new husband, the rector Barnabas Smith, he had learned to stop himself from running to the window every time a carriage rumbled up the gravel path to their home. It had been more difficult to keep still when he was three. The slightest crunch of pebbles had made him jump from his chair and stand on his toes to peek out the window. He had not understood why his mother had hugged him as tightly as she had on her wedding day when he asked her when she was coming back home. He was seven now and fathomed the meaning of her embrace.

Isaac stuffed another piece of bread into his mouth. His grandmother patted his hand and sipped her soup. He did the same, following their nightly script of soft slurps and silence. The breadth of their exchanges was limited to his weight, their herd of Lincoln Longwool sheep, and the apples in their orchard. If the sun was particularly bright, they talked about the weather. Their conversations thinned over lunch, and by dinner their stew was much thicker than anything they had left to say. Still, he tried. He liked seeing his grandmother smile. "The apples look good this year, Gran."

Her faded face brightened. "They do, don't they? I think we shall have a lovely crop. We should give some to your mother the next time she visits."

"Yes." Isaac looked out the window. "I'm sure she'd like that."

"She always said your cheeks were as red as those apples." His grandmother stroked the side of his face. "Do you remember?"

He dropped his eyes to his bowl and gulped down six spoonfuls of the pottage. "May I be excused?"

He watched his grandmother's reply take shape in her cloudy irises. A month ago, he would have tried to guess what she was going to say. Tonight, he didn't have to. Four weeks' worth of experimentation had given him enough information to allow him to confidently predict the decision that was making its way from her eyes to her lips.

He had attempted and failed numerous times to get away with eating less soup. His grandmother had scoffed at two spoonfuls, frowned at three, and dismissed four with a wave of her hand. Five rendered mixed results. Six was the most consistent. There was still a one out of ten chance of failure, but he liked his odds. He folded his hands over his lap and waited to hear the decision the numbers had already made.

"All right," she said, "but please take some bread up with you."

"Bread?" He broke off a small chunk of bread and enclosed it in his fist. He opened his hand, waved around his empty palm, and grinned. "What bread?"

"How many times must I tell you, Isaac?" His grandmother shook her head. "These amusements of yours are unnatural. I don't care if the farmhands find your little tricks entertaining. Magic is the devil's work. I forbid any form of it under this roof."

Isaac rolled his eyes.

"Did you hear me, young man?"

"I did."

"And?"

"I will stop. I promise." He kissed her on the cheek. "Good night, Gran."

ISAAC STRODE INTO his bedroom and shook his sleeve over his desk. A chunk of bread fell out of it and tumbled on top of its stale cousins from the previous evenings. He made a mental note to smuggle the leftovers to the chicken coop in the morning. He was glad that he did not have to lie to his grandmother. Making bread disappear up his sleeve was losing its novelty and he had every intention of mastering apples next. His favorite tree was heavy with them. In the morning, he would take his pick. The night held other amusements for his hands. When his fingers were busy, it was easier to forget that he had a mother who had chosen to forget him.

He crouched by his bed and heaved a wooden chest from under it. Rocks, blocks of wood, pieces of metal, and an assortment of small tools he had made filled it to the brim. He made his selection for the evening and arranged his materials on the desk he had inherited from his father. The scratches and dents on the table had multiplied fourfold since he'd convinced his grandmother to move it into his bedroom. His illiterate father had left it in near-pristine condition, preferring to spend his day keeping his sheep from straying into the neighbor's corn.

Or so he heard. What little he knew of the man was stitched together from the rare times his grandmother spoke of her late son-in-law. The only things he was confident that they had in common were their dark hair, their hazel eyes, and their name. He also knew that his father would approve of this night's project. A new apple cart was a welcome addition to any orchard—even one that could carry only two smallish fruits.

A breeze blew through the window above his desk, perfuming his bedroom with ripe apples. The candle's flame cowered in its wake. He cupped one hand over the candle and reached for the window latch. White light flickered on his timber-framed wall. He turned, expecting to find a firefly that had lost its way. A pair of bright green eyes proved him wrong.

The girl who owned the eyes waved at him from the small glowing hole in his wall. Isaac toppled off his chair. His left knee slammed on the floor. He clenched his teeth. If there was anything that life in Woolsthorpe had taught him, it was how to bear pain without making a sound. His grandmother scowled at the slightest whimper. Boys were not supposed to cry. Isaac clambered to his feet and locked his eyes on the girl behind his wall. His heart pounded in his ears, but he forced himself to smile. Boys were also supposed to have good manners. He waved back at his visitor and took a step toward her.

The girl retreated. He extended his arm to coax her back. The girl trembled where she stood. Isaac searched his room for something to show her that he meant her no harm. Three pieces of stale bread caught his eye. He grabbed them from his desk and tossed them in the air.

The shepherds at the manor did not care for his questions or thoughts, but his juggling never failed to elicit applause. They could not look at him oddly or think him strange when he kept them entertained. He hoped his red-haired guest was going to be as easy to amuse. He couldn't let her leave without discovering who she was or how she had come to live inside his wall. Getting her to stay and smile was worth breaking his promise to his grandmother. He caught the chunks of bread and made each of them disappear with a flourish.

The girl's green eyes grew wide. Her mouth moved as though she gasped, but Isaac couldn't say for sure. Like the large string instrument she had been playing, her voice made no sound. He grinned anyway. Magic had not let him down. He thrust his empty hand to the girl and beamed. A chunk of bread came loose from his sleeve and fell to the floor. A blush seared Isaac's cheeks and melted his smile.

The girl jumped up and clapped for him, her applause as vigorous as it was soundless. It inflated Isaac's chest. He picked up the bread that had given his trick away, determined to earn every clap. He waved his hand over the stale chunk. Two pieces of bread appeared next to it on his palm. Isaac stuffed them in his mouth, hoping to win more of the girl's mute glee. Her sides shook from laughter. Isaac rummaged through the shelves in his mind for other tricks to keep her happy.

The girl took a small step toward the wall. Isaac took a smaller one. The glow around the crack faded. Woolsthorpe's limestone bricks filled in its edges. Isaac ran to the shrinking hole. A layer of plaster sealed it.

"No! Wait!" Isaac scrambled to his treasure chest and grabbed a mallet he had fashioned from pieces of a broken plow. He swung at his wall. Plaster crumbled. "Are you there, girl? What is your name? Tell me who you are."

He pressed his cheek against the wall and waited for a reply. The bricks did not answer. He hoisted his mallet over his shoulder. Knobby fingers closed around his wrist and shook the mallet from his grasp. It crashed on the floor, an inch from his toes.

"Just what do you think you are doing, young man?" His grandmother tugged him away from the wall, her nostrils flaring.

"Gran, I can explain." His eyes scoured his wall for an answer his grandmother might accept. He would have told her the truth had he had the words for it. "I saw a spider."

She jumped back from the wall. "Did you kill it?"

"I missed."

She yanked the hem of her wool skirt off the floor. "Oh . . . well . . . carry on then." She shuffled to the doorway. "But Isaac . . ."

He straightened his face and tried not to giggle. "Yes?"

"Use your shoe."

Isaac shut the door and waited for his grandmother's footsteps to fade behind it. He raised his foot over an invisible insect and stomped as loudly as he could. His Gran deserved to go to bed with peace of mind.

He heaved his mallet and aimed at his wall. His eyes fell on the chipped plaster before the mallet's head did. He dropped the mallet and sighed. He had lived in Woolsthorpe Manor long enough to know that behind his bedroom's stone wall was nothing but a clear view of the barn. He rubbed his forehead, conceding that he was not going to find answers inside its bricks. He had to look elsewhere. He took the candle from his desk, tiptoed past his grandmother's room, and crept downstairs.

The candle's flame cast a yellow glow over the small parlor's cream walls. Brass glinted in the light. He took a step toward the lantern-shaped clock above the stone fireplace. He took note of the time and returned to his bedroom.

Isaac retrieved a leather-bound notebook from his desk drawer and flipped through it. A quarter of its pages were filled with the phrases his grandmother had made him copy from the Bible during his writing lessons. His penmanship was shaky at first, but by the middle of the book, his letters' curls, loops, and tails had grown steady enough to keep his secrets. They guarded the questions that made Woolsthorpe's farmhands snicker whenever he made the mistake of asking them out loud. *Why does my ball only move when I push it? Why does it slow down and stop?* Tonight he entrusted the notebook with his most difficult question yet: *Who is the girl behind my wall?*

He dipped his quill into a small pot of oak gall ink. He steered the nib across the page and listed everything that he remembered about their encounter.

9 o'clock. White light. Crack. Girl.

He doubted he would forget anything about this evening, but committing the details to paper was going to help him believe it in the morning.

Green eyes. Red-brown hair. Large violin. Silence.

He underlined the last word. He closed his eyes and painted the girl inside his eyelids, recalling how her fingers flitted over her instrument's neck and how her bow glided over its four strings. Her music was mute, but he heard its loneliness in his heart. The hollow his mother had left in his chest echoed with the same song.

And that, my dearest Andrea, is how we first met—through a crack, in silence, at the first blush of youth. I know that there is no magic that I can perform to make you fully fathom the letter that is in your hands. I regret that I cannot tell you more at this writing other than that you shall hear from me again. I do not wish to burden you with more than I must—despite the devastating temptation to tell you how everything ends.

Yours always,
Isaac Newton
1666

1, 1, 2, 3, 5, 8, 13, 21, 34, 55

7

PROOF

A man may imagine things that are false, but he can only understand things that are true, for if the things be false, the apprehension of them is not understanding.

—ISAAC NEWTON

San Francisco
Present Day
Andrea is seventeen.

THANK GOD FOR SEVEN-YEAR-OLDS. SINCE Andrea had read Isaac's letter two and a half weeks before, Sebastian was the only person she could sit across from without fidgeting. The Monopoly board between them helped. If she happened to wince when any of Isaac's words came loose from the knot in her gut, she blamed it on not passing Go, not collecting two hundred dollars, and going directly to jail. Sebastian believed her and, it seemed, so did Nate.

Nate landed on Sebastian's Boardwalk property with its little red plastic hotel. He slapped his forehead. "Again? Seriously? Be honest, Bas. You rigged the dice."

Sebastian grinned and read the back of his title deed card. "That will be seventeen hundred dollars. Pay up."

Nate counted out the rent he owed. "You've wiped me out and your hotel didn't even have a minibar."

"Want to play again?" Sebastian asked.

"I'm game if your sister is." Nate turned to Andrea. "What do you say?"

Andrea checked the time on the grandfather clock in the living room. It was getting late and there was another dice she needed to roll. "No, thanks. I'm done. My pride can only take declaring bankruptcy once a night."

Sebastian stuffed the Chance cards back into the Monopoly box.

Nate stowed the game's tokens. "I should get going."

"I'll walk you out." Andrea stood up.

"Hey, Nate," Sebastian said. "Knock, knock."

"Who's there?" Nate asked.

"Monopoly."

"Monopoly who?"

"Monopoly is bigger than your nopoly."

Andrea giggled louder than the joke was funny. It was likely going to be the last time she was going to laugh that evening and she wanted to make the most of it. Her wall and Isaac's letter were waiting for her upstairs.

"Don't quit your real estate job, Bas," Nate said with a chuckle. He walked into the hallway and turned to Andrea. "I had fun tonight."

"Me, too."

He reached for her hand.

Andrea's dad stepped out of the music room. "Heading home, Nate?"

Nate dropped his hand to his side. "Yes, Mr. L."

"Don't be late for your cello lesson tomorrow."

"I won't. Promise."

Andrew Louviere nodded and shut the music room's door.

Andrea smirked. "Liar. You know you're going to stand him up."

"You know me too well." He leaned over to kiss her. "Good night."

Andrea tilted her head, diverting Nate's lips to her cheek. "Good night."

THE FACE OF Mr. Penelo, Andrea's third-grade science teacher, popped into her head as she sat at her desk in her bedroom later that evening. He was a short man with stubby arms and gray hair that was pasted in a wispy spiral around his head, but from the way his voice boomed across the classroom, you would have sworn that he was at least six feet tall. Andrea had scraped by with a C in his fourth-period class but had paid enough attention to recall a lesson he had taught her class one muggy Monday afternoon.

"For every action there is an equal and opposite reaction." Mr. Penelo sat on his chair and pushed against his desk, sending his chair rolling in the opposite direction. "Ta-dah. Isaac Newton's third law of motion. Can anyone give me other examples?"

Nate raised his hand. "Hopping."

"Bouncing balls," said the wiry kid next to him.

"Rocket launches," Laura Thomson volunteered from behind Andrea.

No one had mentioned receiving a love letter from a man who died more than three centuries ago. They should have, Andrea thought, as she stared out of her bedroom window. Isaac's words sent her reeling harder than any brick wall. She locked her door at nine o'clock each night, clinging to the hope that if she read his letter just one more time, she would find answers somewhere between its minuscule handwritten lines. Her search led her in one direction: 1666.

Isaac had turned twenty-four that year and was waiting out the Great Plague in his home at Woolsthorpe. His time at the manor was dubbed his *annus mirabilis*, his "miracle year." It was during this period that Isaac made the three mathematical and scientific discoveries that would forever change the way man understood the world: calculus, the composition of white light, and the universal law of gravity. But no matter how many times Andrea pored over Isaac's equations and scientific laws, she did not get any closer to understanding their correspondence.

Textbooks and history told her nothing of the message he had sent across time and less of the crack that connected them. His letter remained her only clue. She fished it out from her desk drawer just as she did every evening. Tuna rubbed her head against Andrea's leg. She turned to the letter's last page, no longer needing to keep her eyes on it to know what was coming next.

1, 1, 2, 3, 5, 8, 13, 21, 34, 55

A quick Google search told her that they were Fibonacci numbers, an integer sequence, but it did not give any clue to their purpose. They still did not make any sense.

Andrea had come close to blurting everything to Nate, but she bit her lips until they bled each time she felt the urge to ask for his help. It wasn't fair to pull him into the rabbit hole with her. She was feeling crazy enough for the both of them.

She kneaded the bridge of her nose and refolded Isaac's letter. Bits of red wax fell over Tuna's back. She brushed them off, savoring the softness of the cat's orange fur against the swollen pads of her fingers. Playing the cello for hours every evening had left them red and raw. Failing to open her wall made them feel worse than they looked. But from the way her dad's eyes lit up when he noticed the state of her hands, one might have thought they were the loveliest things he had ever seen. He pressed his fingers to his lips to keep his glee from slipping out. He was only partially successful. The corners of his mouth twitched whenever he tried to rein in a grin. Andrea guessed that he would not have been as happy about her sore fingers if he knew why she was playing her cello again.

Andrea unhooked a reusable shopping bag from the back of her chair and pulled out a tin of Bag Balm. Until she grew her calluses back, the ointment was going to be her fingers' best friend. She was not going to get any answers if she bled out over her cello's fingerboard. She slathered the thick salve over her fingertips, desperate to apply the same to her soul. Cradling her cello was at once like throwing her arms around a lost friend and searing them against white-hot coal. It was impossible to pry the pleasure from the blistering pain. For a few hours each night, she was whole again, and acutely aware of each passing second and note that brought her closer to the evening's end. Holding on to something that she knew she could not keep taught Andrea a new kind of despair.

Wanting.

Waiting.

Having.

Losing.

This cycle was her heart's clock, her sole sense of time.

She pulled out her next purchase, leaving greasy prints on its clear plastic box. She wiped away the excess balm on her jeans and read the instructions for her new mini audio recorder. The device was nowhere near as fancy as the one her father owned, but it had been on sale and was good enough for recording and reviewing her attempts to crack her wall open. She popped two AA batteries inside it and pushed the record button.

Andrea pressed the cello's strings. Heat flared in her fingertips. She gritted her teeth, shut her eyes, and played on. Light glowed behind her eyelids. She kept them closed. Flashing cellphone screens had disappointed her before. The light grew brighter. "Please be there," she whispered, parting her lids halfway.

A crack, no bigger than her backpack, broke through her wall. The glowing hole opened into a large room filled with rows of tall bookshelves. A lean, dark-haired man stood with his back to her, returning a book to a shelf. His broad shoulders tensed through his coarse black coat. He spun around. His hazel eyes darted over her face.

Andrea? he said without making a sound.

Andrea recognized the shape of her name on the young man's lips. She nodded, wondering if she looked as different to him as he did to her. The three years that had passed since she'd last seen him on Carnegie Hall's stage had polished his features into an assembly of handsome angles and lines that was difficult to tear her eyes from. "Isaac?" she asked, daring for the first time to say his name out loud. Its syllables tickled her tongue, effervescent and sweet like ginger ale.

His eyes widened. He strode toward the wall and waved, inviting her to come closer. *Come,* he said silently. *Please.*

Andrea glanced at her cello. She was less than three feet away from Isaac and answers, but her instrument kept her pinned to her seat. She pushed it away and lunged toward the crack, unsure how long it would remain open after the music stopped. Isaac thrust his hand through the shrinking hole. She sucked in a breath and pressed her palm against his.

A wave of warmth spread through Andrea's fingers. History told her that she was standing in front of one of mankind's greatest minds, but all she could see was the boy whom she had shared a secret with for more than half of her life. His long fingers closed around hers. Pieces of plaster appeared between their palms. She gripped his hand, digging her nails into him. A thick book materialized and pried their hands apart. The rest of the wall reappeared, sealing the crack.

Andrea staggered from the wall and knocked the audio recorder from her desk. Its tiny red light flashed from the carpet. She scooped up the recorder, her hand tingling from the heat of Isaac's palm. She pressed the play button and waited for the song she had recorded to call the dark, beautiful, and magical creature behind her wall back.

8

HANDS

What was before is left behind; what never was is now.

—OVID

Sri Lanka
Present Day
Andrea is eighteen.

SWEAT DRIPPED FROM ANDREA'S SCALP and stung her sunburned cheeks. She was almost convinced that she could hear her skin sizzle. She could not spare the time to listen closely and know for sure. It was her last day as a volunteer for Habitat for Humanity's Global Village program in Sri Lanka and she had a house to finish building. Matt, her mother's boyfriend, worked for the organization and had suggested the two-week trip as a way to celebrate her eighteenth birthday. Andrea leapt at the chance to get as far away as she could from her bedroom's walls. She was tired of scouring them for cracks.

For a year, her walls had ignored the recording she had made of Isaac's song and all her other attempts to see Isaac again. He had promised her another letter, but her hands were too raw from playing his song to hold on to hope.

"Earth to Dre. Earth to Dre." Nate waved a muddied trowel in front of her face. "Back to work, slacker."

"Remind me again why I agreed to let you come with me on this trip?" Andrea rubbed the sweat from her eyes.

"Hang on. If I recall correctly, it was your dad who suggested I tag along. His little girl needed a chaperone."

She punched his arm. "Oh, shut up."

Nate chuckled. "How are you holding up? Besides your lapses in memory, I mean."

"I don't think my armpits will ever be dry again." Andrea laid a brick on her chin-high wall. She stepped back and admired the three-hundred-square-foot home she had helped build. "But I'm good."

"Don't worry. Eau de Sweat becomes you."

"You don't exactly smell like roses yourself, mister." Working with his hands in a white T-shirt that was molded to his broad chest suited Nate, but Andrea decided to keep that thought to herself. He had more than enough fangirls to boost his ego back home, girls who slipped him their numbers whenever he played with his band.

He took a long sip of water from the plastic jug they shared. "But this is quite something, isn't it? I'm glad I came."

"Me, too."

"You're glad that I came, too?" He leaned closer to Andrea and flashed a dimpled grin that lit his face, transforming him the way fairy lights turned pine trees into Christmas memories.

Andrea's breath caught midway in her throat. She coughed to clear it. "What? No. . . . I . . . uh . . . meant that I'm glad I—" She took a quick step back and tripped on a brick.

Nate caught her by the wrist and laughed. His lucky disc-shaped pendant swung from his neck and sparkled in the sun. "I'm kidding," he said without letting her go.

Andrea kept her eyes from his smile, refusing to lose her footing again. During their weeks in Sri Lanka, Nate's smile had knocked her off-balance more often than she cared to admit.

Tiny bolts of electricity prickled the spot where he held her. Without her cello and Isaac's wax-sealed words, there was nothing to distract her from the current shooting up her arm.

"I know what you meant. I think I know you pretty well by now." Nate slipped his hand from her wrist and held her hand.

Andrea's fingers stiffened, ready to flee. The warmth of Nate's palm fused them in place. Andrea met his eyes. With Nate there was no need to hurry. There was no song that was ending or plaster to push them apart.

"And you know me," he said softly, resting his forehead on the top of her head.

Andrea tilted her face to catch the whisper. The tips of their noses touched. She inhaled sharply, drawing air from the sliver of space between their lips.

"Happy birthday, Dre." He leaned closer.

Andrea closed her eyes, waiting to feel his lips. She had refused their sanctuary since she had received Isaac's letter. Today, she longed to remember what it was like not to be ignored. Nate's upper lip grazed hers. Andrea tiptoed to seek shelter in his kiss. A familiar sweet warmth welcomed her, but its flames grew quickly like rum set on fire. The last time their mouths had touched, Nate was more boy than man. This Nate was intoxicating. Andrea circled her arms around his smooth nape to claim more of him.

A man cleared his throat behind Nate.

Andrea jumped back. "Oh . . . uh . . . hi, Matt."

Nate spun around. "Hey. We were just . . . um . . ."

"Taking a break?" Matt smirked.

Nate blushed and picked up his trowel. "Back to work."

Matt took off his yellow hard hat. He wiped his shiny scalp with a towel. "How's the birthday girl?"

"I wish I didn't have to leave tomorrow," Andrea said, willing the flush on her cheeks to fade. "The trip went by so fast."

"Yeah," Nate said. "This was a great experience, Matt. Thanks again for letting me come along."

"We need all the help we can get," Matt said. "You should tell your friends about this when you get back."

"I will," Nate said.

Matt pulled out a box wrapped in brown paper from his backpack and handed it to Andrea. "This is from Julia."

"Thanks." Andrea took the gift from him. She knew without unwrapping it that it was another journal. Her relationship with her mother was best when it was predictable and from a distance, and after Carnegie Hall, Andrea thought that Julia had even learned to love her a little bit more. She wasn't as lucky as her mother thought she was.

"And this is from me." Matt held out a crumpled paper bag. "Just a little something to help you remember this trip."

Andrea peeked inside. A locally handcrafted silver-and-glass-beaded bracelet caught the sun. "It's beautiful. Thanks, Matt."

"You're welcome. We'll celebrate with the rest of the team tonight."

"You don't need to go through the trouble. I'm sure everyone will be beat after work."

"Nonsense. They're all looking forward to it. It will be fun. Besides, I told your mother I'd look out for you, and I don't think I'd be much of a guardian if I didn't let you blow out a candle on your birthday. I can't promise you a cake to go with that candle, but there's a good chance we'll be able to find some chapati." A boyish smile creased his leathery cheek. "What do you say?"

"Throw in some beef curry and you have a deal."

"Great. I'll see you at quitting time."

A truck, piled high with bags of cement, rumbled into the site. Matt waved at it, directing it to park on the far side of the construction area.

"Do you need help unloading, Matt?" Nate asked.

"Sure. Thanks." Matt planted his hard hat on his head. "Follow me."

Nate squeezed Andrea's shoulder. "Try not to destroy anything while I'm gone."

"I'll do my best." She watched Nate walk away, towering over most people at the construction site. His build and blond hair, she thought, made him look like a Viking that had lost his way. Andrea smiled to herself and touched her lips. They were still warm from his kiss.

"Good day, Ms. Louviere." A voice, grainy and dark like coffee grounds, snaked over her shoulder. "Lovely house."

Andrea twisted around. Except for the sweat that dripped from his brow and the red-gray mud that caked his wing tip shoes, Mr. Westin looked the same as he had the year before. "How . . . how did you know I was here?"

He smiled and handed her a rectangular package wrapped in parchment. "Happy birthday."

Her fingers trembled as she took the delivery from him.

"You've been playing the cello again," he said.

She jerked her head back. "How did you know?"

"Music leaves marks."

She glanced at the calluses on her fingers. Each was a reminder of the nights she had failed to find Isaac. "Ugly ones."

"You should be proud of them, Ms. Louviere. Not many people are blessed with such talent, myself included."

"It's never too late to learn," she said, choosing to be polite rather than truthful.

"Are you offering to teach me?"

"Teach you? No. No way. I can't."

"Why not?"

"I'm not a teacher."

"Last year you said you weren't a cellist. Who can say what you will or won't be next year? Time has more twists and turns than any road, don't you agree?" He tipped his fedora. "Enjoy the rest of your day."

She grabbed his arm. "You haven't answered my question. How did you know that I'd be here?"

"My delivery instructions are quite precise."

"Who gives you your instructions?"

"I'm afraid I can't help you. I'm sorry, Ms. Louviere. I simply follow the instructions I am given."

"Is there a person I can contact? Someone who can tell me more about these letters? Please, Mr. Westin. I have to know."

"I truly wish that I could be of more assistance, but I simply—"

"Follow instructions. I know, I know." Andrea rubbed her forehead. Red mud streaked over her skin.

"Here." Mr. Westin offered her a white handkerchief. "Don't worry. It's clean. You can return it when you give me my first music lesson."

ANDREA KEPT MR. WESTIN'S delivery buried deep in her backpack until she flew home. She couldn't have risked Nate seeing it, and it wouldn't have seemed right to open it so far away from her cello or wall. Now she sat on her bedroom floor and leaned against the white and gray stripes that had taken the place of the room's yellow paint. She pulled the package out from her carry-on bag and ripped its wrapper. A book's mottled leather cover stared up at her. Ovid's *Metamorphoses*. A yellowed piece of folded paper stuck out from its pages. Andrea tugged it free. Isaac's wax initials sealed its flap. She held her breath and cracked the seal open.

My dearest Andrea,

Much time has passed since we first touched, but my hand still remembers the shape and softness of your palm. I also recall the puzzle you left me with when your lips shaped my name. I struggled to comprehend how you came to know it, not having had the privilege of introducing myself before then. I have a better understanding of the nature and sequence of these events now, and one day, you shall, too.

I confess that I gave no thought to propriety that day in the college's library. I do not, however, regret my boldness. If I were permitted just one memory to keep, I would choose that moment. I have known you since I was a boy, but it was only then that you truly felt real.

Trinity College, Cambridge
1661
Isaac is nineteen.

Isaac swept the last of the leaves into a small pile in the corner of the university's courtyard. Of all his chores as a sizar at Trinity College, this was the one he detested the least. When the air was crisp and the sun dappled the courtyard's stones with gold, he admitted to finding some enjoyment in it. His other duties as a scholar and servant at the college held no such pleasure. Fetching meals from the kitchen for his wealthier classmates, waiting in the hall while they dined, and carrying wood for their fires weren't things he looked forward to in any kind of weather. But he did them anyway. His mother did not leave him with a choice.

Though she could have easily paid for Isaac's full tuition and spared him from having to empty his classmates' chamber pots to pay his way through school, she had sent him off to Cambridge with barely enough money to purchase a notebook, a lock for his desk, a bottle of ink, and two weeks' worth of candles. She'd made it clear that she was disappointed when he chose his studies over following in his father and grandfather's footsteps. She held the hope that he would come to his senses, pack his trunk, and come home. Some days, Isaac almost did.

He reminded himself at least 101 times a day that his menial tasks as a school sizar paid for his tuition and that it was still better to be a servant to his fellow students than to Woolsthorpe's sheep. Sizarship was an arrangement that allowed him to trade service for school aid and meant that his education was not at his mother's expense, only his pride's. He found it tolerable because it was temporary. Life as a sheep farmer was not. But there were times when he walked head-down through the halls of Cambridge in a sizar's requisite coarse sleeveless gown and black cloth cap that herding sheep didn't seem so awful. Sheep didn't turn their noses up at him.

"Newton," a voice snickered behind him.

Isaac turned.

"You missed a spot." A tall student who sat in front of Isaac in the lecture hall and obstructed Isaac's view with his pit-riddled nape kicked the pile of leaves that Isaac had just swept. He laughed and sprinted away.

Isaac chased after him and grabbed his arm.

"Gentlemen." An elderly mathematics professor with a hooked nose that would put eagles to shame marched out from the cloisters surrounding the yard. He narrowed his eyes at Isaac. "Is there a problem here?"

Isaac let go of the student's sleeve. "No, sir."

The pockmarked boy smirked and straightened his cloak. "None at all."

"Good." The older man glanced at the leaves rolling across the courtyard. He turned to Isaac. "And I suggest, young man, that you get back to your chores. Those leaves aren't going to sweep themselves."

Isaac nodded. "Yes, of course."

"Good day, gentlemen." The professor straightened his cloak and walked away.

Isaac clenched his fists.

A tight smile sliced the tall student's pitted face. "Know your place, Newton," he said, brushing off invisible dirt from his sleeve. "Never put your filthy hands on me again."

Isaac strode between rows of bookshelves in the college library, clutching a small embroidered coin purse with one hand

and a weathered book with the other. The purse's contents bulged against its intricate needlework. Isaac tossed it onto a desk at the end of the aisle. Silver coins clinked against the desk's dark wood. Though sitting in plain sight, the purse was going to collect a fine layer of dust before it was found. Its owner did not haunt the library like Isaac did.

Isaac had had no interest in the pockmarked student's money when he lifted it from his coat. He merely wished to repay him for the extra work he'd given Isaac in the courtyard. The small inconvenience of scouring Trinity's grounds for the missing coin purse was nearly an equitable exchange. Isaac had stolen his money, but the student had robbed him of part of his day. Coins could be returned. Time could not. Though settling the score would have been swifter with his fist, it would have been less satisfying. The mathematics professor who had walked in on their altercation, Isaac thought, could not have come at a more perfect time. The interruption made it easier to part the coin purse from its owner.

Isaac left the purse on the desk. The beginnings of a grin teased his lips apart. A measure of disappointment weighed it down and kept the smile from spreading. The distraction he had required to surreptitiously lift the purse made it evident that his fingers were not as nimble as they'd been when he'd easily made bread magically vanish into thin air. If the girl behind his wall happened to pay him a visit, he would no longer be able to make her smile.

The years that had passed since he last saw the girl had made him grow weary of his little sleights of hand. None of them made her reappear. More than country fair tricks were required to crack open Woolsthorpe's walls. Isaac wandered past the library's mathematics section to its rows of Greek classics, searching for real spells in their myths. Poring through dusty pages every afternoon was better than staring at his dorm room's walls, waiting for a crack to materialize.

"Andrea," he whispered beneath a sigh.

The name came unbidden. It slipped out of his mouth just as it always did when he felt alone. The girl behind his wall had formed the name with her lips when he'd asked her who she was. He had not heard her voice and could not be sure of her answer. *Andrea* was his best guess. It was an unusual name for a girl, but he wasn't surprised. Nothing about her was common. He closed his eyes and pictured how her hair fell around her shoulders, untamed by braids or ribbons. She moved with the same freedom. She was a fairy from a fable, above all natural laws and norms.

Isaac came to a gap in a row of books. He laid the book he had been carrying on the edge of the shelf. The *Iliad* had brought him no closer to solving Andrea's puzzle. He made his way down the row and stopped. His grandmother had passed away years before, but her raspy voice was never too far from his mind. He could not eat a bowl of stew without hearing her urge him to finish it, and he could not leave his notebooks scattered over the table or his bed unmade without her telling him to tidy up. Anything he had taken, she reminded him, had to be returned to its proper place. The student's coin purse was an exception.

But Homer deserved more respect. Isaac pushed the *Iliad* into the gap on the shelf, making sure it was flush with the other books. Bright white light shimmered over his fingers. He spun around. A crack glowed on the bookshelf across from him. Through it, a woman with the same shade of autumn in her hair as his secret childhood friend played a silent song. He searched her face for the familiar. The delicate lines of her porcelain features distracted him, but when he saw her gentle green eyes, he realized who she was. "Andrea?" he gasped.

Andrea confirmed her identity with a nod. She moved her lips, posing a silent question. His heart stopped. Had she said his name? He brushed the thought aside and hastened to the crack, consumed by the need to get as close to her as possible. He held out his hand, daring her to prove to him that she was real.

Andrea cast her instrument aside and accepted his challenge. She pressed her hand to his, soldering the memory of her touch into his flesh. He laced his fingers around hers, feeling the muscle and bone beneath her skin. She was as real, warm, and alive as he was. A weathered copy of Theocritus's *Idylls* reappeared next to her wrist. Isaac grasped her fingers, trying to keep her longer.

More volumes filled the crack around their clasped hands. Andrea clung to him, digging her fingers behind his knuckles. He tried not to flinch. The pain was worth it, if it meant that she was going to stay. Ovid's *Metamorphoses* crushed that possibility. The book took shape between their palms and pushed Andrea away.

ISAAC WAITED UNTIL his roommate John Wilkin's breathing grew even. He looked over at his bed to make sure he was asleep. Wilkin snored.

Isaac carried a candlestick to his desk, casting shadows over his small dorm room. He sat down and cracked open his journal. Anagrams of his name were scrawled in the borders of an entry lamenting the conditions of his sizarship. Shuffling the letters of his name soothed him whenever he wanted to pretend that he was someone else. Isaac flipped to a blank page and began that night's journal entry the same way he began every entry about Andrea. *Hypotheses non fingo.* Beneath it, he scribbled its English translation. "I frame no hypotheses."

A man of science, Isaac thought, might have ransacked every shelf in the library to try to explain how his hands had grazed another world. But he was not such a man and felt no compulsion to reduce what had happened to him into theorems and numbers. He did not need equations to know how he felt. He required only one book.

Isaac retrieved from beneath his pillow the fifteenth-century edition of Ovid's *Metamorphoses* that he had stolen from the library. He traced the scratches Andrea's fingernails had left on its leather binding, envying how they were going to last longer than the five tiny crescent-shaped wounds she had scraped over his skin.

> *The scars you gave me have faded, my dearest, but I can still feel them. They soothe me with the veracity of your existence. I pray that my humble gift and the tale I have left for you between its pages offer you the same comfort.*
>
> *Yours always,*
> *Isaac*
> *1666*
> *1, 1, 2, 3, 5, 8, 13, 21, 34, 55*

Ovid's *Metamorphoses* had not been on Andrea's wish list for her birthday, but holding it in her arms, Andrea realized that there was nothing that she had needed more. The warmth of its leather, the weight of its pages, and the five small scratches her nails had left on its cover kindled the embers of her faith in the man and world behind her wall.

Another sheet of paper stuck out from between the book's covers. Andrea pulled it free. The edges of the page were ragged, cruder than the kind Isaac used for his letters. Neither was it sealed with wax. Andrea's pulse quickened as she unfolded it. An excerpt of Ovid's ancient tale of Pyramus and Thisbe, written in Isaac's hand, filled the page. The story of the forbidden lovers who whispered their love for each other through a crack between their homes drew her in and refused to let her go. Stone walls. Fleeting whispers. Stolen time. Untasted kisses. Each passage knew her pain.

Andrea came up for air. Isaac had intended the tale to comfort her. Instead, envy tunneled inside her. The bricks between Pyramus and Thisbe seemed like such a feeble barrier compared to the centuries that kept her from Isaac and answers. But Andrea could not bring herself to resent the book that had delivered the lovers' story. Its scarred cover pushed away all doubt. She had touched Isaac's world and he had touched hers. And now she had proof. She picked up her phone and dialed Nate's number.

9

SECRETS

A man is sorry to be honest for nothing.

—OVID

San Francisco
Present Day
Andrea is eighteen.

THE DRUM SOLO OF JIMI HENDRIX'S "If 6 Was 9" pounded against Nate's garage door. Andrea's heart thundered louder. She adjusted her backpack's straps over her left shoulder and knocked on the door's white wooden slats. "Hey, you. It's me."

The drums fell silent. The garage door opener hummed. Nate waved at her with his drumsticks. "So what's this big secret you couldn't tell me over the phone last night?"

Andrea licked her dry lips. "You sounded great."

"Thanks, but you didn't come all this way to tell me that, right? Is something wrong? You've been acting weird since we left Sri Lanka."

Andrea took her usual spot on a threadbare couch that had more springs than stuffing. It sank under her, remembering her shape. "No. Nothing's wrong."

"Then why do you look like you're carrying a severed head in that bag of yours? Come on, Dre. Whatever's bothering you, just spit it out. Unless, of course, you really have someone's head in there."

Andrea clutched her bag. The top of Ovid's *Metamorphoses* peeked out from under its flap. She had spent the night researching all she could about it and Isaac. History made no mention of the scratches she had left on its cover, but it chronicled a darker secret Isaac made its verses keep. An auction of the contents of a three-hundred-year-old metal chest at Sotheby's in 1936 brought them to light. The British economist John Maynard Keynes had purchased 39 out of the auction's 329 lots. What he discovered in Isaac's private handwritten manuscripts drastically altered his image of the scientist and mathematician he thought he knew.

Isaac's encrypted laboratory notes revealed an illicit pursuit he had taken great pains to hide. Though he was heralded as one of the world's foremost scientific intellects, Isaac was a devoted alchemist who based his clandestine experiments on ancient Greek myths. The verses that he believed hid secret alchemical recipes burned a hole in Andrea's backpack.

"Well? Are you going to go all *Dexter* on me or not?" Nate leaned against his pickup, a blue Ford held together by equal amounts of duct tape and willpower.

"Nate . . . I . . . well . . . there's something I've been wanting to tell for a while."

"Should I be sitting down for this?"

"That might be a good idea."

"Scoot over."

Andrea made room for him. His hip grazed hers. Nate was sweaty from playing the drums, but he still smelled like soap. And safety. Andrea rested her cheek on his toned shoulder. On this side of the wall, Nate was her oldest friend. She tilted her face to find his eyes. They still looked at her the way they did when they'd traded snacks at recess and didn't flinch or laugh at her when she insisted that "Something" by the Beatles tasted like warm bread pudding. Today, she counted on them to do the same. She held Nate's hand.

"You're trembling," he said.

"In a good way."

"What do you mean?"

"We've been friends a long time."

"We have."

"And we've told each other everything."

"Yes."

"But there's one thing I haven't been able to tell you." Andrea lowered her eyes. "Believe me, I've wanted to. I . . . just haven't found the right words."

"Look at me, Dre." He tilted her chin with his finger. "It's okay. You don't need words. I already know."

"You do?" She squeezed Ovid's book through her backpack.

"I love you, too."

Nate's words struck Andrea an inch and a half below her rib cage, two inches to the left of a small leaf-shaped pale pink birthmark, and landed squarely on the spot where her soul and the truth lived. She had loved Nate for as long as she could remember but did not know if it was in the way that he wanted her to. The laws of physics prevented her from ever knowing for sure. Pauli's exclusion principle applied to hearts as much as it did to identical fermions. *"No two objects can occupy the same place at the same time."* A boy had broken through her bedroom wall and tunneled into her heart a long time ago and filled more of it with every letter he wrote. Andrea clutched her stomach and clamped her mouth shut. Five words lodged in a wet ball in her throat. She swallowed them back. *I love you, too, Nate.*

Andrea scrambled off the couch and grabbed her backpack. Her shoulder hunched under the weight of an old book and its secrets.

"Dre . . ." Nate stood up. "What's wrong? I thought—"

"I have to go."

He grabbed her elbow. "No. Wait. I'm sorry. Forget what I

said. Why did you come here? What did you want to tell me? Look at me. Please. I'm still me."

"You are." Andrea fought the tears rising inside her. "But I'm not."

"I don't understand."

She looked away.

"What's his name?" He clenched his jaw.

"What?"

"The guy you came here to tell me about. That's why you came here, right? To tell me that you met someone?"

"You're being ridiculous." She marched to the door.

"Am I? Then come back here and kiss me the way you did when we were in Sri Lanka. Tell me you love me the way that I've always loved you."

Andrea looked away. "I can't."

"Tell me his name. You owe me that much."

"Isaac." She hugged Nate and leaned her face against his chest so that he wouldn't see her cry. "His name's Isaac."

Nate exhaled slowly. A tear trailed down his face, dripped from his chin, and continued the course gravity had set for it on Andrea's cheek. Andrea made the mistake of looking up. She met his eyes and saw what she had done. The man that Nate had grown to be no longer stood in front of her. In his place was the boy she'd met in fourth grade. And yet, Andrea almost didn't recognize him. His cheeky grin and the naughty glint in his eyes were gone. The last time she'd seen him look this way was when he had first walked into her class, clutching two drumsticks as though they were his only friends. With two syllables of another man's name, Andrea had sawed through the muscle, tissue, and veins that had bound them since they were ten years old. Nate was bleeding out. And so was she. She prayed that it was not too late to stitch them back together. "Nate . . ."

He shoved her away. "Go."

"I'm sorry. I—"

"Don't." He gritted his teeth. "Don't you dare pity me."

"Please, Nate. Let me explain."

"There's nothing to explain, Dre. It's really quite simple. I'm a fool. All these years with you I've been seeing things that weren't there." He laughed bitterly. "I was worried about ending up like my mother. It turns out that I'm exactly like her. She saw fairies. I saw you. An imaginary you who loved me back."

"No. You're wrong."

"About what? Being crazy? I'll tell you what crazy is, Dre. It's standing here looking at you after hearing you tell me that you love some guy named Isaac and still hoping that in the next second you'll burst out laughing, take it all back, and say that you got me good. So what are you waiting for, Dre? Come on. Stop crying. Laugh. Tell me that this is your idea of a joke. I'll believe you."

Andrea wept too hard to speak.

"Yeah. I thought so." Nate turned his back to her. "Please go."

"See you on the bus?" Andrea choked through her tears.

"I said get out."

10

APPLES

Millions saw the apple fall but Newton was the one who asked why.

—BERNARD M. BARUCH

San Francisco
Present Day
Andrea is nineteen.

PYRAMUS POUNDED ON THE WALL that kept him from his lover, ripping the skin from his knuckles. He turned to Andrea and reached out to her with his torn hands. Andrea held on to him, but his hands were slick with blood and slipped from her fingers. She fell backward. Her head slammed against her pillow, jolting her awake.

Pain bit into her palms. She opened her eyes and found her fingernails digging into her flesh. The weathered leather spine of *Metamorphoses* shifted in the circle of her arms. In the year that had passed since she told Nate about Isaac, the characters that dwelled in its pages were the only company she dared to keep. They didn't care about her secrets.

Andrea relaxed her fingers and gathered the book to her breast. The nights she spent wading through its myths led her to tragic dreams, but she found an odd comfort waking up next to tales that were stranger than the one she lived in. Andrea had hoped to share the entirety of her story with Nate, but the tip of it had crushed him more than she could bear. She had given Nate Isaac's name and, in exchange, she received the contents of his heart. Her two oldest friends now lived behind walls. Isaac was locked behind a thicker one that was deaf to her cello's pleas. Andrea was one song away from giving up trying to find him.

"Hey, kiddo. You awake yet?" her dad asked through her bedroom door.

She sat up and shoved Isaac's present back in its hiding place. "Yup."

"There's someone looking for you downstairs. Do you know a Mr. Westin?"

Her heart stopped. She yanked open her night table's drawer and pulled out a crisp white handkerchief that she had washed and pressed herself. A hint of the red Sri Lankan mud that had stained it a year ago remained on one of its corners. Andrea jumped out of bed and scrambled to the door. "Thanks," she said, squeezing past her dad.

"Who is he?" he asked.

Andrea heard the real question in his voice as she bounded down the stairs. It had thinned over the years since she had given up on his dream, but it was still loud enough to ring in her ears. "No, Dad. He's not a cello teacher. I bought something on craigslist. He's delivering it."

"Oh."

The word hung in the air. It was funny, Andrea thought, how a sound so heavy with disappointment defied gravity as long as it did.

MR. WESTIN STOOD at her doorstep looking like he always did: smiling and lint-free. "Good morning, Ms. Louviere. Did I wake you?"

"No." She wrestled her hair down. "I . . . I didn't expect to see you today." She handed him his handkerchief. "Here. Thanks for lending it to me. I washed it, but I'm afraid I couldn't get all the mud off. I'm sorry."

"That's perfectly all right. Thank you." Mr. Westin tucked his handkerchief into his pocket.

"Do you have something for me?"

"I do." He slipped his hand into his suit jacket and drew out a yellowed letter. "Have you changed your mind about giving me cello lessons?"

She took the letter from him. "I didn't think you were serious about that."

"I couldn't be more serious." He buttoned his jacket.

"I can give you the numbers of some cello teachers I know."

"I'd like to learn from you."

"Why?"

"Because I'm old and I know that you're one of the finest cellists in the world. I'd like to learn how to play the cello as soon as possible."

"Learning how to play isn't something you can rush, no matter how good your teacher is. And I'm certainly not qualified to teach you."

"I respect your decision. Have a good day."

"Hold on," she said. "Do you know how many letters I have left?"

"I do."

She leaned forward on the balls of her feet. "How many are there?"

"I'm afraid I can't divulge that sort of—"

"Please, Mr. Westin. I won't tell anyone if that's what you're worried about. No one has to know. I won't get you into trouble. I promise. Besides, what harm is there in giving information about letters that belong to me?"

"I wish I could help you, Ms. Louviere, but I can't. I'm truly, truly sorry."

ANDREA LAID ISAAC's letter on her desk and ran her fingers over his monogrammed seal a fourth time, memorizing the swells and valleys of the wax. Not knowing how long she would have to wait until she heard from him again, she needed to make his latest letter last as long as possible. She was not in a hurry to be alone. She broke his wax initials and unfolded his note. The passages of Pyramus and Thisbe's tragic fate leapt from the first page. The story of the lovers' untimely deaths had spurred Shakespeare to write *Romeo and Juliet,* but it'd had a less inspiring effect on her. She gnawed her bottom lip and turned to the next page of Isaac's letter.

My dearest Andrea,

By now, I am certain that you are more than well acquainted with Pyramus and Thisbe's tale. They defied their families and dared to love each other through a crack. For this, they paid with their lives. I would have wanted more than anything to assure you that our story bears no similarities to theirs, but I swore a long time ago never to lie to you.

We defy rules just as surely as Pyramus and Thisbe did. The difference lies in the gravity of the laws that we break. Pyramus and Thisbe went against their parents' wishes. We flaunt time itself. Such a crime has its own consequences. I would offer you my protection, but the wall between us allows me to send you no more than words of caution—and my deepest gratitude—for the risk you take whenever you open our wall and for the lovely gift that you are about to send through it.

Andrea yanked her night table drawer open. A gift, wrapped in lilac paper, jostled against Ovid's book. Andrea did not understand how Isaac knew about the thank-you present she had planned to give him, only that he was waiting for it on his side of the wall. She could not imagine a danger great enough to keep her from sending it to him. She pulled her cello from its case and played.

Notes tumbled out of the instrument's strings in several false starts. Andrea paced the room, wringing a year's worth of calcified disappointment from her fingers. She returned to her chair with knuckles that were red but less stiff. It was easier to play through pain than self-doubt.

A damp October afternoon flowed from her bow. She played on, ripening the song into a crisp, golden fall. A silvery white crack spread over her corkboard, coming to a stop between her class schedule at the University of San Francisco and a birthday card Sebastian had made for her. A curtain of leaves draped over it from the other side of the wall. A shadow lurked behind the green veil. Isaac poked his head through the leaves. His lips shaped her name with a smile.

"Isaac . . ." Andrea dropped her bow and tossed the gift through the crack. "Catch."

The box flew through the corkboard, rustling her class schedule. The crack flared. Andrea squinted through the glare. Isaac caught her gift. The crack shrank around his grin. Andrea pushed the edges of the corkboard back with a flurry of notes. Isaac stepped away from the crack and disappeared behind the leaves.

"Come back," she yelled, not caring that he couldn't hear her. She abandoned her cello and ran to the wall. "How did you know about the gift? How do you send me your letters? Isaac? Are you there?"

An apple flew through the crack. The hole burned bright and closed. The red-green fruit rolled across the carpet and came to a stop by Andrea's foot. She scooped it up. A crudely carved smiley face that mimicked the one that she had drawn on a music sheet years before grinned at her from the apple's peel. A chuckle snorted through her nose. She set the apple on her desk and read the rest of Isaac's letter.

Your gift puts mine to shame. The apple I gave you was hardly a fair exchange. For you, our most recent encounter happened but moments ago. The same is not true for me. Much time has passed between this letter and the afternoon the crack opened in my orchard. Still, the memory of you and the little box you hurled through the crack remains fresh in my mind.

Woolsthorpe Manor
1666
Isaac is twenty-four.

Isaac leaned his shoulders on the makeshift table he had set up behind the barn. He clutched his playing cards, trying not to smile at his pair of queens. It wasn't too difficult. Compared to his other secrets, his hand of cards was a fairly simple thing to keep close to his chest. He placed his bet inside the circular compartment of the wooden Pochspiel board and looked across the table. "Tom?"

The stocky farmhand ran his eyes over the chips Isaac had tossed on the board. He glanced down at his cards. His stubby fingers pinched them tighter. He wrinkled his bulbous nose, grunted, and threw his cards down on the table. "I fold."

Isaac turned to the man on his left. "John?"

The scruffy man knitted a hedge of graying brows. He scratched his ear with mud-encrusted fingernails. "Er . . . pardon me, sir, but are three kings a good or bad thing to have? I haven't quite gotten the rules straight in my head. There seem to be more of them than the manor's sheep."

Isaac chuckled. "It is a very good thing, indeed."

The old shepherd broke into a grin that displayed more gums than teeth. "In that case, sir, I shall raise you," he said, tossing chips into the game board's compartment.

"I fold. Well done, John." Isaac patted the shepherd's shoulder. Secretly dealing the man a winning hand had been a challenge, but the manor's longtime servant was taking his wife's recent passing roughly and Isaac thought he could use some cheering up. Isaac could not take back the hand that fate had dealt John, but he could control the playing cards he received. He knew too well what it was like to live under the shadow of loss. "Congratulations."

"Thank you, sir," John said.

"Better luck next time, Tom," Isaac said, winking at the farmhand who was in on his plan.

The farmhand nodded. His mouth twitched as he did his best to look disappointed.

"Thank you for the game, gentlemen. I enjoyed it very much." Isaac stood up, savoring the taste his words left in his mouth. The truth was clean and sweet and it had been a long time since he had been able to speak his thoughts plainly. "Have a good day."

Isaac strode into the apple orchard. He weaved his way to a tree with a crooked trunk. Of all the apple trees in the orchard, he liked this one the best. Its trunk curved into a shape that cradled his back and neck, rivaling the comfort of his bed. He had frequently sought sanctuary in its shade in recent months. It was the only place in Woolsthorpe where it was quiet enough for him to hear himself think.

The bustle in the manor had grown when his mother had returned after her second husband had died. She had brought his three half siblings, Mary, Benjamin, and Hannah, with her. It was almost the family that he had prayed for every night when he was a little boy, but not quite. He did not know any of them well enough to trust them with his secret. Trees were easier to confide in.

He approached his old friend. The whorl on the side of its trunk glowed behind a low branch. Isaac's pulse raced. A crack broke through wood. Andrea appeared on the other side. Isaac ran to her. She called his name and tossed a box wrapped in lilac paper through the glowing hole. Isaac caught it. His eyes flew around the orchard, searching for something to give her in return.

THE FOG SWALLOWED the lantern's light, leaving only the scent of apples to guide Isaac through the maze of mist. Damp grass squished under his feet. He raised his lamp higher, grazing his elbow against bark. He reached blindly through the fog and rested his palm against a crooked trunk. The evening air seeped through his coat. Isaac shivered. He rested his cheek against his favorite tree. "Andrea?" he whispered.

Isaac turned his collar up against the chill and the colder certainty that he was not going to get an answer. He had documented the details of Andrea's visits in enough pages to know that she never came when he begged her to, nor appeared in the same place twice in the same day. But hoping was the hardest of habits to break. He pressed his face closer to the bark. "Are you there?"

Only the leaves rustling above him offered a reply. Isaac sank to the ground, molding his spine to the curve of the tree's trunk. He pulled Andrea's gift from his coat and opened it. He did not have a name for the little rectangular black object inside the box. The letter that came with it was sparse, leaving him with only the briefest of instructions. He had fumbled during his first attempt to follow them, but now he navigated them with ease. He turned the object to its side and pushed a silver button with a drawing of a small triangle on it.

Music spilled from the tiny holes in the object's back and floated into the fog. The song danced in the air, traipsing over mist and moonlight. It found its way into his soul as swiftly as it did the first time he had heard it. Andrea's song broke his heart and put it back together with every note. The apple and the grinning face he had carved on it seemed ridiculous in comparison to her song, but he knew it would make her smile.

He looked up at the stars twinkling through the tree's canopy and wondered if it was evening wherever Andrea was. A dark object fell through the branches and struck her music box from his hand. The box crashed against a rock, shattering her song. Isaac swung the lantern around him, searching for the culprit. A shriveled apple wobbled next to Andrea's broken gift. He picked it up. A carved face grinned at him from the fruit's withered black flesh. His hand grew limp. The fruit slipped from his grasp and crumbled into dust in midair. The shattered pieces of Andrea's music box glowed beneath the gray shower. Isaac retrieved a silver button from the ground. Its light faded through the gaps between his fingers. He held his lantern over it and illuminated a fistful of fog.

And so it seems, Andrea, that some gifts are not meant to be kept. One day soon, I shall make it up to you.

Yours always,
Isaac
1666
1, 1, 2, 3, 5, 8, 13, 21, 34, 55

Isaac's letter had described how the apple he had thrown through the crack had returned to him and rotted before his eyes. Andrea looked at the shiny fruit in her hands and wanted to tell him that he had been mistaken. His gift was ripe, plump, and begging to be bitten. She raised it to her lips. A bright white light ignited under its peel as her teeth sank into its glowing flesh. She spat it out.

The apple vanished from her carpet in a burst of light. Her lilac gift box took its place. Andrea tore it open. A mini audio recorder, wrapped in purple tissue paper, sat inside it. She pulled it out and pressed play.

The song she had recorded years before crackled out of its tiny speaker. A bright white light bled through the recorder's plastic and glowed in time with the music. Andrea fumbled with the pause button. The recorder broke apart under her thumb and swirled into a tiny dust storm over her palm. The gift box met the same fate. Ice rose up from her ankles. The crack's message was clear. Their wall was not meant to be crossed. She wrapped her dusty fingers around her bow and threw it out the window.

11

GIFTS

Anything cracked will shatter at a touch.

—OVID

San Francisco
Present Day
Andrea is twenty.

THE CURSOR BLINKED AND BROUGHT Andrea half a second closer to a paper deadline she was not going to meet. She took a long sip of her tall macchiato on the odd chance that the two thousand words she needed were swimming at the bottom of her cup. Her phone vibrated on the café's table. She licked the foam off her upper lip and answered it. "Hey, you."

"Hey, you," Nate said. "How's it going?"

"Oh, you know me. Every day's an adventure. Today, I put *two* packets of *real* sugar in my coffee."

Nate chuckled. "How can you stand all that excitement?"

"What can I say? I like to live dangerously." Her words had slipped out with a laugh, but Andrea heard the irony coating each of them.

A recorder crumbling to dust lived in the edges of her mind. Andrea was quick to push it away whenever it got too close but took care not to shove it too far. She needed to know that she could summon it whenever the compulsion to open her wall became too strong. The crack had given her fair warning of the dire consequences of breaching it. Over the year that she had heeded it, there was not one second that she did not wonder whether turning to dust might be less painful than keeping away from Isaac. She pressed her phone closer to her cheek and blinked twice, trying to drag herself from the mire of questions back to Nate.

"Dre? Are you okay?"

"Oh . . . uh . . . yeah. Sure. I was just thinking about this paper I need to finish. So how have you been? How's the tour going? Where's your next stop?" she said, without taking a breath.

Nate had dropped out of college, choosing his band over an advanced math degree. He had called a few times from the road and Andrea found herself really listening to what he had to say. In the year that had passed since she had thrown her bow away, she and Nate had learned to become friends, albeit from a distance. His voice kept her mind off gifts that turned to dust.

"Whoa. Slow down. If I didn't know any better I'd think you were excited to talk to me."

Heat flared in her cheeks. "Of course not."

"Don't worry," he said with a chuckle. "I believe you."

"So . . . um . . . how's the tour?"

"Okay, I guess. It could be better, but playing in a half-empty venue is still better than snoring through a political science class, right?" he said. "Say 'yes' and pretend to agree with me."

Andrea laughed. "Okay, but only if you get me another snow globe. And don't forget, the cheesier . . ."

"The better. Naturally. Although I have to say that it might be difficult to top that last glow-in-the-dark one I got you from New York."

"I have faith in you." Andrea had amassed a tiny collection of globes from the stops on Nate's tour. She liked holding each one up to the light knowing that none of them were going to disintegrate between her fingers. "When are you coming home?"

The line went silent.

"Nate? Are you still there?"

"I miss you, Dre."

"I . . . miss you, too." Nate's absence had proven Wolfgang Pauli wrong. Andrea had discovered that two desires could exist in the same place at the same time. She missed Nate just as much as she longed to see Isaac.

"Good morning, Ms. Louviere. Is this seat taken?"

Andrea jumped in her chair. Mr. Westin smiled at her from across the table.

"I . . . uh . . . have to go, Nate," she stammered over the phone. "I really need to finish this paper."

"Okay," Nate said. "I'll see you soon."

Andrea stuffed her phone in her bag and steadied herself with a breath. She looked up at Mr. Westin. "You just pop up everywhere, don't you?"

"I try my best." He settled into his chair. A smile lit his eyes. "Your packages can't deliver themselves."

"About that . . ." Andrea wrung her fingers. She rehearsed the speech that she had prepared in her head. She was going to tell Mr. Westin that she did not want to receive any more wax-sealed letters. Trying not to think of what Isaac was doing behind her wall was hard enough without reading his words. The speech had seemed simple enough when she'd recited it in front of her bathroom mirror. With Mr. Westin and Isaac's letter two feet away from her, it crumbled like Isaac's apple. She wrung her fingers.

Mr. Westin frowned at her hands. "You've stopped playing?"

"Yes." Andrea directed her gaze to her fingertips. The year without her cello had smoothened away their calluses. Isaac's face was harder to erase. She saw it whenever she closed her eyes. "For good this time."

"I suppose that means that our music lessons are out of the question?"

She nodded.

"That is unfortunate. I had come up with the perfect way to compensate you for your time."

She narrowed her eyes. "How?"

"Answers."

"But I thought you said—"

"You were right, Ms. Louviere. These letters are yours and you have every right to know about them. I have decided to help you."

Andrea folded her arms over her chest. "For a price."

"Yes, but a small one, I assure you. A cello lesson each time I deliver your letters isn't too much trouble, is it?"

"And in return you'll answer my questions about the letters?"

"One lesson. One question. One answer."

"But why not just get a teacher who could give you lessons on a more regular basis?"

"Is that your question for this year?"

"What? No. Of course not."

"So you have another question, then?"

"Yes. I mean no. If this is a trick—"

"It is not. You have my word. Do you agree to our arrangement?"

Andrea picked at her fingernails. She had scraped the remains of her mini recorder from under them a long time ago, but an invisible layer of dust still seemed to choke every inch of her skin.

"I understand if you need some time to think about it." He drew out a wax-sealed envelope from his suit pocket.

Andrea stared hard at the letter, trying to summon the courage to refuse it. Three words in Isaac's elegant handwriting leapt at her from the back of the envelope. *"Read this now."* Andrea's voice faltered as she read them out loud. She gaped at Mr. Westin. "What does this mean?"

"I have been instructed to wait while you read it," Mr. Westin said, laying the letter on the table.

"What? Why?"

"I can only give you the rest of the delivery once you've read the letter."

Andrea's nape turned to ice. "The rest of the delivery? I have another letter?"

"No. A package."

"Give it to me."

"I will. After you read the letter."

"No way. I can't read that letter. Not here. Not in front of you."

"As you wish." He slipped the note back into his pocket and stood up. "Enjoy the rest of your day, Ms. Louviere."

She watched Mr. Westin walk to the door. Andrea's heart screamed with every step he took. Andrea squeezed her eyes shut and clamped her hands over her ears. The screams grew louder, drowning out every thought in her head except for one. It burst out of her. "Stop!"

Heads twisted in her direction. Mr. Westin turned.

"I'll do it." Andrea gritted her teeth. "Give me the damn letter."

Mr. Westin nodded, returned to his seat, and handed her the letter. Andrea cracked its seal as quickly as she could without ripping the letter in two. She did not want to give herself time to change her mind. "My dearest Andrea . . ." Her voice trembled.

"You misunderstand, Ms. Louviere," Mr. Westin cut her off. "You need not read the letter out loud. The instructions require only that you read the letter at this precise moment and in my presence."

Andrea exhaled. Her eyes raced back to the yellowed page.

My dearest Andrea,

I thank you for indulging my request. It is not my intention to diminish the intimacy of our conversation. My sole purpose is to ease the fear that has grown in your heart. While it was necessary that you be made aware of the deathly consequence of crossing the crack between our walls, it is as necessary for you to believe me when I tell you that dust need not be the fate of all that dare to traverse it. I know that this decaying letter is far too fragile a thing to hold on to, thus shall I attempt to give my words more weight. I offer you a story, Andrea, but one that is different from those that I have already shared with you. This is not a tale of things that have passed, but of things to come.

In a moment, a woman in a blue frock shall walk through the doors of the establishment you are presently seated in. She will request a beverage—mint tea in a small cup. While retrieving payment from her scarlet purse, a coin bearing the image of a king by the name of Kennedy shall fall to the floor. It shall roll in your direction and come to a stop at your heel. My statements are not prophecy or conjecture. They are merely a narration of fated steps. To the woman they belong to, they are nothing more than meaningless fragments of her day. To you, my beloved, they are my hands, extended from the time and place I write this note, offered so that you may have something to grasp when faith threatens to fail. Lift your eyes from the page, Andrea. Witness how the truth of my words defies the centuries between us and take as much courage as you can from what is about to take place.

Andrea looked up. A slim brunette in a navy shift dress entered the coffee shop. She walked up to the counter and ordered a cup of peppermint tea in the shop's smallest size. As she fished for her wallet, a coin tumbled out of her red shoulder bag and rolled to Andrea's table. It hit the heel of Andrea's sneaker and toppled head side up on the floor. President John F. Kennedy stared up at Andrea from the half dollar, waiting to be rescued. Andrea's hand shook as she picked it up. The coin fell from her fingers. Mr. Westin caught it and returned it to the woman in blue. Andrea watched her thank him.

"You look pale," Mr. Westin said, settling back into his chair. "Can I get you anything? Water perhaps?"

"No . . . I'm fine." Andrea could hardly hear her own voice over the blood rushing in her ears. "You said you had another package for me. Give it to me." She gripped the edges of the table to keep herself from jumping on Mr. Westin and tearing whatever Isaac had sent from his suit. "Now."

He handed her a small leather box. "Do take care opening it. I believe that it is rather fragile."

She pulled the top off the leather case and shook the box over her palm. A triangular piece of faceted glass and a small piece of paper fell into her hand. Andrea read Isaac's note.

A prism to bridge the present and the past, a handful of hope when I am far away.

Andrea held Isaac's present up and caught a sunbeam streaming through the café's door. The light shot through the glass and painted a rainbow over Mr. Westin's suit jacket. The memory of another gift, a fiery one with a red-green peel, trembled through Andrea's fingers. The prism slipped and shattered next to Mr. Westin's polished shoes. Andrea's hand flew over her mouth. She swore into her palm.

Mr. Westin clucked his tongue. "What a pity. It was a rather lovely prism."

Andrea stared at the jagged glass on the floor.

"It's fortunate that you have a spare." He pulled out a leather case that was nearly identical to the empty one on the table. "I was told to give this to you in case something happened to the first one."

Small golden words were embossed on the new box's lid. FATED STEPS. Andrea ran her thumb over the words, feeling their meaning melt into her skin and slither through her veins. She lifted the box's lid slowly. Sunlight twinkled over beveled glass. She lifted her eyes from the second prism. "Mr. Westin?"

"Yes?"

"Can you start your lessons now?"

THEY SAT ON opposite sides of a park bench beneath the shade of one of the park's cypress trees. The chirping of birds stood in for conversation. Andrea took her brand-new bow out of its box and adjusted its strings. She did not want to play Mr. Westin's game, but she wanted answers more. "What do you know about the cello?"

"I like the way it sounds."

"I see." She hauled her cello out of its dusty case and yanked out its end pin. She set the instrument on the ground. "Pay attention. I don't want to repeat myself."

He nodded. "I shall do my best."

"Body. Front. Back. Ribs. F holes. Neck. Fingerboard. Scroll. End pin. A string. D string. G string. C string. Pegs," she said, pointing out the cello's parts. "Got it?"

"Body. Front. Back. Ribs. F holes. Neck. Fingerboard. Scroll. End pin. A string. D string. G string. C string. Pegs," Mr. Westin said. "Did I miss anything?"

"Er . . . no. That was perfect." She tugged an eyebrow down and pointed to the parts of the bow. "Stick. Hair. Pad. Frog. Screw. Clear?"

He smiled. "Stick. Hair. Pad. Frog. Screw. Clear."

"We'll start with getting the bow grip right."

"Whatever you think is best."

Andrea positioned the bow at a ninety-degree angle to the cello's strings the way her dad had taught her when she was three. The only difference was that Andrew Louviere had demonstrated the straight bow principle without scowling. Andrea looked up at Mr. Westin. "You have to keep the bow straight at all times. Since the bridge of the cello is curved, this position will vary from string to string. See?" she said, demonstrating how to shift the angle of the bow. "Here. You try it."

THE LESSON WENT more quickly than Andrea expected. Mr. Westin was a fast learner, but she was not about to tell him that.

"Thank you, Ms. Louviere. I learned a lot today." He handed the cello back to Andrea. "Now what would you like to know about your deliveries?"

Questions raced to the tip of her tongue. One squeezed past the rest before she could decide which one to ask first. "Where do you get these letters and packages?" If she could find out where Isaac's letters came from, she would not have to wait for Mr. Westin to show up to get her hands on them.

"From a rather filthy box. All your deliveries were packed inside it with great care. Their sender must have really thought that it was important that you receive each and every one of them."

"Where did the box come from? Where is it now?"

"One lesson. One question." He buttoned his jacket and smiled. "Thank you for the lesson, Ms. Louviere. I'm looking forward to the next one."

ANDREA BUILT A little fort of textbooks around her desk to keep her thoughts from drifting from her general psychology homework. They clambered over an Erik Erikson book and escaped. She slammed her book shut, wedging her yellow highlighter between its pages. Isaac's glass gift sat on top of her stack of textbooks and twinkled in the light of her reading lamp. She had learned that Isaac had used two prisms to study the composition of light. Before Isaac, two thousand years of optical doctrine proclaimed that impurities in prisms tinted light and produced color. Isaac debunked this. He funneled sunlight through a slit in a boarded-up window into one prism to make a rainbow over his bedroom's wall. He used a second prism to catch the rainbow's ray of red light. Had the popular doctrine been true, the second prism would have tinted the red light and produced another rainbow. The ray, however, passed through the second glass and remained red, proving Isaac's theory that light was made up of a spectrum of colors.

Andrea had found illustrations of Isaac's experiment, but the man in these drawings looked nothing like him. Ink and an artist's limited imagination made him appear as lifeless as the tools on his worktable. She ached for the Isaac she knew. She took Isaac's prism from its red leather case and angled it beneath her reading lamp. She traced the rainbow it splashed over the desk with her hand. Notches rubbed against her forefinger. A thin coat of white paint covered the indentions, but it could not keep the frustration etched into the desk from prickling her skin. It stung as much as it did when she had carved it with a ballpoint pen when she was fourteen. She slid her fingers over the desk and found a quarter note. Next to it was a musical sharp. The marks screamed into her skin, begging to find their place in an old song. She turned to her wall. For too long, an apple that had vanished in an explosion of white light had scared her away from attempting to open it. Today, Isaac had sent her a rainbow and a story. Both gave her courage. She reached for her cello and switched off her reading lamp. Music had always been easier to find in the dark. She cradled her cello and played Isaac's song.

A flash of white light streaked over her wall in the middle of the melody. She drew more notes from the cello's strings and urged the crack to open wider. Inky black spread out behind it. She squinted at the crack, trying to find Isaac in the dark. A lance of red light shot past her, pierced the prism on her desk, and splashed onto the opposite wall. Andrea's bow hand fumbled and nearly missed a note. Isaac's theory of light had just been proven over her bed. Science and history would never know of her accidental role in Isaac's milestone experiment. Andrea didn't care. What she discovered was more important than the composition of light. The crack's rules were not absolute. She now knew of at least two things that the crack could not turn to dust: light and hope. Sunlight poured through the crack and washed the red beam away. Andrea forced herself to look into the glare.

Isaac stood next to his bedroom window, holding a wooden screen. He dropped the screen and sprinted toward the crack, bumping into a low table. A prism and a set of circular lenses wobbled on top of it. Isaac leaned close to the crack and peered into Andrea's dark bedroom. Andrea stopped playing the cello and flicked the switch of her reading lamp. The lamp's light shone on Isaac's elegant face. He smiled and raised his arm to the crack.

"Stop!" she screamed, picturing his fingers crumbling.

His hand stopped a breath from the wall. He rolled up his sleeve and pointed to a round piece of metal strapped to his wrist. Andrea raised her chin to get a better look as the crack shrank. A 1950s Omega Seamaster's glass face shone in the crack's light. Andrea gasped.

Isaac slipped the watch off his wrist and displayed its back. Two entwined rings, the symbol for infinity, were etched on the stainless steel. Isaac thrust the watch closer to the crack. Andrea leaned forward and learned the engraving's secret. The infinity symbol was not made up of circles, but two loops of tiny, delicate words.

For Isaac. Love, Andrea

12

ANSWERS

If I have ever made any valuable discoveries, it has been owing more to patient attention, than to any other talent.
—ISAAC NEWTON

Seattle
Present Day
Andrea is twenty-one.

ANDREA PULLED OUT A BASS guitar from the back of a dented blue van and handed it to Nate's bandmate Ross.

"Thanks, Andrea," he said, pushing back greasy black hair from his eyes. "See you inside."

Andrea nodded.

Nate shut the back of the van. "Tell me again why you decided to ditch graduation to watch us play? Don't get me wrong. I really like having you around, but the places we play at . . ." He glanced at the small bar and the nearly empty parking lot around it. "Well, they aren't exactly Carnegie—" Nate snapped his mouth shut. "Sorry. I didn't mean . . ."

"It's okay, Nate. It's been seven years. I'm a big girl." Andrea hid the lie behind her best impression of a smile. Unlike clowns with purple hair, Carnegie Hall's stage still gave her nightmares.

Sometimes she was naked. Sometimes all her hair fell out when she took a bow. She had skipped out on her graduation ceremony because she couldn't stand the thought of walking onto a stage, with or without her cello. Irrational fears were the hardest to talk herself out of. They talked back. "Why can't you just accept that I'm here because I want to hear you play?"

"You spent half of your spring break with us and sat through two gigs this week. You must be sick of our sets by now."

"And I spent the other half of the break and my entire summer in Cambodia with Matt. That didn't make me sick of building wells or houses." Andrea shrugged. "I wouldn't be here if I didn't want to be."

Nate was a pleasure to watch even if the rest of the band was not. Behind his drums, Nate was in a different place and time. When he played, he took her with him. She leapt at any chance to escape the chaos of questions Isaac had left in her head. He had given her a glimpse of something she could not understand. The engraving on the watch on his wrist implied that she had given it to him, but comprehending how it had come into his possession was like trying to figure out where a circle ended or began. She had tried for a whole year to see Isaac again and find out how he had gotten it, but her wall refused to let her see him. Neither had Mr. Westin shown up with any new letters. She had almost convinced herself that she hadn't seen Isaac's watch and its engraving at all.

"Come on," she said, tugging Nate's arm. "Let's go inside. Your set's about to start."

"Hang on a sec." He ducked inside the van. He came out holding two wrapped gifts, one slightly larger than the other. "Happy graduation, roadie. This one is from me and this one is from your dad."

"My dad?"

"Yeah. He sent it to the hotel. He wanted it to be a surprise."

"Oh." Andrea bit her lower lip, remembering how her dad's smile had slipped off his face when she told him she had no intention of attending her graduation. He had quickly pasted it back on and told her that he was fine with whatever she decided, but Andrea saw how his new smile fell short of his eyes.

Nate offered her the smaller gift. "But you should open mine first. I'm sure that it will look pathetic compared to whatever your dad got you. And before you get too excited, let me tell you right now that I got it at the hotel gift shop. I didn't have time to go shopping. Sorry."

"You really didn't even have to bother with getting me anything." Andrea tore open the blue wrapper printed with the hotel's logo. She opened the box and pulled out a snow globe containing Seattle's Space Needle. Andrea shook the globe. A storm of silver glitter swirled around the tower. Andrea laughed. "Thank you. I love it."

"Next time we'll go see the actual needle."

"Next time." Andrea smiled. Nate did not know it, but these two short words were the best gift he could have given her. It held the promise of an hour, a place, and a date in the future, the kind of certainty she did not know with Isaac.

Nate handed Andrea her dad's gift. "Open it. I'm dying to know what he got you. I shook it. It sounded a lot like car keys to me."

"You wish." Andrea ripped the wrapper, revealing a red leather box. She lifted the box's lid. A 1950s Omega Seamaster caught the light from the bar's flickering neon sign.

EVERY SECOND THAT ticked over the face of Andrea's graduation present made her believe that she was getting closer to solving the mystery of Isaac and his letters. The blank steel on its back reminded her that she wasn't. She strapped it on each day, not knowing how much longer it would have to wait until she engraved it with the words she had seen on Isaac's watch. Three centuries was a huge leap for even the loneliest heart to take.

Her eyes flitted around her dark bedroom as she lay in bed. Without the dog-eared Agatha Christie books on her bookshelf or the mountain of clutter on her desk, the room belonged to a stranger. Sleep was not going to find her on her last night in it. She rolled out of bed and dragged her feet past the boxes she had stuffed her childhood into. Her battered cello case leaned on the wall between a "Toss" and "Keep" pile. The studio apartment waiting for her in Los Angeles barely had room for a bed, much less for Isaac and his secrets. Andrea hauled her cello over to the boxes destined for the attic. Her fingers twitched around its handle, begging her to let them say goodbye to their old friend.

The cello screeched beneath her bow. She took her time tuning it, making sure every string sounded just right. It deserved a proper farewell. She arranged her fingers over the strings and played the opening strains of "Le Cygne," the thirteenth movement of Camille Saint-Saëns's *The Carnival of Animals.* The melody tugged at her heart. She shut her eyes to see it better. An apple orchard stretched before her. She was three measures into Isaac's melody when she realized that she had strayed from her swan song.

"Hey, kiddo." Her dad knocked on her door.

"Just a sec, Dad." She set her cello and any hopes of a glowing crack aside and opened the door.

"Can't sleep either, huh?" Andrew said. "I'm making tea. Want some?"

ANDREA SLIPPED INTO her usual seat at the bleached pine breakfast nook.

"Have you finished packing?" Andrew asked.

"Nope."

"You know it's not too late to change your mind."

"I'm moving to L.A., Dad, not Mars."

"I wish you were. Martians are less scary."

"Unfortunately, there aren't very many openings for PR assistants on Mars. Besides, I won't really be alone. Nate's apartment is just a couple of doors down from mine."

"So . . . is he . . . um . . . still with that band of his?"

"Yes."

"Good for him."

Andrea smirked. "I thought you said that you didn't care for drums?"

"Yes, but I still have to admire the guy for sticking with his passion."

Andrea folded her arms over the table. "You mean unlike me?"

He answered her with a heavy breath and pulled a tin of green tea from the shelf. "Did you know that the San Francisco Symphony has an opening for a cellist? I've heard you play, Andrea. You're still very good. You could easily—"

"Dad, please. We've talked about this. You do realize that I can do other things, too, right? Believe it or not, I actually learned a thing or two in college."

He dropped tea bags into their cups. "Does it have a name?"

"Does what have a name?"

"Your song."

"What song?"

"The song you just played upstairs. You used to play it all the time."

"Oh. That." Andrea fixed her eyes on a whorl on the table. "It doesn't have a name."

"It's an excellent piece." The kettle whistled over her dad's voice. He emptied it into their cups and settled into the chair across from Andrea. "It deserves a name."

Andrea watched the steam curl over the rim of her cup. "I guess so, but—"

"But what?"

She wrung the strap of her Omega. The image of its twin on

Isaac's arm snaked under her skin. "I don't know how it ends yet."

Her dad's gaze drifted to the date he had circled with a red marker on their kitchen calendar. It was the day she was moving out. "Endings are always the hardest part."

Andrea sipped her tea. "Any expert advice?"

The lines around her dad's eyes crinkled from a smile that made him look more sad than happy. He reached across the table and squeezed her hand. "It's not a question of knowing how to end a song, kiddo. It's about deciding when the time has come to let it go."

NATE STRODE INTO Andrea's new studio apartment carrying a large pepperoni pizza box in one arm and balancing a stack of DVDs in the other. He set the DVDs on the floor next to the TV and the pizza down on the only table Andrea owned. Her coffee table wobbled. "I can fix that for you," he said, pointing to the table's uneven leg.

"Don't worry about it." Andrea arranged a bowl of popcorn and a couple of glasses of Coke on the other end of the table to counter the pizza's weight. "There. Fixed. See?"

"If you say so." Nate pulled out a small gift box from his pocket. "I got you a housewarming present."

She stood on tiptoe and kissed Nate on the cheek. "Thanks," she said, lifting the box's lid. She pulled out a small white plastic hook. Her brow furrowed. "Oh . . . uh . . . this is great."

Nate chuckled. "One thing I've learned from living on my own is that you can't have too many hooks. There's always something to hang on them. Keys, towels, corkboards, and . . . um . . . pot holders."

"Pot holders?" Andrea laughed. "Do you even own a pot? Or a stove?"

Nate grinned. "Well, no, but now that we're neighbors I was thinking we could have movie nights and cook dinners together.

And of course by *we* I mean *you.* It's only fair. After all, I've already done the hard stuff. I bought the hook. I'll even hang it for you if you want."

"How thoughtful. And after I cook dinner, would you like me to do your laundry for you and rub your feet?"

"You read my mind."

Andrea punched his arm. "Come on. Let's eat. The pizza's getting cold. What are we watching?" she said, eyeing the DVDs Nate had brought.

"I think you will be pleased with the selection we have for this evening, madam. *Five Graves to Cairo,* an oldie but goodie from 1943 full of espionage, action, and hidden treasure. Next, we have *Sneakers.* Admittedly, this is more caper than spy film, but what can I say? I'm a sucker for anything about ultimate-super-secret-encryption-decoding machines. And lastly, we have *Tinker Tailor Soldier Spy,* a critically acclaimed movie starring Gary Oldman, Colin Firth, Benedict Cumberbatch—"

"Stop." Andrea waved her hand. "Say no more. You got me at Cumberbatch."

"I thought so. You've had a crush on that guy since forever. What is it about him that you like so much anyway? The dark hair? The English accent?"

"All of the above."

"Well, I hate to break it you, Dre. In this movie he's blond and gay."

"But is he English?"

"Yes."

Andrea smiled. "Then what are you waiting for?"

Nate laughed.

He wouldn't have, Andrea thought, if he knew the real reason why she liked the actor. Unlike the journals she kept, Nate did not know how, on the cold nights that her fingers found their way back to her small collection of yellowed pages and broken wax seals, she lent the actor's voice to the words she had never heard their sender speak.

Nate inserted the DVD into the player and pressed play. He settled into the sofa bed and patted the empty space next to him. Andrea grabbed a slice of pizza and sat down. Her cheek found her old spot on his shoulder. It was more muscular than she remembered and warmer. Nate put his arm around her and drew little circles on her bare shoulder with his thumb. She kept her eyes on the TV, trying to ignore the ripples of heat spreading to her toes.

NATE WAITED AT the curb outside Andrea's office on his black motorbike. He picked her up from work on days when his band wasn't booked on any gigs. "Hey, you. How was work today?" he said, handing her the purple helmet he had bought for her.

Andrea shrugged and strapped on the helmet. "If you consider spending the day on the phone confirming the guests for a launch event and collating a hundred press kits about a new flavor of milkshake fun, then you may say that I had the most amazing day of my life."

"Hey. Don't knock milkshakes. A chocolate one and Sylvia's vegetarian meatloaf saved me from getting a black eye once, remember?"

Andrea hopped onto the motorcycle and hooked her arms around Nate. She cleared her throat and gave him a squeeze. "For the record, *I* saved you."

"And one day, I hope to return the favor." Nate twisted around, smiled, and adjusted the helmet strap under her chin.

A black leather glove covered Nate's hand, but that didn't stop Andrea's face from flushing at his touch. "Can we . . . um . . . stop by Trader Joe's? I need to pick up some artichokes for the pasta we're having tonight."

"Nope. Sorry, Dre." Nate switched on the engine and sped down the road.

"Why not? It's on the way home."

Nate grinned. "We're not going home."

THE SPRAWLING DOMED white building was perched on a hillside on the eastern edge of the Santa Monica Mountains. Nate parked his motorcycle and pulled off his helmet. He raked his fingers through his hair, letting the blond waves fall where they pleased. Nate's hair, Andrea thought, always somehow managed to find the right balance between perfection and disarray.

"I thought we'd change up movie night a bit tonight," Nate said, walking up to the building. "I know you were looking forward to a Benedict Cumberbatch marathon, but I figured that spending the evening at the Griffith Observatory might be more fun than rewatching the *Sherlock* series."

Andrea took in the sprawling views of downtown Los Angeles. She looked up at Nate and smiled. "*Sherlock* can wait."

Nate checked his watch. "We have some time before the planetarium show starts. Want to take some photos to prove to your dad that I'm being a great, responsible friend and showing you the city's sights? I can't shake the feeling that Mr. L's been stalking my Facebook page to check if I've dragged you into some dark, drugged-out rock band scene."

Andrea chuckled. "He doesn't think that."

"Really?"

"Well, no." She laughed and pointed to a large white concrete monument towering over the observatory's front lawn. Six stylized statues surrounded the marble pillar. "Let's take a picture over there."

"Good choice. That's the Astronomers Monument." Nate positioned Andrea in front of the monument and stood next to her. He put his arm around her shoulder and stretched his other arm out to hold his phone in front of them. He adjusted the angle of his phone to frame the shot. "It pays tribute to six of the greatest astronomers of all time. Hipparchus, Copernicus, Galileo, Kepler, Herschel, and Newton. Say cheese."

Andrea blanched. She wriggled free from Nate's arm and

darted past Isaac's sculpture, keeping her eyes from his carved face.

"Dre," Nate called after her. "Where are you going? I didn't get the shot yet."

Andrea wrapped her arms around her stomach and hurried across the lawn to the observatory's door. "It's cold. I want to go inside."

THE AUDIENCE FILED through the bronze and leather doors of the Samuel Oschin Planetarium. Andrea followed Nate to their seats near the center of the circular theater. A cool blue light suffused the large dome above her, mimicking clouds. Andrea watched them drift across the fake sky. The illusion did not make breathing any easier. Every inch of the Griffith Observatory seemed to bear Isaac's imprint, from the principle of inertia that governed the operations of the gentle swaying of the Foucault pendulum at the W. M. Keck Foundation Central Rotunda to the laws of motion and gravity that explained forces acting on the planets at the Gunther Depths of Space exhibit. The observatory's walls chafed her heart, ripping off the scabs that covered her longing for the boy in her wall.

"Are you going to tell me what that was all about?" Nate whispered.

"I told you. I got cold."

"You look like you saw a ghost."

"Don't be silly."

"Dre, is something—"

"The show's about to start."

An actor strode to the middle of the theater, flourishing a small glowing sphere. His silky voice wrapped around the audience like a ribbon, capturing their attention for the length of his introductory spiel about how various cultures interpreted celestial phenomena. It missed Andrea. While the orb's light pulsed to emphasize the actor's words, all she could see was an apple that had burned bright and turned to dust. She dug her fingernails into the arms of her seat to keep herself in her chair.

Andrea watched the orb fade and give way to a digital laser projector that filled the darkened dome with stars. Groups of stars gleamed, forming the constellations ancient peoples invented to understand the randomness of the night sky. Naming the patterns of light and weaving their tales gave the stars purpose and sense. When sailors crossed the seas, Polaris, the brightest star of Ursa Minor, the son Zeus was forced to turn into a bear, guided their way. Andrea envied the certainty of their direction.

Nate slipped his hand over hers as the constellations above them dissolved into a scene in the Great Library of ancient Alexandria. Andrea let him hold her. For the next thirty minutes of the planetarium show, she was determined to pretend that there weren't two stars over her piece of sky, pulling her in opposite directions. She anchored her fingers in the closest one, convincing herself that it was the one that showed her the way home. The other star only led her to a wall.

ANDREA'S SECOND MONTH in L.A. began as all the thirty days before it had: with dawn, a stretch, and the promise of dark-roasted coffee drifting over her nose. She yawned and rubbed her eyes open. The sun stretched its arms across her studio and brushed its fingertips against the rusted hinges of the cello case tucked into the farthest corner of the apartment.

"Good morning, sleepyhead." Nate sat by the kitchen counter and looked up from a nearly empty bowl of Honey Nut Cheerios. He had let himself into Andrea's apartment with his key just as he did every Sunday morning. In exchange for her breakfast cereal, he made coffee. According to Andrea, the Sumatra Mandheling tasted better when he brewed it. "Coffee?"

"Yes. Please." Andrea walked over to him and found herself smiling at the perfect mess of blond hair flopping over his forehead and the wrinkled navy-blue T-shirt he had slept in. The shirt had seen better days, but it made him look shipwrecked in the best way.

Nate poured coffee into one of the three mismatched mugs Andrea owned. A tattoo peeked out from under his wrist.

"Is that new?" she asked.

"Yeah. I got it last night." Nate held out his wrist and showed off the latest addition to the gallery on his skin. His left arm was home to three swallows, one phoenix, and a chameleon. His right had a G clef formed by a blue snake entwined around a rose. Once, when they were stretched out on his couch for movie night, Andrea caught a glimpse of the jewel-toned dragon that lived on his left hip. But it could have been a koi fish. Andrea had glued her eyes on Jason Bourne's face before she could tell for sure. The ink on his wrist was Nate's first tattoo of words.

"*Nitimur in vetitum semper, cupimusque negata,*" Andrea said, reading the Latin phrase out loud. "What does it mean?"

"May the force be with you."

"Please tell me you're kidding."

"It means, 'We try to get what has been forbidden for us, and we always want whatever we have been refused.' Or at least I hope it does. I might have been slightly drunk when I picked it out from the shop's catalog."

The Latin words summoned a memory of Isaac's smile. Andrea forced a laugh to chase it away. "The *Star Wars* quote was better."

"Without a bottle of tequila, I suppose it does seem a bit silly."

"Not silly. It's sad."

"Sad? Why?"

"Because it's true." Andrea retreated into her coffee mug.

Nate chewed on his lip. "So . . . um . . . what are your plans for today?"

"Vacuuming. Laundry. Bills," she said, trying to look miserable. Nate would not understand why she cherished her chores.

They grounded her day in routine and set the limits of what was possible and what was not. Isaac fell into the latter category. "If there's time, I might paint my nails."

"Don't."

"Don't what?"

"Paint your nails."

Andrea arched a brow. "Why not?"

"Because you'll only ruin them."

"Why?"

"Because of this." He pulled out a small mint-green gift bag from behind the kitchen counter.

"What is it?"

"It's an I'm-really-sorry-that-you'll-be-alone-for-a-month-while-I'm-touring gift. I'm leaving tomorrow, remember?"

Andrea tried to laugh. "A month. Right. I forgot." Andrea had done her best to push Nate's upcoming tour with his band out of her mind. His was the last voice she heard before she went to sleep. Without him, her days were going to feel endless.

"Aren't you going to open your present?" Nate asked.

"Yes. Of course. Thanks." She took the gift bag from him and gave him a peck on the cheek. Heat flared over his skin, marking the line she took care not to cross. She and Nate had learned to be neighbors and friends, but it was a lesson she needed regular refresher courses on. She kept Nate at an arm and a half's length. The border of love and lust was like the world behind her wall. It was a place old friends did not return from intact.

Andrea opened the gift bag and pulled out a miniature cello case made of wood. "It's adorable."

"Open it," Nate said.

Andrea unlatched the wooden case. A dark amber cake, molded in the shape of a cello, lay inside it. "Rosin?"

"I won't be around to bug you for a month and I figured that you might want to get some practice in while I'm gone. You haven't touched your cello since you got here. You've neglected it long enough, don't you think?"

Andrea glanced at the wall. "But—"

"No *buts*, Dre. I already picked out a song for us."

"For us? What are you talking about?"

"Get dressed and I'll show you. Bring your cello."

THE SMALL BAR was closed when they got there. Nate fished out a key from his jeans. "The owner's a friend of mine."

Andrea stepped inside, carrying her cello. "Why are we here?"

"The bar doesn't open until tonight so we have the stage to ourselves."

"You play. I'll watch."

"Come on, Dre. You already lugged your cello all this way."

"Only because you promised to do my dishes for a week when you get back from your tour if I did. I brought my cello. That was our deal. You didn't say I had to play it."

Nate reached inside his leather jacket and pulled out folded sheets of paper. "This might change your mind."

Andrea unfolded the sheets and saw a cello arrangement for Coldplay's "Clocks" in Nate's handwriting. The notes leapt from the page and sang in her head. "You wrote this? It's beautiful."

Nate smiled. "Believe it or not, I did manage to pick up a thing or two from the few cello lessons I had with your dad." He pulled a second set of music sheets from his jacket. "And I made another arrangement for drums. It's a duet. What do you say? Shall we find out what we sound like together?"

ANDREA TOOK HER seat in the center of the small stage. Nate's drum set was behind her. She looked out at her audience of empty tables and chairs and took a deep breath. She wiped her sweaty palms on her jeans.

"Ready?" Nate asked.

Andrea answered with a long pull of her bow. Her heart was

pounding too fast to let her speak. The haunting opening notes of "Clocks" flowed from her strings. Nate's drumbeat joined them. Each beat throbbed in Andrea's chest. They had kissed, held hands, and touched, but for the first time in all the years that she had known Nate, Andrea listened to the music they made and felt what it was like to have him inside her.

ANDREA LAY IN bed, her spine still tingling from the song that she and Nate had played that morning and the kiss they shared when it ended. Nate would be on a plane long before she woke up. She dreaded the month without him. When she was with him, she could think clearly. She could hear his voice and breathe in the scent of his skin. She could run her fingers through his hair and nuzzle his cheek. Nate was made of flesh, bone, logic, reason, and blood. He didn't come wrapped in mystery or magic, but his music entranced her as strongly as any spell. The world was simple and made sense when he was around. When he wasn't, it grew silent enough for Andrea to hear the questions behind her wall.

She stared into the face of the vintage Omega on her wrist. There were so many seconds in a month and in any one of those seconds, a silver-haired man in a crisp gray suit and wing tip shoes could show up with a letter, or a crack could open in a wall. At any moment, she could split in two, torn cleanly in half by what she had and what could be. Andrea closed her eyes and slipped into a dream about clocks with two faces and hands that ran both forward and back.

A KISS ON her cheek woke her. Andrea's eyes adjusted to the dark. "Nate? What are you doing here? What time is it?"

"Ridiculous o'clock in the morning. Sorry. I just wanted to say goodbye before I left. The guys are waiting downstairs."

"Don't go."

"What?" Nate frowned.

"Don't go on tour."

"Come on, Dre. You know I can't do that." He stroked her cheek. "I wouldn't leave if I really didn't have to. You'll be okay by yourself here, right?"

Andrea searched the shadows for her cello and sighed. "Right."

SHE RUBBED NATE's gift over her cello's bow and set the rosin cake on top of the only table in the apartment. The table shook. She had not gotten around to fixing its uneven leg but had mastered the delicate art of arranging her coffee and laptop on it so that it wouldn't wobble. She flipped her laptop open and reviewed the keynote presentation she had spent the morning revising. She turned the laptop's screen toward the wall and opened her cello case. There were things that she needed to tell Isaac if and when she managed to open the wall between them. Nate had kissed her on the bar's stage and she had kissed him back. She didn't know what it meant or where it would lead them, but she owed Isaac the truth. She begged the wall to give her a chance to say it face-to-face. Living with a heart that was torn in two made her a cheater, but she refused to let it make her a coward.

Notes felt their way around the studio. A glowing hole opened on the wall in front of her in the midst of a frail staccato. Isaac's hazel eyes greeted her from behind it. Blood rushed from Andrea's head to her heart. She gripped the cello's neck. The time that had passed since she had seen him had not dulled Isaac's gaze. It pierced every layer that hid her secrets from the world. Skin. Muscle. Soul. Each shivered, naked and—though none would admit it—happy to be seen.

She laid her bow down, making her table wobble. Her fingers fumbled over her laptop's track pad. A black-and-white slide appeared on its screen and asked Isaac a question in bold sixty-point Arial type. *Hello, Isaac. How have you been?*

Isaac cracked a notebook open and held it up to the shrinking crack. *I have been well, thank you.*

Andrea jolted back from the ready answer on his notebook. Her laptop was more composed and automatically transitioned to her second slide. *I have moved.*

Isaac turned the page and revealed his waiting answer. *I know.*

Andrea blinked, trying to keep up with the thoughts streaming past her. Each tried and failed to grasp how Isaac had prepared his replies to her questions. Her third slide posed her next one. *How did I give you my watch?*

Isaac held his notebook closer to the crack. *1, 1, 2, 3, 5, 8, 13, 21, 34, 55.*

The series of numbers twisted inside Andrea just as they did at the end of each of his letters.

Isaac flipped to a new page. *I have missed you, Andrea. Your eyes, your smile, the sound of your voice.*

Voice? Andrea gasped. She slammed her laptop shut before the next slide appeared. The lopsided table shook. She grabbed the first piece of paper she could find and wrote a more urgent question on the back of a grocery receipt for milk, bananas, and instant oatmeal. She crumpled it into a ball and hurled it through the crack. Her wall closed behind it. She staggered back. Paper crunched under her foot. The note that she had just thrown glowed beneath her heel. Andrea smoothed it over her lap, unsure if Isaac had had the chance to read it. The page crumbled over her jeans, taking with it the only question she cared to know the answer to.

A KNOCK ON the door stole Andrea away from the In-N-Out burger she was picking at. Seeing Isaac had left her insides quivering too much to digest anything. She pulled the door open.

"Hello, Ms. Louviere." Mr. Westin tipped his hat.

Andrea staggered back.

"May I come in?" Mr. Westin asked.

Andrea let him through without speaking. She had waited so long to see him again that she didn't know whether she wanted to jump up and throw her arms around him or slap him for taking so long. She clenched her hands at her side, trying to decide.

"You have a lovely apartment," he said, looking around.

Andrea found her voice and relaxed her fingers. "If you like shoe boxes."

"I do. My wife feels the same way. Small homes make you feel safe."

Andrea looked at Mr. Westin as though she were seeing him for the first time. Until then, she had never stopped to imagine the life he lived outside of delivering Isaac's letters. He, his wife, and his little house were a part of a world governed by time and nature. She had never envied him more.

"Is there something wrong, Ms. Louviere?"

She shook her head. "I'm good."

"Would you like me to give you your delivery now or after our lesson?"

"Lesson?" Andrea wrinkled her brow.

"My second cello lesson—that is, if you are still interested in continuing our little arrangement."

"I . . . I am," Andrea stammered, remembering her part of the bargain. "Where did we end last time? It's been so long."

Mr. Westin smiled. "Bow movements."

Andrea nodded. "Right. Let's get started then."

Andrea ushered him to one of the two chairs in her apartment and gave him her cello. Mr. Westin drew the bow just above each of the strings, shifting the angle of his arm and wrist to keep the bow straight.

Andrea tried not to look impressed. "You've been practicing."

He nodded. *"Repetitio mater studiorum est."*

"'Repetition is the mother of all learning.' I'd be rich if I had a dollar for every time my dad said that whenever I groaned about my cello exercises. He'd be richer if he had a dollar for each time I complained. It's his prescription for anything you want to physically control. Hands. Arms. Bows. The two of you would get along. You really should be taking lessons from someone like him."

"Perhaps," he said. "But your father doesn't have any questions for me."

Andrea smoothed away the beginnings of a frown. Until she found another way to get answers, she was going to have to play by Mr. Westin's rules.

THE A STRING sang a slow note, ending Mr. Westin's second cello lesson. Andrea took the bow from him. "Good. Keep practicing and remember what I've told you."

He nodded. "Don't play over the bridge or fingerboard. The 'down bow' stroke is from left to right. 'Up bow' is from right to left. A 'slow bow' is produced by moving the whole arm. Faster bows are produced by the lower arm, wrist, and finger strokes. Did I miss anything?"

"No. Just do these open string exercises as often as you can."

"I will. Thank you." He cleared his throat. "So, what answer would you like in return for your patience?"

Andrea sifted through her options. She had already learned that Isaac's letters had been packed inside a box. She didn't know where the box was or how it had come into Mr. Westin's possession. Was Mr. Westin the sole caretaker of this box or was he getting his instructions from someone else? What other things did the box contain and when was he going to give them to her? Her head spun.

"Ms. Louviere? Do you have a question for me?"

"Mr. Westin . . . your job is to deliver letters, yes? And no, that does not count as my question."

Mr. Westin smiled. "That is correct."

"So if I wrote a letter back to the sender . . . would you be able to deliver it for me?" It was an impossible request, but so was her correspondence with Isaac. She had to try. She didn't care whether delivering her letter meant that Mr. Westin had to get a degree in astrophysics and build a time machine from scratch or if he simply had to drop her letter into the box that all of Isaac's letters came from. He just needed to agree to her request. She didn't have to know what he did next. She was going to be able to take it from there. All she needed was half a sliver of hope to be able to make herself believe that her letter would somehow find its way to Isaac's hands. If she did, she could empty out her heart onto a page and make it ache a little less.

"Deliver it?" Mr. Westin's silver brows knitted as though he were rearranging a large living room somewhere deep behind them. "Yes, Ms. Louviere. I believe I could."

THE SMALL TABLE wobbled under Andrea's elbows and the letter she had laid on top of it. The yellowed paper bulged behind Isaac's seal. The wax strained to keep the letter closed. Andrea relieved it of its duty and broke it in two. The thought of finally being able to write letters to Isaac made her head spin with everything she was going to tell him and ask, but, for now, the only letter that mattered was the one in her hands. She unfolded it slowly, begging it to contain the answer to the question she had tossed through her wall.

A small, square piece of wood, as thick as two Scrabble tiles, tumbled out of the letter and onto the table. She set it aside. Isaac's words were waiting for her and she did not have the time to figure out what the wooden tile was for.

My dearest Andrea,

Your note vanished before I could answer your question. I suppose this was for the best. Had it lingered but half a moment longer, I would have, without hesitation, revealed to you all that is to unfold. But our wall was good enough to re-

mind me that the time for such revelations remains ahead of us. For now, I can only share with you what has already come to pass.

Stourbridge Fair, Cambridge
1665
Isaac is twenty-three.

The Leper Chapel of St. Mary Magdalene was glad for the company. When the leper colony the small stone church had served closed, its duties diminished to providing the town extra storage and to watching over the animals that grazed in the nearby pasture. But the arrival of the annual Stourbridge Fair brought it better companions than cattle and sheep. One of the country's most important fairs had seemingly sprouted overnight on the common grazing grounds, replacing stretches of grass with a small, temporary town overflowing with all manner of wares and trade.

Isaac walked past the chapel and waded through the fair's narrow, well-trampled streets, struggling to keep his head above the flood of visitors, craftsmen, and merchants. He kept a firm grip on his coin purse, well aware of how stealthy and quick determined fingers could be. The scent of produce, sweat, and horses swirled beneath his nose. He tilted his chin up, searching for pockets of sweet air. He didn't find any. He forged ahead, inhaling through his mouth. He couldn't have been happier. The bustle of the fair drowned the constant chorus of questions in his head.

He had grown up with a swarm of queries buzzing in his ear, like the flies that annoyed the horses at Woolsthorpe's stables, but louder. The horses were luckier than he was. At night, their tiny tormentors had the decency to give them a few hours of peace. Isaac's questions gave him no such courtesy. They compelled him to figure out how the pieces of the world around him fit together and challenged him to discover how they worked. He did not care for their chatter. They distracted him from the only riddle that mattered. Andrea.

Isaac roamed the fair's measured rows of wooden booths, savoring his respite. The stalls, bursting with produce and wares, doubled as accommodation for the traders that had descended on the town. Isaac spied their straw mattresses tucked in the back of their booths. He imagined that he might enjoy their transient, simple life, their happiness measured by the amount of goods they sold. He changed his mind midstep. Math equations, floating lanterns, and magic tricks weren't things that would sell well next to the fair's other offerings. To his left, goldsmiths competed with braziers and turners for his attention. To his right, milliners, haberdashers, and mercers puffed up their chests and boasted of the best deals. His skills would leave both his coin purse and stomach empty.

A wave of elbows and boots swept him toward the edge of the fair near the River Cam. Isaac kept his eyes ahead of him when he marched along the rows of freak shows. He took no pleasure in the misfortune of a stranger's deformities. He was acutely aware that he would just as quickly be thrown in a cage and put on display if anyone learned of the secrets he kept. He saw glowing cracks in solid walls and ached for a girl that science said did not exist. He did not need twisted limbs to be the worst of the freaks.

Glass sparkled in his periphery. Isaac stopped and glanced its way. Two prisms glittered on a table of tipcats, tops, sap whistles, balls, and teetotums. He had no practical use for them, but they were the brightest things at Stourbridge. They reminded him of the smile in Andrea's eyes. He didn't bother haggling for them. Missing a meal was worth it to feel Andrea near. He paid for the prisms and turned to leave.

A tattered copy of Euclid's *Elements* called to him from a stack of secondhand books next to the toy stall. Isaac offered to buy it for half its price. The merchant refused but proposed to give Isaac a second book at no extra cost. The dusty music book's pages dangled from its spine, but free was a price that Isaac found impossible to resist. One day, he reasoned, he might even find a use for the volume on acoustics and the vibration of instrumental strings.

Woolsthorpe Manor

1666

Isaac is twenty-four.

Isaac rummaged through his traveling trunk. He pushed his collection of mathematics textbooks to the side. His purchases from the Stourbridge Fair the year before poked out from under them. He pulled the music book out, leaving Euclid's book behind. He balanced his two prisms on top of it and brought them to his desk. All three were a part of a tool kit he had assembled for one purpose: to understand the wall that kept him from Andrea and learn what it took to break it down.

What he knew of the nature of the crack that gave him glimpses of Andrea and her world was limited at best. He knew that it opened when she played her silent song and shut when she didn't. He dusted his old music book off, praying that somewhere between its covers was something that would give him a better grasp of the vibration of strings. Sound, in the right volume and pitch, could shatter glass. Andrea's song broke through walls. To see her again, he needed to know how her music worked.

The white light that illuminated the borders of the crack befuddled him equally. He had used his prisms to lend clarity to it. His recent experiment had proved his theory on its composition but explained little else. He set the prisms aside. The night was best for tools that required more discretion. Magic had brought Andrea into his life and Isaac swore to master the art beyond his childhood card tricks. Alchemists were hanged for their dark art, but life without seeing Andrea was worse than the slowest of deaths.

Isaac pushed his candlestick next to a large flask in the middle of his desk. Spidery silver branches bloomed inside the glass, growing into what appeared to be a small metallic tree. It had taken him several attempts to grow the *Arbor Diana,* or "Diana's Tree," but on this night, he appeared to be successful. He scribbled the amounts of silver, mercury, and nitric acid he had used in his notebook. Four ounces of nitric acid made the tree's shiny twigs sprout the fastest. His hope flowered from its branches.

He checked the hour on the Omega on his wrist. There was still time to package Andrea's presents before dawn. He wrapped the two prisms in parchment and twine. The first was a gift. The second was a spare. Andrea was going to need it when she broke the first prism he sent.

THE SECOND HAND ticked away on the 1952 Omega Seamaster. The morning rushed past him. Time, Isaac thought, seemed to move faster ever since he had started wearing it around his wrist. He pulled his sleeve over the watch's glass face. Loneliness was not a luxury he could afford. There was still much he had to do. He turned his attention to the notebook lying open on his desk. He reviewed the calendar of dates and times scribbled on it and checked his watch again. His heart pounded two beats faster. Andrea was arriving soon. He reread the answers he had prepared for the questions she was going to ask him.

> *I have been well, thank you.*
> *I know.*
> *1, 1, 2, 3, 5, 8, 13, 21, 34, 55.*

Andrea would not be pleased with this last response, but it was the truth. She did not understand it now, but when the time was right, she would.

He read the rest of his message and chewed on his thumb. His next words were not a response to any question that she was going to ask him. They served only as a release for his longing. He gripped the page to rip it out. The white glow on his wall stopped him. It was too late to change his mind. Isaac stood up, squared his shoulders, and waited for Andrea to appear.

The wall cracked open. Andrea played her silent song on the other side. The ache in Isaac's heart grew with every stroke of her bow, but he did not want to waste any fraction of this moment by feeling sad. There was plenty of time for that later. He smiled at Andrea and waved.

Andrea set her bow down on a crooked table, next to what looked like a small blackboard. She turned to the board and pressed a button on its stand. White words scrawled over it.

Hello, Isaac. How have you been?

Isaac took a step back. He had expected her question but not the manner in which she presented it. Like the music box she had given him, the words that magically appeared on Andrea's board fell beyond his understanding. He opened his notebook and presented her with his response.

I have been well, thank you.

Andrea asked more questions and his notebook answered each in turn. His fingers trembled over the page he had failed to rip out.

I have missed you, Andrea.
Your eyes,
your smile,
the sound of your voice.

Andrea recoiled from his words. His chest sank. He had said too much too soon. He glanced at the watch sticking out from under the ruffle of his sleeve and hoped that she would remember the engraving he had shown her during her last visit. She could doubt the honesty of his words, but she could not question her own.

Andrea shoved away her cello and scribbled over a slip of paper. Her table shook beneath her pen. She crumpled the note and tossed it through the shrinking crack. Isaac caught it. He read the shaky question Andrea had written on it as the crack closed.

When will I cross over?

The paper glowed and vanished in a flash of white light. A constellation of stars sparkled in Isaac's eyes. He groped his way to his wall and leaned his cheek on the spot where the crack had been. He whispered his answer to Andrea's question to Woolsthorpe's bricks.

"Isaac?" a woman called through his door.

Isaac rubbed his eyes clear and staggered to his desk. He crossed out the date of Andrea's latest appearance from his calendar and shoved it into his drawer. He straightened his shirt and pulled his shoulders back.

"Isaac? Are you awake?"

"Come in, Mama."

Hannah Ayscough carried a wooden tray into the bedroom. "You didn't come down for dinner. I thought you might be hungry. I saved you some pie."

His mother's voice was barely louder than a dying breeze, and Isaac strained to catch what she was saying. Every word that came out of her mouth since she had returned to Woolsthorpe sounded like an apology.

"Thank you," he said as gently as he could, forgiving her for whatever it was she seemed to regret. He took the tray from her and set it on his desk. The scent of mutton, cloves, and orange peel rose from the golden-brown pastry resting on it. "It smells delicious."

The smile slipped off his mother's lips.

"Is something wrong, Mama?" Isaac asked.

She wrung her hands. "Won't you ever tell me where you have been? You were gone for ages—"

"I want to." Isaac squeezed Andrea's watch through his sleeve. "But I cannot."

Andrea, I do not take any pleasure in keeping secrets from you or anyone else. One's chest can only hold so much before it becomes impossible to breathe. But I choose gladly to gasp for breath rather than risk altering the course you are on. I shall keep the question you asked close to my heart until the time comes when I shall be permitted to answer it freely. I regret most profoundly that I cannot make the ground you are treading now tremble less, but I nurse the hope that my little gift shall make at least one thing in your life feel a fraction steadier. I would be most pleased if you could let me know what you think of it when I see you tomorrow evening. Play your song at half past the hour of eight. I shall be waiting for you then.

Yours always,
Isaac
1666

1, 1, 2, 3, 5, 8, 13, 21, 34, 55

Andrea tossed aside Isaac's letter and grabbed the little wooden block he had sent. Realizing what it was for, she crouched, lifted the table, and wedged the block beneath its uneven leg. She laid Isaac's letter on the steady tabletop, her hand trembling over the appointment he had set.

13

ROUTINE

Nothing is stronger than habit.

—OVID

Los Angeles
Present Day
Andrea is twenty-one.

HER TABLE HAD STOPPED SHAKING, but her knees had not. Andrea had played Isaac's song as he had instructed and waited for her wall to do its part. It cracked open in the middle of the melody's second strain. Isaac waited for her behind it. He did the same the next evening. And the evening after that.

Andrea wrote off the first week that the silver crack opened every night as a fluke, but by the end of the third week, she built her day around it. She filled in *Johann Sebastian Bach* with every detail of Isaac's nightly visits. She thawed her beef and broccoli dinner at seven, did the dishes at seven twenty-five, and tried, for the next endless hour, to exhale. In between half breaths, she checked, double-checked, and rechecked all the things she needed before Isaac arrived: a stack of paper planes, a bowl of *fleur de sel* caramel popcorn, and her cello. Sometimes while waiting, she remembered to answer Nate's texts.

Isaac's visits were always brief, and Andrea refused to waste a moment of them. In the beginning, the crack between their walls stayed open for only the first few strains of Isaac's song. An accidental twist in the melody changed that. Andrea discovered that by changing a few notes, slurring some, and shortening others, she could stretch Isaac's visits. The tweaks allowed her to pause from playing the song long enough to exchange short notes and tokens with Isaac across the crack. The additional time she bought for them fluctuated, but all of them began the same way: with the wall's white glow twinkling in Isaac's irises. *Good evening, Andrea.*

Andrea watched her name slip from his lips and wished that her parents had given her a longer one. Every syllable ignited the golden embers in his eyes. Andrea hoarded every detail of his face.

You look lovely. As always.

Candlelight danced over Isaac's hair and invited her fingers to wade into its dark waves. Draped in half light, Isaac promised the best kind of danger.

Magic came next. He had made white smoke rise from his fingers and made flames leap from candlesticks. On this night, he juggled fireballs with his bare hands. Andrea applauded with her eyes, keeping the crack open with steady strokes of her bow.

Isaac grinned, acknowledging her applause with a deep bow. He plucked a wooden apple from an invisible tree and threw it through the crack. His presents were always tiny and light, and flew through the glowing backpack-sized hole in the wall with ease.

Andrea lifted her bow from the cello's strings to catch this evening's gift. The carved apple, she thought, would have made a lovely paperweight if the crack allowed her to keep it. But like the wildflowers, floating paper lanterns, and little sundials he had sent before it, the apple was destined to vanish from her grasp, return to the seventeenth century, and turn to dust. She set the wooden fruit down on her once wobbly table and plucked a piece of popcorn from the large red bowl next to it. She fixed her eyes on the hole in her wall and aimed the popcorn at Isaac's mouth. M&M's had not agreed with Isaac and made his lips itch, but salted caramel popcorn was an instant favorite. Andrea tossed the popcorn through the crack. She played his song and counted down the seconds he had left to chew it.

Ten.

Nine.

Eight.

Seven.

Six.

Five.

The caramel-coated snack reappeared intact and lightly salted in front of the couch. On some days it took longer. The other night, it took two seconds less. The piece of popcorn glowed, dimmed, and, with a soft poof, became the newest addition to Andrea's collection of little ash piles scattered around the apartment. A fully charged Dustbuster sat on the kitchen counter next to the coffee machine, ready to tidy up.

Isaac scribbled on his notebook and held it up to the crack. *Knock. Knock.*

"Who's there?" Andrea asked.

He scribbled a new line. *Peas.*

"Peas who?"

He wrote down his answer and broke into a lopsided grin. *Peas let me in.*

Andrea rolled her eyes and laughed. Old English didn't lend itself to knock-knock jokes, but Isaac had caught on quickly. She was planning to teach him Pictionary next. She had already bought a set.

Are you ready? He formed the words slowly so that she could read his lips.

Nothing was less necessary. Andrea knew their nightly ritual by heart and anticipated to the second what was going to happen next. She stopped playing and picked up the first of the planes she had made out of the pale blue craft paper she had bought from the Dollar Store that afternoon. On his last visit, she had sent him purple ones. She hurled her blue messenger through the crack.

Isaac snatched it from the air and read the short note she had written across its wings.

It had taken Andrea a few days and dust piles to figure out the optimum number of words Isaac could comfortably read before the plane returned to her side of the wall and crumbled. Her daily challenge was to select the best forty or so words in her vocabulary to express the volumes of thoughts, questions, and emotions written over every page of her life since she was seven years old. While she overflowed with all of the things she wanted to know, Isaac had an equally long list of questions he refused to answer. After his third visit, she learned to rein in her curiosity to the things that really mattered.

Do you remember the second time we saw each other when we were children? You were in a smaller, darker room than the one you are in now. You were curled up on a bed. Crying. What made you so sad?

Isaac hurriedly scribbled a reply on the wings of his own paper plane and threw it to Andrea.

I was sent to live with another family while attending grammar school in Grantham. I was utterly lonely and did horribly in school. Each day that I languished at the bottom of my class made a future beyond the fate I had inherited from my father seem more and more like a frivolous dream.

You changed that.

Andrea grabbed a fresh plane and scrawled her surprise over it.

Me? How?

Another plane ferried Isaac's reply to her.

You were a magical girl who smiled at me when no one else would. If an angel had thought enough of me to break through stone just to pay me a visit, I could not be as worthless as everyone in school believed. I swore to be worthy to ask your name the next time you came. That day was the last day I sat in the back of the class, and from that moment my life's compass knew only one direction. You.

Isaac's plane vanished from Andrea's lap, but his words lingered in her mind as she played the final strains of his song. She knew the path of greatness that Isaac was on, but her own trajectory was less clear. She refused to think about the possibility of Isaac's nightly visits ending, but every history book ever written told her that she was not even a footnote in his life. Her fingers snagged on the A string.

A new plane landed on her lap.

A shadow has fallen over your face. Have I caused it?

Andrea looked up and shook her head. Her nights with Isaac made her feel a lot of things, but sadness was not one of them. Each fleeting second with him was too precious to taint with the smallest tear. She hurriedly scribbled on the wings of a third blue plane.

Your visits make me happy, Isaac. Very happy. But I am neither magical nor angelic. I am greedy. I want more. More time. More you. More us. I'm tired of secrets and waiting. When will you tell me what the numbers in your letters mean?

Andrea balanced on the edge of her seat as Isaac's eyes reached the end of her note. The blue plane vanished from Isaac's hands in a flash of white light. It reappeared on her knee. She shook it off before it crumbled. She had worn her jeans only once that week and wasn't in the mood to do laundry. She played the song's final note. Isaac's visit was coming to an end. Encores, regardless of how flawlessly she played them, were not going to crack her wall open a second time that evening.

Isaac reached for a blank plane on his desk, scribbled on it, and sent it sailing past Andrea's shoulder. Andrea dropped her bow and caught it, crumpling it between her fingers. She smoothed it out and read Isaac's reply.

Do you love me yet?

Isaac's latest paper messenger vanished almost as soon as Andrea finished reading it. Andrea watched it turn to dust on Isaac's side of the wall. The glow around the edges of the crack dimmed. Isaac picked up his notebook and walked over to the crack. Andrea set her cello aside. They had come to Andrea's favorite part of his visit. Both of their unanswered questions would have to wait.

Repetitio mater studiorum est. Her time with Isaac gave her dad's motto new meaning. Her bow arm was no longer the only body part it applied to. Repetition had the same effect on her heart. It taught it well. It beat faster as she joined Isaac at her wall. From the way his neck muscles tightened, she could tell that he did not wish to wait until the next evening for her reply to the question he had sent. She stretched her hand toward him. He raised her hand to his lips and brushed the softest kiss over each of her fingers. Syrupy heat trickled through her arm, down her thighs, and pooled in the back of her knees. She clung to his hand to keep from puddling on the floor.

Good night, Andrea.

"Good night, Isaac. I'll see you tomorrow."

Isaac's face paled. He flipped through his notebook. His eyes raced to the bottom of a page. Their rims reddened and quivered.

"What is it?" Andrea said. "What's wrong?

"Isaac?"

We shall not see each other tomorrow.

"The next night then?"

He shook his head.

Andrea tiptoed and tilted her face closer to the hole in the wall. "So when—"

His lips silenced hers and shattered every law the universe had wedged between them. She melted into his mouth. Time blushed and looked away, stranding them in the second they stood in.

The wall sealed Isaac behind it. Andrea collapsed onto the sofa bed. The phone vibrated beneath her leg. Nate's name flashed on the screen.

"Finally," he said. "I've been trying to call you for the past fifteen minutes. I thought you were picking me up from the airport?"

"Oh . . . uh . . . was that today? I'm sorry. I forgot. I'll be right there."

"Forget it. I'll get a cab."

14

INERTIA

Every body continues in its state of rest, or of uniform motion in a right line, unless it is compelled to change that state by forces impressed upon it.

—ISAAC NEWTON'S FIRST LAW OF MOTION

Los Angeles
Present Day
Andrea is twenty-one.

DO YOU LOVE ME YET? Isaac's question had turned to dust months ago, but Andrea could not exhale without choking on it. The paper planes that Isaac had sent her through the crack had carried more than just his words. They ferried the invisible, the immaterial, and the ignored. They were like the wind in history's hands, but they fit snugly in the cup of Andrea's palms. Isaac's first memory, favorite color, and the way he liked to lie half-curled on his left side when he slept were not the things that made him significant, much less great. They were far more precious than that. The many little nothings added up, giving Isaac substance. They made Isaac as real as the other man who lived in her soul.

"Dre, open up." Nate pounded his fists on her door.

Since Nate had returned from his tour, his eyes asked Andrea the very question that Isaac had written on his plane. But giving her heart to one of them meant carving it from the half the other owned. Refusing to look Nate in the eye was the least painful choice she could make.

"I lost my keys," he said, slurring his words through her door.

Andrea let him in. The stench of alcohol, dried sweat, and cigarette smoke trailed him. "Again? Seriously? You look like shit and you smell worse."

Movie nights with Nate had gotten fewer and far between. Her stock of Honey Nut Cheerios grew stale when he stopped coming by for breakfast. Andrea heard him stumble drunk down the hall outside her door at dawn on more days than he was sober, and on some nights, he didn't bother going home at all. Tonight Andrea wished that he had chosen the latter.

"Well, hello to you, too." He grabbed her by the waist and pressed his mouth against her lips. Whiskey coated his tongue.

Andrea shoved him away. "Get the fuck off me."

He grabbed her elbow and tugged her to him. "Come on, Dre. We used to do more than just kiss, remember? Let's have some fun. For old times' sake."

Andrea wrestled free. "Stay away, Nate," she said, backing into the sofa bed. "What the hell's wrong with you?"

He flopped onto the sofa and laughed. "How much time do you have?" He patted the space next to him. "Come sit. This may take a while."

"I won't talk to you when you're like this," Andrea said.

"Oops. Sorry. My mistake." He stretched out on the sofa. "I thought you just didn't like talking to me in general."

"Why are you doing this?" Tears stung her eyes. "Just tell me what's bothering you. Let me help."

"You can't."

"Let me try."

"All right. Then love me. Can you do that for me, Dre? Do you think you can help me out? No? Too difficult?"

Andrea's mouth moved, but the truth came out of her in a grating sob rather than any meaningful sound. Nate was a thread woven into her, stitched into every tissue and fastened between every joint and bone. Watching him fall apart, Andrea came undone, too.

"I don't blame you," he said. "You made it perfectly clear a long time ago that you didn't feel the same way about me. I guess I've just been sticking around all these years stupidly hoping that one day you'd wake up and see me as more than just . . . me. But that hasn't happened, has it? I'm not blind. I wish I were. That way, I wouldn't be able to see how far away you are."

"Nate, please. Don't be this way."

"Don't you think I wish I could? I wish I could be in the same room with you and not think about wanting to kiss you. I wish I could be happy just keeping things the way they are. But I can't. It's too hard." He pushed himself off the sofa and marched to the door.

"Wait." Andrea ran after him the way she used to when they were children when he stomped away after one of their playground spats. All she had to do then to make him come around was punch him in the arm and pout. Fixing things between them had been easy when the worst things they broke were drumsticks and cello bows. People shattered less easily, but when they did, they were harder to mend. "Where are you going? Let's talk about this."

"Why?"

"Because . . ."

"Because what, Dre?"

"Because before we were anything else, before we grew up and began wanting more than just to share our lunches or joke around, we were friends. Friends who looked out for each other. Friends who knew how to make each other laugh the way no one else could. Nothing can change that. I'm here for you, Nate. I've always been here. You can't walk away like this."

He clutched her hand. A stream of tears had washed away

the glaze the liquor had left in his eyes. He gazed directly at Andrea, restored to the Nate she knew. "Then make me stay."

Her fingers entwined around his. All she had to do was open her mouth and say the words he wanted desperately to hear. Nate would smile. He would kiss her. She would kiss him back and all would be forgotten, forgiven, and well. But loving Nate had never been the problem. Loving *only* him was. She turned her face and hid from the plea in his eyes.

"Yeah." Nate let go. "That's what I thought."

ANDREA FOUND A new apartment that week. She left a note on Nate's door and told him that she was sorry. She didn't bother listing what she was apologizing for. There wasn't enough room on the page.

15

WISHES

Love and dignity cannot share the same abode.

—OVID

Los Angeles
Present Day
Andrea is twenty-two.

CHEAP RED WINE SPLATTERED ALONG the side of the overstuffed trash can. Andrea shoved her hand through the bin's plastic flap and pushed down an empty Pinot bottle and pizza box to make more room. She gathered the last of the empty lipstick-stained cups from her Ikea dining table and tossed them in the trash. She wiped the water rings and pizza crumbs off the frosted glass tabletop and set her birthday cake on it. Like the impromptu dinner party she had thrown for some of the staff from the office, the dark chocolate fudge cake made her new apartment feel less empty.

Upgrading to the one-bedroom unit had seemed like a good idea when she had been promoted to account manager, but she had since realized that moving had been a mistake. A larger apartment meant only that she had more walls to stare at without glowing cracks.

Andrea headed to the kitchen to hunt for matches to light her striped candles. Her birthday present from her father and Sylvia sat on the faux-granite counter next to the new Moleskine journal from her mother. This year, *Johann Sebastian Bach* was mint green and matched the Monet-inspired chiffon scarf Sylvia had picked out. Andrea had never been happier to see fresh, blank pages. Its predecessor was nearly stained from cover to cover with all the guilt, hurt, and helplessness that flowed out of her whenever she thought about Nate. On the rest of its pages, Andrea wrote, scratched out, and rewrote drafts of the letter she was going to ask Mr. Westin to deliver to Isaac. She paused her match hunt to review the latest draft she had written on the first page of this year's journal.

Dear Isaac,

It feels beyond strange to be on this end of the conversation. I've bottled up what I'm about to tell you for so long that I'm afraid that when it gushes out over this page all at once, it will make no sense. While we shared more than I could have hoped for or imagined in the month the crack allowed us to see each other every night, there was one thing I could not let my little paper planes carry. It was too heavy for their wings. I cannot let you spend another second thinking of me or writing to me without knowing who I really am.

More than my wall breaks open whenever the crack appears. I split in two. One half is the part that dies a little every time the wall closes with you behind it. The other is the part that remains devoted to a boy who made school less lonely. He no longer speaks to me, but this has not diminished how I feel about him. What he was to me is frozen in place like a shard. I do not know if it will ever melt away or if I want it to. It's the punishment I deserve for lying to him all these years. I refuse to make the same mistake with you. Now that you know the truth, I leave it to you to decide whether the half of me that is completely, utterly, and wholly yours is worth another drop of ink.

Andrea closed her journal, clipping an envelope between its pages. The envelope contained the final version of her letter to Isaac. She pulled the envelope out, sealed it, and slipped it back inside her journal. Sunlight sparkled in the glass face of her Omega. She had just gotten it back from the engravers. The answer she owed Isaac's paper plane warmed her wrist.

For Isaac. Love, Andrea

The words were coiled in the shape of an infinity symbol, mimicking the design Isaac had shown her. She wasn't sure if *love* was the right word for what she felt for him, but it was the best the online thesaurus could suggest. The right words to describe the constant, aching pull she felt across time had not been invented. Labeling the path of wonder, gratitude, curiosity, and attraction she had traveled on since she was seven was simple, but the point where it branched off in every direction was not.

Courage and fear. Resolve and weakness. Certainty and doubt. Andrea hurtled down every road. She felt everything all at once, including the compulsions to stay put and run away. It was impossible to feel just one thing for a man who was both long dead and very much alive. She had the engravers etch the word *love* on Isaac's watch knowing that it fell terribly and painfully short.

Andrea set her journal on top of the two-month-old invitation her dad had sent.

The invitation was buried deep beneath a hill of junk mail and bills, but adding to the stack that kept it out of sight was not going to hurt. Her dad was organizing a Beatles tribute concert with the San Francisco Symphony and had invited her to perform as the show's guest soloist. He had already picked out her song and sent her a copy of the score he had arranged for the show. She tossed a kitchen towel over the pile, fished a box of matches from her kitchen junk drawer, and returned to her cake.

She straightened the two-layer cake in the middle of the dining table. It was too large to eat by herself, but a cupcake didn't have enough space for all of her candles. She pushed the yellow-striped candles into the fudge frosting. She lit each, counting out the twenty-two years they marked. She had known Isaac for fifteen of them. In all of that time, she blew out the candles on her birthday cakes, stole a glance at the wall, and made the same wish: *Open.*

Wax dripped along the sides of the candles and pooled over the dark chocolate icing. Andrea closed her eyes and breathed out a new wish.

Open.

Wider.

She fanned the candle smoke, whisking her wish away. Two loud knocks rattled her front door. Andrea scampered to answer it.

"Good day, Ms. Louviere," Mr. Westin said.

"Mr. Westin . . ." After all his visits, Andrea was still startled whenever he showed up.

"You've moved."

"Yes. I had to because . . ." Next to the many paper incarnations of *Johann Sebastian Bach,* Mr. Westin was the closest thing she had to a confidant. The slightest twitch around his eyes was all the prodding she would have needed to unravel the tangle of thoughts wound around her lungs. Andrea chose to believe that she was feeling bold rather than lonely.

His gaze remained steady.

"I needed a bigger shoe box," she said, shoving her secrets back.

"I see."

"Please come in." She led him to the dining room. "We can have your cello lesson in here."

Mr. Westin followed her to the dining table. His gaze drifted over to her birthday cake. "Are you expecting company?"

"No. Would you like to have some cake before we begin?" She'd made her wish and no longer had any use for it.

"Thank you, but chocolate doesn't agree with me, I'm afraid."

"That's too bad."

His eyes skimmed over the top of the cake. "Twenty-two."

"Yup, getting old. I think I'll have to switch to those number-type candles next year. There isn't enough space to squeeze in more."

Mr. Westin smiled and sat down. "When you are my age, I doubt very much that you will think that twenty-two is remotely old. Enjoy your youth, Ms. Louviere. It is not something you can wish back."

Andrea opened her cello case and took her instrument out. "Would you like to be younger again if you could?"

"Of course. Who wouldn't want such a thing?"

"Really?" She handed him her bow. "I didn't expect that answer from you."

"Why not?"

"I don't know." She shrugged. "I guess it's because you look so comfortable, well, being you." She tightened the cello's strings.

A tired smile added years to his face. "Silver hair and sagging skin are tricks of nature, Ms. Louviere. They make you look more content than you really are. Old age makes everyone look the same. Wrinkles don't care whether the years they mark are happy or sad. It is time's way of being kind, I suppose. Loneliness and regret are hard to look at in the eye."

MR. WESTIN KNITTED his brows as he played the C major scale in two octaves. He plucked the last note and exhaled. "How was that?"

"You're a fast learner." Andrea took the cello from him. She had made him spend an hour learning how to find the notes on the fingerboard by plucking the strings, pizzicato style, the same way her dad had taught her. "That was really good."

Mr. Westin stretched his fingers. "Real musicians make it look easy."

"Practice will make finding the notes second nature. You have to be aware of where your fingers are at all times and what note they're playing without having to think about it. You need to have blind and deaf security in your hand."

He massaged his wrinkled fingers. "Learning to trust this old hand might take a while."

Andrea smirked. "If I can bite my tongue for over a year while waiting to ask you one question, I know that you can have the same patience."

"Indeed," he said. "And I don't want to keep you waiting one moment longer."

Andrea walked over to her kitchen counter and pulled her letter for Isaac from between the pages of her journal. She turned to Mr. Westin. "You said that you would be able to deliver this for me."

"I can deliver it, but . . ."

"But what?"

"Not directly into the hands of the person sending you your letters. There are—"

"Rules." Andrea sighed and pressed her letter into his wrinkled hand. "Just do what you can."

"I will," Mr. Westin said, slipping the envelope into his jacket. "But I can only do this for you once." He drew out a wax-sealed letter from his suit pocket and gave it to Andrea.

"Why?" Andrea took Isaac's letter from him.

"Will my answer to that question be my fee for this lesson?"

"Absolutely not."

"Then tell me what it is that you really wish to know."

"You told me that these letters and packages were inside a box."

Mr. Westin nodded.

"Where did you find this box?"

"Woolsthorpe Manor, England."

"Is . . ." Andrea drew a breath. "Is it still there?"

"That's another question."

"And I'm not letting you leave until you answer it." She blocked the door.

"Very well." Mr. Westin smiled. "It is your birthday today. Consider it a present."

Andrea exhaled and relaxed her shoulders. "So is the box still there?"

"Yes."

SHE CURLED UP in bed with Isaac's letter. She had thought that finding out where the rest of his letters were would feel like the afternoon she had discovered that her dad had hidden her Christmas presents behind the vacuum in the closet under their stairs. As soon as Mr. Westin had walked out of her door, it became clear that she was wrong. Knowing that Isaac's letters were at Woolsthorpe posed a dilemma. If she jumped on a plane to search for them before the dates Isaac meant for them to be sent, she feared that she might endanger their correspondence. If she didn't, the image of a box containing Isaac's words was going to gnaw at her until there was nothing left.

She pressed his latest letter's seal against her mouth. The red wax bore none of the warmth of Isaac's lips, but it was all she had of him. Several lifetimes had seemed to pass since they had exchanged a kiss through her wall, and in each, she withered away slowly. She hungered to find a trace of Isaac in each elegant stroke of his pen.

> *My dearest Andrea,*
> *I received your letter.*

Andrea's chest heaved. She had wished for the impossible and Isaac had granted it. Her desire to devour his letter was matched only by the blinding urge to throw it away. She steeled herself for Isaac's response to her truth.

I thank you for your honesty. To reveal such a thing was not a trifling task. I am certain of this not through any power of conjecture, empathy, or imagination, but because I have, until now, hesitated to commit to ink a confession of my own.

I lay no claim to your life on your side of the wall. I have no right to. I possess not the audacity to ask for your complete devotion when yellowed pages and dusty pieces of glass are the most I can offer you as proof of mine.

Companionship. Conversation. Warmth. The distance between our worlds prevents us from sharing the basic elements that are as necessary to life as food, water, and air. To seek them out beyond the wall we share does not make one selfish or cruel. It makes one human. How can I deny you the very things that I do not have the power to provide? If this man you speak of loves you half as much as I do, then I take comfort in the knowledge that even when the wall keeps us apart, your heart will never be alone.

You are not mine, Andrea. Not yet. And years ago, before I was the man you made me, neither was I yours.

Grantham, Lincolnshire
1659
Isaac is seventeen.

Seeds and herbs crunched beneath William Clarke's pestle. The tall, slightly built man hunched over the counter of his dimly lit apothecary, grinding the contents of his mortar into a paste. "Could you fetch the absinthe, Isaac? It's between the—"

"The alecost and betony on the second shelf of the first row," Isaac said, making his way across the apothecary's back room to the shelves where his landlord, William Clarke, kept his ingredients. In the four years that he had lived with the Clarke family while studying at the Free Grammar School of King Edward VI in Grantham, Isaac had spent more time in the apothecary than in his room above it.

Isaac had lost track of the hours he had spent browsing the apothecary's rows of densely packed dark wooden shelves, imagining the potions he might create if he mixed the colorful contents of William Clarke's neatly labeled glass jars. Candied rose petals and oil of sulphur. Lungwort and aurum potabile. Alum and sweet cicely. The combinations of ingredients and the wonders they might produce seemed endless.

He stopped at a shelf and read the label pasted on a small bottle of green liquid. ARTEMISIA ABSINTHIUM. He took the absinthe, an essential oil extracted from wormwood, and winced at the memory of the afternoon he had made the mistake of tasting a few drops. His tongue darted over his lips, trying to wipe off the remembered bitterness.

Isaac handed the absinthe to William Clarke. "What are you making?"

"A purge for worms. It's for Mrs. Norton's son."

"Good evening, Father." A smile adorned Katherine Storer's delicate lips as she walked into the apothecary and greeted her stepfather. It spread to her wide brown eyes when she glimpsed Isaac. "Good evening, Isaac. Mama sent me to fetch you for dinner."

Isaac felt the usual warmth that flushed over his cheeks whenever he was in the same room as Katherine. They had grown up together, but it was only in recent months that his blood rushed up his neck when he saw her. Katherine was slightly older than he and moved with such grace that she appeared to be floating across the floor rather than walking. But what entranced Isaac was not her gentle manner or doll-like face. What drew him to her was the secret they shared.

He and Katherine enjoyed experimenting with the herbs,

spices, and potions in the apothecary when everyone else in the Clarke household had gone to sleep. When one of them happened to break a jar, they could count on the other not to tell. They had authored a fine collection of recipes for chalk, balms, dyes, and candied earthworms that didn't taste too bad. After William Clarke locked the store up later that evening, they were going to try their hand at making gold ink.

ISAAC PUNCHED A small hole into an egg Katherine had spirited out of the Clarkes' kitchen. The sleight-of-hand lessons he gave her were paying off. Today was the first time Katherine hadn't got caught.

She peeked over Isaac's shoulder. "What must we do next?"

Isaac felt her sweet breath on his neck. "We . . . uh . . . need to add mercury."

"I shall do it." Katherine pried the top off a small jar of the silver liquid. "How much do we need?"

Isaac checked the recipe in his notebook. "A few drops should suffice."

Katherine took the egg from Isaac. She knitted her dark brows and poured the mercury into its yolk. She looked up and beamed. "Done."

"The final step is to seal it." Isaac melted the stick of red wax William Clarke used to seal his letters and plastered the hole on the egg.

Katherine examined the sealed egg by the light of the candlestick. Her alabaster skin glowed in the halo of the flame. Isaac's chest pounded. The only other girl that had made him feel this way was behind his wall. She had last visited him more than three years before, when she had seen him weeping in his bed. His life had changed vastly since that evening. He was at the top of his class and no longer had any reason to cry himself to sleep. The only thing that burdened him was the thought that he might never see her again to thank her. The clandestine nights with

Katherine lightened that weight. The girl in his wall was the wish in his heart. Katherine was the wish he could touch.

"When will it be ready?" Katherine's thick eyelashes fluttered with excitement.

"In a few weeks. The recipe suggests we store the egg beneath a chicken for best results."

"A chicken?" Katherine lifted an elegant brow. "And where do you propose we get one?"

Isaac chuckled. "Well, I suppose we could take turns sitting on it."

Katherine laughed. The egg slipped from her grasp and shattered over the floor. Mercury-tinted yolk spattered on the hem of her skirt. "I . . . I'm sorry."

"We've broken worse things than eggs." Isaac smirked and wiped the floor with a rag.

Katherine knelt across from him and gathered the broken eggshell pieces. Her fingertips brushed Isaac's knuckles. She pulled her hand away, stealing a glance at Isaac through her lashes. Isaac caught her hand before it could escape. Katherine drew a sharp breath.

"Katherine . . ." he whispered.

"Yes?" Her voice quavered.

"Do you know how beautiful you are?"

Katherine blushed. "Isaac . . . I . . ."

"If I asked you if I could kiss you . . ." He paused to gather courage. "Would you allow it?"

"I might be an egg thief, Isaac, but I am still a lady. A proper one."

"I . . . I apologize." Isaac let go of her hand. "Please forgive my boldness, Katherine."

"But," Katherine smiled, drawing his hand to her corseted waist, "I could certainly not be faulted if you stole one. Or two."

And so, Andrea, with Katherine's help, I became a rather skilled thief. But we were like Serpentine powder and flame.

We burned brightly and brief. At the end of that summer, only the embers of our engagement remained. It was about that time you broke through our wall and gifted me with a soundless version of your name. I knew then that the magic my soul was missing was not to be found in apothecary jars or in my Katherine.

Andrea squeezed her eyes shut. *My Katherine.* The phrase burned a hole through the page. She gritted her teeth. Though she told herself that Katherine was long dead and that the feelings she harbored for Nate meant that she had given up her right to feel bitter, every cell in her body blistered. Jealousy was not only an ugly creature. It was fucking deaf. Andrea forced herself to read the rest of Isaac's letter.

You are proof of the mystical and the miraculous and I am grateful for whatever piece of your heart you can spare. But do not mistake this gratitude for contentment. I will not rest until you are returned to me. For now, I console myself with frayed strands of memories of the days that I once had so much more of you to hold. The letters that ferry my words to you are my only release, a sanctuary where my heart is free to speak. An old friend shall guard them until the hour fate appoints for their delivery, along with the key that unlocks the door between our worlds. When the time to open it draws near, Pyramus and Thisbe will light your way.

Yours always,
Isaac
1666
1, 1, 2, 3, 5, 8, 13, 21, 34, 55

Isaac's last words tumbled in Andrea's head, shoving one another around to find an order where they made sense. Andrea squeezed her temples to keep them still. She pulled out Ovid's book from her drawer and reread the handwritten excerpt Isaac had tucked between its pages. Pyramus and Thisbe led her nowhere. She massaged her nape. A sunbeam streaming through her bedroom window ignited a thought. *Pyramus and Thisbe will light your way.* Andrea gnawed on the cuticle of her thumb and held up the yellowed excerpt against the windowpane. A watermark in the shape of a tree blossomed in the corner of the page. Five pale words accompanied it.

Come home to me now.

16

WARNINGS

All Science is necessarily prophetic, so truly so, that the power of prophecy is the test, the infallible criterion, by which any presumed Science is ascertained to be actually & verily science. The Ptolemaic Astronomy was barely able to prognosticate a lunar eclipse; with Kepler and Newton came Science and Prophecy.

—SAMUEL TAYLOR COLERIDGE

On a Plane to London
Present Day
Andrea is twenty-two.

THE FASTEN SEATBELT LIGHT SWITCHED off. Andrea leaned back in her aisle seat and unbuckled her seatbelt. She stretched out her legs, trying to find a comfortable position to spend her ten-hour flight to Heathrow. Mr. Westin had told her that Isaac's box of letters was at Woolsthorpe Manor, and thanks to the tree Isaac had hidden in Pyramus and Thisbe's tale, she knew exactly where to look for it. The watermarked words beneath gave her the assurance she needed to book her flight. The need to hide from her father gave her the reason to book it immediately.

A business trip on the week of her father's Beatles tribute

concert offered Andrea the perfect excuse to turn down his invitation to perform. As it was a pretext made up of two half truths, Andrea didn't think it counted as a whole lie. The business she needed to conduct was the unfinished kind and not PR, and London was a stopover rather than her destination. There were no direct flights to Woolsthorpe's apple orchard.

PINK RIBBONS OF sunlight frayed and gave way to a purple twilight. A sprinkling of stars flickered in the darkening sky, giving the small group of telescope-wielding tourists a preview of the show they had paid £6 to see. Andrea trailed behind the group with her hands stuffed in her red trench coat's pockets. Not owning a telescope did not stop her from booking the last slot in the National Trust's Stargazing at Woolsthorpe tour. What she was searching for was not in the sky.

A man's voice, rich and deep like Earl Grey with a splash of cream, rose over the tour group's shuffling feet and hushed chatter. "Good evening, everyone. It is my great pleasure to welcome all of you to my home."

Andrea craned her neck to see their tour guide. An elderly man dressed in a wavy white wig and period clothes stood in front of the group. Though he fairly resembled the stylized portraits of Isaac as an old man, he looked nothing like the Isaac she saw through her wall. He gestured to a small T-shaped stone farmhouse with shuttered windows.

"I know that it's hardly a manor by today's standards, but it is home. I was born here on Christmas Day in 1642 to a young widow named Hannah Ayscough Newton. I was born premature and was the size of a quart mug. None of the servants had much hope that I was going to survive. My mother nursed me through the night with a broth of herbs and proved all of them wrong. She named me Isaac, after my father, who died three months before I was born. It is, I believe, the only thing that my father and I have in common. Sadly, I did not inherit his fondness for sheep and grew up pursuing far less practical hobbies such as discovering gravity and calculus."

The tour group laughed. Andrea pretended to. Isaac's apple orchard was in sight and it took all her willpower not to run to it.

"Before we proceed to stargazing," the tour guide continued, "we shall be taking a tour of the manor itself. I think you will find its rooms quite fascinating. The furniture isn't original, of course, but the good people at the National Trust have been able to preserve some of the sketches and diagrams I made on its walls as a child and young man. I can tell you that they appreciate it more than my grandmother and mother did when they saw my 'art' on their walls. Let's go inside, shall we?"

Andrea's eyes roamed over the manor's stone façade. She would have loved to scour every corner of the manor and trace each of the marks, scratches, and scribbles Isaac had left in the building where he had come upon the three great discoveries that secured his position as one of history's greatest minds. But she had not come to Woolsthorpe to look at old furniture. When the last of the group stepped inside the manor, she seized her chance to slip away.

ANDREA CLIMBED OVER a low wooden fence bordering the small field across the manor. She switched her flashlight on and made her way past the half dozen young Flower of Kent apple trees that had been grown from the cuttings of the orchard's oldest and most famous tree.

A low, circular wooden fence emerged in the edge of the pale blue beam of her flashlight. A gnarled tree gazed up at the night sky from inside the barrier, its twisted limbs branching into two directions from the ground. One trunk ended abruptly in a short stump. The other climbed upward, curling into the shape of half a heart. A handful of shiny red-green apples clung to its frail branches. Andrea had never seen anything look so lonely.

Andrea jumped over the fence and landed on the apple tree's ancient roots. Their stubbornness rippled against her soles. She crept beneath the tree's canopy, careful not to make a sound. She waved her flashlight over the tree's trunk, remembering how Isaac had described seeing her appear through a glowing crack in one of its whorls. He had tossed her an apple from his side of time and she had given him a recording of his song. Both gifts were now dust. She slid her palm over the apple tree's bark, searching for a secret she hoped had fared the centuries better. Her fingertips found it in the middle of a large whorl.

Anyone else might have missed the tiny carving or dismissed it as one of the tree's many random marks and scars. But Andrea was well acquainted with its shape. It had warmed the skin of her wrist ever since the day she'd had it engraved into the back of her watch. She leaned close to inspect the infinity symbol.

A tangle of broken branches and twigs brushed against her leg. The pile fell to its side. Andrea directed her flashlight at the ground. A freshly dug hole swallowed the blue beam. Andrea dropped to her knees. She thrust her hand into the hole. Loose, damp soil brushed against her fingers. Blood drained from her limbs. If Isaac's secrets had been buried in the ground, the freshly dug hole meant one thing. Someone had beaten her to them.

Andrea clawed at the emptiness, grabbing handfuls of nothing and despair. And wax. Andrea gasped. She could not see what her hand had found, but her fingers knew every ridge of Isaac's initials almost as well as her heart did. She could only assume that whoever had beaten her to Isaac's hiding place must have accidentally left a letter behind. The wax and the letter it sealed slipped out of her hand. Andrea squeezed as much will as she could find down her trembling arm and into her knuckles. Her thumb was the first to calm down. Andrea groped the ground. Paper grazed the tip of her forefinger. She clasped her fist around it and drew Isaac's words from the darkness and dirt.

—

MUDDY WATER DRAINED into the inn's sink. Andrea lathered her palms with lavender-scented soap and scrubbed between her fingers. An invisible stain seeped deeper into her skin the more she thought about the dark hole beneath the apple tree's gnarled limbs. The image of Isaac's most intimate thoughts being ripped open by a stranger's hands burrowed into her flesh. Andrea could scrub her hands until she stripped off her skin, but she could not wash away the thoughts that had taken root in her bones. She splashed water over her face and twisted the faucet shut.

The letter she had taken from Woolsthorpe waited for her on the bed. She sat on the edge of the mattress and dusted off the bits of soil that had fallen on its white duvet. She picked up Isaac's letter and snapped its seal in two.

My dearest Andrea,

Your absence has made my days in the manor seem much longer. I find that it is easier on everyone here if I keep my gloom to myself. The barn has become a convenient retreat, as have the dusty projects stored beneath its eaves.

As of late, I have kept myself busy tinkering with the water clocks and other crude toys I made as a boy. When I was younger, I was filled with a brash confidence that my little inventions would help me understand how you reached across my wall to find me. Today, they serve only to keep me occupied until your next visit. The sundial I made with a penknife two years after you first appeared in my bedroom has weathered the years exceptionally well. I carved a message into the stone this afternoon and there it will stay until your eyes fall upon it. It is not necessary that you understand what I have left for you. What matters is that you remember it. If you do, everything that lies ahead of you shall fall into place.

Andrea stopped reading. If another of Isaac's messages was waiting for her, she had no time to waste. She had learned the consequences of being late. She stuffed the rest of Isaac's letter in her bag and reached for her laptop.

ANDREA'S FOOTSTEPS ECHOED inside St. John the Baptist Church, marking her progress down the limestone building's ancient nave. Tracking down Isaac's childhood sundial online had been easier than she expected. Spending the night on the steps of the church, waiting for it to open, was harder. She had hailed a cab and sped over to the church as soon as she had learned of the sundial's current home only to find that it was closed for the day. Returning to her hotel was the practical choice, but Andrea could not bring herself to leave. Somewhere inside the church, Isaac's message was waiting for her, and this time, she was not going to let anyone steal it away. She read the rest of his letter huddled in the corner of the church's steps.

ANDREA'S GAZE WANDERED through the intricately carved Saxon-era herringbone stonework over the chancel. The ancient design was a testament to how well stone weathered time. Whatever secret Isaac had etched into his limestone sundial, he had wanted to ensure that it would last.

Andrea had learned that the sundial had been donated to the St. John the Baptist Church by a certain Christopher Turnor after he purchased Woolsthorpe Manor in 1733. Turnor had believed that the sundial, built by Isaac when he was nine years old, would have a better home at the church where Isaac's family was buried than in the barn where it was found. Andrea hurried to the organ chamber where the sundial was kept.

An effigy of an aged, though dignified, Isaac Newton peeked out from behind a large pipe organ. The artist had carved Isaac's image posthumously, copied from heavily stylized paintings that bore no resemblance to the Isaac Andrea knew. The elderly face's blank gaze and the wig that Isaac often wore in portraits made him a stranger. Andrea peered into the effigy's face, searching for the passionate young man she desperately missed. Dead wood stared back at her. Her eyes escaped to the limestone sundial beneath it. The sundial, shaped like a half circle, was missing a gnomon and was mounted upside down in a frame of carved red marble. She scoured it for Isaac's message.

Andrea lost track of how long she searched. Her chest sank. She took a step back and released a sigh. A faded Roman numeral, as minuscule as Isaac's handwriting, leapt at her from the bottom left corner of the stone.

VIII

Andrea stared at the number, uncertain if it was part of the sundial's design or if it was the message Isaac had left for her. She laid her palm over the tiny Roman numeral. It chilled her skin. Andrea recoiled. She was in the church where Isaac had been baptized and had attended Sunday services, but he had never felt farther away. She hurried to the exit, wrestling with the number in her mind.

A starling flew above her head. Andrea followed the bird's path out the doorway to the graveyard on the church's grounds. She needed air. Well-tended paths led her to rows of weathered gravestones. She accepted their invitation to linger. She was not eager to return to her hotel room empty-handed.

Andrea took small steps, taking time to read the names on each of the old graves. Husbands lay beside their wives, fathers beside their sons, mothers beside their daughters. Death, she thought, found a way to bring families back together. She made her way through the cemetery and reached the last of its rows. A crumbling tombstone leaned to its side, propped up by the breeze and a prayer. A smaller headstone carved with a cherub rested next to it. A similar angel watched over Andrea's infant sister Wendy's grave. Andrea knelt by the cherub and brushed the moss from the name beneath the little angel's wings. MARGERY.

The rest of the name was worn away, but the date beneath it was clear enough to break her heart. The child buried beneath it had lived only for a day, shorter than the time she had been allowed to keep her sister. Andrea wondered if it made her family's grief less or greater than her own. Tears welled in her eyes. She tore her gaze away from the child's grave and fixed it on the lopsided tombstone beside it. A faded epitaph pierced her tears.

HERE LYETH THE BODY OF ANDREA LOUVIERE
WHO DEPARTED THIS LIFE IN THE YEAR 1666
AGED 23 YEARS

Ground and logic gave way beneath her feet. Andrea clutched the side of the tombstone, her knuckles cold and white. She forced herself to read the rest of the weathered engraving. Verses from the story of Pyramus and Thisbe screamed at her from beneath the date of her death.

ONE NIGHT SHALL DEATH TO
TWO YOUNG LOVERS GIVE,
BUT SHE DESERV'D UNNUMBER'D YEARS TO LIVE!
'TIS I AM GUILTY, I HAVE THEE BETRAY'D,
WHO CAME NOT EARLY, AS MY CHARMING MAID.
WHATEVER SLEW THEE, I THE CAUSE REMAIN,
I NAM'D, AND FIX'D THE PLACE,
WHERE THOU WAST SLAIN.

Andrea crumpled to the grass. She pulled out the letter she had found at Woolsthorpe from her bag. She was a guest at her own funeral and did not want to be alone. She unfolded Isaac's letter and skimmed through it, searching for the part that had confused her the night before.

I carved a message into the stone this afternoon and there it will stay until your eyes fall upon it. It is not necessary that you understand what I have left for you. What matters is that you remember it. If you do, everything that lies ahead of you shall fall into place.

She turned to the next page.

But for now, cast your thoughts from the message I have left for you on the sundial. You must not sit in the rain. This letter has already waited awhile to be read. It can wait a little bit more.

A fat raindrop splashed on Andrea's cheek and slid down her neck. What had been nonsense the previous evening had turned into prophecy. A flurry of drops splattered over Isaac's words. Andrea clambered up from the grass and ran back to the church. She settled into a pew in the back of the church, dried her hands on her jeans, and returned to Isaac's rain-spattered letter.

My words cannot shelter you from a storm but they can warn you of its approach. There is a storm coming and it is not the one you have just sought shelter from. Forgive me for not being able to reveal more than this. I will, however, chance this one slip. I know too well what it feels like to long for something you can never have back. So run home, Andrea. Run home now. I am so, so terribly sorry for your loss.

Yours always,
Isaac
1666
1, 1, 2, 3, 5, 8, 13, 21, 34, 55

17

STORMS

People are slow to believe that, which if believed, would work them harm.

—OVID

San Francisco

Present Day

Andrea is twenty-two.

ANDREA RAN. TRIPPED. PICKED HERSELF up. And ran again. The walkway of her family's home seemed to have a grown a hundred feet while she was away. She sprinted across the stretch to the front door. Her sides burned. Isaac had told her to run home and she did. If he could predict the rain, she was not going to take any chances with storms. She banged her fist on the door.

"Hey, I thought you were in London," Sebastian said, pulling the door open. "What are you doing here?"

Andrea grabbed his forearm. He had grown a foot over the summer and she needed to stand on her toes to look at his freckled face. "Bas, are you okay?"

"Sure." He pulled his arm away. "Why?"

"And Dad? Sylvia?" Andrea dragged her suitcase into the foyer. "Are they okay? Where are they? Are they home?"

"Mom's doing laundry and Dad's in the music room. Is something wrong?"

Andrea ran past him and pushed the music room's door open, breathing hard. "Dad?"

Her dad's bow screeched to a stop in the middle of his cello arrangement for "Hey Jude." "Andrea? What are you doing here? Don't you have a business trip this week?"

Andrea searched the nooks and crannies of his face. The way his cancer used to shadow his bravest smile was as clear in her mind now as it was when she was a little girl. There were no traces of it that afternoon. She threw her arms around him. "You're okay."

"Of course I am." His shoulders stiffened. "Why wouldn't I be? What's going on? I thought you said you couldn't make it back for the concert."

"The concert . . . right. I . . . um . . . wanted it to be a surprise so . . ." She threw her hands up in the air. "Surprise."

"I wish you'd told me you were coming home. I could have picked you up from the airport." He narrowed his eyes. "Are you sure everything's okay?"

Andrea exhaled for the first time since she'd raced out of St. John the Baptist Church. There had been no need to hurry home. Isaac had made a mistake. "Everything's fine."

A smile crinkled the corners of her dad's eyes. "Well, this is the best surprise. You won't regret it, kiddo. I'm really happy that you changed your mind. You'll learn your piece in no time."

"My piece?" Blood drained from her face and arms. "Wait. That's not why I'm—"

"You'll do great." He massaged the muscle around the metal rod in his arm.

"Dad, I . . ." Andrea shook her head. She had seen her grave and run home to face a storm that didn't come. There shouldn't have been any more space in her chest for other fears, but her ribs expanded to make room for a stage. She strained to breathe under the old weight. She was tired of it. She straightened her shoulders and looked her dad in the eye. "I'm willing to make a fool out of myself if you are. Do we have a deal?"

EACH DAY THAT passed without any of her family suffering so much as a paper cut blunted Isaac's warning, but the icy needles stabbing her lungs twisted each time she picked up her cello. Her house did not have enough steps to count. She tiptoed downstairs and slipped into the music room the night before the show.

She had mastered her dad's cello arrangement for "Eleanor Rigby" on the first try, but she preferred to tremble on her own. Tuna poked her head out from behind her dad's chair. Andrea scooped her up and stroked her back. The ridges of her spine rubbed against Andrea's fingertips. She looked up from Tuna's thinning fur to her dad's concert posters. Making believe that Tuna was still the little kitten that popped her head out of a gift-wrapped box was easier if she couldn't see the bald patches on her back.

Her eyes drifted to the foam panel where a glowing white crack had first appeared. Though she had never heard Isaac's voice, her heart had heard him calling her name through the wall from over three hundred years away. Every fiber in her body ached to answer him. She hugged Tuna tighter. Her watch snagged on the cat's collar. Tuna jumped from Andrea's arms and knocked over the music stand. Her dad's "Let It Be" arrangement scattered over the floor. Andrea gathered up the music sheets. Notes sang from the pages. Andrea took the Beatles' advice and pulled her cello out of its case.

Isaac's song flowed out of her, answering his silent call. She didn't know what she wanted to say to Isaac if the crack opened. All she was certain of was that holding his hand was going to make her fingers shake less. Worrying about her crumbling grave could wait. Her twenty-third birthday was still a year away. The disaster waiting for her on Louise M. Davies Symphony Hall's stage was much closer.

Tuna's hiss sliced a C note. Andrea raised her eyes from the strings and caught the scent of apples. A glowing crack spread below her dad's Lisbon concert poster. A small sunlit bedroom appeared beyond it. A swallow, perched on a windowsill, was the room's sole occupant. It hopped onto Isaac's desk and pecked at chunks of stale bread. Tuna perked her ears. She locked her eyes on the bird, crouched, and sprung through the crack.

"No!" Andrea leapt to the wall.

Tuna landed on Isaac's floor. The crack closed behind her. Bile surged up Andrea's throat. She slumped against the wall and waited for Tuna to come home.

A furry head nudged her hip. She cradled Tuna on her lap and pulled her sweatshirt's sleeve over her watch. She did not want to know how much time Tuna had left. Andrea held her close and waited for the storm Isaac had predicted to arrive. She rubbed her old friend's belly until her fingernails filled with dust.

APPLAUSE BOUNCED OFF the convex acrylic panels hanging from the ceiling of the symphony hall. Her dad made his way to his seat on the stage. Andrea almost didn't recognize him. It might have been his black tuxedo or the way the spotlight ignited the red streaks in his hair, but whatever it was, it made him a lifetime younger and a hundred feet tall. He took a bow, turned to where Andrea was standing in the wings, and winked.

"The Magical Mystery Tour," "The Fool on the Hill," and "Penny Lane" seeped backstage. Icy beads of sweat dripped down Andrea's back. The audience clapped at the end of "Strawberry Fields Forever." Her duet with her dad was next. She walked across the stage and took her place next to him.

Sebastian waved at Andrea from the front row. He had spent the better part of the day looking for Tuna. Andrea did not have the heart to tell him that unless he found the dust she had scattered over their backyard in the middle of the night, he was never going to see her again. Andrea turned from his smile to the music sheets in front of her. She squeezed her eyes shut and made her way down Abbey Road.

The last note of "Eleanor Rigby" hung in the air. Applause soared over it. Her dad did not wait for it to end. He leapt out of his seat and hugged Andrea tighter than he ever had in his life.

THE EVENING BREEZE kissed Andrea's cheek. She hooked her arm around her dad's. Andrea had waited eight years to take this walk with him. She looked up at his eyes and smiled. For the first time since she walked off Carnegie Hall's stage, she didn't see them twitch.

"I told you there was nothing to be nervous about. You were great out there, kiddo."

"Says the man who couldn't stop pacing his dressing room and stuffing his face with M&M's. Do I need to remind you of how many bags you went through tonight?"

"Hey, I only ate the orange ones." A bright and brand-new laugh tripped over his lips. "I'm really glad we—" his face contorted.

"Dad? What's wrong?"

He rubbed his forehead. "I . . . I'm not feeling too good."

"Let's go back home."

Her dad nodded, gripped her wrist, and fell in a twisted heap on the ground.

18

MONSTERS

Everything comes gradually and at its appointed hour.

—OVID

San Francisco

Present Day

Andrea is twenty-two.

THEY WERE ESPRESSO-COLORED DANSKO SHOES, possibly a size ten. Andrea counted the tiny creases in the oiled leather, refusing to look at the doctor's face. She didn't want to see the news he carried in his eyes.

"Mrs. Louviere," he said to Sylvia in a voice that sounded like suede.

Sylvia gripped Sebastian's hand. "How is my husband?"

"He suffered a major aneurysm. I'm sorry. We did—"

Andrea bolted out of the hospital's waiting room. If she didn't hear the next words the doctor said, everything was going to be okay. She was going to run home and find her dad in their music room. She was going to listen to four ice cubes clinking inside her glass of chocolate milk, he was going to drink his Earl Grey tea, and they were going to play the "Butterfly Lovers" Concerto and never stop.

WHEN SHE WAS a little girl, Andrea prayed to God to keep her safe from monsters. Now she wished that he had sent her one. If her father had been killed in a car crash by a deadbeat drunk who hit his kids, she would have had a monster to blame for his death. But the aneurysm that had killed her father left Andrea with only one man to hate.

Isaac had known about her father's death, and all he had chosen to tell her was to run home in the rain. This was her last thought before she slept and the first when she woke up. She reread his letter at least a hundred times, hoping to arrive at a different conclusion. Still, she was grateful. Blame was the best balm. She slathered a thick layer over the hole in her chest.

Sebastian did not have the same luxury. After the funeral, he sat in front of the television, drowning in the empty spot his dad had left on the couch. Andrea sat next to him and pretended to watch the local news. She tried to fill up as much space on the sofa as she could but fell a foot and a father short. The doorbell rang in the middle of the weather report.

"I'll get it," Andrea said.

Sebastian nodded and returned to staring blankly at a forecast for fog and rain.

Andrea walked to the front door, hoping that a neighbor's pizza had lost its way. She would have tipped the delivery guy just to see a face that wasn't sad.

"Hey, you." Nate stood on the welcome mat.

"Hey." Andrea couldn't decide if the glassiness in Nate's blue eyes was his grief or a reflection of hers. He had flown in for the funeral, but they had barely spoken. It wasn't personal. She had avoided all their guests, not trusting her lips to keep her thoughts to herself. No one would have understood why she cursed Isaac's name.

"I just wanted to check in on you guys. We weren't able to talk much at the funeral."

"I know. Sorry about that. There were just so many people. But thank you for coming. Bas was really glad you came." Andrea mustered a smile. The old warmth of Nate's voice seeped inside her and melted away the whiskey-stained memory of the last time they had spoken. He was the boy who debated about the colors of songs with her again. "I was, too."

"Your dad was an amazing man, Dre. I had to come. Oh, I almost forgot. I ran into this guy at your door. He asked me to give you this." Nate handed her a letter sealed with red wax. "He said his name was . . . um . . . Wesley? No. Westin. He looked kind of familiar. Was he a friend of your dad?"

Andrea paled. She took the letter from Nate and stuffed it into the back pocket of her jeans. She would have ripped it apart right then and there, but that would only have made Nate ask questions she couldn't answer. "Yes. He's an old friend."

"Yeah. I figured I must have seen him around your house or something." Nate's arms hung at his sides as though he wasn't sure where to put them. "Can I come in?"

"No."

"Oh. Okay." Nate lowered his head. "Good night, then."

"I mean . . ." Andrea reached for his hand, wincing from the hole Isaac's letter burned in her jeans. "I don't want to stay here tonight."

NATE PUSHED THE door of his hotel room open and groped the wall for the light switch.

"Don't." Andrea pulled his arm away from the wall. "Keep it dark." She shut the door behind them. She wrapped her hands around his nape and drew him to her mouth.

Nate pulled away. "What are you doing?"

She pressed against him and found his lips in the dark. She didn't have an answer for Nate. All she knew was that while she kissed him, she couldn't cry, and that while she kept her eyes closed, she could pretend that she felt something other than pain.

ANDREA WATCHED NATE dream. She gently pushed the hair from his brow to see more of his face. Her breathing fell in time with his. It was easy to fall into their old rhythm. Andrea exhaled. "I love you." The words slipped out with her breath so quietly that Andrea wasn't sure if she had said it at all. She tried to say it again. Nate stirred and she bit her lip. She could not have felt more for him. And that was the problem. She only had half a heart to spare. The other half had grown bitter and cold, but it wasn't empty. Hating Isaac took up space. Nate deserved so much more love than her chest could hold. She slipped out from under his arm and rolled out of bed.

She felt around the floor for her clothes. They felt heavier than when she had stripped them off. She pulled on her jeans, trying not to make a sound. Isaac's letter fell out of her pocket. She crumpled it and aimed at the steel trash can beneath a small desk. The letter bounced off the bin's stainless-steel rim. She grabbed the letter from the floor. Its wax seal cracked. Her resolve followed. She opened the letter and read it.

Look up.

Andrea frowned at the minuscule words in the center of the page. Her father was dead and all Isaac had sent her was another puzzle. She balled the letter in her fist.

"Hey, you." Nate yawned. "Good morning. Do you want to order room service for breakfast?"

"No, thanks." Andrea shoved the letter into her pocket. "I have to go."

Nate wrapped the blanket around his waist and stood up. "Why?"

Andrea slipped her arms through her blouse. "I'm sorry."

"Did I do something wrong?"

"No. I did." Andrea fumbled with the buttons of her blouse. Tears blurred her vision. "I shouldn't have come here. I'm sorry."

"I love you, Dre."

"I know." Andrea kissed his cheek, wetting it with tears. "Maybe now you'll finally be able to stop," she said, giving Nate the monster she wished she had.

THE TWO WORDS Isaac's letter contained screamed in her head on the taxi ride home. The TV was still on in the living room when Andrea let herself in. Sebastian was asleep on the couch. She crept past him and slipped into the closest place she could reread Isaac's letter in private. She locked the music room's door and fished the letter from her jeans.

Look up.

White light flashed in front of her. Andrea lifted her eyes. A crack spread over an acoustic foam panel. Whoever opened it was playing Isaac's song from the other side. Andrea could not hear a single note, but they resonated in her marrow. She held her breath and waited for the silent song's player to appear.

Isaac emerged from the darkness beyond the crack. His head hung low. He uttered silent words. Andrea read his lips.

I am sorry for your loss, Andrea.

Andrea clenched her fists. "You're sorry? Why didn't you tell me what was going to happen? Why did you let him die? We didn't have to take that stupid walk. I could have taken him to the hospital. I—"

I am deeply, deeply sorry.

Isaac stepped away from the crack and vanished into the shadows.

"Isaac!" Andrea lunged at the wall. "Come back. Answer me!"

A paper plane flew through the shrinking crack and slammed into her chest. She picked it up. Its wings were crisp and bleached white. The plane was not made from any sheet from Isaac's journals. It was crafted from a page torn from one of hers. Her large block-print handwriting leapt at her from its wings.

Find Nate. Come home.

19

NUMBERS

When one body exerts a force on a second body, the second body simultaneously exerts a force equal in magnitude and opposite in direction on the first body.

—ISAAC NEWTON'S THIRD LAW OF MOTION

Los Angeles

Present Day

Andrea is twenty-two.

IT TOOK ANDREA THREE WEEKS to bring herself to stand in front of the door of Nate's apartment. He pulled it open before she could steady her hand to knock. Andrea lowered her head.

Nate gripped the edge of the door. His jaw hardened. "What are you doing here?"

Andrea forced herself to meet his eyes. It was the first time she'd seen him since she left his hotel room. Looking at his face was like staring into the sun. "Can I . . . uh . . . come in?"

"No. I was on the way out. I have a date."

"A date." The words sliced her tongue. "Oh."

"You should go."

"I need your help. It's about my dad."

Nate frowned. "Your dad?"

"Yes."

Nate heaved a sigh. "Fine. But make it quick." He pulled out his phone and dialed. "Trish. It's me. Sorry. I'm running a little late. See you at eight? Okay. Great. Bye. Yeah. Me, too."

Andrea stepped inside the studio apartment. It had more furniture and was much neater than when she used to live down the hall from it. "Her . . . um . . . name's Trish, huh?"

Nate folded his arms over his chest and stood by the door. "You said you wanted to talk. So talk. I don't have much time."

"I can't begin to tell you how sorry I am about what—"

"You said this was about your dad."

"It is."

"Then stop apologizing. We are two adults who had sex. Life goes on."

"Nate . . ."

"Are you going to tell me what you need my help for or what?"

"But—"

"Dre, stop. If you're just here to talk about that night, please go. I get it. Your dad had just died. You were sad. I was, too. We both made a mistake. You told me to stop loving you. I have. I'm fucking a girl named Trish. Is that what you wanted to hear?"

The air squeezed out of Andrea's lungs. She steadied herself against a wall. "That's not why I'm here. I'm here because I need you to tell me the truth."

"The truth? About what?"

"Do you remember the day I let you listen to the song I made for Sebastian?"

He flinched. "Why?"

"You saw something on the music room's wall."

"I don't know what you're talking about."

"I think you do."

"Jesus, Dre. I've told you a million times. I didn't see anything. It's been years. Let it go. And how the hell does one stupid afternoon when we were kids have anything to do with your dad?"

"You saw a glowing crack on the wall, Nate. I know because I saw it, too. I've seen it all my life." Andrea planted her backpack on the coffee table. Paper rustled inside it. "And I can tell you what's on the other side."

NATE'S PHONE VIBRATED on his kitchen counter. A pretty brunette's face flashed on its screen. Nate ignored it just as he had for the past hour. His eyes flew across the page of the letter where Isaac had written to Andrea about the number he had carved on his stone sundial. Andrea had told Nate about Isaac, his song, and the crack, but had kept one secret to herself. Nate did not need to know about her grave. If he did, he was never going to agree to what she was going to ask of him.

He set the letter next to the pile he had finished reading. "This can't be true. Isaac Newton lived more than three hundred years ago. How could he have written these letters? How can he be in love with you? This is beyond absurd."

"Don't you think I know how crazy all of this sounds? I wish I were insane. It would make things so much easier," Andrea said. "But I'm not crazy. In these letters is the truth I've lived with since I was seven years old."

"Then prove it. Play your cello and open the crack."

"I told you. It doesn't work all the time. That's why I'm here."

A wrinkle crept over Nate's forehead. "I don't understand."

"You read what Isaac said about the numbers he's been sending me."

"Yeah. So?"

"He said that they're important, but I don't know what I'm supposed to do with them. I thought that they were related to our song in some way, but I couldn't match them up with any notes. I was hoping you could make sense out of them."

"Me?"

"You've always been great at math. If you take a look at them you might be able to figure out what they're for. Isaac used codes to keep his alchemy experiments a secret. Maybe these numbers work the same way."

Nate rubbed his forehead. "Let's just assume for a minute that what you're saying is true—just what do you think this code will do?"

"I'm hoping it will open the crack wide enough so that . . ." She drew a deep breath. "I can cross over."

"*What?* But you said that everything that crosses that wall turns to dust. Why on earth would you want to go over to the other side?"

"The wall isn't going to turn me into dust."

"And how do you know that?"

Andrea reached into her backpack and pulled out a crumpled paper plane. "Because this didn't."

"Find Nate. Come home," Nate said, reading the words on its crisp wing. "What is this? Where did you get it?"

"It came through the crack."

"This is insane."

"Hear me out. I think this plane proves what the numbers are for. They'll make the crack safe to cross. Just take a look at them. If you won't do it for me, then do it for my dad."

The crease in his brow deepened. "What does your dad have to do with these letters?"

"Everything. Behind my wall is all the time I need to save him. Three hundred years' worth. If I cross over, I'll be able to convince Isaac to change his letter and warn me about my dad's death. I might be able to do something to—"

"Let me get this straight." Nate rubbed his face. "You want me to believe that playing a song can open a crack in time, Isaac Newton is sending you love letters, and that you are planning to change the past by walking through a wall. Did I miss anything?"

"You saw the crack with your own eyes. You know that I'm telling you the truth."

"Look, I'll admit that I don't know what I saw in your music room, and I won't even pretend to understand the letters you've shown me, but I do know what the numbers in the letters are. I know how badly you want your dad back, but these numbers aren't going to help you. They aren't codes. They're Fibonacci numbers, an integer sequence." He grabbed one of Isaac's letters from the stack beside him and pointed to the numbers beneath his signature. "They're formed by adding the first two numbers and the rest are formed by adding the previous two together. One plus one equals two, two plus three equals five, three plus five equals eight."

"I know. I figured that part out. But there must be something more to them. Why would Isaac send them? Why would he say that they were important? Check them again."

"Looking at them again won't change anything. Even if you're right about the numbers being a code, we'd need some sort of message key to decrypt it."

She clasped his hand. "Then let's look for the key. If we work on this together I'm sure that we could—"

"Dre, stop." Nate pulled his hand away. "I'm not doing this."

20

KEYS

God created everything by number, weight and measure.

—ISAAC NEWTON

Los Angeles

Present Day

Andrea is twenty-three.

THE X-RAY FILM LODGED IN the flap of the hospital's trash can. Andrea left it there and marched away, clasping her bow arm to her chest. She had wasted her money and time. This was the third doctor she had seen and he had told her the same thing. There was nothing wrong with her wrist. The pain that burned through her ligaments whenever she tried to play the cello knew better. It was the same pain she'd felt when her father had gripped her arm before he fell in a heap on the street. She had buried him a year ago, but she still felt his hand holding her tight. He died all over again each time she floundered at playing the songs he had taught her. After months of struggling with her *Cello for Beginners* book and Isaac's song, her apartment manager served her with a formal notice to stop.

A FIGURE IN gray stood outside her door when Andrea returned to her apartment.

"Good morning, Ms. Louviere." Mr. Westin pulled off his hat. His gray suit was too large for him and slightly rumpled as always, but the line of his mouth was less familiar. It dipped toward his chin. "Did you receive the last letter? I stopped by your home to deliver it and heard about what happened to your father. I would have given you my condolences, but I didn't want to intrude. I asked a young man to hand you the letter instead. I am terribly sorry for your loss."

"Thank you. I got the letter." Today was the first day that she wasn't surprised to see him. Apart from the pain in her forearm, she had not felt much about anything lately. She kneaded her wrist and unlocked her door. "Shall we get started on your next lesson?"

"We don't have to if you don't—"

"I insist, Mr. Westin."

He arched a silver brow, deepening the lines on his forehead. "Are you certain?"

"Yes. You're playing your first song today." Andrea led him to the dining room. "I'm looking forward to hearing it."

"I see. I wouldn't get my hopes up, if I were you."

Andrea sat down and opened her cello case. Her fingers left marks on the layer of dust that covered it. She stared at her bow.

"Is everything all right?" Mr. Westin asked.

"It's been a while since I've played." Andrea pulled the bow over the cello's strings to tune them. It wobbled and screeched. Her arm burned. Sweat dripped down from her neck and soaked into her collar.

"Ms. Louviere, we don't have to do this today."

"Do you know how many cello lessons my dad gave me?"

"Quite a few, I imagine."

"And do you know how many of them I remember as though they happened yesterday?"

He shook his head.

"One. It was the day I played my first song. The piece wasn't anything complicated, but the way it made my dad smile . . ." Her voice broke.

"Ms. Louviere . . ."

"I want to smile like he did that morning. I want to remember what it's like to be happy."

Mr. Westin's shoulder sagged. "I'm just an old man who delivers your packages. I'm afraid that I can't make you happy like that."

She placed the cello in his arms. "Try."

MR. WESTIN USED his wrinkled hands in unison for the first time, putting together the basics Andrea had taught him. She made him do exercises to improve his fingers' agility and showed him how to shift his hand's positions over the fingerboard as he played scales.

"Well done. You've made a lot of progress." She handed him a piece of paper. "I made you a list of finger patterns to practice. Just keep on doing the exercises until they feel natural to you. Thirty minutes. Every day. Minimum."

He smiled. "Thank you, Ms. Louviere, for your patience and your time."

Andrea gave him a folder of sheet music. "These are some songs by Catherine Colledge. 'Stepping Stones,' 'Wagon Wheels,' and 'Fast Forward.' They're fairly simple and you should be able to play them soon. I also included 'In Aller Frühe' by Alexander Gretchaninoff. It's a little bit more complicated than Colledge's pieces, but I'm sure you'll be able to handle it with enough practice."

"I'll do my best. So what question can I assist you with to compensate you for this lesson?"

"Question?" Andrea cracked a joyless smile. "Are we still doing that?"

"Of course. We had an agreement."

"I thought we did, Mr. Westin, but then you lied to me about the box of letters at Woolsthorpe. I asked you if it was still there and you said that it was. I went to the manor to look for it, but the box was gone."

"I have never lied to you, Ms. Louviere. At the time you asked me about them, the box and all the letters it contained were still there."

"You took them." She looked away. A part of her had known ever since she discovered the empty hole at Woolsthorpe that it had been Mr. Westin who had taken Isaac's letters from his hiding place. "You took them because you knew that I was going to search for them, didn't you?"

"Will any answer I give you make you feel the slightest bit better?"

"No."

"These might." He laid two wax-sealed letters side by side on the dining table. "This is to be opened today," he said, pointing to one of them. "And the second is to be read after your trip."

"What trip?"

"Have a good day, Ms. Louviere." He smiled, stood up, and walked out the door.

ANDREA SAT ON the floor beside her bed and laid the two letters over a coffee stain that had come free with the apartment's cream carpet. She selected the thinner one and opened it as Mr. Westin had instructed. Her bold block-letter handwriting was scrawled over the weathered page.

> *I do not know exactly how this letter will find its way, but I am trusting that time will deliver this message from my hand to yours. I know that nothing that I can say will make what I must tell you easier to believe. I can only offer you my word that everything in this letter is true.*

I know you and the anger and grief inside your heart. I am not writing to console you. I am writing to you to tell you the truth: Fate isn't anyone's fault.

Isaac told you what he could just as I am telling all that I can now. It destroyed him that he couldn't give you more. It was not his choice to make. He didn't take Dad away. He gave you an extra week with him and one last embrace. In time, you will heal enough to feel grateful. You will be happy again. Everything will be okay. I promise.

Her lungs collapsed. She grabbed the second letter Mr. Westin delivered. She ripped it open, ignoring his instructions.

My dearest Andrea,

I cannot tell you what you can and cannot do, nor do I have the right to. I hope, however, that the trust we have built over the lifetime we have lived behind each other's walls is enough to persuade you to defer reading the remainder of this letter until you return from your journey. Seeking Nate's assistance is a far more urgent matter. It is he who shall send you on your way. Andrea, I beg you, make haste.

Andrea shoved the letter deep beneath her mattress to keep herself from reading another word. Her watch snagged on a bedspring. She ripped it off and tossed it onto her nightstand, weary of the constant push and pull of time's hands. The looping engraving on the steel back of the Omega glinted in a small pool of sunlight. It posed the same riddle the infinity symbol carved into Isaac's apple tree had asked her. Andrea squinted at it, just as she had inspected it many times before. This time, she noticed a change. From the angle her watch lay on her nightstand, the two intertwined circles looked less like the symbol of infinity and more like a number. An eight. Andrea gasped, remembering where she had seen the number before. Isaac had carved its Roman form into his sundial.

—

THE SOLES OF her shoes stuck to the floor of the bar where Nate's band was playing. Andrea took her pick of empty tables in the room. She sat down and ordered a Corona she had no intention of drinking. She needed to be sober when Nate finished his set.

The veins in the neck of the band's wiry lead singer bulged as he screeched through a cover of a Queen song. Andrea sifted his voice from the music and found Nate's drums pulsing behind it. Nate kept his eyes closed. A smile hovered over his lips. He didn't need an audience to be happy.

Nate walked over to Andrea after the set, his black T-shirt clinging to the sweat on his chest. "Why are you here?"

Andrea stared at the water rings on the table. "That was a good show. I enjoyed it."

"You're still a horrible liar."

"No. I mean it."

"Why are you here, Dre?"

"I found it."

"Found what?"

"The key to Isaac's code."

"Jesus. Not this again." He turned on his heel.

"Nate, please. He told me to see you."

He stopped and looked at Andrea. "Who told you to see me?"

"Isaac did. In his last letter. He said that you could help."

Nate shook his head. "This is crazy."

"I know it isn't fair of me to drag you into all of this."

"Then don't. And you don't have to be stuck in it, either. Just walk away. Forget the crack. Forget Isaac. Forget all of it."

"I can't."

"You can't or you won't?"

"I can't," Andrea said. "It's not just Isaac that's behind my wall."

"What do you mean? Who else is there?"

"I am."

NATE DOODLED LITTLE eights on the back of a Chinese takeout menu and sipped his coffee. An hour had passed since he and Andrea had returned to his apartment after she had told him about the engraving on the watch and the sundial. He had not looked up from the paper once.

Andrea balanced on the edge of the barstool in his kitchen. "Any progress?"

He shook his head. "I've tried using number eight as the code key, but it doesn't break down the sequences into anything that makes the slightest sense."

"But it can't just be a coincidence, right? The same number on two different types of clocks must mean something."

Nate slapped his forehead. *"Clocks. Of course."*

"Clocks?"

"Have you heard of clock arithmetic?"

"No. What is it?"

"It's the way we tell time on a twelve-hour clock. It's also called modular arithmetic. The twelve-hour clock divides the day into two twelve-hour periods."

"So? What does this have to do with Isaac's code?"

"What time is it?"

Andrea glanced at her watch. "Almost three a.m. Why?"

"What time will it be twelve hours from now?"

"Three p.m."

"Wrong."

"What are you talking about? Of course it will be."

"Not if you used simple addition. If you added twelve to three, the answer should be fifteen, right?"

"Well, yes, but . . ."

"But clock addition makes your answer correct," Nate said. "Twelve hours from now is three o'clock and not fifteen o'clock.

Clock time starts over every twelve hours. When you add hours in a twelve-hour clock, whenever the answer goes over twelve, you subtract twelve to find the answer. This is known as modulo or mod twelve."

"Okay, I get it," Andrea said. "But I still don't see how clock arithmetic helps us."

"This means that your first hunch about the numbers being related to music was correct."

"But I told you, I couldn't match them up to notes. Isaac's numbers run up to double digits but an octave only spans . . ." Andrea's eyes grew large. *"Eight notes."*

"Exactly. If we think of the musical scale as an eight-hour clock and use eight as our modulus instead of twelve, we could apply clock arithmetic to Isaac's code—"

Andrea's heart pounded. "And make Isaac's numbers fit into the musical scale."

Nate nodded. "All we'd have to do next is assign each note a number, match the code to the numbered note, and convert the sequences into music. One would be C since it's the first note in the scale, two would be D, and so forth. For numbers that are higher than eight, we would have to subtract eight or a multiple of eight to get the right note. Thirteen, for example, would become five and correspond to G on the scale."

Andrea threw her arms around him. "Thank you. Thank you. Thank you."

He shrugged her arms off him. "Do you know why I decided to help you?"

"Because you believe me."

"Because I'm the guy who killed Santa. I helped you because I know that the only way you're going to be able to forget about all of this is when you have proof that you're wrong. So go ahead. Hurry up and play this song. The sooner you see the truth, the sooner you'll come back to the real world where the real people who care about you live."

21

DOORS

I am dragged along by a strange new force.
Desire and reason are pulling in different directions.
I see the right way and approve it, but follow the wrong.
—OVID

Los Angeles
Present Day
Andrea is twenty-three.

NOTES ROSE AND FELL INSIDE Andrea's chest as she lay on her couch. The melody was a variation of a tune that she had played her entire life, stripped down to its raw and most fragile form. Isaac had arranged the song that opened the wall into strains Andrea's arm could play.

Andrea sat up and rested her cello between her legs. The new, naked song felt its way to the cello's strings. The pain in her wrist fought every note. Every inch between her shoulder and wrist turned to cement. Sweat dripped into her lashes. She shut her eyes. Music found her in the dark. It led her by the hand and took her to a place where the pain could not follow. Every measure pulled her farther away. Bright white light called her back.

A crack grew to the size and width of a door on her living room wall. Blackness stretched beyond it. She laid her cello at her feet and lunged through the crack before her legs could tremble.

Liquid white light swallowed her whole and drowned out every sound. She swam, unable to tell if she was moving forward or staying in place. Air bubbled from her lips and rose past the tip of her nose. A silver bubble drifted by her eye. A breezy morning when she was six months old flickered inside it like a firefly in a cage.

The moment was small and she had been too young to remember it, but as she gazed into it, it came back to life. A high chair pressed against her back. The airplane noises her dad made as he steered a pink spoon into her mouth tickled her ears. Applesauce slid over her tongue. Andrea did not have the words to describe the mush, but she knew that she liked it. She cooed for more.

Breath rushed out of her mouth and bubbled around her. Slivers of memory and time swirled inside each translucent sphere.

A math quiz she had in fourth grade.

A heart-shaped rock she found in the garden when she was six.

The third tooth she lost.

Isaac's kiss.

Her lungs burned. Drowning inside a wall, though painful, looked pretty.

Her face slammed against stone. Pain radiated through her left cheek. Heaven, she thought, hurt. She groaned and opened her eyes. The crack dimmed and sealed shut on a timber-framed wall.

She clambered to her feet. Her legs swayed. Andrea staggered into plastered brick. Familiar shapes emerged from the shadows. A small desk sat by a window and a dark wooden bed was pushed against a wall. Isaac's bedroom and the scent of apples spun around her. A woman's voice drifted through his door.

"I am beyond relieved that you are home, Isaac," she said. "We have been hearing such dreadful news about the plague in the city. I pray it does not spread. Thank God they closed the university."

"Woolsthorpe is quite a distance from London, Mama. I would not worry."

Andrea had waited all her life to hear Isaac's voice, and in that moment she realized how crude her imagination had been. His words were made from the darkest hot chocolate, every sound creamy, comforting, and spiced with cinnamon, nutmeg, and cloves. She leaned closer to hear more.

Footsteps stopped inches from the door. Andrea squeezed herself into the darkest corner of the room.

"Would you like me to have some dinner brought up for you? You must be starving from the journey," Isaac's mother asked.

"Thank you, but I am more exhausted than hungry, to be honest. I think I shall go straight to bed."

The door swung open. Candlelight spilled into the room and lapped at the tips of Andrea's navy-blue flats. She muffled a gasp with her hands and stood on her toes.

Isaac stepped into the room and took the candlestick from his mother. He kissed her on the cheek. "Good night, Mama."

"Sleep well, Isaac," she said. "I shall have your things sent up shortly."

"Thank you." Isaac shut the door behind him. He held up his candle and swept away the last of the room's shadows. Light fell over Andrea's face.

She swallowed hard. "Hello, Isaac."

Isaac stumbled back. *"Andrea?"*

She nodded.

The candle trembled in his hands. "Surely this must be a dream."

"Your numbers worked. We figured out your code. We used clock arithmetic to turn the numbers into music and—"

Isaac wrinkled his forehead. "Numbers?"

"The numbers you sent in your letters."

"Letters?" The crease on his brow carved deeper into his skin.

"The letters you wrote to me."

"I have written no such letters."

"What are you talking about? You've been sending them to me since I was seventeen."

"Andrea, I swear to you, I have not." He set his candle on his desk. His sleeve fell back from his wrist, exposing his naked arm.

Andrea gasped. "My watch . . . where is it?"

"Your watch?"

"The watch I . . ." Her next words evaporated. She fixed her eyes on Isaac's bare wrist. "When was the last time you saw me?"

"Do you not remember?" The tips of Isaac's ears flushed red. "It has been four years since I saw you at the library. I . . . I held your hand."

Her mouth fell open. "What year is it now?"

"The year of our Lord sixteen hundred and sixty-five, of course." He frowned. "Is it not the same where you are from?"

She leaned against his desk, reeling from time's latest trick. Isaac was a year away from writing his first letter to her. "I must have played your song wrong. I've come too soon."

"Too soon?" Isaac's eyes flashed. "Andrea, where do you come from? Or should I ask from *when*?"

She drew a breath. "Three hundred years ahead of you."

"I never imagined . . ." Isaac gripped the corner of his desk. "So this place . . . this moment . . . this is your—"

"Past." The word exploded inside Andrea. She was not early. She was right on time. Isaac had yet to write a single letter. Nothing needed to be undone. There was no better time to convince him about warning her about her father's death. She flung her arms around him. He was still the man she loved.

His spine stiffened. "Andrea . . ."

Heat flared in the back of her neck. She stepped away from him. This version of Isaac, she thought, did not love her yet. She cast her eyes down. "I'm sorry."

"No. Wait." He took her hand and drew her closer. "Stay."

She inhaled the early spring on his skin. More than three hundred years away from her life, she was home. Every muscle in her body screamed when she pulled away.

Isaac dropped his arms to his sides. "Is something wrong? Have I offended you?"

"No. Nothing's wrong. Not anymore. I don't know how much time I have here and there's something I need to ask you to do for me."

"Anything."

Her eyes darted around the bedroom, chasing the thin hope that she would find the right words to plead her father's case. A young boy's loneliness was soaked into the floorboards and walls. Andrea breathed in the scent of old tears and found what she needed. "Isaac, do you remember how sad you were when your mother left you? How you ran to the window each time a carriage passed and stood there until your toes hurt, hoping to see her again?"

His jaw tensed. "How have you come to know of this? I have not spoken of this to anyone."

"You told me," she said. "I mean, you *will*. A year from now, you will write letters to me and tell me all about your childhood and Cambridge, and—"

"Stop." He took a step back. "Are you saying that you know of my future?"

"I . . ." All that Andrea knew of him—the greatness he would achieve and the man he would become—rushed to the tip of her tongue. She bit down hard. As eager as she was to tell him about the legacy he was going to leave, she did not dare tamper with his destiny by revealing things that might alter it in some way. "I don't. Not all of it. I only know that you will write me letters about—"

"Andrea, I beg you, do not tell me any more. Such things are not meant to be revealed. We are taking too many liberties with God's laws as it is. I dare not be greedier than I already am."

"I understand. Believe me, I do. But there is one thing that you must know, and it is important that you remember it. It's about my father."

He nodded. "Go on."

"My father left me." Her voice shook. "But unlike your mother, he can't come back. Not on his own."

"I do not grasp your meaning."

"He's dead."

"I'm so sorry, Andrea."

"But he doesn't have to die." Her eyes locked into Isaac's. "Not if you warn me about it. This is the past and what you do here can fix my future. If you tell me not to let him go for a walk after his concert and to take him to the hospital instead, he might . . . *will* live."

"I do not understand."

"But I will. Just write down what I'm telling you in the letter you will send me on my twenty-second birthday. My twenty-second, Isaac. It cannot come later than that. Will you do this?"

"Andrea . . ." The muscles in his neck twitched as though he were trying to wrestle his voice from it. He pointed to Andrea's arms. "You are aflame."

She glanced down. Light flowed through her veins and seeped out of her skin, erasing the border between her body and the candlelight. In a flash of light, she was gone.

THE OLD COFFEE stain on her bedroom carpet tickled the side of Andrea's face. She tried to stand, but every breath dragged her closer to sleep. She made a pillow of her arms. Her watch ticked in her ear, falling in perfect rhythm with the dull pain throbbing in her cheek. She brushed her fingertips against the bruise left by her introduction to Isaac's floor. It had swelled into a small bump and was her sole souvenir from her trip. When she turned to dust, it was going to crumble with her. She sank into a syrupy dream, hoping that she would not leave too much of a mess for her landlord to clean up in the morning. Her Dustbuster sat fully charged on top of the kitchen counter just in case.

22

TOOLS

If I had staid for other people to make my tools and things for me, I had never made anything of it.

—ISAAC NEWTON

Los Angeles
Present Day
Andrea is twenty-three.

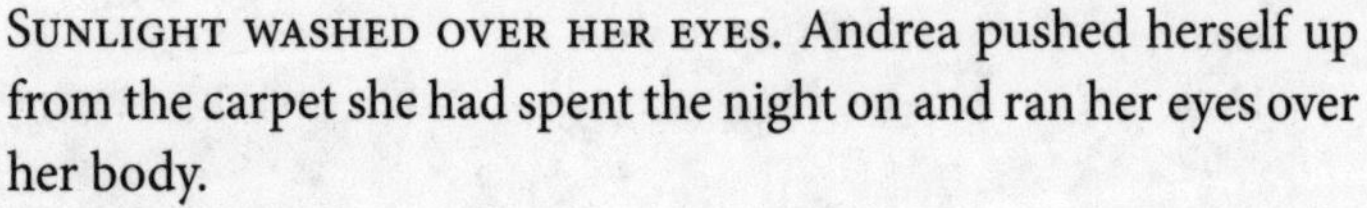

SUNLIGHT WASHED OVER HER EYES. Andrea pushed herself up from the carpet she had spent the night on and ran her eyes over her body.

Two hands.

Two feet.

Ten fingers.

Ten toes.

She ran to her phone and called her dad. His cellphone was still disconnected. The old pain in her arm, in the shape of his fingers, squeezed her wrist. She dropped the phone. Isaac's song had worked; her plea had not. The crack had not turned her to dust, but she had not changed the past. Her dad was still dead. She drew a breath that should have been heavy but was not. The crack had let her live and she was going to cross it as many times as it took to make Isaac listen.

The doorbell rang over her thoughts. Andrea wobbled out of her bedroom and answered it. Nate stood outside her door.

"Dre, we need to . . ." His eyes fell over the large purple bruise Isaac's floor had left on her cheek. "What the hell happened to you?"

Her hand flew to her cheek. "I tripped in the shower."

He frowned, his gaze glued to her bruise. "We need to talk."

Andrea straightened her shoulders. "About what?"

"What do you think? I doubt this is a conversation you want to have in your hallway."

Andrea stepped aside and let him in.

Nate eyed the music sheets on the coffee table and the cello on the floor. "You've tried playing the song?"

"Yes."

He exhaled. "It's over then."

"It's not over."

"Come on, Dre. You've played the stupid song. You know it doesn't work. What else do you need to show you that none of this is real?"

"But, Nate, the song . . ."

He pulled a piece of paper from his pocket. "I have something for you."

"What is it?"

"Something you need to hear." Nate unfolded the paper. *"In 1727, Isaac Newton collapsed. His niece's husband, John Conduitt, recorded that his pain 'rose to such a height that the bed under him, and the very room shook with his agony, to the wonder of those that were present.'"*

Andrea clenched her teeth. "Why are you telling me this?"

"Because you need to face the truth. There is no such thing as cracks through time, and Isaac Newton is not writing you love letters from the other side of your wall. My mother died in an institution because she was convinced that little fairies flew around our living room, and because she believed it, I believed it, too. She swore to me that they were real. But what's real is the padded room they lock you in when you won't stop talking about things that aren't there."

"But Isaac *is* real."

Nate tightened his grip on his research notes. "After two weeks of intense suffering, Newton died in his home at Kensington at the age of eighty-four. Mercury was later found in his hair, a possible consequence of his extensive alchemical experiments. Mercury poisoning was thought to be behind his odd behavior toward the end of his life."

"Are you done?" Andrea folded her arms.

"No." He turned to the next page. "Newton never fell in love nor married. In 1733, French writer and philosopher Voltaire wrote that the scientist 'had neither passion nor weakness; he never went near any woman.' He died as he lived, alone." Nate looked up from his notes. "Now I'm done," he said, tears eroding the edges of his words. "I couldn't stop them when they took my mother away. I don't want to lose you, too. I'm begging you. Stop chasing ghosts."

Andrea touched the bruise on her cheek. "Nate . . . I—"

"Please, Dre."

She nodded.

"I want to hear you say it."

"I promise." She hugged him tight and didn't flinch. She wasn't lying. Isaac was not a ghost. Behind her wall, he was as alive as Nate.

ANDREA CROUCHED BY her bed after Nate left. She pulled out Isaac's letter from under her mattress. She was back from her "trip" and it was time to read the rest of it. After sixteen years, she no longer had to imagine what Isaac's voice sounded like.

Welcome back, Andrea.

You said that night that you came too early. I disagree. I have waited for you all my life. You could not have come sooner. I will forever remember the night I found you in my bedroom and heard your voice. It told me all that I needed to know. And more.

Woolsthorpe Manor

1665

Isaac is twenty-three.

A burst of light stole Andrea from him. Isaac dropped into his chair and pressed his palm to his forehead. He had heard that the plague gave its victims fevered dreams, and Andrea had vanished without leaving him with anything to prove that she wasn't a delusion. She had spoken of letters he had not written, a code he had not made, and a song he had never heard of. None of it made any sense, but there was nothing he wanted to believe in more. A knock jolted him from his seat. Isaac steadied himself and opened the door.

"Good evening, sir." A stocky man flashed a gap-toothed smile from the hallway. Isaac's traveling trunk was on the floor by his side. "Welcome home."

"Thank you, Tom."

"Where would you like me to set your things?" Tom asked.

"By the door is fine."

Tom arranged the trunk next to the wall. "Will you be needing anything else?"

"That will be all. Thank you. Have a good evening."

"Good night, sir."

Isaac shut the door and slumped against it. His insides had not stopped trembling since Andrea had appeared and told him where she was from. He had always known that she was not remotely from anywhere near Lincolnshire, but he had not expected her to be from quite so far away. Years of poring over musty history books had taught him how to scour the past, but nothing had prepared him to cast his gaze three hundred years into a future where he was long forgotten and dead.

He unlocked his traveling trunk and pulled out the battered journal buried beneath his clothes, textbooks, and a thick leather-bound book he had stolen from Cambridge's library. The journal had been his confidant since he was a child. Between its covers was the only place where he could speak freely about Andrea. He opened it. Half of its pages were filled with detailed accounts of her visits. The other half contained the equations, charts, and graphs that failed to explain them.

Isaac scribbled down all that he remembered of the evening. His fingers shook. In all the years that Andrea had appeared through the crack, he had never feared for her safety when it closed. A part of him always knew that she was coming back. Tonight, he wasn't so sure. This was the first time she had burst into flames.

ISAAC ROSE LATE, just as he had every day since Andrea's visit. He had spent the past month toiling over the puzzle she had left him. The grand sum of his efforts was the shadow under his eyes. He still had no idea if he was ever going to see her again. He dragged himself to the oak dining table and helped himself to what remained of his family's breakfast. He tore a piece of brown bread and sprinkled a poached egg with vinegar, black pepper, and salt.

His mother walked into the room, her lips pressed together in a terse line. "You are awake. Finally."

Isaac looked up from his plate. "Good morning, Mama."

"Is something troubling you, Isaac? You have hardly left

your room since you returned and you never join the family for meals."

"I apologize." Isaac poked at the egg with his fork. It bled over his plate. "I have been studying."

"You should go out more and get some air. Spend some time with your brother and sisters. We can go to the village this afternoon and—"

"I can't," Isaac said. "I have to finish my work."

His mother sighed. "Isaac, Cambridge is closed. What possible work do you have that requires all your attention? Whatever it is, it surely cannot be as urgent as you think."

Isaac's fourteen-year-old half brother, Benjamin, barged into the kitchen. A grin stretched across his square face. Isaac could not look at him without seeing the face of Benjamin's late father, the Reverend Barnabas Smith. The man had been dead for several years, but Isaac doubted that he would ever be able to forget the face of the man who had once stolen his mother from him.

"Mama, look what I found. It was in the barn." Benjamin set a dusty wooden chest on the table and rummaged through the cupboards. He pulled out a knife and used it to pry the chest's rusted lock. He dug through the box, pulling out little handmade tools, odd-shaped pieces of wood and metal, and a miniature apple cart that was missing a wheel. He tossed the cart back into the chest and pouted. "It's all rubbish."

"And mine," Isaac said.

Isaac's mother patted his hand. "We stowed some of your things in the barn when you went away to school. They were gathering dust in your room. I did not think you would mind. We can have them brought up, now that you are home."

"No. Leave them there. I shall be returning to Cambridge as soon as it reopens. But I shall take this." He picked up the wooden chest and squeezed his half brother's shoulder. For the first time in his life, Isaac smiled at him and meant it. "I had forgotten all about it, but it is exactly what I need for my work. I am grateful for your assistance, Benjamin. Truly."

Benjamin shrugged. "What are you going to do with a box of rusty tools and wood scraps?"

Isaac got up from the table. "A lot, I imagine."

THERE WERE TWO things that Isaac had come to rely on in this world: numbers and Andrea. On the surface, they were polar opposites. The first existed in the universe of logic, the other in the realm of magic and dreams. But they shared the one thing that mattered. Together, they made the world make sense. Numbers gave life order. Andrea gave it meaning.

Isaac brushed the dust from his wooden chest. He did not bother opening it. He knew what it contained. Inside was the answer to Andrea's puzzle, the solution traditional mathematics failed to provide.

In school, numbers had allowed him to do sums, measure distances, and estimate volume. It gave the physical world a common language with which to speak and be understood. But Andrea's last visit had made it clear that she was not from his world. She had journeyed across three hundred years to break through his wall and make him smile. He could not use the math that measured tables and trees on Andrea for the same reason he had not been able to use Woolsthorpe's bulky tools for his projects when he was a boy.

The farm's breastplows, chaff cutters, and sheep shears were too cumbersome and crude to create the things he imagined. He'd handcrafted tools that served him better. He had made each with a specific function but had not foreseen their most important purpose: to remind him of the boy who built them all those years ago. His younger self had created the tools he needed. If he was to understand Andrea, he had to do it again.

ISAAC SAT IN the shade of his favorite apple tree, reviewing the equations in his notebook. His thirteen-year-old half sister, Hannah, sat across from him, darning an old skirt. Isaac looked up from the page and watched her sew. Her name was not the only thing she shared with their mother. She had her pale skin, straight dark hair, and slim nose. Her brown eyes, however, were rounder and less tired. She pulled her needle through the skirt and smiled.

"Why are you smiling like that?" he asked.

"I am not used to seeing you outdoors," she said. "Or seeing you at all."

"I know. I apologize. I have been terribly busy."

She snatched his notebook from him and giggled. "With this?"

"Give it back."

"Let us see what you have been scribbling away in here, shall we?" She flipped through the notebook and rolled her eyes. "Numbers. How dull. I thought you kept more thrilling secrets."

"I am sorry to disappoint you." Isaac leaned against the tree trunk and stretched his legs over the grass. Sunlight weaved through the apple tree's leaves and found his face. He had forgotten what the sun felt like on his skin.

"So what are they for?" Hannah nudged his leg with her foot.

"That, I cannot tell you."

She pouted. "Why not? I am your sister. Do you not trust me? I will not tell anyone. Not even Mama. I promise."

"Very well." Isaac looked her in the eye. "Hand the notebook back and I shall tell you their purpose."

"You will?"

Isaac nodded.

Hannah gave the notebook back to him. "Go on then. Tell me."

"To catch the wind."

"*The wind?*" Hannah huffed. "Do not tell me then if you do

not want to. I do not care." She scooped up her sewing basket and stomped away.

Isaac chuckled. He had not meant to tease his younger sister, but neither had he lied. He had been holed up in his room attempting to do exactly what he had just told her. The wind was not an easy thing to predict, much less grasp. He had been trying to catch it since it first blew through a crack in his bedroom when he was seven.

Andrea darted in and out of his life as she pleased, wanton like the breeze. At times there were only months between her visits and there were others when she stayed away from him for years. She was in flux and slipped through math's fingers. To hold on to her, Isaac needed something with a firmer grip. The notebook on his lap was filled with a new method he'd crafted to do just that. It found order where there was none and calculated change.

He had worked until dawn over the past months, wrestling with equations that pursued his theory that if a constantly changing thing was chopped into small enough pieces, one would find that within each piece, things remained the same. If he could apply such a method to Andrea's visits, he could predict when she was coming back. Or so he hoped.

Isaac opened his notebook to an ink-stained page. In the sunlight, the jumble of minuscule equations appeared even more chaotic. Isaac reviewed his new math for the tenth time since he had risen. He wasn't entirely convinced that he wasn't dreaming. Proof was going to have to wait for the sun to set. If his calculations were correct, a glowing white crack was going to appear on his wall that evening.

"Hannah. Wait." He stood up and ran after his sister.

Hannah turned and planted her hands on her hips.

"I was only teasing." He smiled. "Please do not be cross with me."

"Give me one reason why I should not be mad at you."

Isaac waved his hand in front of him. A curd cake appeared

in his palm. "Because I'm your big brother and I still know how to make you smile."

My dearest Andrea, my new math did not lie. You came as it predicted. You do not remember this. You cannot. Despite all the rules that we flaunt, there remain a sacred few that we cannot break. You cannot recall an event that, for you, has yet to come to pass. The crack shall open an hour before midnight two weeks from today, and when you come to me this second time, you will linger longer than I ever dared to hope. No words can ever express the depth of my gratitude to your friend for his assistance. Without him, I would not have known the joy of having you by my side.

Yours always,
Isaac
1666

23

1665

The result justifies the deed.
—OVID

Los Angeles
Present Day
Andrea is twenty-three.

Isaac called his new math "Fluxions" after the word *flux*. The world renamed it "calculus," the mathematics of change, and immortalized it as the method Isaac had invented to prove his theory on gravity. Andrea knew the truth. Before Isaac had employed his math to study the universe's physical laws, he used it to break them and find her.

The day she had circled with a red marker on her calendar arrived swiftly. The nausea from her first trip across the wall was fresh in her mind, and she did not dare try to hold down anything more than two saltine crackers and half a cup of instant tomato soup. She finished her dinner and put away the dishes with an hour left to decide what she was going to take with her through the crack. A carry-on toiletry kit would have been her default choice, but an extended trip to the seventeenth century required something more than just travel-size toothpaste and shampoo.

Andrea completed her packing list with twenty minutes to spare. She used it to carefully apply rosin to her bow and tune her cello. This was not the time for second thoughts or squeaky strings. The alarm on her phone beeped. She massaged her wrist and arranged her fingers over the cello's neck.

Her bowing was flawed but Isaac's coded score was forgiving. On its second measure, it kindled a white glow on her wall. The doorbell cut through a vibrato. Andrea ignored it.

"Andrea?" Nate yelled. "Open the door. I know you're in there."

Her fingers flew over the cello's strings, urging the glowing crack to widen faster.

"Don't do this."

"Go away," Andrea said, raising her voice over Isaac's song.

Nate pounded his fists against the door. "Dre, I'm begging you. Stop. Let me in."

Andrea kept her eyes on the large glowing hole taking shape on the wall. "I can't."

The apartment door broke open with a loud crack. Andrea glanced over her shoulder without missing a note. Nate stumbled through the doorway. His eyes flew to the crack on the wall. Color fled his face.

"Don't come any closer," Andrea pleaded.

He sprinted toward her.

The wall glowed brighter. Andrea slipped her backpack over her shoulder, grabbed her cello and bow, and dashed to the crack. She stopped half a step from it and turned to Nate. "I'm sorry. I'll come back. I promise."

Nate lunged for her hand. "Don't—"

His voice was the last sound she heard when the wall closed behind her.

Her memories swirled inside silver bubbles rising around her.

The spotlight bouncing off Nate's silver pendant when he kissed her after they had played Coldplay's "Clocks."

The Post-it note Nate gave her before her performance at Carnegie Hall.

The weathered tombstone that bore her name.

Andrea thrashed her arms at the bubble containing the grave. If she could break the past open with a stroke of her bow, surely she had greater power over her future. A crumbling epitaph was not going to dictate her fate. Her palm slammed into the bubble. The memory of the tomb leaked out, dissolving into silver froth. Andrea kicked her legs and pushed herself away.

The swim across the crack's silver pool was as endless as it had been the first time around. The nausea was worse. Andrea burst free of the wall and fell to the ground, her head spinning one direction one moment and the opposite way the next. Something dry and rough prickled her cheek. She opened her eyes. Darkness surrounded her.

"Andrea," a voice, more air than sound, whispered.

Andrea twisted in its direction.

Isaac ran to her. "You came back."

"Where am I?"

Isaac offered her his hand. "The barn."

Andrea gripped his fingers and pulled herself to her feet. He was as warm as she remembered. She squinted and looked around. Bales of hay took shape in the dark.

Isaac held on to her hand. "My calculations told me that you were coming back tonight, but I did not dare to believe them. When I saw a white light glowing in the barn, I ran here as fast as I could. I had prayed every night for two months to catch the faintest glimmer—"

"Did you say *two months*?"

"That is correct."

"It's only been two weeks for me."

Footsteps shuffled outside the open barn doors.

"Hide," Isaac whispered.

She ducked behind a bale of hay.

"Isaac? Are you in here?" The voice warbled midsentence.

"Yes, Benjamin."

Andrea peeked from behind the hay. A thin boy in his early teens raised his lantern higher. His angular brow and jaw resembled Isaac's, but his brown eyes, even in the lantern's light, were not as bright.

Benjamin raised his head to peek over Isaac's shoulder. "Is there someone in here with you?"

"No. I am alone."

Benjamin narrowed his eyes at him. "I heard a woman speaking."

Isaac shrugged. "It was probably just the wind. Did you want anything?"

"Mama sent me to fetch you for supper."

"I shall be along shortly."

"What are you doing here at this hour?"

"I am collecting a few of my old things for a project."

Benjamin rolled his eyes and slipped out of the barn. Isaac shut the door behind him and waited for his footsteps to fade. "Andrea, you can come out."

She stood up. Hay clung to her jeans. "You better go inside."

"Supper can wait. I shall stay here until you leave."

"No. Go." She adjusted her backpack's straps over her shoulder. "Don't worry. I think I'm going to be here awhile."

ANDREA LEANED AGAINST a barn post and hugged her knees to her chest. They didn't stop shaking. Isaac had been gone for more than an hour, and every leaf that rustled behind the barn's doors made her jump. She dragged her cello to her side. It was the first thing that she had decided to take with her through the wall and the one with the least practical use, but it helped her hold on to the belief that she could go home anytime she wished. The second item was her backpack. Though she knew that it was not going to help her blend into the seventeenth century, it was the most convenient way to carry the last, and the most important, items on her packing list.

"Andrea?" Isaac slipped inside the barn like a cat. A rough sack was slung over his shoulder. "Where are you?"

Andrea stepped out of the shadows. "Over here."

"I apologize for keeping you waiting for so long. I could not leave until everyone retired to their rooms. I gathered a few things we might need for the journey."

Her breath caught in her throat. "Journey?"

"There will be no shadows in Woolsthorpe to hide in come morning. We cannot stay here."

"Where will we go?" Her heart pounded faster.

"There is a village a half night's ride from here." He dug through the sack and pulled out a long gray dress and a cream-colored coif embroidered with tiny flowers. "These belong to my sister. They look to be about your size."

WOOLSTHORPE'S GABLES DISAPPEARED into the fog rolling behind the carriage. Andrea shifted in her seat to face the road. Isaac shook the horse's reins, urging the animal into a trot.

"Won't they look for you?" she asked.

"I left my mother a letter. I told her that I needed to fetch some things at Cambridge for my projects."

"Do you think she'll believe you?"

"No."

"But . . ."

"Do not let this trouble you. This is not the reason you are here. I have not forgotten about your request."

Her chest tightened. "You've come to a decision then?"

"What you ask of me is no trifling thing. It goes against nature and God. I wanted to be ready with my answer when you returned. I devoted all my waking hours to crafting a math that could predict when the crack would let you through."

"Fluxions."

Isaac twisted toward her. "How did you know?"

"You told me."

"In one of the letters I have yet to write and send?"

"Yes."

A smile flitted over Isaac's lips. "I do not think that I shall ever grow accustomed to you knowing of things that I have only entrusted to my notebooks, but my new math has helped me come to understand it."

"It has?"

"When I was a boy, I imagined what your life was like behind my wall. I prayed every evening that you would break through it more often. God did not answer and I now know why. He could not. The crack did not open because you were not behind it."

"That's not true," Andrea said. "I was there. I played our song. Every night for years. I was there."

"No, Andrea, you were not."

She shook her head. "I know where I was."

Isaac pointed to the side of the road. "Look over there. What do you see?"

Andrea peered into the night. Moonlight outlined the tops of tall trees. "A forest. I think."

"And what do you see beyond it?"

"Nothing. It's too dark."

"An old Roman road lies beyond the shadows. No one uses it anymore. It is a good distance from here, but there are points where the wall of trees between that road and this one thins."

"Why are you telling me this?"

"Because the same is true for the worlds we are from. Your time runs near this one, but our paths are not parallel roads. They twist and turn. Sometimes they are closer to each other; at others, they are farther apart. This is why your song does not always work. It can open the crack only when the wall between us is at its thinnest. While we may both swear that we spent every day of our childhood planted in front of our wall, on most of those days, only an endless stretch of nothing was on the other side. It did not matter how flawlessly you played your song. I was too far away."

"But how does music open the crack?"

"The circumstances of your appearances suggest that it is linked to your instrument. The way its strings vibrate could affect the barrier that keeps our worlds apart, the same way certain sounds can shatter glass. I would need to hear your song and study its notes to be certain."

"I'll write it down." Andrea reached inside her backpack.

"There is no need for urgency."

"Why not?"

"The most important question has already been answered."

"And what question is that?"

"I have always believed that our connection was meant to serve some purpose. Growing up, I could think only of selfish reasons for your visits. I believed that you came into my life to push me to solve mysteries beyond the problems posed by my professors. I was convinced that the universe sent you to be my muse."

"And now?"

"I have come to see the real reason why we have been allowed to meet." He looked at her. "We are meant to save a life."

Andrea's heart lurched ahead of the carriage. She reeled it back with a slow breath.

Isaac turned to her. "I asked myself a hundred times what harm would come of averting the death of your father. I could not come up with an answer. The only consequence I foresee from this choice is your happiness. If it is within my power to soothe your grief, I see no reason why I should not. If I had a chance to change the past and know my father even for just a little while, I would. I know how you feel. You are my oldest friend." He drew a piece of folded paper from his coat pocket and handed it to Andrea. "There is nothing I would not do for you."

Andrea's fingers trembled over the red wax that sealed her father's new fate. The engraving on the vintage watch on her wrist fused into her skin. The etched words surged through her veins and found her lips. *For Isaac. Love, Andrea.* She clamped her mouth shut. Isaac would not understand how she felt about him. He was a year away from feeling the same way. Andrea reminded herself that he did not love her yet. She leaned on his shoulder and whispered words that would be easier for him to believe. "Thank you, Isaac. Thank you."

THE GOOSE AND Gander's fireplace crackled over Isaac's voice as he spoke with the graying innkeeper. He asked for a room for himself and his wife. It was a lie for the sake of propriety, but Andrea's ears could not tell the difference. They burned beneath the coif that tamed her hair.

"How long will you be staying?" Gossamer fluttered between the innkeeper's words.

"One night," Isaac said.

The old man's cloudy eyes shifted Andrea's way. She held her breath behind a stiff smile, certain that he had seen her sneakers peeking from the hem of her skirt.

The innkeeper turned to Isaac. "That will be four farthings for the room and a halfpenny to stable your horse."

A SWEET MÉLANGE of hyssop, sage, and anise rose from the inn's small kitchen garden and drifted through their bedroom's sole window. Andrea leaned her cello next to the windowsill and took her fill of the breeze.

Isaac shut the bedroom door. "I would love to hear it."

Andrea turned from the window. "Hear what?"

"The song that brought you to me. I have tried to imagine what it might sound like since I was a boy. Will you play it for me?"

Andrea stroked the cello's neck. She had intended to use it to reopen the crack and return to her side of the wall, but standing a bed away from Isaac, she did not feel the need to rush home. "No."

A furrow formed between Isaac's eyes. "Why not?"

Andrea sat on the edge of the bed. "The crack might open. I don't want to go back. Not just yet."

A blush rose behind Isaac's collar. "You . . . uh . . . must be exhausted. I shall not keep you up. Good night, Andrea," he said, spreading a blanket over the floor.

A DARK ANGEL, wingless and mighty, slept on the floor at the foot of her bed. His skin glowed golden in the firelight as though he were still smoldering from his fall. A traveling sack cradled his head. Its coarse, stained cloth was a sin against his smooth cheek. He didn't seem to mind. His eyes shifted behind his lids, darting after a dream. Even from behind the veil of sleep, they pulled Andrea to him. Andrea forced herself to look away. She tiptoed past him, clutching his letter to her breast.

Andrea sat by the fireplace and cracked Isaac's wax seal. The letter's paper was crisper than any of the ones Mr. Westin delivered, but Isaac's tiny handwriting remained the same.

My dearest Andrea,

I know that I risk offending you by addressing you in such a familiar manner, but calling you anything less would be a lie. Though we had never spoken until your visit, you are, in truth, my most cherished friend. It is impossible for me to explain within the confines of one letter how you have steered the course of my life and so I shall not attempt it. There will be time for such stories in other letters. For now, I am writing you about a much more urgent matter.

I do not know how or when you shall receive this letter, but I hope most fervently that it reaches you in time. My next words shall be blunt for I am at a loss for any other way to convey the dreadful message that you have requested that I send to you across time. If you are standing while reading this, I must insist that you find a place to sit. I beg you to be strong.

Your father will meet his death soon after your twenty-second birthday. The nature and circumstances of this terrible event are not clear to me. All that I know of it are the words you have instructed me to convey. Forgo a stroll with your father after his concert. Seek a doctor and make haste. His life depends on it.

Always,
Isaac Newton

Andrea exhaled. In three hundred years, Mr. Westin would stand at her door with a letter containing the words she had just read. Every ounce of grief she had hoarded pushed against her ribs, demanding to be released. They no longer had anyone to mourn. Andrea let them roll down her cheeks.

"Is it as you hoped?" Isaac walked up behind her.

She wiped her tears. "I thought you were asleep."

"My words have saddened you." He reached for his letter. "I am sorry. I shall rip them apart and compose ones that are more to your liking."

"No. You don't have to change a thing."

"Then why do you weep?"

Andrea smiled through her tears. "Trust me. This letter is perfect."

The fireplace cast shadows over Isaac's face. "But how shall it reach you in the future? Shall I slip it through the crack?"

"You have to bury it."

"Bury it? Where? How will you find it? How will—"

Andrea pressed her lips against Isaac's mouth. There was a time for telling him about his apple tree and Mr. Westin's deliveries, but on this night, they had a fire, a bed, and a letter that made everything right. Only their clothes kept them apart. Andrea led his fingers to her waist.

Isaac searched her eyes for permission he didn't need. "Andrea . . ."

She clasped her hands behind his neck. "Do you want me?"

"In the most hopeless and terrible way." He undid the ribbon that laced up the bodice of her dress, taking slow breaths.

Andrea slipped the dress from her shoulders and let it pool on the floor. "Then have me."

Isaac's eyes wandered over Andrea's body. Heat flared where his gaze caressed her skin. If he explored her nakedness a fraction of a second longer, she was going to burst into flames. She raised her hands to cover herself.

Isaac drew her hand away from her breast. "I want to see you," he said, sliding his hand down to her hip. "All of you." He hooked his arm around her and lifted her off the floor. He carried her to the bed, kissing her fiercely and deeply. He laid her over the sheets and planted a trail of kisses from her ankle up to the curve of her neck. "You own me, Andrea," he whispered behind her ear. "We do not stand beneath a church, but you are my altar, and in front of you, I make a vow as unbreakable as any blessed by a vicar. Tonight and always, everything I am and will be is yours."

ANDREA WOKE UP, naked except for the warmth of Isaac's arms. She exhaled into his chest. The morning had not stolen him away.

"You are still here." He stroked her cheek. "We have another day."

"But it feels like a trick." She pressed herself closer to him. "I'm afraid that if we talk too loud . . ." She lowered her voice. "The crack will hear us and realize that I'm still here."

"You said that my letter told you that you would linger."

"But it didn't say exactly how much time I have."

He sat up. "Then let us remove ourselves from this place. Let us live this day like two people with all the time in the world."

Andrea watched his lips intently, reading them as though he were still speaking soundlessly through the crack. She had not yet gotten used to hearing his voice. His words trembled through her spine just as the "Butterfly Lovers" Concerto did every time she heard it. Andrea rolled to her side and stared at the wall. "But that would be a lie."

He planted a trail of kisses over her nape. "I am willing to believe it if you are."

THE LATE AFTERNOON sun dyed the winding brook with swirls of orange, red, and purple. The water gurgled in appreciation. Two leaves meandered through the brook, twirling to its song. A rock halted their dance. Isaac sat up from the pillow he had made of Andrea's lap, leaving the shape of his head creased into her skirt. He dipped his hand into the water and nudged the leaves free. He rested his cheek over her thighs and watched them drift away.

Andrea stroked his hair. She had read that his hair had gone snow white before he'd turned thirty and that he had blamed it on his extensive alchemical experiments with mercury. That afternoon, there was not a single strand of silver on his head. His dark waves framed his handsome, unlined face, better than any of the ornate wooden frames mounted over portraits of him as an old man. He had yet to accomplish any of the great things that would secure his place in history, but she could not help but think that here, with his head cradled in her lap, his eyes on the water, and his lips curled in a lazy smile, he was most himself.

"Do you think they will make it to the end?" she asked.

Isaac craned his neck to follow the leaves as they drifted down the brook. "They are afloat."

Andrea sighed. "For now."

He reached behind her ear. A small wildflower crowned by intense blue petals appeared in his hand. "*Gentiana verna*. You can make a tea from it that eases digestion." He handed it to her. "And doubt."

Andrea smiled. "You still do magic."

"You are magic." He kissed her hand. "It is getting late. We should head back to the village."

The inn's walls pressed against Andrea's mind. "Do you . . . um . . . suppose we could spend the night here?"

Isaac raised a brow. "You wish to sleep outdoors?"

"Sure." She patted the grass. "Why not?"

Isaac smirked. "Is sleeping on the ground common on your side of the wall?"

"Well, no, not really. Unless you like tents, bug bites, and s'mores."

"S'mores?"

"Heaven between two graham crackers. Or biscuits. Or whatever it is you call them over here."

Isaac chuckled. "You are a strange one, Andrea Louviere. Come, tell me more about the world on your side of the wall."

"I thought you didn't want to know about the future."

"I do not wish to know about *my* future, but I am curious about the rest of the world. I greatly wish to know more about where you are from."

Andrea chewed the side of her thumb. Isaac's contributions in math and science were inextricable from the world he was asking her to describe. Man would not have landed on the moon if he had not understood gravity. Planes would not fly across the sky if people did not comprehend his laws of motion. Even rainbows would be a mystery without his experiments on the nature of light. "What would you like to know?"

His eyes flashed. "S'mores. People. Everything. Do you still use carriages? Horses? Lanterns? I imagine that the world has made great strides in three hundred years. It must be filled with such wondrous inventions. I'm embarrassed to think about how terribly dull my world must appear to you."

Andrea looked around the meadow, breathing in the scent of flowers and grass. She had never smelled sweeter air. The sounds floating in it were just as lush. Birds chirped, leaves fluttered, and the brook sang. She didn't need to play her cello to hear music. "Not at all."

"But surely your side must be at least a thousand times more beautiful and grand."

"Beautiful?" Traffic, global warming, and L.A.'s smog tumbled around in her head. "Let's just say it's different."

A crease marred Isaac's brow. "Do you not like your world, Andrea?"

She twirled a weed around her forefinger and tugged it from the ground. "It's just that I never really felt that I truly belonged there. Not since I was seven and saw you through the crack. I saw something no one else wanted to believe or understand."

Isaac stared into the brook. The gold flecks in his eyes dimmed with the setting sun. "If I ask you a question, will you promise to tell me the truth?"

"Of course."

"Do you regret seeing me, Andrea? Do you wish that none of this ever happened?"

She cupped his cheeks, turning his face toward her. "How could I possibly regret any of this? You. This day. This place. All of this is beyond magical."

"Perhaps." Isaac threw a pebble into the river. "But none of it will last. I dare not blink because I fear that when I open my eyes you will be gone."

"Don't blink." She kissed him deeply and clung to him. Even in the open, miles away from the nearest town, she could feel the crack pulling them apart. "Don't let me go."

"Death itself could not pry you from my arms." He held her face. "You have no inkling of the depth of beauty you possess. If you did, you would not be as blithe with it."

"Blithe?" Andrea frowned.

"You are a dangerous creature, Andrea." He pulled the ribbons of her bodice free.

Andrea breathed hard. Her dress fell open, exposing her breasts. "Isaac . . ."

He drew her close and kissed her neck. "I can take my fill of the little pleasures of this place, its brook, its sky, its grass, without consequence or worry. But I must take the utmost care when I look upon you. I could drown in your eyes and lose myself in your mouth." He caressed her breast. "I could wander over your skin for days and not want for food or drink. You could kill me with a kiss, Andrea, and I would not lift a finger to stop you."

Andrea pushed him down on the grass. She fumbled with the buttons of his breeches and straddled his hips. She slipped him inside her, out in the open for any passing stranger to see. She didn't care. Decency was for those with the luxury of time. Their bodies moved as one, falling into perfect rhythm with a silent song they had heard all their lives.

24

CRIMES

The acceleration of an object is directly proportional to the net external force acting on the object and inversely proportional to the mass of the object.

—ISAAC NEWTON'S SECOND LAW OF MOTION

Andrea and Isaac's Home
1665
Andrea is twenty-three.

Dear Mister Johann Sebastian Bach,

I'm glad I took you with me. Without you, I'm bound to forget.

My name is Andrea S. Louviere. My parents are Julia and Andrew Louviere. My stepmother's name is Sylvia. I have a brother named Bas. Nate was my best friend, but we don't speak anymore. At least, I don't think we do. The last time I saw him was the night I stepped through a crack in my wall. I now live in a little village in England, three hundred years in the past. I've been here two months, one week, and four days.

I haven't got the accent quite right, but the butcher seems to understand me well enough when I order mutton or veal for the evening stew. He seems to think that I'm from France. Some days, I believe him. My old life is so far away. One day soon, if I don't write down who I used to be, I'm going to wake up and forget that I was anyone else but the strange, possibly French, woman living in a little limestone cottage at the edge of a village in Lincolnshire with the man she has loved all her life.

Andrea signed her name at the bottom of the journal's page. She paused, trying to decide whether to add the new last name she went by. Though there were no witnesses to their wedding and their hearts kept the sole record of their vows, here she and Isaac lived as man and wife. But as much as she relished her new life, Andrea was acutely aware that every step she took in it brought her closer to its end. She shut her journal and squeezed it into her backpack. The bag was stuffed to overflowing, filled with all the bound pages that had chronicled her life on the other side of the wall, her only tethers to her old world. She shoved her backpack deep beneath the bed she shared with her husband and checked the time on her Omega. Isaac was teaching at the local grammar school and wasn't going to be home for another two hours. She threw on her coat, grabbed her cello, and fled their bedroom.

She carried her instrument across her little garden, taking slow, deep breaths of the crisp air. Outside, Andrea found it easier to breathe. It didn't tremble the way it did inside the cottage's walls, crackling with all the seconds she and Isaac burned through. Growing up stealing time, Andrea found it difficult to stop feeling like a thief. She could not sit through supper without sneaking a peek over Isaac's shoulder, checking for glowing cracks.

An old oak tree's thinning canopy rustled in the wind beyond the border of her garden. The little bench Isaac had built waited for her and her cello beneath its shade. Andrea hurried toward it.

It had taken Isaac nearly a month to persuade Andrea to pick up her cello again. Playing still made her sit on the edge of her seat, wary of cracks, but it made the seventeenth century feel less strange. While the pages of her journal kept her memories of her past life safe, only music could bring them to life.

Andrea settled on the bench and positioned her bow over her cello. Playing in a meadow allowed her to play to her heart's content, without worrying about walls.

SHE HAD NEVER missed her microwave and frozen chicken and broccoli dinners more. The thin reddish-brown liquid that bubbled over the fire looked nothing like mutton stew and smelled like it even less. Her fourth attempt at making Isaac's favorite childhood dish had gone the way of its predecessors. Andrea rubbed her forehead, wondering where she had gone wrong.

Isaac walked through the cottage door and made his way to her. "That smells lovely."

"Liar. Let's call for pizza. If I call now . . ." She checked her watch. "Dinner should be ready in about three hundred years. We get a free pizza if it's late."

Isaac laughed. Andrea had brought him up to speed on a lot of the modern conveniences she missed. She mentioned her craving for Papa John's original crust pepperoni pizza and ice-cold Coke only every other day.

She took a sip of the stew and grimaced. "It's worse than I thought."

Isaac grabbed her by the waist and kissed the side of her neck. "But you, my dearest, are delectable." He slid his hand over her thigh. "Who needs supper?"

"Not me." Andrea pulled off his coat and kissed him.

Isaac carried her onto the dining table, knocking their water jug on the floor.

Andrea laughed. "That's the second one you've broken this week."

He lifted up her skirt and drew her legs apart. "Shall we break some more?"

THE COOKING FIRE cast shadows over Isaac's face as he lay half-dressed next to Andrea on the cottage's floor. Broken dishes were scattered next to him. Andrea rested her head on his chest and listened to him breathe. These were the moments when time almost seemed to slow down and allowed her to believe that they could grow old together. "How was school?"

"Half of the boys were asleep during arithmetic and the rest spent the hour staring at their feet. During the Latin lesson, I heard them groaning in their heads. So you might say that it was better than yesterday. I am a better student than teacher, I'm afraid."

"Nonsense. They're sleepy because school begins at the crack of dawn."

"Is it not the same in your time?" Isaac asked.

Her lips quivered. "Her time" lurked behind their cottage's bricks, waiting for her to trip and stumble against it.

"Did I say something wrong?" Isaac asked.

"No."

"Then why are you frowning?"

"I just don't like it when you say things like that. You aren't a bad teacher. You're one of the most brilliant men that has ever lived. You discovered gravity, calculus, and—"

"Andrea, stop. We have discussed this. You gave me your word. Time is a fragile thing. I do not wish to risk what we have now by prying into the future."

She pursed her lips. Isaac had made her swear not to talk about what she knew of the future, but there were times when her promise pushed against her teeth. He was destined to be one of the world's greatest minds and yet only one of them knew who he really was.

"There is only one thing I wish to know about what your history books say about my future." Isaac clasped her hand and met her eyes. "Are you in it?"

Andrea's fingers froze in his palm. "Isaac . . . I . . ."

Isaac sat up. "Then the future you know of is not the future I want. Everything that I have done, every book I scoured, every equation I solved, every elixir I concocted, all these, Andrea, were for one purpose. To find you. And now you are here. All that I have dreamed of and ached for is under this roof. I no longer have any use or interest in math, science, potions, or spells. I live with real magic every day. Forget the man you have read of. He does not exist. I do. I would suffer a wretched death if I were to walk down any path that took me one step away from a life with you."

"But this isn't the life you are supposed to lead. You are meant to do the most amazing things."

"Tell me this, Andrea. What could possibly be greater than being happy? Than being content? I have loved you all my life. I desire nothing more than to continue loving you for the rest of it. My one ambition is to grow old by your side."

"That's just it. You should want more. You shouldn't be content. You can't give up your destiny."

"I am not giving up anything."

"You have no idea what you're turning your back on."

"But I do know what I am getting to keep in return. You are not a choice, Andrea. You are in my bones. I have seen our life together. I am living it. That is all that matters to me. I thought you wanted the same thing."

"No." Andrea turned from him. "I don't."

"You do not mean that."

"I do. Every second I'm here in the past erases a little more of your future. This cottage . . . this little pretend life we have . . . all of this is a mistake. My mistake. I should never have come here. You aren't meant to be mine. You are meant to be great."

THE BORDER BETWEEN the last of her dreams and morning was thinner than a butterfly's wing. Andrea rolled over in bed, hiding from the rising sun. In the shadow of Isaac's shoulder, she could make the foggy sliver of half sleep last a few moments longer. She lingered in the haze, convinced that she could live forever curled in that exact spot on her bed, her cheek against Isaac's back. The part of her that remembered the argument they'd had the night before was still asleep. It stirred when Isaac shifted his legs beneath the blanket.

She had told him that their life together was a mistake, and her cold words had crawled into bed with them, wedging a wall of ice down the length of their mattress. Isaac had turned his back to Andrea and shut his eyes, believing them. Andrea had wanted to tug on his arm and tell him that she would readily rob the world of him so that she could have him to herself. She would hide him in their tiny cottage, away from his destiny and future achievements, to live out days that were as obscure as they were ridiculously happy. But she was fully awake now and remembered why they could not be together. Stealing time was a petty crime compared to murdering the man Isaac was born to be.

ANDREA TWISTED THE pegs on her cello. She had been trying to tune the instrument for more than half an hour, but every string screeched in her ear. Her cello did not want to be played almost as much as her hands did not want to play Isaac's song. But as she had yet to discover a way to open their cottage's wall by bashing her cello against it, she was going to have to force both heart and bow to do what was right. Floorboards squeaked from their bedroom. Andrea's chest sank. Attempting to leave Isaac was going to be a million times harder when he was awake.

Isaac entered the sitting room and picked up a chair. He planted it a few feet from Andrea and sat down. His mouth sculpted silent words. *Good morning.*

Andrea frowned. "What are you doing?"

Apologizing.

"For what?" A lifetime of silent conversations through their walls made it a simple to task to read Isaac's lips.

For believing you.

Andrea tightened her fist around the cello's neck, bracing herself for Isaac's next words. If he was going to tell her that he hated her, she was thankful that he chose to speak without sound. His voice would have shredded her.

Isaac leaned forward.

For believing you when you said that you thought that this . . . that we were a mistake.

For listening to my anger and not to what you were trying to say.

For not saying that I would unravel all of the universe's mysteries, create every single invention mankind would ever need, and publish every scientific principle that governed the world just to make you stay.

The ribbon of mute words slipped from Isaac's tongue and wrapped itself around Andrea's heart. And squeezed. Isaac's silence allowed her to hear the truth the way she used to when he spoke them through the crack.

Isaac rose and drew her to her feet. "We've lived behind walls our entire life, Andrea. I do not wish to take part in erecting any more between us. I swear to you that I will do whatever it takes to keep you by my side."

Andrea pulled him to her, savoring the promise on his lips.

THERE WERE DAYS when Andrea would have sold her soul for a refrigerator and a washing machine, but she never missed her television. The seventeenth century's night sky put on the best show she had ever seen. There were more stars that evening than all the other nights she had lain beneath the oak tree behind their cottage. Andrea squeezed Isaac's hand and pointed to the sky. "See that group in a circle?"

"Where?"

"There. To the left. The circle with two pointy ears. It looks like a cat."

Isaac squinted. "Does it?"

"Yup. And according to our rules, the one who discovers the constellation gets to name it."

"Very well. Let us hear it."

"Tuna," Andrea said with a smile. "After my cat."

Isaac laughed. "You come up with the oddest names. My turn." He pointed to the right of the newly dubbed constellation. "That cluster over there. The group shaped like a heart."

"Sorry, mister. You can't name that. It's part of the Tuna constellation. That's her, well, you know, behind."

Isaac chuckled. "Surely you must admit that it looks more like a heart."

"No way. Are you blind?" Andrea smirked. "But because I'm such a kind and generous person, you can have it. On one condition. You better give it a kick-ass name."

"Er, kick-ass?"

Andrea laughed. "A really good one."

"That should not be a problem. As it is my heart, only one name is suitable." Isaac bent down to kiss her. "Yours."

A METAL CLANG woke Andrea up. Isaac was not by her side. She found him at his makeshift worktable in the back of their cottage hammering a strip of metal into a circular band. "What are you doing?"

Isaac looked up and broke into a wide smile. "Good. You are awake. Could you help me with this?"

"With what?"

"Could you affix this mirror inside that tube? You have smaller hands. It needs to be set at an angle. Like this." Isaac demonstrated a forty-five-degree angle with his fingers.

Andrea admired the highly polished coin-sized metal mirror and fastened it inside the short cardboard tube. "Did you make this?"

Isaac pushed a sweaty lock of hair out of his eyes and nodded. "It took a bit of grinding on a pitch lap to get the metal to the proper sheen." Isaac slipped a larger cardboard tube over the smaller one and attached a second, slightly curved metal mirror to the bottom of the tube. He blocked one end of the connected tubes with a piece of cork and clamped the metal bands he had fashioned on both ends of the tube. "Almost done," he said, fastening a thumbscrew to the bottom of the device. "Do you mind fetching that little sculpture I made last week while I finish up?"

"Sure." Andrea stepped inside the cottage and took a mounted wooden sphere from their mantle. It currently served as a bookend and reminded Andrea of a globe. It was part of a growing collection of strange objects Isaac crafted in his free time. Andrea was running out of places to store them, but she enjoyed how they cocooned her. Some even had an actual purpose.

Andrea got the most use out of the little machine that peeled potatoes and cored apples, though only after she convinced Isaac that it didn't need to be powered by a mouse. As it was, she wasn't too fond of the field mice that regularly helped themselves to the contents of their cupboards. Isaac had sought the help of the cats that roamed the meadow to get rid of their unwanted guests, and installed two cat flaps in their back door to encourage them to come in for tea. He built a larger door for a gray striped cat and a smaller one for her kittens. While Andrea was impressed that he had probably invented the world's first pet door, she tried not to laugh too loud when the kittens promptly followed their mother through the larger hole.

Andrea set the wooden sphere on the worktable. "Here you go."

"Thank you." Isaac centered his cardboard tube on the top of the wooden ball and affixed the metal rod that ran along the length of the tube to the sphere. He tested the range of motion of the tube, tilting the wooden ball on its stand. He stepped away from his creation and beamed. "Come. Look through it."

Andrea bent down and peered through the eyepiece at the top of the tube. She could see the whorls in the bark of their favorite oak tree as clear as though it were right in their garden. She gasped. On a dented worktable, behind a small limestone cottage, in a village no history book thought worth noting, the world's first reflecting telescope had just been invented. Isaac's innovative design had solved the problem of the blurry images produced by the crude refracting telescopes of that time by replacing the conventional image-blurring glass lenses with metal mirrors that eliminated this distortion. His new telescope was one-twelfth the size of traditional telescopes and had far more powerful magnification. On Andrea's side of the wall, nearly all observatories used a variation of Isaac's original design to explore the stars.

But this was not what made the device in front of her remarkable. Her research had revealed that this groundbreaking invention had earned Isaac entry into the ranks of the prestigious Royal Society of London—in 1668. This morning, he had invented it two years early. Isaac's fate had not changed. It had accelerated. "Isaac, do you realize what you've just made?"

"Something slightly more useful than my kitten door, I hope. It is a project I have been toying with for a while now. I decided that it was time to finish it. It was the only way we could settle our little debate." He flashed a grin.

"Debate?"

"Tonight, you, my dearest, shall have to concede that the 'Andrea Constellation' looks nothing like a cat's arse."

SLEEP FOUND ANDREA swiftly. For the first time since she crossed over, she did not have to drown out the scratching in her head. The doubts she had about Isaac securing his spot in history ceased clawing inside her. The telescope sitting on their windowsill made her see more than just the stars clearly. Destiny would find Isaac wherever he was.

A WAVE OF nausea washed over Andrea before she opened her eyes. Her stomach heaved and pushed its contents up her throat. The crack, she thought, had taken her back in her sleep. She flipped to her side and threw up. She lifted her lids. A pool of vomit spread over the rough wooden floor. Unless her landlord had pulled out the carpeting, she was not in her apartment. She had not fallen back through the crack. She wiped her mouth with her nightgown's sleeve.

Isaac ran into the bedroom. His eyes flew from her face to the vomit by their bed. He pushed the hair from her face and laid his palm over her forehead, checking her temperature. "What happened? Are you ill?"

"I must have eaten something bad. Maybe it was the stew."

"I shall fetch the doctor."

"Don't." She rested her head on the pillow. "I'm sure it's nothing."

After another week of nausea and vomiting, she learned that she was wrong.

25

CHOICES

Thus all things are but altered, nothing dies.
—OVID

Andrea and Isaac's Home
1666
Andrea is twenty-three.

NOT ALL HISTORY BOOKS SPOKE of Isaac the same way. Andrea knew this because she had read as many as she could about him. Some showered him with praise while others dwelt on the eccentricities of his later life. But all agreed on one thing: Isaac had no direct heirs. Andrea stroked her stomach through her dress, feeling the small swell where his story was being rewritten. She sat at her desk and wrote in her journal.

Dear Mister Johann Sebastian Bach,

Her pen hovered over the page. She crossed out the greeting and closed the journal. This was the most she had dared to write in all her five attempts at making a new entry. She did not know what to say next. It might have been easier if all she needed to confess was that she had been reckless and that her pregnancy was an accident. It was harder to admit that her abandon with Isaac was tinted with a shade of hope. The silver hands of her watch never let her forget that her time with him was limited, but they could not reach deep enough to find the spot where she hid away a tiny world of possibility, a place where they were a little family with nothing to set them apart from their neighbors other than their two cat doors.

Nursing the possible in her heart turned out to be very different from finding it growing in her belly. Fear grew along with it. It was now 1666, the year she had seen on her crumbling grave at St. John the Baptist Church. The date entwined itself around her spine. She had convinced herself that by knowing what was ahead, she could be more wary of danger and stay a step ahead of fate. Now she wasn't so sure. She was looking out for not just one life but two.

"How are you feeling?" Isaac strode into the room and set his textbooks on the table. He kissed her on the cheek. "You still look pale. Are you certain you do not wish to see a doctor?"

She drew a pillow over her belly. "Isaac, do you remember the calculations you made? The ones that you used to predict when I would be coming back?"

"Of course. Why do you ask?"

"Would you be able to do them again and find out the next time it will be possible for the song to crack the wall open?"

His face blanched. "Are . . . you leaving me?"

"No."

"Then why do you wish to know such a thing?"

"I came here to convince you to save my father's life."

"And I have done as you have asked."

"And I am grateful for it. But now I have to ask you for one more thing."

"Anything. Ask and it is done."

"Rip your letter apart."

"*What?* Why?"

"I love my father, but if we change his fate and save his life"—Andrea wiped away a tear—"we would take someone else's."

Isaac rubbed his temples. "Andrea, you are not making any sense. Who are you talking about? Whose life would be in danger?"

Andrea pressed his hand against her belly. "Our baby's."

"A child . . ." Isaac said, his voice a fraction louder than a whisper. He caressed the small swell, his lips quivering as though he were about to laugh or cry. "Our child."

"If we change the events that led me to this point, I may not make the same decisions that got me here. I may not choose to cross over and . . ." Andrea clutched her stomach.

"It is a terrible, cruel choice." Isaac held her hand. "But you are making the right one. A man can never truly perish if his line persists. Your father would live on in our child. He would understand your decision."

Andrea sighed. "But I won't."

"What do you mean?"

"I blamed you for his death."

The light in Isaac's eyes faltered. "Why?"

"Because not once, in all your letters, did you warn me about it. I hated you for it. But the night after my father's funeral, something happened. I . . ." Andrea pushed the night she spent in Nate's bed away. "I was in the music room and the crack opened. But I wasn't playing your song. You were standing behind the wall. That was the night I received the message that led me here."

"I do not recall any of this."

"That's because it hasn't happened yet."

"What was the message I sent you?"

"You didn't send it. I did. The message was written on a paper plane made from a page of my journal. It had my handwriting on it. That's why I need to know when the wall can be opened. I have to play the song from this side of time and deliver this message to myself. The Andrea on the other side needs to find her friend Nate so I can come home to you."

ISAAC'S QUILL FLEW over the pages of his notebook. The candle by his side had melted into a stub, but he didn't seem to notice. A fire, brighter than the candle's flame, flickered in his eyes. It was the same fire Andrea had first glimpsed when he hammered away at a small apple cart. He set his pen down. "I have it."

"When can we open the wall?" Andrea leaned forward on her toes. "Tell me."

"Tomorrow at nightfall. That is when the paths of time on either side of the wall will be closest to each other. If you play the song at the right moment, the crack should open. But remember that this is merely a prediction. I cannot guarantee that my calculations are completely accurate."

"I can," Andrea said. "Your numbers brought me here. They are correct. I just need to make sure I can play your song tomorrow without making any mistakes."

ANDREA PRACTICED ISAAC'S song in the meadow while Isaac was teaching at the grammar school. Mistakes were easier to live with in front of an audience of wildflowers. A lifetime had seemed to pass since she had played Isaac's song and crossed over. While its measures were simple, no other piece of music made her fingers tremble more.

ISAAC PACED THE width of the cottage's little sitting room, his breath racing in and out of him.

"Stop. Please." Andrea twisted the peg on her cello's neck and tightened the A string. "You're making me nervous. Relax."

"How can I?" He folded his arms across his chest. "The woman I am about to see behind that wall loathes me."

"That woman is me," Andrea said.

"No. Not yet. The Andrea behind that wall just lost her father. I am the last person she wishes to see tonight. I will only cause her more grief."

Andrea held his hand. "That's why we need to do this. This is the night that sets everything in motion. This is when I learn that I need Nate's help to decipher your code. It's when I give myself hope. Without this night, I wouldn't be here."

"But can you not tell yourself about all that has happened to you here? That you are carrying our child and that you are happy?"

"I wish I could. But everything needs to happen exactly as it did." She placed her hand over her belly. "We can't risk altering the path that brought me here."

Isaac stroked Andrea's stomach. "I just wish I knew the right words to say to you—*her*—when the crack opens."

"Don't worry." Andrea played the first notes of his song. "You will."

The song sprung from the cello and touched Isaac's ears for the first time. His eyes brimmed with tears. He clasped his hand over his mouth. A gasp expanded his chest. "I never imagined—"

White light broke through the wall's plaster. Isaac turned toward it and pulled his shoulders back. The wall cracked open. Andrea ended the song before the hole grew too large. She needed to pass a message, not cross over. Isaac stepped in front of her, blocking her view of the woman behind the crack.

"I am sorry for your loss, Andrea," he said.

Andrea pictured herself clenching her fists on the other side of the wall. She could not see past Isaac, but she knew that her past self was screaming at him.

"I am deeply, deeply sorry." Isaac stepped away from the wall. The light from the crack glistened on the tears streaming down the finely chiseled angles of his face.

Andrea kissed him on the cheek. "Thank you."

He squeezed her arm. "Go on. She is waiting."

Andrea picked up the paper plane she had made from a page of her latest journal, careful to stay out of her past self's line of sight. She hurled the plane through the crack. Her twin's face paled as she read the message on its wing. Her resolve to stick to the script that time had written for both of them shuddered. She laid her palm over her belly and reminded herself why she could not allow it to crumble.

SYBIL'S DARK RINGLETS framed her chubby, round face. It took every ounce of Andrea's will not to reach out and pinch the little girl's rosy cheeks. If she made her cry, Andrea feared her mother would no longer bring the five-year-old over. Sybil and her family lived down the lane from their cottage, and sometimes her mother asked Andrea to watch her when she had errands to run in town. "Would you like something to eat, Sybil? I made some snow." Andrea offered her a bowl of the sweet dish she had just learned to prepare, a dessert made by whisking cream, rosewater, and sugar until it resembled a little snowy hill. It was one of Isaac's favorite treats.

"Yes, please." Sybil clambered onto the chair at the dining table.

Isaac sat down next to her and ruffled her hair. He reached behind her ear and made a small spoon appear in his hand. Sybil giggled, grabbed it, and scooped up snow. "Do it again, Uncle Isaac."

"As you wish, princess. But my magic isn't free." Isaac grinned and tapped his cheek.

Sybil kissed his cheek, smudging it with cream.

Isaac laughed. Cream dribbled down the side of his face. He waved his arm and pulled two pink wildflowers from the air. He tucked one into Sybil's hair and the other one in Andrea's. He laid his palm on her growing belly. He did not say a word, but Andrea heard his heart sing.

26

GOODBYES

Love is a thing full of anxious fears.

—OVID

Andrea and Isaac's Home
1666
Andrea is twenty-three.

IT LIVED UNDER THE COTTAGE's thatched roof, beneath its uneven floorboards, and inside its limestone walls. It crackled in the tinder in the fireplace and whispered in Andrea's ears. She often caught herself wondering how death would find her. Was she going to meet an accident? Was she going to catch the plague? The happiness growing in her belly pushed her fears away. But not far. The inevitable is nothing if not persistent. It hovered close, waiting to tear her little family apart.

Each day her baby grew inside her counted down the time she and Isaac had left. There was only one person Andrea could share her fears with and she lived centuries away. One night, after Isaac had gone to bed, she dipped a quill into a pot of ink and wrote to her.

I do not know exactly how this letter will find its way, but I am trusting that time will deliver this message from my hand to yours. I know that nothing that I can say will make what I must tell you easier to believe. I can only offer you my word that everything in this letter is true.

The rest of the letter flowed onto the page just as she remembered it. The day Mr. Westin had delivered it was fresh in her mind. All his visits were. Her journals housed every memory she had of him since her seventeenth birthday. Sweeping herself back to the morning a silver-haired man dressed in a gray double-breasted suit that was slightly too large for him rang her doorbell was as easy as breathing. She wondered what he was doing and then remembered that he had not yet been born. She scribbled the last lines of her letter:

Everything will be okay. I promise.

She intended her words for her past self as much as for her present one. Both of them needed to believe it.

"Why are you still up?" Isaac rubbed his eyes.

Andrea tucked her letter between the pages of her latest journal, along with her fears about a crumbling grave. "I was just writing."

Isaac pulled the blanket from his hips and walked toward her. Andrea watched his every step, memorizing the way his muscles moved in the candlelight. She wanted to remember as much as she could.

"I miss you." He tilted her chin up and kissed her. "Come back to bed."

A PALE MORNING crept over the wool blanket. Isaac rolled over and laid his cheek on Andrea's stomach. "Good morning, little bean."

The baby kicked.

Andrea chuckled. "I don't think he likes that name."

"He?" Isaac grinned. "So you think we're having a boy?"

Andrea smiled. "No. I have no idea if we're having a boy or a girl. It just feels weird to refer to our baby as an 'it.' Do you have a preference?"

"It does not matter as long as he or she looks like you." He kissed her belly. "If you happen to look like me, little bean, you have my deepest apologies."

Andrea propped herself on a pillow. "Would you like to start your cello lessons today?"

Isaac's eyes brightened. "I thought you were not keen on giving me lessons. I have been begging you to teach me for months."

"I figured that it was now or never. I don't think I'll be able to hold the cello if I get any bigger, and finding time for sleep, much less cello lessons, once the baby comes is going to be next to impossible."

He grinned and patted her belly. "Sleep shall certainly be a luxury in a few months. Shall I fetch the cello? I am eager to get started."

Andrea watched Isaac's eyes as he spoke, checking if they narrowed or hardened. They looked back at her, bright, wide, and happy. They had not caught her lie. Andrea thought it was best to spare him from the truth behind her change of heart. She was going to teach him how to play because her music was the only thing she could leave to him and their child.

"Hang on, mister. Not so fast. Nothing gets between a pregnant lady and her breakfast. I believe that it's your turn to make the porridge."

Isaac jumped up from bed and bowed with a flourish. "Right away, madam."

ANDREA STRAIGHTENED THE sheets of paper on her lap and dipped her quill into the inkpot she had propped against one of the oak tree's protruding roots. A drop of ink fell over her skirt and added to her collection of stains. Composing lullabies beneath the shade of an oak tree wasn't the neatest of endeavors, but it was easier to find notes in the meadow than in their house. The wind carried them over the grass. All she had to do was listen and write them down. She jotted down the last measure of her newest song.

Isaac walked across the meadow, a chair hooked on one arm, a small wooden box with a slanted lid tucked in the other. He glanced at Andrea's stained skirt and smiled. "Good writing day?"

"I have a couple of songs to show for the mess. Whether they are any good is another matter."

"I am certain that they are wonderful." He set his chair down and handed the wooden box to Andrea. "But I thought that this might help the state of your dress."

Andrea admired the box's carved panels. "What is it?"

"A writing box." Isaac lifted the box's slanted lid. Paper and inkpots were neatly arranged inside its compartments. "You can keep your music sheets inside it and write over its lid like a desk. I imagine that it will be easier to compose your songs on this than on the grass."

Andrea laughed. "The world's first laptop. And I have the perfect logo for it. How do you feel about apples?"

"Er, 'laptop'?"

"Never mind. I love it." Andrea kissed him on the lips.

Isaac pulled her closer. His hand slipped under her dress and cupped a breast.

Andrea wriggled away and smiled. "You have a cello lesson, Mr. Newton."

"Shall I get a reward if I do well?" Isaac grinned.

"We'll see. That depends on how well you do." She handed him a music sheet. "You will be playing this piece for today's lesson."

He glanced over the notes. "Is it one of yours?"

Andrea chuckled. "I'd love to take credit for it, but it isn't. Let's begin, shall we?"

"Twinkle, Twinkle, Little Star" trickled from the cello's strings and flitted through the oak tree's branches. Its last note screeched. Isaac threw up his hands. "This, by far, is the most difficult thing I have ever done in my life."

"Don't be so hard on yourself. You've only had a few lessons. You're actually a rather fast learner."

"I sincerely doubt that."

She kissed his cheek. "You're my best student. Honest."

"I am your only student."

"You're my second."

"Oh?" The corners of his eyes twitched. "Who was the first? Was it your . . . um . . . friend, Nate?"

"Mr. Newton, don't tell me you're jealous. You've already knocked me up."

He frowned. "'Knocked up'?"

She laughed. "No, it wasn't him. And I've told you a million times that Nate's a friend." On this side of the wall, Andrea thought, her answer almost seemed true.

"Thirteen, actually."

"What?"

"That is how many times you have told me about the nature of your relationship with Nate."

"You've kept track?"

"Not on purpose. I remember numbers whether I wish to or not. I am an odd one, I know."

"Odd." She sat on his lap and put her arms around his neck. "And funny."

He brushed a kiss on her collarbone. "And?"

"Intelligent."

"And?" He kissed her neck.

"Witty."

He nuzzled the back of her ear. "And?"

"Handsome."

"And?" He leaned close, his lips a whisper from her mouth.

"Mine."

"Yours." He drank her in. "Always."

ANDREA UNSTRAPPED HER Omega from her swollen wrist. None of her clothes fit her anymore, and her watch only made her fingers look more like sausages. She set the Omega next to the writing box on her desk. She had stopped writing music in the meadow when her belly edged the box out of her lap. She took every step with great care, ate as well as she could, and avoided the village to reduce the risk of catching the slightest sniffle. She was determined to make it as hard as possible for a crumbling tombstone to find her. In her pregnancy's ninth month, she allowed herself to believe, for a few moments before she opened her eyes in the morning, that her death was not carved in stone.

She smoothed a fresh sheet of paper over the desk and waited for the music to come. A lullaby trickled from the quill's nib, but dried out after a handful of notes. New songs were more difficult to catch inside the cottage, much less keep. She borrowed someone else's music to keep her thoughts in place. Songs kept her mind from wandering down a path of old graves.

The classics worked best. They were solid, safe, and easy to hold. Andrea would have played any one of them, but her bulging stomach kept her from her cello. The orchestra in her head filled in for her. Their afternoon's selection was the "Butterfly Lovers" Concerto. Andrea leaned in her chair, shut her eyes, and listened.

A harp opened the concerto's sole movement. A flute, followed by a violin and oboe, unraveled more of the tale. None of them hinted of the tragedy ahead. The legend's lovers would die as they always did, and Andrea could do nothing to warn them. She sat on her hands. A cello weaved through the violin's strains and steered the story down its inevitable course. Chords pounded through the string duet and marched one of the lovers to his death. His lover cast herself into his grave after him. The violin wept for her. The lovers' spirits, in the form of two butterflies, emerged from their grave and flitted through the concerto's bittersweet notes. Andrea drew the butterfly lovers on the corner of the writing box's slanted lid, giving them a place to rest their wings.

Isaac walked into their bedroom carrying a bowl of stew. "Why are you out of bed? The midwife said you need your rest." He set the bowl down and fluffed up the pillows on the bed.

"I'm going. I'm going." Andrea waddled to the bed and climbed in.

Isaac sat beside her and tucked her in. He spooned the stew and fed her.

"It's good," Andrea said. "Well done, Mr. Newton."

"Thank you." He caressed her belly. "I hope the little bean likes it, too."

"Our bean isn't so little anymore. I think it's time we settled on a name, don't you think? The midwife said I could give birth any time now."

"Very well. If we have a boy—"

"How about . . ." Andrea looked at her cello. "Andrew?"

Isaac held her hand. "Your father would like that. And if it is a girl?"

"You pick as long as it's anything but Anabentine or Philochrista. I don't care if they're fashionable in this century."

Isaac grinned. "Margery."

The name knocked the air out of Andrea. "What did you say?"

"Margery. After my grandmother."

A cherub's face pierced the fog in Andrea's head. It stared at her from its perch on the small tombstone beside her grave. Its young charge's name, half-erased by time, caught the raindrops in its shallow grooves. MARGERY. Tears flooded Andrea's eyes. She had lived in terror of one grave, when she should have feared two.

Isaac wiped her tears. "Why do you weep? Do you not like the name? We can change it if you like. Elizabeth? Abigail? Rachel? Grace? Choose anything you like."

Andrea sobbed and threw her arms around Isaac. "There's something I need to tell you."

"What is it?"

A sharp pain shot through the lower part of Andrea's stomach. Andrea bit down the pain. The baby grew restless. She clutched her belly and groaned.

Isaac grew pale. "Is it time?"

A contraction twisted inside her. "Yes."

ANDREA MOANED. THE night had grown dark as she lay in labor. The midwife, Mrs. Hadfield, drew Andrea's skirt down over her legs to cover her. She pulled Isaac aside and looked at him as though she were threading a needle somewhere inside her head. "I am sorry."

"Sorry?" The blood drained from Isaac's face.

"The baby is not coming as it should," the midwife said in a hushed tone. "There is nothing I can do."

"What are you saying?" He gripped her wrist. "You cannot give up. We can make a potion of dittany and mugwort or a powder from ergot. They can help with her labor and—"

Mrs. Hadfield shook her head. "The baby's feet are bearing down first. It cannot be delivered no matter what herbs we give your wife. There is nothing to be done except to say your goodbyes."

Isaac cursed and tightened his hold on the midwife's arm. "Do something, woman, or I swear to God that—"

"Isaac . . ." Andrea said weakly. "Let her go."

Isaac dropped his hands at his sides and clenched his fists. He glared at the midwife. "Get out."

Mrs. Hadfield nodded and left the room.

Isaac ran to Andrea's side. "I shall go out and fetch some

herbs for a potion. I won't be long. Everything will be all right. I promise."

"No. Don't go," Andrea said. "Potions can't save me or our baby."

"Be strong, dearest. Have faith. I must go." He kissed her and stood up.

"I saw my grave."

"What?" A shadow fell over Isaac's face. "You are ill. You don't know what you are saying."

"I do. On my side of the wall, I saw my grave with my own eyes. And our baby's. You buried us at St. John the Baptist Church."

"Stop. Do not say another word." Isaac backed away from her and knocked down her cello.

Andrea's eyes widened. She struggled to sit up.

"What are you doing?"

"My cello . . . give it to me."

"*Why?*"

"Our baby might have a chance on my side of the wall. There are doctors. Hospitals. Medicine." Andrea threw a glance at the wall. Her heart sank. "But the crack . . . it may not open tonight."

"It will. It must." Isaac grabbed the cello and placed it in Andrea's hands.

Andrea struggled to position the cello over her belly. She pulled the bow across the strings. A note quivered in the air and faded before she could gather the strength to play another. Her fingers slipped from the cello's neck.

Isaac took the bow from Andrea.

"What are you doing?" she said. "Give it back. We don't have much time."

"Let me play it." He arranged the cello against him.

Andrea's vision blurred. She squinted, trying to keep Isaac in focus. "But you don't know how."

"Then I shall have to learn quickly."

"Do you even remember how it goes?"

Isaac drew a breath. He sat on the edge of the bed facing the wall and drew the bow. A note squeaked from the strings. Isaac rearranged his fingers over the cello's neck. The strings shrieked under his bow. He fixed his eyes on the wall and tried again. A note, as shrill as the two that came before it, ripped the air.

Andrea cradled her stomach. The cello's screeches made the name etched on the small tombstone in her mind grow more vivid. She wanted to tell Isaac to be with them while he could, but she could not bring herself to tell him to lay his hope and bow down.

Light glowed in the corner of Andrea's eye.

"The crack!" Isaac gasped. "The song worked."

A doorway of white light broke through their wall. Isaac ran to Andrea and gathered her in his arms. "Hold on," he said, carrying her to the crack. The hem of Andrea's skirt slipped through the opening and disappeared behind the glow. Isaac took a step through the wall.

"Isaac, stop!" Andrea clung to the edge of the crack. "What are you doing?"

Isaac's eyes held on to Andrea's gaze tighter than his arms were wrapped around her body. With one look, they told her all that his words would have taken a lifetime to say. He was choosing to hold her hand every single day of his life instead of any pen, to cradle their child instead of any book, to embrace his family instead of any question he had ever asked about the world. "I am coming with you."

"You can't." Isaac's destiny twisted inside Andrea. With one more step, all that he was fated to be was going to be erased. With one step, he could always be hers on her side of the wall. Her mind screamed over her heart's pleas. "You mustn't. Your life is here."

"Andrea, you are my life."

She gripped his shoulders. "But you aren't mine."

Isaac's face crumpled. "What?"

"On the other side of this wall, I . . . love someone else."

"You are lying." Tears crept up the rims of Isaac's eyes.

"I'm not. I never belonged here. I just got stuck. But now I can go back to my time, to my real home and the man that I'm supposed to be with."

"I do not believe you." Isaac's voice flooded with tears. "Why are you saying such things? You love me just as I love you. The life we built was . . . *is* real."

"What we had, Isaac, was a mistake and now I'm going to fix it."

" '*Fix it*'?" Isaac backed away from the crack. "You're carrying my child, Andrea. Is that a mistake? Is it truly your wish to deprive him of a father? You told me about my legacy, but what use is even the greatest legacy without a child to inherit it? Such a future without him—or you—would be a curse."

The light around the crack dimmed, casting shadows over Andrea's tear-streaked face. "Your child won't have a future if you don't let us go now. Give him a chance to live."

"I intend to." Isaac held Andrea tight and lunged toward the glowing doorway.

"Forgive me. . . ." Andrea pushed herself off from Isaac's arms and tumbled into the crack. The wall closed behind her.

27

PROMISES

Neither can the wave that has passed by be recalled,
nor the hour which has passed ever return.

—OVID

Los Angeles
Present Day
Andrea is twenty-three.

CARPET SCRATCHED ANDREA'S CHEEK. SHE opened her eyes, but her vision was too blurry to let her see where she was. The words she had spoken to keep Isaac from following her through the crack shredded her soul. The pain tearing through her belly almost equaled it. She cried out.

Footsteps sprinted toward her. "Andrea!"

Andrea raised her head. A tide of bile surged up her throat. She swallowed it back. A blurry figure stood a few feet in front of her. "Isaac . . ."

"Jesus, Dre. You're bleeding."

"Nate?" Her eyes focused. Nate's outline sharpened. A cello lay next to his feet. She felt his arms scoop her up before the world turned black.

ANTISEPTIC AND AIR-CONDITIONING. The cocktail of scents filled Andrea's nostrils. She opened her eyes. Her hands flew to her stomach. Her fingers found bandages over where her baby had been. Andrea gasped.

"She's in the NICU," Nate said from her bedside. "They had to perform an emergency cesarean to get her out. The doctors are monitoring her. They said she's doing much better. She'll be okay. Both of you got here just in time."

"She?" Andrea choked on her tears.

"Yes. She's beautiful."

"Her name's . . . Margery."

"Margery," he said slowly and tentatively, like the way one might sip hot soup. When the last of it passed from his lips, his face softened into a smile that broke Andrea's heart. "That's a nice name."

"You saved her. And me."

"I dialed 911. That was about it."

"You know you did more than that. You opened the crack. I saw your cello. How did you know that I needed to come back at that exact moment?"

"I didn't."

"Then how—"

"You promised to come back, Dre." He lowered his gaze. "And I believed you. But I couldn't just sit and wait."

Andrea's eyes widened. "Do you mean you've been—"

"I've been playing Isaac's song every day since you crossed over, hoping that the crack would open and I would get a chance to—"

Nate turned his face away from her to hide a thought or a tear. Andrea was not able to tell for sure. "To get a chance to do what, Nate?" she asked quietly.

"Nothing." He rubbed his eyes. "It doesn't matter anymore."

Andrea clutched his hand and felt the calluses that had

thickened on his fingers. Tears swelled in her eyes and fell on the back of Nate's hand. "How . . . how long have I been away?" she asked, uncertain if she wanted to hear his answer.

Nate's hand clenched into a fist. He drew a breath and exhaled. "Four months," he said, as though dragging the words from some place so deep inside him that when they reached his lips, their edges were faded and frayed. "Your family has been frantic. The police have been searching for you."

Andrea stared up at the ceiling, letting Nate's words sink in. "It's been longer for me."

"I kind of figured that out when I saw you and . . . Margery." Nate anchored his eyes on one of the blinking lights of the monitor she was hooked up to. "I tried to imagine your life behind the wall. Heck, I even searched for you in every history book I could find. Can you believe it?" he said, and smirked. His fingers relaxed in Andrea's hand. "Me reading history books? You turned me into a certified library card–carrying nerd, Dre. I even wear glasses now." He pulled out a black-rimmed pair from his pocket and wore them. "See? This is your fault."

Andrea chuckled. After everything that had happened between them, Nate still had the power to make her laugh. "Well, you look good in them. You're welcome."

"I scoured museums, hoping that I might find you peeking from an old painting. Sometimes I convinced myself that I did. Silly, right?" Tears found their way back into his voice. "I just really needed to believe that you were okay. That you were happy there with . . . him."

"I'm so sorry, Nate . . ." Andrea wept. She knew how useless her words were. The kind of wound that waiting inflicted never closed. Apologizing would not be able to give Nate back a single second of the months he had wasted calling her back through the wall. "I'm sorry that I broke my promise to you."

"You didn't break it," he said, the way parents assured their children with lies that sounded so earnest you wanted to believe them. "You're here."

Andrea laid her hand over her bandaged stomach. She refused to hurt Nate any more than she already had.

Nate stared out the window. "But you aren't staying, are you, Dre?"

"I can't stay, Nate. We can't."

Nate nodded. "I know. You're . . . a family now."

"As soon as both of us are well enough, we're going to go back."

"Do you know when the crack can open again?"

"No." Andrea fixed her eyes on the white wall across the bed. "But one of these days it will. It has to."

28

MAGIC

He very rarely went to bed until two or three of the clock, sometimes not till five or six, lying about four or five hours, especially at spring or the fall of the leaf, at which time he used to employ about six weeks in his laboratory, the fire scarce going out night or day. What his aim might be I was unable to penetrate into.

—HUMPHREY NEWTON, ISAAC NEWTON'S COUSIN AND SECRETARY, ON NEWTON'S ALCHEMICAL PURSUITS

Colsterworth, England
Present Day
Andrea is twenty-four.

HER GIGGLE TICKLED THE AIR. The breeze swept through her auburn curls and laughed along with her. Like her father's, Margery's joy was contagious. She had just turned one and it didn't take much to make her smile. The little rocks strewn along the grassy path obliged. Margery waved her chubby arms and laughed as her stroller rumbled over them. She and her mother were not strolling through their usual route in their neighborhood, but she didn't seem to notice.

The graveyard at St. John the Baptist Church had not changed much since Andrea had last seen it, though the moss over the graves seemed a brighter shade of green in the sun. The weather report had said that it wasn't going to rain, but Andrea had brought an umbrella just in case. It swung from her arm as the notes of Isaac's song filled her head.

Her mind was the only place she could bear to listen to the melody. Playing it on her cello had become too difficult. It had been easier to play Isaac's song during the first few weeks she was back, but as time passed without a hint of a crack, her bow and cello grew heavier. As her cello became more difficult to haul out of its case, she sought other ways to tear down the wall that kept her little family apart. Science and math had once led her to her life in a little cottage in Lincolnshire, and she had hoped that they would help her do it again.

Isaac had imagined their worlds to be winding roads that ran alongside each other. Sometimes they were close enough to touch; at others, they were an inconceivably vast distance apart. Most modern-day physicists, Andrea learned, agreed with him. They imagined the universe floating on the fabric of space and time, like a bead bobbing on the surface of a jar of water. To allow the bead to reach the other end of the jar, a whirlpool was required to serve as a tunnel between the top and bottom surfaces of the water. Physicists contended that space and time could be distorted the same way to form bridges between worlds.

But such passageways, like whirlpools, were not stable. They were extremely tiny and in flux. They existed one moment and vanished the next like a Snakes and Ladders board that morphed each time you blinked. To make the wormholes in space and time large and stable enough to pass through, some scientists proposed expanding them with negative energy. Andrea only had her cello and a song. After three months of playing to deaf walls, she stopped. She looked for a job, surrendering to the possibility that Isaac was not going to be able to hold his daughter anytime soon.

But Margery did not miss out on cuddles or hugs. Bas and Sylvia gave her more than her fair share. They were beyond ecstatic when Andrea called them after she was released from the hospital, but they weren't as shocked about Margery as Andrea had expected. She guessed that learning she'd had a daughter out of wedlock made her disappearance make more sense to them. An unplanned pregnancy had made people do odder things than run away. As Andrea navigated her first year as a mother, Nate held her steady.

Nate and his bandmates had parted ways and he had moved on to being an on-call drummer for three studios and an on-call classical percussionist for two. When he was not recording, he was happily volunteering to change Margery's diapers and sing her to sleep. A video he had posted of his latest lullaby had gone viral, and at the time Andrea left for England, Nate was in talks with a producer who was interested in the lullaby and his other compositions.

Andrea stepped on the stroller's brake near the end of the cemetery's last lane and unbuckled Margery. Her daughter smiled and squealed. Andrea kissed her rosy, round cheek and carried her on her hip, inhaling the hint of lavender baby shampoo in her curls. Andrea held the scent in her lungs and walked down the lane, reading the names on the graves that lined it. Her chest burned as she came upon the last one.

HERE LYETH
MARY ELLEN
WIFE OF RICHARD HARRINGTON
AGED 56
DIED 15TH OF SEPTEMBER 1678

Andrea stepped back from the tombstone and exhaled. Margery wriggled in her arms. Andrea set her on the grass and watched her toddle to the patch of dandelions growing over the spot where two crumbling tombstones used to stand. Each morning that Margery smiled up from her crib soothed Andrea with the thought that they had tricked time and changed their fate, but they did not stop her from going to bed with the same fear. Mary Ellen Harrington's tombstone promised Andrea her first night's sleep without a dream about two graves.

"Miss Louviere . . ."

Andrea spun around.

Mr. Westin's hat bobbed as he approached. From the way his brows were knitted, it appeared as though this year, he was the one who had the questions.

"Mr. Westin!" She threw her arms around him, crushing herself against the suit pocket that held Isaac's letter. She begged the wax-sealed note to contain three things: forgiveness, a time, and a date. She needed to know when she and Margery could go home. "I'm so glad you're here." Andrea breathed hard into Mr. Westin's lapel.

"It's . . . lovely to see you, too."

"Can I have my letter?"

Wind swept over the dandelions and sent them swirling around Margery. She grabbed at them with her chubby fingers and giggled.

Mr. Westin glanced the little girl's way. His eyes lit up, making him look years younger. "And who do we have here?"

"My daughter."

"She's beautiful. Like her mother."

"She has her father's eyes." Andrea picked her up. "Say hello to Mommy's friend, Mr. Westin."

Margery held out her hand and offered him a dandelion stem.

"Why, thank you." He took her gift. "What a clever little girl you are."

"I'm sorry to rush you." Andrea lowered Margery into her stroller. "But I'd really like to have my delivery now."

"Of course." He slipped his hand beneath his jacket and pulled out a yellowed letter.

"It's been a pleasure being of service to you all these years, Ms. Louviere. This is your last letter."

Andrea clutched it to her chest. She and Margery were going home. "Thank you, Mr. Westin. Take care."

He nodded. "I wish you and Margery well."

Andrea buckled Margery into her stroller and watched Mr. Westin walk in the direction of the church. Their goodbye was abrupt, but there was no time to be polite. Isaac had waited for his family long enough. Andrea pulled his final letter out.

The red wax lay like a rose over the parchment. Andrea could not decide whether it was at its peak or was about to die. She explored its brittle ridges with her fingers. The tip of the *I* bled into the wax and the lines of the *N* were thin. It did not matter. She knew whom the letter was from. She gripped Isaac's seal and broke it in half.

> *My dearest Andrea,*
>
> *Our correspondence has reached its end. It has been many months since you crossed back into your time carrying our child, and I am left to guess what has become of my family. I still feel you slipping from my grasp and falling into a sea of silver and silence. I can only pray that you and our child are well and that the man you love on your side of the wall knows how truly blessed he is to have you back. Though I hate him as I have hated nothing and no one before, I am forced to put my faith in his love for you, to hope that he cares for you and my child in all the ways I cannot. But make no mistake, I swear on all that is sacred, that I will not stop fighting to win you back.*
>
> *I have returned to Woolsthorpe in your absence. Without you, no amount of kindling could make our cottage warm. I have seen you on numerous occasions since you left, but they are past versions of yourself that have no knowledge of the life we shared. Today, you sent me a list of answers on paper wings and I sent you a query in return. I asked you if you*

loved me, but you did not respond. I stole a kiss from you, seeking a reply from your lips. I pray to remember the taste and warmth of your mouth, for I know that it will be all I have of you for a while.

There is nothing more I wish to see through the wall than the woman who is my wife, and the child we had. Work provides me with my only respite, but it has proved, most recently, to be cruel.

Woolsthorpe Manor
1666
Isaac is twenty-four.

Sunlight poured through the small hole in the wooden screen leaning against Isaac's window. Isaac nudged the screen to the left, directing the sun toward a low table in the middle of his bedroom. The beam slipped through a prism and splashed a rainbow over the wall's cream plaster. Isaac checked the calendar he had drawn in his notebook. If his calculations were correct, he was going to see Andrea soon.

It had been three months since he had seen her, and each day that passed without her and their baby carved out a little more of his soul. The crack had opened on several occasions since Andrea had left, but it had allowed him only glimpses of days when she was younger, when so much had yet to come to pass. It was impossible to look at her and not long for more.

This afternoon's experiment was the latest in the slew of projects he had designed to unravel the mystery of the crack. He found the strength to breathe by believing that if he understood the light that made it glow, the laws that governed its comings and goings, and the force that drew their worlds together, he would get his family back.

Isaac set his notebook on his bed and hauled out his traveling trunk. He lifted its lid and pulled out a light green journal. He had never asked Andrea if he could see any of her diaries, but when she left, he lost his battle to keep his distance. The map of his future was written in the pages of her past and he was determined to stay the course that had brought her into his arms. He had even found drafts of a letter in which her younger self confessed her feelings for another man. He wondered if she was with this man now. He composed a letter in response, struggling to hide the bitterness he felt. Andrea's journal entry told him that his reply to her letter had been understanding and kind, and he strove to live up to her expectations.

He constantly wrestled with the temptation to reveal everything to her all at once, to forgo all the clandestine clues and codes her journals had spoken of, but he did not dare to deviate from destiny's script. If there was anything he had learned at William Clarke's apothecary, it was that tinkering with an elixir's recipe could produce the most disastrous results. The paradox of his life with Andrea was more volatile than any ether and more fragile than any prism. If he broke it, he did not have a spare.

Isaac checked the time on the 1952 Omega that Andrea had left behind. He stood by his boarded-up window and waited for her to appear. The wall glowed in front of him. Andrea's journal had detailed what was to happen next, but Isaac held his breath and clung to the hope that this time, the Andrea he would see on the other side would be his.

The wall cracked open and swallowed the rainbow his prism had splashed over it. The sunlight from his window pierced a second prism on Andrea's desk and shot a red beam onto the opposite wall of her dark room. The theory he had long held about white light had just been proven, but he could not bring himself to care. He squinted, trying to find Andrea in the shadows behind his wall. The crack shrank.

Isaac pulled the screen from the window and flooded his bedroom with light. He ran to his wall, slamming his knee into the table where his equipment was set up. A lens toppled to the floor and shattered. Isaac leapt over the broken glass and peered through the crack. Plaster reappeared around the hole.

"Andrea, where are you? Show yourself."

A lamp came to life in the corner of her bedroom. Light fell over Andrea's face. Isaac exhaled through a smile. She was not his Andrea yet, but he ached for her just the same. He reached out to remember the warmth of her skin.

"Stop!" she yelled.

Isaac could not hear her voice, but he saw the fear flashing in her eyes. He rolled up his sleeve and offered her the only comfort he could. The Omega's face sparkled in the crack's light. Isaac pulled it off and shared the words Andrea had etched in its steel.

For Isaac. Love, Andrea

Isaac watched the wall close over the shock on Andrea's face. He wanted to explain everything to her right then and there, but his words would have to wait three centuries to meet her eyes. His trail of wax-sealed clues required the same patience.

He sat at his desk and twisted a thin wire into the shape of his favorite apple tree. Beneath it, he looped and pinched the wire to spell out a phrase he had come to know of through Andrea's journals. He had considered several options to discreetly convey the key to Andrea, from the invisible ink Ovid wrote of in his tales about secret love letters, to the disappearing ink made from the milk of the tithymalus plant used by the ancient Roman general and scientist Pliny the Elder. Isaac opted to pursue a course that, though more mundane, had been proven to stand the test of time.

Paper mills across Europe had been using wire to embed their trademark onto their work for hundreds of years. The translucent design became visible when held up against light, identifying the paper's source. Isaac counted on fate to reveal the watermark he was creating in the same way. He twisted the last of the wire and reviewed his work.

Come home to me now.

He sewed the wire phrase onto the paper's mesh mold. His experience in purifying antimony and boiling mercury far exceeded any he had in papermaking, but he could not trust the mill's most skilled vatman with this task. He filled the mold with a pulp made from linen rags and lowered it into a small vat of water. He lifted the mold, allowing the water to drain from the pulp. He had to press the pulp and wait for it to dry before he could set his quill upon it, but Isaac permitted himself to exhale. Compared to crafting the watermark's design, writing down the excerpt of Ovid's tale was easy. He knew the verses of Pyramus and Thisbe's tale by heart. He set the pulp aside and pulled out a sheet of paper that didn't require drying.

The time that he sat down to write his letters to Andrea was the best part of his day. Ending them was the worst. His hand turned to marble every time he signed his name. Each farewell felt like it was for forever. Only the numbers he left for her at the bottom of the page consoled him.

Leonardo Pisano, nicknamed Fibonacci, had introduced the number sequence to Western Europe in his 1202 mathematics book, *Liber Abaci.* Fibonacci had used the numbers to describe the population growth of rabbits, but Isaac discovered an alternative use for them. When converted into music, they opened cracks.

On the surface, the Fibonacci sequence was a simple numerical pattern, but its significance in nature could not be ignored. When the numbers in the series were divided by the number before it, they derived an intriguing ratio that was first described in Euclid's *Elements.* The ancient Greeks called it the "golden number" or "golden mean." Its other name, *sectio divina,* or "divine section," hinted of its true importance.

The ratio's ubiquitous presence in nature and frequent appearance in geometry suggested a fundamental order weaved into the very fabric of the world. Sunflower seeds and pinecone pods spiraled in accordance with it. Tree branches sprouted following the same pattern along the tree's trunk, as did the arrangement of leaves on a stem, the spirals of shells, and the curl of an ocean wave rushing to the shore. The golden mean, Isaac noted, was likewise present in the human body. Each section of his fingers, from fingertip to wrist, was longer than the one before it by approximately the same ratio. The numbers were everywhere around him, waiting to be discovered. Andrea's cello gave them a voice.

The song that Andrea had stumbled upon as a child molded the numbers into a form that could be hurled at her side of the wall. Each time the winding paths of time he and Andrea traveled on brushed close, the energy that lived in the music's notes broke through. But though the original song could lay down a bridge that was long enough to exchange presents across, it did not keep it steady. Tiny flaws in the song's measures spread like cracks across the path, ultimately crumbling it. Paper planes and apples were pulled back, wracked by the tunnel of time collapsing around it. They returned aged, weathered to ash by the centuries they traversed. The numbers Isaac sent to Andrea in his letters fixed this.

The notes the numbers corresponded to mirrored the pattern infused into the very building blocks of nature. The new song built a bridge, note by note, on the same foundation that the universe stood on. When the separate roads he and Andrea were on wound close enough, this bridge would let Andrea travel safely back to his arms.

Isaac signed his name at the end of his letter, wrote out the numbers Andrea would need for her song, and sealed his words with hope and wax.

—

ISAAC DEVOTED THE next months to employing his new math to calculate the date when Andrea would appear next. He wrote out a date at the end of a string of equations. He glared at the date and spat out a curse. He ripped the page from his notebook and threw it on the floor. He dipped the tip of his quill into the inkpot and scribbled out a new set of equations. Andrea had opened the crack on every date he had predicted and had proven the reliability of his method over and over again. He wished she had not. It would have made it easier for him to doubt the latest date that repeatedly spilled from his pen. He flung his notebook across the room.

Isaac hauled Andrea's old writing box from its hiding place beneath his bed. Two butterflies perched on the upper corner of its slanting lid. Their ink wings had faded from all the times he had rubbed his fingers over them, trying to find the warmth of Andrea's hand. He opened the writing box and surveyed its contents. Ovid's book. Two prisms. Andrea's letter to herself. He shut its lid and grabbed the knife he stowed under his mattress. He laid the box on its side and carved out the pain wrenching his heart. It twisted into two intertwining loops. Infinity was supposed to look hopeful, but against the wood's grain, it looked dark.

He dropped the knife and hid his face in his hands. The date on the crumpled sheet on the floor found him and screamed the truth: The crack would open and he would see Andrea again, but Andrea was never going to see the man she knew.

And so, my dearest Andrea, this is goodbye. I have no more stories to tell and no more visits to remember. I am writing this letter because it helps me believe that you and our child are living your lives behind my wall, happy and safe. Whether this farewell is for now or forever is beyond my knowledge. There will not be a day that I will not devote to finding you and our child, but I cannot write this letter in good conscience and promise you something that has no certainty. Though the wall may keep you from my arms, you will eternally be in my heart's embrace.

Yours always,
Isaac

ANDREA'S EYES CLUNG to Isaac's name. As long as she kept it in sight, his letter was not going to end and she was not going to have to say goodbye. A tremor in her fingers shook his letter from her hands. It fell onto their daughter's lap. Margery grabbed it, giggled, and ripped it in two.

"No!" Andrea yanked the pieces from Margery's grasp.

Margery burst into tears. Andrea bundled her to her breast. "Hush. Hush. Mommy didn't mean it. I'm sorry, Margery."

Margery. Though her daughter's name slipped off her tongue, it was Mr. Westin's voice that Andrea heard speaking it. He had called Margery by name when he bid them goodbye. A realization ruptured over Andrea as cold and sharp as the rain that had fallen the last time she had stood at the graveyard. She had not told Mr. Westin her daughter's name. She tightened her hold around Margery and sprinted to the church, her heart beating faster than she could run.

ANDREA SCRAMBLED DOWN the church's nave. Her eyes flew around the empty pews. Mr. Westin and the answers she needed from him were gone. Andrea sat down in the last row and held Margery against her heaving chest. Margery wriggled. Andrea cradled her tighter. The back of her leg brushed against rough cloth. She looked under the pew. Her old backpack sat on the floor. Mr. Westin had delivered more than just a letter this year. She set Margery by her feet and gave her the pieces of Isaac's last letter to play with. They were all she could give her of a father she was never going to know. Andrea pulled the backpack out.

A jumble of journals were stuffed inside it. She arranged

them on the pew like a multicolored Moleskine road. Their pages had guided Isaac to her like a trail of breadcrumbs dropped across time. She laid a battered journal near the end of the pew and reached into her backpack for another. Her hand scraped its cloth bottom. Her story had run out. She turned the bag over and shook it, begging for another chapter. A letter fell into her lap. Andrea steadied her hand and broke its seal.

My dearest Andrea,

This is the letter that I did not bury and in its pages are the words I had hoped I would never have to write. I compose it with a heavy hand and an infinitely heavier heart.

A Shed, Cambridge University
1676
Isaac is thirty-four.

His shirt was soaked through with sweat and clung to his chest. Isaac shielded his nose with a sticky sleeve that had once been white. The fumes spewing out of the small shed's furnace pierced the cloth and mingled with the odor of his unwashed skin. Isaac gagged but forced himself to take another breath. Fainting was not an option. He could not leave his experiment unattended. He stood by the furnace and kept his eyes on the small ceramic crucible inside it. He checked his Omega. In a few minutes, he was going to find out if he was right about Ovid's ancient tales.

In his book *Metamorphoses,* the poet had written about Vulcan and the night the god had caught his wife Venus in bed with Mars. Consumed with anger, Vulcan trapped the lovers in a net and left them hanging on the ceiling for all to see. Isaac believed the myth to be a chemical recipe, with the gods representing the metals he required. Venus was copper, Mars was iron, and Vulcan was fire. Isaac watched them melt into each other inside the glowing furnace, locked in their ancient, illicit embrace.

Isaac gripped the white-hot crucible with a pair of iron tongs and pulled it from the flames. He set it on a narrow wooden table next to his stained laboratory notes. He fidgeted as it cooled. A shadow stirred in the corner of his eye. Isaac turned. His reflection greeted him from a large, round-bottom bottle. The candlelight swimming over the glass curves warped his face, but he could make out the fine lines that marked the years since the crack had wrenched his family from him.

A decade had gone by since Andrea had disappeared through the crack. His child would have no memory of him, but he wondered if Andrea would still know his face. Time had turned his hair prematurely silver and carved creases around his eyes and mouth. Even his voice had changed. The soup of smoke he waded through in his little shed had added a grit to his voice that he feared Andrea would not like. He exhaled a heavy breath and shoved away his aged reflection. The bottle shattered over the floor. Shards of glass twinkled in the furnace's light. If he squinted and tilted his head just so, Isaac could pretend they were stars. He did not bother to name the new constellation but made a wish on the largest of its stars: His experiment had to work.

He struck the crucible with a small mallet. The ceramic shattered over his table. A purple alloy, striated with a web of thin silver lines, rolled out of the broken cup. Isaac held it to the furnace's light. "Vulcan's net" gleamed between his tongs. A grin, the lopsided kind that had lit his face as a boy when his floating paper lanterns glowed in the sky and scared his neighbors, found its way back to his lips. He was one step closer to the end of his alchemical quest.

The secret he housed in his little shed restored the hope that science and math had stolen from him. His calculations had declared that forty-seven years would pass before the crack would let him see his family. He would wither in that time, shriveling into a man his wife would not recognize. Alchemy was the only tool he had left to change his fate. Behind the doors of his shed, he was forced to commit the crime that men were hung on gilded scaffoldings for. Here, until dawn seeped through its windows, he toiled in a haze of fumes to create the *lapis philosophorum,* the philosopher's stone. But unlike those who sought it out to transmute base metals into gold, Isaac required its fabled power for a simpler task. He needed it to help him remain the man Andrea loved. He had already lost ten years. He could not afford to age another day.

A Shed, Cambridge University
1696
Isaac is fifty-four.

Today was his last day in Cambridge and when he left for London to assume his new post as Warden of the Royal Mint, he was leaving the world of academe, science, math, alchemy, magic, and Andrea behind. He had chased a fable for thirty years, but the time had come to accept defeat. Had the *lapis philosophorum* he had desperately sought magically appeared in front of him at this very moment, he would no longer have found any use for it.

He had lost his youth a long time ago, and all that was left for the mythical stone to preserve was a man as dusty as the notebooks on the shed's shelves. More than half of his life had passed, while Andrea's whole life remained ahead of her. They had met as wide-eyed children and had grown up alongside each other through a glowing crack. They had fallen in love, as only young lovers could, recklessly, fiercely, and fast. Behind the wall, Andrea was still the same young woman who had lain beneath the constellations and dared to claim them. Without her by his side, he had lost all interest in lying on the grass and pondering the night. There were no stars in his sky. Lonely decades had worn him down and where dreams had once lit a fire in his heart, only their ashes remained. He and Andrea had always been from different times; now they were from very different places in their lives.

He scanned the empty table that had once been heavy with all manner of bottles, crucibles, and flasks. It appeared much larger than it had looked in all the years he had ground metal over it and splattered elixirs over its wood. He had discarded all of his equipment in recent weeks, careful not to leave a trace of his experiments. All that was left to do was pack away the notebooks and manuscripts that documented his covert pursuits inside a large metal chest.

Isaac took a stack of manuscripts from the corner of the shed and stuffed them inside the chest without bothering to go through them. He knew exactly how many times his experiments had failed without reading his records. But no matter how much he loathed what his notebooks contained, he could not bring himself to get rid of them. It was all he had left to remind him of the family he'd briefly had.

He thought about the letters he had buried in Woolsthorpe. All he had to do was dig them up and burn them to sever the chain of events that had led him to this moment. Andrea would never receive his letters, cross over, and steal his heart. And he would not be sitting alone in a dark shed, filling a metal chest with lost years and regret. A tear rolled off his wrinkled cheek and splattered over his aged reflection on the chest's lid. He looked into his own eyes and promised himself to go back to his apple tree and change his past. One day. Perhaps.

87 Jermyn Street, Westminster, London
1713
Isaac is seventy-one.

Isaac hunched over his desk at the London home he had lived in since taking on his responsibilities at the Royal Mint. He scribbled away on a sheet of paper, indulging in a pastime he had enjoyed since he was a boy. He shuffled around the letters of his name and listed down as many anagrams as he could. Even in his old age, there were still days that he took pleasure in making himself believe that he was someone else. Queen Anne had knighted him and he found amusement in rearranging the letters of his new title.

Sir Isaac Newton
A cast-iron swine
Is now Cartesian
Creation's swain
Oscar Ian Westin

He liked the sound of the last one best and wrote it down again. He did not smile often and when he did, it never lasted long. He seized the moment to enjoy a grin. An old loneliness closed in on him before he could tug his lips into place. Though he was miles away from Woolsthorpe Manor, there was no escape from blank walls. Today, they pressed close and crushed his lungs.

The date the numbers had told him the crack would open again had arrived. His fluxions had calculated the time when their worlds were close enough to build a bridge across, in the same way his equations had helped his friend Edmond Halley predict the return of his comet. Halley would have to wait forty-five more years to be proven right. Isaac's wait was significantly less. He rose from his desk, walked over to a polished armoire, and pulled out Andrea's cello from inside it.

In Andrea's absence, he had taught himself to play the songs she had left behind. His rendition of "Twinkle, Twinkle, Little Star" was impeccable, while his attempts at mastering the melody that summoned the crack left him deflated. He took a seat in front of his bedroom wall and placed the cello between his legs. He angled his bow arm, gathering confidence from the knowledge that the crack was going to forgive his flaws. According to Andrea's journals, all that was to happen next had already taken place.

He had no inkling that the silver-haired man that Andrea had written of in her journals would turn out to be himself, but as his body aged, Isaac had come to see the face of Andrea's elderly messenger in his mirror. He did not know the mechanics of how he would come to deliver his own letters, but he knew that when the crack opened, he was going to step through it and become the man who showed up on Andrea's doorstep with his sealed messages. He was no longer the man she loved, but he was too old to be greedy. He pulled the bow across the cello and played her song.

THE SILVER, SILENT sea of time between their walls was exactly as Andrea had described. His memories bobbed around him in little silver bubbles. The white in his grandmother's hair. The smell of leather in Cambridge's library. The fresh custard pies he passed over at the Stourbridge Fair. Isaac lost himself in each, happy to be young again. A bubble drifted past his chin. Andrea was in it, heavy with their child, vanishing through a glowing crack. Isaac screamed her name and tried to swim after her.

Something hard slammed into his cheek. Isaac opened his eyes and gasped for breath. His eyes adjusted to the dim light. The walls of a room took shape around him. He knew them well. His old bedroom at Woolsthorpe was the last place he had expected the crack to lead him. He did not recognize the furniture inside it. It appeared worn and older than any he had owned. He strode to the window, the bedroom's only source of light. A pink twilight veiled Woolsthorpe's grounds, but he could see that the orchard had far fewer trees than he remembered. Footsteps shuffled over the gravel path below. Isaac moved to one side of the window, leaned against the wall, and listened.

"The stargazing tour group will be arriving soon," a woman's voice said. "Your costume is inside."

"I hope they were able to change the wig. The last one itched," an older man's voice said.

"Yes, I believe that's been taken care of."

"Wonderful. Thank you."

"No, thank you, Harold, for volunteering to do this and for being such a good sport about the costume. I must say that you do bear a striking resemblance to Isaac Newton once you have the wig on."

"Don't mention it. It's a nice little break from the bank."

"This tour will be exactly the same as the one we did last week. You'll first take them on a tour of the manor and then lead them to the orchard so that they can set up their telescopes. The staff will be waiting for you there."

"The sky looks brilliant tonight. Perfect for stargazing," the old man said. "Well, I better get changed. I think the tour group would be rather disappointed to find the great Isaac Newton in a rumpled gray suit."

ISAAC WAITED FOR the costumed tour guide to step outside the manor before stealing his clothes. Andrea's journals were very precise about what Mr. Oscar Ian Westin looked like, and the tour guide's gray suit and hat matched the picture in his mind. He buttoned his double-breasted jacket. The suit's jacket drooped at his shoulders, and the sleeves were too long for his arms. From what he remembered of Andrea's description of Mr. Westin, it was a perfect fit. He slipped on the brown wing tip shoes and pulled off his wig, donning the tour guide's hat. He checked his reflection in the mirror. Mr. Westin appeared to be a much happier man than he was. He crept out of the manor's back door and into a strange new world, armed with a library of Andrea's stories about her time. The hours they had spent talking and laughing beneath the stars had filled his mind's shelves.

He kept to the shadows. He could think of only one reason why the crack had led him to his old home, and it was buried in its orchard. The gravity that drew him to Andrea extended beyond her. It exerted its pull, it seemed, on everything that she had touched. The hopes she had stowed in her writing box had called to him from across time.

A garbage bin stood in place of the shed where the manor's tools used to be stored. Isaac kept to the shadows as he searched the nearby buildings for a spade. A rake leaned against a wooden fence. Isaac grabbed it and made his way to an old friend.

Time had been less kind to his apple tree than it had been to him. Its branches were more gnarled than he was and its bark bore more creases than his skin. Isaac patted its crooked trunk. The infinity symbol he had left for Andrea found his palm, reminding him of a young man's hopes. He took a measured step away from it and dug. He had been at the peak of his youth and strength when he buried his secrets beneath the tree, and every tug of the rake reminded him of how much the years had taken from him since then.

His rake struck wood. Isaac crouched and brushed the mud from the writing box's slanted lid. Etched words whispered an old plea.

Come home.

He had carved the words for Andrea's eyes, not knowing that the task of delivering his letters would fall on his own shoulders. He broke the box's wax seal and pried its lid open. The cold, damp smell of age flew into his nostrils. He recoiled and shielded his nose with his sleeve. He held his breath and peeked inside the box. His gifts for Andrea, wrapped in parchment and twine, were scattered over its bottom. His letters, bound by a frayed black ribbon, sat on top of the pile. He picked up the bundle. The ribbon fell apart, scattering his letters on the ground.

Voices drifted across the orchard. The tour group had arrived. Isaac gathered the letters and stuffed them inside the box. He collected whatever branches he could find and tossed them over the hole. He grabbed the box and held it close. Light broke through the sleeves of his suit. Isaac drew a deep breath and waited for the crack to call him back.

ISAAC REAPPEARED IN the bedroom of his house in Jermyn Street, clutching Andrea's writing box. He waited for the nausea to pass. He brushed off the mud from the box. The etched designs were badly worn, but he could still make out a few of the flowers along its sides. He rubbed a patch of mud from the box's front panel. The crude grooves of the infinity symbol he had carved, half-erased by time, brushed against his hand. Even "forever," it appeared, could fade.

He stared at the box. The decision that he had put off for so long demanded action. His fireplace crackled next to him. If he threw the box and its contents into the flames, his heart would never know pain. Or happiness. He remembered the moments he had stroked Andrea's growing belly and whispered to his little bean. He did not know if Andrea had been able to save their child, but he knew that if he cast his letters into the fire, he was throwing away its very existence. No amount of despair or loneliness could drive him to kill his own blood. The mere possibility that his child had lived was worth every ounce of pain. He arranged the cello over his shoulder and prepared himself to introduce Andrea to the silver-haired man who would one day lead her home.

HIS SECOND TRIP across the crack left him twice as nauseous. Isaac opened his eyes and found himself lying on the floor of a room he had glimpsed from his side of the wall. Except for one difference. Andrea was not in it. A tall, handsome man with blond hair and drawings over his skin had taken her place. The man staggered away from him and bumped into a music stand.

"You . . ." The man clutched a cello at his side. "Who are you?"

Isaac stood up. He steadied his legs and straightened his suit. He had read Andrea's journals so often that he slipped into Mr. Westin's mannerisms like a well-worn coat. Her pages had also told him about the other people she held dear. "I believe you already know the answer to that, Nate."

Nate's jaw dropped. "I've seen you before. You gave me a letter to give to Andrea and . . ." He clutched the metal disc he wore as a pendant. "You're Isaac? But why are you so old? Why are you dressed like that? Where's Andrea?"

"Andrea?" Isaac's heart stopped. "Is she not here?"

The color drained from Nate's face. "She was with you. She crossed over. She's been gone for months. Did you leave her behind? Where is she?"

Isaac glared at the wall. "Dear God . . ."

"What? What's wrong? What have you done with Andrea?"

"This moment!" Isaac gasped. "This is not the first time I am to see Andrea."

"What do you mean?"

Isaac hung his head. "It is the last."

"I don't understand," Nate said. "You're not making any sense."

Isaac's skin glowed bright. "There is no time to explain. I beg you, Nate. Save Andrea. Play her song *now.*"

> *My dearest, the wall stole me back before I could witness you cross into your world. It has opened several times since then, allowing me to deliver my letters to you. Each time I stepped through the crack, I emerged at the date and time you recorded in your diary entries about my visits, and in the same order that you narrated my deliveries had transpired. The pages of your journal have been my guide and have served as my script. I did my utmost to be faithful to every detail of your chronicles, delivering my letters to you in the sequence that you listed. For you, my visits happened over the course of several years. For me, they transpired in one day.*

On each sojourn, I looked at you and wondered if you could see a glimmer of the man you used to love in my tired eyes. The first time you crossed over to my time, you told me that you feared you'd come too early. It is now my turn to apologize for coming too late. The story in your journals has ended and I have run out of pages to tell me what shall happen next. I am ending this letter not knowing if it shall find its way to you and if I shall see you once more. All I know is what the numbers have told me.

My calculations show that this is the last day that the crack shall open in my lifetime. If it does not permit one more visit before this day ends, I pray that you shall somehow know in your heart that you and our child shall be my last thought before I leave this earth. Perhaps in the next world, in a little limestone cottage by a meadow, we shall be permitted to be the family that we were not free to be in this one.

I love you now
and always.
Isaac

TEARS SOAKED THE letter in her hands. Andrea looked up from the page, unable to see beyond the river flowing from her eyes. She tried to take a breath, but her lungs could not hold anything but sorrow. Margery's giggle echoed in the church and pierced her sobs. She wiped her eyes clear and glanced at her daughter. Her chubby pink hands pointed to the side of the pew. Andrea turned.

Mr. Westin's cloudy hazel eyes smiled at Margery. He bent down, reached behind Margery's ear, and plucked a dandelion from thin air. He handed it to her. A 1952 Omega peeked from under his sleeve. Margery played with the flower and giggled. He looked around the church. "This place has not changed much. It echoes the same way."

"You lied to me," Andrea hissed through her tears. "Why didn't you tell me the truth about who you were?"

"I told you who I was the day I delivered your first letter. Oscar Ian Westin."

"Stop playing games." Andrea stood up.

"An anagram is amusing but not quite a game, wouldn't you agree? I found that it was a good place to hide the truth, if one was reluctant to lie. . . ." He looked down at his wing tip shoes. "And half-hoping to be discovered."

Andrea moved her mouth to speak, but her voice died in her throat. One word squeaked out, heavier than any she had spoken before it. *"Why?"*

He exhaled a tired breath, breaking the line of his perfect posture. "Do you need to ask? I am an old man."

Andrea stared at Isaac's face, searching for the man she loved behind its doughy skin and lines. "That wasn't what I was asking."

"Then tell me what you want to know. You can have more than one question on this visit as it appears to be our last. Go on. Ask. Why didn't I tell you? Why am I here? Why now? What would you like to know first?"

"None of them. None of that matters." She picked up Margery from the floor. "What I want to know is why aren't you holding us? Why are you standing there like there's still a wall between us? Do you still hate me for leaving you behind?"

"It would be easier if I did. I could have lived my life without thinking about what I had lost. But I could not hate you, Andrea, as much as I tried. Not after I read your journals. I know why you pushed me away. I forgave you a long time ago."

"Then why won't you hold me?" Andrea sobbed. "Us?"

"Here is your answer. Look at me, Andrea. I'm old and gray. I'm not the young man you fell in love with and left behind."

"You're right. You're more than that. You're the man who found his way back to his family." Andrea stroked his cheek. "I see you, Isaac."

He flinched and turned away. “This was a mistake.”

“How can you say that? This is your daughter. Don’t you want to hold her?”

Isaac’s eyes wandered over Margery’s face. Tears watered them. “More than you can imagine. I did not know what to expect when I crossed over this time. After you left, I had no way of knowing what had become of you. I prayed every second of every day of the past forty-seven years that you were safe behind my wall. I imagined an entire life for both of you down to the smallest details of your days. The porridge our baby might have for breakfast. The sound her laugh might make. The way you might sing her to sleep. This myth was the air I breathed. Without it, I could not live. When I saw both of you in the cemetery, it took every ounce of strength in this feeble body not to run to you and hold my family in my arms.” He reached out to Margery but pulled his hand back before his fingers touched her. “But I know I must not.”

“Why?”

“Because if my arms remember what it is like to embrace you, their emptiness will be unbearable when I let you go.”

“Then don’t go.”

“You know your history. You know that the crack will not let me stay. Your journals have informed me of my future. Fourteen years from now on my side of the wall, on the thirty-first of March, I shall meet my death.” He lowered his eyes. “I should not have come today. I should have been content with my little myth. Instead, I was the worst kind of fool. I thought that if I came here and proved to myself that my family was alive and safe, all the pain from the years we lost would vanish. Though the joy of seeing you and Margery is beyond any words, I already feel the crack wrenching you from me. There is no magic great enough to heal the wound that losing my family a second time will carve into my soul.”

White light broke through Isaac’s skin, lighting his face from within. The light erased the lines around his lips and eyes, and for the briefest of moments, he was Andrea's Isaac again. "You can't leave us. I won't let you."

He looked down the church's nave and sighed. "Life has quite a sense of humor, doesn't it? We are finally here. Beneath the roof of a church, in front of a proper altar. We have a place to say our vows."

Andrea held his wrinkled hand. "We made them long ago."

"And I have kept all but one. I have grown old, though not at your side."

"You've always been with me," Andrea sobbed.

"And now it is time to let me go." He looked into Margery's eyes and then Andrea's. His skin glowed brighter.

"No." Andrea clasped his hand just as she did the first time they touched through the crack in the library. She dug her fingernails into his skin to keep him with her. "Never."

"My dearest, I beg you. Do not follow my path. I have lived a lifetime lonely enough for the both of us. Allow me solely to bear the punishment for our crimes against nature and time. I want a better life for you and our daughter." He kissed the top of Margery's head and brushed his lips against Andrea's cheek. "Find love again, Andrea, one as fierce and strong as the one we shared. I have scoured the pages of your life and if you saw the truth hidden in your words as clearly as I have, you would know, as I do, that you would not have to look far. Give our daughter a father to know and love. If you ever loved me, allow yourself to embrace happiness so I can find peace."

"Isaac . . ." Andrea wept.

"Promise me." He glowed brighter.

"I . . . promise."

His hand vanished from Andrea's grasp. Cold air filled her fingers. Andrea stood there, her eyes fixed on the empty spot where Isaac had been standing. The wisps of candle smoke drifting through the church, the faint chirping of birds spilling through the doorway, and the weight of Margery on her left hip seared into her soul.

ANDREA DID NOT know how long she had been sitting inside the church. She had not run out of tears and her legs were too weak for her to stand. Margery had fallen asleep on the pew next to her, smiling in her sleep the way only children can. Andrea stroked her curls.

"Hey, you."

Andrea twisted around, tears flowing down her cheeks. "Nate? What are you doing here?"

He sat down beside her. "Keeping a promise."

"What promise? What are you talking about?"

Nate pulled out a white handkerchief from his jeans and dried her tears. The shadow of a small stain in the corner of the cloth caught Andrea's eye. She grabbed the handkerchief from him. "Where did you get this?"

"He gave it to me." He unfolded the handkerchief. The name of the church they were sitting in, along with a date and time, were scribbled in the middle of the cloth. "That's how I knew you'd be here."

Andrea stared at the familiar minuscule handwriting on the handkerchief. "Who gave this to you?"

"The same man who gave me this." Nate slipped his pendant out from behind the collar of his shirt. It gleamed like a mirror in the sun.

Andrea rubbed her temples. "I don't understand. You've had that pendant since we were kids."

"Yes. I've had it ever since the day I ran out of your house when I saw the glowing crack in the music room. For years I refused to admit remembering anything about that afternoon, but the opposite was true. How could I forget the day I was convinced that I was becoming like my mother? Every detail about it was branded into my mind. The black sneakers I wore. My Metallica shirt. The way I ran out of your house and collided with an old man who was walking to your door. I slammed into him and knocked down the small wooden telescope he was carrying. It smashed into pieces on the street. I thought he was going to be furious, but he wasn't. He just asked me what my name was. He almost seemed glad to see me. He told me that the telescope was supposed to be a gift for his daughter, Margery, but he said that he was going to get her something better."

Nate glanced at Margery. "He asked me if I believed in magic. I told him I didn't. He waved his hand and made a shiny round metal mirror appear from the air. He gave it to me and said that the mirror was magic because it was touched by a girl who was magic herself. He said that one day I would see my future in it. I told him I didn't believe him. He pulled out a slightly stained white handkerchief from his suit pocket and scribbled an address, date, and time on it. His handwriting was so small that I almost couldn't make out what he wrote. I squinted at the date and thought he had made a mistake. It was fourteen years away. He said the date was correct and that if I went to St. John the Baptist Church at the time he listed, I was going to find that magical girl. I asked him how he could possibly know something that far away in the future. He said it was because—"

"That's where he had just come from. . . ." Andrea gasped.

Nate nodded. "He told me that when he had left, the magical girl had been sad. He wanted to return, but instead, he found himself in front of her old home. He said that when I saw her, she would need this handkerchief to dry her eyes."

"But you never said anything, Nate."

"My mother was locked away in an institution because she said she saw fairies, Dre. I wasn't exactly keen on telling anyone about strange old men, mysterious mirrors, or magical girls. I pushed it out of my mind even though a part of me wished that it were true. I grew up and didn't think any more of it. But then I saw that guy at your doorstep after your father's funeral. He looked familiar, but so many years had passed that I wasn't sure that it was him. The third and last time I saw him was the day you came back. That's when I realized who he really was. He told me to open the crack and save you."

"Why didn't you tell me about him?"

"I wanted to. But you were so hopeful about opening the crack again and returning to your life with him. The man I saw that day was an old man who said that the day you crossed over from his time into this one was the last day he would see you. I understood then that you weren't going to be able to go back to his world."

"So all this time . . ." Andrea closed her eyes, trying to wrap her mind around the chain of events that had led Nate to the church. "You knew that I wasn't going to be able to go back?"

Nate nodded with a heavy sigh. "I didn't tell you because I didn't want to make you suffer more by taking away your last hope. I saw how difficult rebuilding your life and raising Margery on your own was on you. I couldn't bring myself to hurt you more. I'm so sorry, Dre. Can you forgive me?"

Andrea leaned her head against Nate's chest. His pendant, the metal mirror that she had helped Isaac attach to his telescope, cooled the tears on her cheek. Like the writing box that had drawn Isaac to Woolsthorpe the first time he crossed over, the mirror she had touched had pulled him to Nate on the day he needed to save her and Margery. Isaac and Andrea's connection was a natural law, greater than any he had ever discovered: unbreakable, timeless, and absolute. It had bound their hearts just as gravity married the earth to the moon. But now Isaac was gone and he had given her one last gift through the crack, a gift that time couldn't turn to dust. She closed her eyes and sealed him inside the pages of her life with a love stronger than time and molten red wax. She held Nate's hand. "I understand."

A shadow lifted from Nate's face. He exhaled and squeezed her fingers. "It had been so long since I received the handkerchief. I would take it out once or twice every year, reliving the conversation I had with a stranger. There were days the whole thing no longer felt real. But as the date written on the handkerchief approached, a thousand possibilities ate away at my doubts.

"But they were never fully erased. Not even when I booked a flight over here or when I got out of the cab and walked up to the church's door. I didn't know what I was going to find or if I was going to find anyone or anything at all. I just knew what I hoped for."

"And what did you hope for, Nate?"

"I hoped that if I did see that magical girl, she wasn't going to need a handkerchief to dry her eyes." He brushed a tear from Andrea's cheek with his thumb as a hot drop rolled down his own face. "It kills me to see you cry, Dre. I just want, more than anything, for you to finally find whatever it is you need to be truly happy."

"Nate . . ." Andrea dried the little stream on Nate's face with the white handkerchief and glanced at the shiny pendant around his neck. Isaac had told Nate that its reflection held Nate's future. In it, Andrea saw her face. History could not remember what it did not know, but the truth was what Andrea would never allow herself to forget. She recalled everything about the last time she saw the man she had loved her entire life. And the first time she truly saw the man she was going to love for the rest of it. "I think I have."

Epilogue

THE APPLE FELL INTO ANDREA's right palm. She closed her fingers around it and tossed it into the air again. Her eyes followed it along gravity's appointed trail. She caught the apple, polished it on her silk sleeve, and bit into it. This was her new preshow ritual. It was healthier than eating orange M&M's and more calming than counting the steps of stairs. There was nothing more certain than gravity. It kept her feet firmly planted on the ground. She set the apple down next to the pile of music sheets on the table, shut her dressing room door behind her, and made her way to the Isaac Stern Auditorium's stage with steady steps.

Two thousand eight hundred and four pairs of eyes watched her take her seat in front of the orchestra for her latest performance at Carnegie Hall. She took her cello from its stand. A yellow Post-it note was stuck on its back.

> *Hey, you.*
> *Breathe.*

Andrea smiled at the note, took its advice, and played.

Apple pie à la mode. Four ice cubes. And the warmth of her father's arms around her after their "Eleanor Rigby" duet. These were the memories that Andrea drew from her cello's strings. A little limestone cottage and a sky full of stars flowed after them.

The melody swelled and swept everyone in its path along with it. *Loss. Longing. Laughter. Love.* Andrea set each free to tell its chapter of her story. They swirled around her, finding their place in the same song.

Andrea's final note filled every corner of the auditorium. The audience breathed it in and kept it in their chests, reluctant to let it go. Those who could no longer hold their breath released Andrea's song with a sigh. Some quickly wiped away tears; some let them fall.

Andrea stood up and took a bow. Applause roared around her. The loudest came from a tall blond man in the front row who managed to clap while balancing a girl with auburn curls on his shoulders and carrying her little brother in the crook of his arm. Andrea blew a kiss to her family, committing every detail of the evening to the journal in her mind. She filled an entire page with the love that lit Nate's eyes. She was good at remembering things that made her smile.

ACKNOWLEDGMENTS

Oma. Opa. Sibling units. Grandma. Capitol Folks. Rez. PV. Pinky. Dino. Cathy. Johnny. Tina. Jebot. Rochelle. Fino. Mutya. Jinggoy. Kris. Jake. Pierra. Toto. Elay. Tennant. Thank you, thank you, thank you for being there for me through all the ups and downs of this adventure.

Steph, where do I begin? Thank you for being the most patient and persistent person I know. Thank you for never losing faith in me and this book. You are a rock star.

Shauna, thank you for taking a chance on this little story and making it shine. You've taught me so much, and I will forever be grateful.

A huge thank-you to the wonderful team at Ballantine who helped bring this book to life.

Nico and Cai, thank you for putting up with your mother's special brand of crazy. Cai, thank you for lending Andrea your name and teaching me about rosin, bowing, and tuning strings. Nico, thank you for giving me a window into the mind of a thirteen-year-old boy. Nate and Isaac are forever grateful too. I love you, bubbaboos.

And, finally, to my gravity, the man I am blessed to wake up next to every morning: Thank you for the calculus and wormhole tutorials, tireless back rubs, the home-cooked gourmet meals, and the depthless love, that kept me sane, happy, and fed throughout this amazing journey. You keep me standing even when the world shakes beneath my feet.

Ad majorem Dei gloriam.

Read on for an excerpt of ***Water Moon,*** an enchanting fantasy novel about a woman who inherits a pawnshop where you can sell your regrets, and the magical journey she takes when a charming young physicist wanders into the shop.

Available now from Del Rey

Chapter One

THE PAWNSHOP OF ALMOSTS AND IFS

TIME HAS NO BORDERS EXCEPT those people make. On this particularly cold autumn day, Ishikawa Hana fashioned that border out of the thinnest layer of skin. Eyelids were useful that way. Because as long as she kept her eyelids shut, she could keep the two halves of her life apart: the twenty-one years she had lived before she opened her eyes, and all that was going to happen next.

She pulled her blanket over her head and pretended that her hungover first morning as the pawnshop's new owner had yet to begin. It didn't matter that she was now wide awake, that the last of a tangled string of dreams she could not remember had unraveled more than an hour ago. Her head felt heavier and her mouth drier than usual, but she figured that this was less on account of the alcohol she'd had the night before than on what awaited her.

In a few moments, her father, Toshio, was going to knock on her door to start their day.

Hana insisted on clinging to the tiny hope that the unwise amount of sake they had celebrated his retirement with was going to keep him in bed a little longer. This hope—if it indeed could be called hope given its size—was smaller than a mossy river pebble and just as slippery.

In all the years that the pawnshop had been in Toshio's charge, there were only two occasions when it had not opened on time. On both those days, it had not opened at all. But Hana and her father didn't talk about those two days. Ever.

If their pawnshop were like other ordinary pawnshops that traded in diamonds, silver, and gold, the Ishikawa family, who had run the pawnshop for generations, might have had the luxury of sick days and weekends. But Toshio had trained Hana to appraise far more valuable treasure.

They found their best clients when summer ended and the nights grew colder and longer. Melancholy was good for business. It didn't matter that their little shop, tucked along a quiet alley of Tokyo's Asakusa district, didn't have a name. Those who required its services always managed to find it. But, if anyone was curious enough to ask Hana what she thought the pawnshop should be called, she had a ready answer. Ikigai. There was no other word that suited it more.

Hana was a little more than a year old when she learned to walk on the shop's dark wooden floors, and every step she had taken since then had been toward taking over the shop when her father retired. He was a widower, and she was his only heir. The pawnshop was her life's path, her singular purpose. Her ikigai. But not once, in all the time that she had played as a toddler at her father's feet or worked by his side as a young woman, had any of their clients bothered to inquire what the pawnshop's name was. They had far more urgent questions darting behind their eyes when Toshio welcomed them with a polite bow. The first was almost always about where they were, and the second about how they had gotten there.

After all, no one expected to find a pawnshop behind a ramen restaurant's door.

Anyone who stood in line outside the long-standing popular restaurant would tell you that its shoyu ramen was the best in the Taitō prefecture. For some, the wafting scent of steaming bowls of chijirimen noodles and perfectly braised slices of pork belly swimming in a dark and rich bone broth made waiting easier. For others, it made their time in the snaking queue feel twice as long. Still, they all drew deep breaths, taking their fill of the air's savory promise until it was their turn to enter the cramped dining room that might have been considered modern two decades ago. Yellowed walls plastered with autographed photos of the restaurant's celebrity clientele welcomed them as they weaved their way to empty seats. But, despite stepping through its door, some of the hungry did not make it into the restaurant's dining room. Instead, they were greeted by a pawnshop's dimly lit front office and the tinkling of a little copper door chime.

The memory of that chime rang in Hana's head as she curled beneath her blanket. It commanded her to rise and accept the inevitable. She clamped her palms over her ears and fought a losing battle to keep her mind from getting out of bed ahead of her. Some of her thoughts were already almost dressed, fastening the last buttons of the pawnshop's crisp black suit uniform. Others were already at the office beneath her room, imagining how her father was going to spend the first day of his retirement: hovering close, double-checking everything she did.

He would not say anything if he caught a mistake. He never did. The slightest twitch of his right eyebrow sufficed. Toshio preferred silence to words, reserving his energy and breath for his clients. Hana had become rather adept at interpreting his quiet breathing, half smiles, and glances. Her only memory of him losing his temper was of the stormy afternoon when she was ten and had misplaced a pawned antique watch. His eyes had grown darker than the clouds churning above their home's courtyard garden, and when he gripped her by her thin shoulders and lowered his mouth to her ear, her heart dropped to her toes. His voice was as quiet as the breeze, but his words howled inside Hana louder than any typhoon.

Find it.

Now.

Hana did not know what would have happened if she had not found the watch later that day behind a stack of books in the back room. All she was certain of was that she never wanted to hear her father speak to her that way again.

Hana drew a ragged breath, reeling her thoughts back to the present. An invisible weight pushed down on her chest. She had expected her future to feel heavier, or at least heavier than a well-fed cat, but instead the pile of days teetering on top of her chest felt as light as a mountain made of mere husks, each hollowed out and spent before it began. She knew every second of the days that lay ahead of her by heart. After all, she'd spent her life watching her father live them. And now her father's life was hers, and from here on, nothing was ever going to be new.

She rolled to her side. The edge of a yellowed photograph peeked from under her pillow. Hana pulled the faded photo out and squinted at it beneath her blanket. The eyes of a young woman who could have been her twin gazed back at her. "Good morning, Okaa-san," Hana greeted the mother she never knew and tucked the only picture she had of her back into its hiding place. She pulled her blanket off and peeped through her dark lashes. A sliver of sunlight pierced her irises. She squeezed her eyes shut and pushed herself out of bed. She didn't need to see to navigate her bedroom. This room and the pawnshop beneath it made up her entire world, and today, that world felt even smaller.

And quiet.

Hana cocked her head, straining to hear the familiar clinking of cups and bowls from the kitchen downstairs. But only silence seeped through her door. She bit her bottom lip.

Retirement, she was certain, would not be enough to keep a man like Toshio from his rituals. Though the small shrine her father kept in their home honored the spirits, the god her father really worshiped was routine. The steaming cup of roasted green tea he had every morning was sacred, no matter how much sake or whiskey swam inside him from the night before.

Hana pressed her ear to her door. There were only two possible reasons the pawnshop was this quiet, and neither of them was good.

Chapter Two

ISHIKAWA TOSHIO'S LAST CLIENT

The day before

AUTUMN HAD COME EARLY, AND since its arrival, the number of the pawnshop's customers had doubled.

Toshio shifted his weight, relieving the bunion on his left foot. His stomach growled twice through his black suit. He ignored it and adjusted his tie. This was not the first day he had been too busy to have lunch, but it was going to be his last. When they closed shop in less than an hour, he was going to be officially retired and would never have to work through lunch again. He had expected the thought to make him smile, but the corners of his mouth refused to be persuaded to curl the slightest angle upward. A copper bell tinkled, heralding the arrival of his last customer.

"Irasshaimase." Toshio bowed with a practiced smile, his voice smooth like warmed sake.

Hana peeked out from the back room with this month's record book tucked under her arm. Toshio waved her back inside and turned his attention to the elegant woman who had just walked through their door. "How may I help you?"

The woman met Toshio's smile with a bewildered look. Though her porcelain features made her appear to be younger than Toshio, her hair, tied in a loose knot at her nape, shared the color of the single strand of white freshwater pearls she wore around her neck. "I'm so sorry. I made a mistake. I thought that the line outside was for the ramen restaurant."

"It is," Toshio said.

The woman glanced around the room. "This is the restaurant?"

"No. This is my pawnshop."

"Is the restaurant upstairs?"

Toshio shook his head. "It is not."

A wrinkle deepened across the woman's handsome forehead.

"You must be tired from standing in line this whole time. Perhaps you'd like to sit for a while?" Toshio gestured to a low table surrounded by a set of silk floor cushions in a corner of the room.

The woman tilted her chin and touched her thin lips. "I . . . I could have sworn that this was the restaurant. I watched the man in line in front of me walk through its door. I saw tables and chairs and . . ." She dipped her head in a small bow. "I am sorry for bothering you."

"There is no need to apologize. May I offer you something to drink? Some tea?"

"Thank you, but I—"

"Please, I insist. It is no trouble at all." Toshio walked out from behind the counter and called over his shoulder, "Hana? Will you bring out some tea? We have a guest."

HANA SHUT THE record book and stood up from a desk that had once belonged to her mother. She knew her cue as well as she knew the single thought presently rolling around the woman's mind.

Tea. At this point in their conversation with her father, all clients pondered the same thing. It was a simple thought, small and as light as air, without any sharp edges they could cut themselves on. They had all drunk tea before and remembered how it washed over their tongues, slipped down their throats, and warmed their souls. No harm had ever come from a cup of tea, and they could not think of a single reason to refuse the pawnshop owner's kind offer. If anything, it would be impolite to say no, seeing as they had been the ones who had mistakenly wandered into his shop. They tried to remember where they had been headed in the first place, but the most they could recall was feeling a cold emptiness in their stomachs. Tea could soothe that. Perhaps it was tea that they had been standing in line for all along. Hana filled a kettle with water and set it on the stove.

"Tea would be nice." The woman nodded with a smile.

"Wonderful. My name is Ishikawa Toshio." He gestured to a floor cushion. "Please, have a seat."

"Thank you." The woman settled onto a cushion that was the same shade of gray as the day outside. "I am Takeda Izumi."

"Thank you for choosing to visit us today, Takeda-sama. I am certain that you will find that we make very fair, if not generous, offers at this pawnshop."

"But I'm not here to . . ." Izumi rolled a pearl from her necklace between her forefinger and thumb, her brow furrowed as though she were rummaging through drawers inside her head, trying to find what she had meant to say next.

Hana carried over their tea on a black lacquer tray.

"Hana, this is Takeda-sama," Toshio said.

Hana bowed. "Welcome to our pawnshop. Please enjoy your tea," she said, setting the tray on the table.

Izumi turned to Toshio as Hana took her leave. "You have a lovely daughter, Ishikawa-san."

"Thank you. She takes after her . . ." Toshio banished his next words with a stiff smile.

He anchored his eyes on their tea and poured it into small clay bowls. The bowls were the color of the calmest sea, but cracks of varying sizes crawled over their glaze. If not for the kintsugi technique used to repair them, they would have fallen apart. Gold dust and lacquer filled the cracks, streaking over the bowls like lightning.

"Those are exquisite," Izumi said, admiring the bowls.

"Thank you. I was rather upset with myself for tripping and dropping them, but in this instance, I will admit that I am grateful for my clumsiness." Toshio handed Izumi her tea. "Broken things have a unique kind of beauty, don't you think?"

Izumi traced the bowl's delicate gold joinery with the tip of a perfectly manicured finger. "Some things wear their damage better than others," she said softly, so softly it was as if she were worried that her voice might shatter the bowl.

"I have found beauty in all manner of broken things. Chairs. Buildings. People."

Izumi looked up from her tea. "People?"

"Especially people. They shatter in the most fascinating ways. Every dent, scratch, and crack tells a story. Invisible scars hide the deepest wounds and are the most interesting."

Izumi twisted one of her two large diamond rings around her finger, pulling on her skin. "That is a very unique point of view, Ishikawa-san."

"Oh, it is more than a point of view. It is the very reason I run this business. This is a different kind of pawnshop, Takeda-sama. We are not in the business of trading trinkets. Diamond rings and pearl necklaces have no value here."

HANA LISTENED IN on Izumi and her father from the back room. She had heard the same conversation carried on over tea more times than she could count.

But no matter how many times he said those words, her father always sounded sincere. For the most part, he told their clients the truth, regardless of how hard the truth was for them to believe. While what he shared with the clients, in her opinion, was not by any means a staggering revelation, it always took them a few moments to wrestle their eyebrows down. This was understandable. On the other side of the ramen restaurant's door, up was up, down was down, and pawnshops such as this one did not exist. Her father's special skill, as Takeda Izumi was about to learn, was to, in the time it took her to finish her tea, convince her to let go of everything she was brought up to believe and allow her mind to grasp what her hands could not.

Hana strode back to her desk and picked up a book from the pile on top of it. It was a dog-eared paperback whose pages clung to its spine by sheer will. A client named Ito Daisuke had pawned it that morning. She checked the item against the list in her record book and put a little tick mark when she confirmed that everything was in order. It was her favorite among the items that had found their way into the pawnshop that day.

Hana pulled out her mother's old gold-rimmed glasses from a desk drawer. She put the glasses on, adjusted them over her nose, and, through its lenses, saw the book for what it really was: a choice that had changed the course of Ito Daisuke's life.

Its true form was much prettier than that of a book. It had traded its pages for feathers made of wisps of light, transforming into a glowing songbird. It perched on Hana's finger, its colors constantly shifting between blue and gold.

Once, this bird had sung brightly inside Daisuke while he worked on writing a mystery novel every night for five years, after his shift as a convenience store clerk. When he had abandoned it and deleted all his unfinished drafts two years ago, the bird dimmed, grew silent, and turned as black as coal. It pecked at his gut whenever he thought about the series of fictional Harajuku murders he was never going to solve. But now Daisuke had pawned his choice, and he was free. There were going to be times when he would feel a cold emptiness where the choice had once lived, but these would pass. He was not going to remember this choice, or this pawnshop, or the man who had persuaded him to part with a battered mystery novel. Peace of mind, Toshio had told him, was worth the price of never knowing what happened after page 254.

Hana took the glasses off and made room for Daisuke's book on a shelf next to a set of house keys and a plane ticket torn in two. That evening, when the pawnshop closed, her father would take all the items from the shelf and store them in the vault, together with the rest of the day's acquisitions.

TAKEDA IZUMI BLINKED, trying to comprehend the words that hung in the air over two cracked bowls of tea. "That doesn't make any sense. How can people pawn choices?"

"'Sense' is relative," Toshio said. "There are things that make sense in your world that are ridiculous in mine. I have never been able to understand the purpose of televisions or telephones."

"What do you mean by 'your world'?"

"You come from the world outside that door. My daughter and I are from the world inside it. Whenever anyone from your side finds their way to our pawnshop, there is always a good reason for it. Our clients have choices that have become too burdensome to carry. We take these choices off their hands so that they may return to their world lighter. Content."

"Is this a joke?"

"I would not make jokes about such things. We do important work here."

Izumi grabbed her bag. "I do not know what kind of game this is, but it is not amusing."

"It is not a game, and it is not meant to be amusing. I cannot force you to stay, but I do know that no one finds the pawnshop by accident. If you had no need for our services, you would have opened that door and walked into the ramen restaurant just like all the other customers waiting in line outside."

Izumi pulled her shoulders back and lifted her chin. "Assuming that what you are saying is true, which it is not, I still would not require your services. I do not have any regrets."

"I apologize if I have offended you, Takeda-sama." Toshio bowed his head. "But I have been doing this job for a very long time. I can tell when people are happy and when they are not, regardless of how well they are dressed or how bright their smile is. Happiness has little to do with what you have, and everything to do with what you do not."

Izumi tightened her grip on her bag. "You do not know anything about me."

"Perhaps. But what I do know is what I have learned from the collective experience of the generations of my family who have run this pawnshop. Every client who has passed through our door has insisted that they stumbled into our little establishment because they were lost. And they were right. Losing your way is oftentimes the only way to find something you did not know you were looking for."

"I know perfectly well what I was looking for today. Ramen."

"There are many good ramen restaurants in the city. Why were you looking for this restaurant in particular?"

"I used to live in this neighborhood when I was younger. I ate at this restaurant all the time."

"But surely you must have had better ramen since then?"

"Yes, of course, but—"

"And I am certain that a woman such as yourself could easily afford an establishment with better ambience."

Izumi twirled her pearls around her neck, her eyes fixed on her tea.

"But this restaurant isn't like just any other restaurant, is it?" Toshio said.

Izumi looked away.

"Do not worry, Takeda-sama. I have no intentions of prying. I do not need to. I already know why you decided to visit the restaurant today."

Izumi's thin brows shot up.

"You said that you used to frequent this restaurant when you were younger." Toshio clasped his hands over the table. "People revisit the past to relive pleasant memories, chase away bad ones, or both."

"Since you seem to think that you know me so well and are unwilling to accept my simple desire to eat ramen as my only explanation for being here, would you care to share which of these reasons you believe is mine?" Izumi said.

"You came to the restaurant to dine with a ghost."

"That's . . ." Izumi's voice caught in her throat. "That's nonsense."

"So you were joining a friend for a meal, then?"

"Well . . . I . . . no. I was going to eat alone. I like coming here by myself. I visit at least once every autumn."

"But no one ever really dines alone, do they?" Toshio said. "Our thoughts share our meals with us. They keep us company whether we invite them to or not and are especially noisy when they are the only ones at our table. They chatter about all the things we cannot say aloud. In your case, I would guess that they like to reminisce about a time when you were not the woman you are today, a time, perhaps, when you liked to share your table at the ramen restaurant with someone else."

"Stop."

"You argue with your thoughts and insist that they are wrong, but they keep on going until your ramen turns cold. But that does not stop you from coming back whenever you have the chance, because a cold bowl of ramen still tastes better than any hot meal in your home."

"Stop." Tears welled in Izumi's eyes and streamed down her pale cheeks. "Please, stop."

"I'm sorry. You asked me a question and I answered it. There are many things that I wish I did not know, but after spending a lifetime at this pawnshop, I can read the stories of my clients as though they were written on their faces."

Izumi dried her eyes. "I am not your client."

"You are correct." Toshio laced his fingers. "I have not yet decided if what you wish to exchange is of any value."

"Enough. I'm tired of your games." Fresh tears filled her eyes. "Who are you?"

"I am simply a man who offers a unique service to those who require it, a man who can tell that you are crying not because you are sad, but because you are angry. But not at me. You wish you were, but you are not. You were furious even before you set foot inside this pawnshop."

Izumi glared at him, color rising over her neck. "Of course I'm angry. I hate that I have every reason to be happy and yet all I feel are the cracks spreading inside me each time I force myself to smile. Is that what you wanted me to say? Is this what you want me to pawn? A broken smile patched with gold like one of your tea bowls? Because if you will take it, I will give it to you right now."

"So you believe what I have told you about the pawnshop?"

"Prove it. Make me believe."

"Very well. Show me your choice and I will tell you what it is worth."

"Show you? How? A choice isn't something you keep in your pocket or purse."

"You carry around all the decisions you have ever made in your life, Takeda-sama. This choice is no different," Toshio said. "And I think that you already know exactly where to find it."

ABOUT THE AUTHOR

SAMANTHA SOTTO YAMBAO is a professional daydreamer, aspiring time traveler, and speculative fiction writer based in Manila, the Philippines. She is the *New York Times* bestselling author of *Before Ever After, Love and Gravity, A Dream of Trees, The Beginning of Always,* and *Water Moon.*

samanthasotto.com
Facebook.com/samanthasotto
X: @samanthasotto
Instagram: @samanthasottoyambao

ABOUT THE TYPE

This book was set in Minion, a 1990 Adobe Originals typeface by Robert Slimbach. Minion is inspired by classical, old-style typefaces of the late Renaissance, a period of elegant and beautiful type designs. Created primarily for text setting, Minion combines the aesthetic and functional qualities that make text type highly readable with the versatility of digital technology.